DEAD
PAN

Other Jocelyn O'Roarke Mysteries

Murder on Cue
First Hit of the Season
Death Mask

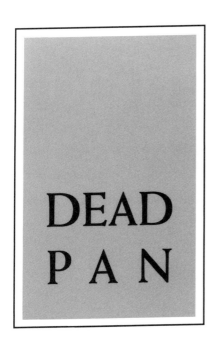

DEAD
PAN

A Jocelyn O'Roarke Mystery

Jane Dentinger

VIKING

VIKING
Published by the Penguin Group
Viking Penguin, a division of Penguin Books USA Inc.,
375 Hudson Street, New York, New York 10014, U.S.A.
Penguin Books Ltd, 27 Wrights Lane,
London W8 5TZ, England
Penguin Books Australia Ltd, Ringwood,
Victoria, Australia
Penguin Books Canada Ltd, 10 Alcorn Avenue, Suite 300,
Toronto, Ontario, Canada M4V 3B2
Penguin Books (N.Z.) Ltd, 182–190 Wairau Road,
Auckland 10, New Zealand

Penguin Books Ltd, Registered Offices:
Harmondsworth, Middlesex, England

First published in 1992 by Viking Penguin,
a division of Penguin Books USA Inc.

10 9 8 7 6 5 4 3 2 1

PUBLISHER'S NOTE
This is a work of fiction. Names, characters, places, and incidents either are the
product of the author's imagination or are used fictitiously, and any resemblance
to actual persons, living or dead, events, or locales is entirely coincidental.

Grateful acknowledgment is made for permission to reprint excerpts from the
following copyrighted works:
    "The Patty Duke Theme (Cousins)" by Sid Ramin and Bob Welles. Copyright
© 1963, 1966 United Artists Music Company, Inc. All rights of United Artists
Music Co., Inc. assigned to EMI Catalogue Partnership. All rights controlled
and administered by EMI U Catalog. International copyright secured. Made in
USA. All rights reserved.
    "I Went to a Marvellous Party" by Noel Coward. © 1938 Chappell Music
Ltd. (renewed). All rights administered by Chappell & Co. All rights reserved.
Used by permission.

LIBRARY OF CONGRESS CATALOGING IN PUBLICATION DATA
Dentinger, Jane.
Dead pan : a Jocelyn O'Roarke mystery / Jane Dentinger.
p.   cm.
ISBN 0-670-84108-0
I. Title.
PS3554.E587D37   1992
813'.54—dc20   92-5463

Printed in the United States of America
Set in Weiss Roman
Designed by Virginia Norey

For RICHMOND CRINKLEY (1940–1989)

A fellow of infinite jest, of most excellent fancy . . .
and the best partner-in-crime a girl ever had.

ACKNOWLEDGMENTS

Many thanks to all my crafty accomplices: my medical team Dr. Mark Dentinger and Dr. Russ Mankes; the L.A. contingent—Alan Heppel (with assists from Mike and Buster), Ron Orbach, David Lee, Marty Blumenthal, Stu Silver and the crew of The Avalon, especially Paul, Colin, Tony D., and Tony R. And my home team, Charlotte Sheedy and Vicky Bijur.

DEAD PAN

1

Dear O'Roarke,

Listen, snookums, after our last phone confab, I feel it's only right that I put my proposition on paper so you'll know it wasn't just a will o' the wisp offer on my part. Do, do, do come out here and work on this wretched TV movie of mine. I've already spoken to the director, Larry Goldstein, and he agrees that you'd be perfect for the part. So it's a 90% sure thing (or as close to it as you'll get in this town). And even if it should fall through, the worst that would happen is you'd end up lolling by my pool for a week or two, stroking my fevered brow as I bitch about the whole mess.

Seriously, I think it's time you got away from the Asphalt Jungle for a bit. As an old friend, let me tell you what I didn't have the guts to say over the phone: Josh—you're as dull as dishwater these days . . . And I say this with deep affection, as someone who knows you from the days when you were considered a "fun kid," a bon vivant. These days you're barely vivant.

I'm not saying that you don't have good reason to be off stride—after the fallout from the Burbage thing and Phillip's—well, let's not go into all that. I just mean that gray has never been your color; depression doesn't suit you. And, odd as it may sound, L.A. may be just the thing to lighten your palette just now . . . Think of it, there's nothing out here you need take remotely seriously. Doesn't that notion hold a certain appeal?

Of course, I leave it up to you. You will, as always, suit yourself . . . Then again, it's not as if I couldn't really use you on this hateful, incredibly lucrative project, you numb nuts.

Unopinionated love from—
Austin

————————————

The Players Club
16 Gramercy Park South
N.Y.C.
May 10

Dear Jocelyn,

I hope this arrives in L.A. shortly after you do because I know how you fret. Rest assured that I've moved my meager belongings into your place so that foul beast you call a cat will not perish from neglect. Actually I cheated and brought fresh crabmeat with me the first night so Angus now thinks I am the way and the light of his culinary future.

To be honest, being here makes a nice break from the Players Club where, as the resident relic of Broadway's ancien régime, I was beginning to feel like a bit like a museum piece.

Per your instructions, I've recorded a new message on the answering machine. It goes: "This is Frederick Revere. Jocelyn O'Roarke is in Hollywood, selling her soul and raking in big bucks while I hold down the fort and pray for her redemption." —or words to that effect . . . Dear me, do I hear the pressing of sour grapes? Sorry, I'm

just so bored without the sound of your evil tongue. You must write
often and give me all the awful West Coast news.

   Actually, I think Austin's right—the change will do you good
(though it's not as if you were going to Bath, is it?). And I've already said my piece about tying up loose ends . . . with Phillip,
etc.—not that we want to go into that again. And, naturally, you
must always please yourself— My God, I can't believe I'm doing
this sort of guilt-mongering! Forgive me, Josh, it's just my way of
admitting how much I'll miss you, nothing else.

   Have a wonderful time in Lotus Land working on Austin's script
(however much they leave intact). I'm certain that, by the time you
get back to N.Y.C., the last of the bad winds will have blown over.
Meanwhile I promise to keep you abreast of all that's going on here.

                                        As always,
                                        Frederick

_____

                        Chez Frost
                        1188 Mulholland Drive
                        Poolside, Calif.
                        May 15

Dear Mr. Revere,

   Thank you so much for your kind inquiry about the state of my
current employment and general personal well-being; also for pertinent
details about said "foul beast" (though I'll tell you right now, crabmeat isn't enough. Angus ain't that easy).

   And the phone message sounds real cute. Thanks a heap, Freddie.
Honestly, everybody and their grandmother goes out to L.A. for part
of the year! I don't see why, when I do it, it's perceived as a major
defection. Don't think I can't read between the lines, toots. And don't
force me to bring up your little piece of Hollywood history circa
1956—what was it called—"Seadogs"? Such an appropriate title.

   On the work front, I really am doing Austin's script; I signed the
contract two days ago—which is why I must cut this short. I'm
having lunch with the leading lady today. Now if you behave nicely
and drop the silly references to yourself as "Broadway's ancien
régime"—unbecoming in an established star who turns down more

work than most of us get offered!—I'll fill you in on all the juicy bits later.

Best love,
Josh

"Ginger, this is Jocelyn O'Roarke. Josh—Ginger Jellicoe!"
Like a circus master, Austin Frost held the sliding glass door open with one arm as he ushered his star through it with the other. Putting down her pen and quickly tying her beach robe, Jocelyn jumped up from the chaise longue, not merely out of politeness, but as an instinctive salute to the geometrically astounding vision that was sauntering toward her. Ginger Jellicoe, twenty-seven-year-old former child star, has-been, and recently resuscitated leading lady, was, even in a town renowned for perfect bodies, a major piece of construction. The broad-brimmed, white straw hat she wore shaded her wide shoulders, full breasts, and narrow hips that dwindled down to long, lovely calves and Oriental feet. She looked like a divinely formed isosceles triangle.

Jocelyn took in the wide-set, china blue eyes against the honey-colored skin and tawny hair and felt herself sinking fast into a mire of physical self-loathing. Then the vision spoke.

"Hiya, Jocelyn. God, I hope you got fruit. I'm starving and that's all I can have for lunch, fruit. It's this damn diet I'm on. And now ol' Frostie says I should go to my natural brunette for this part—dye it back. I dunno. You think Frostie's right?"

Old Frostie was standing behind Ginger, wringing his hands in an elaborate "Oh, please, be kind" signal. So Jocelyn simply said, "We've got tons of fruit. And Austin, for all his faults, is usually dead on about hair color. Plus I read the script and . . . yeah, you should go natural."

"But you're a brunette, too. Won't that be a bit much, us both being brunette?"

"Oh, I dunno. I think it's okay 'cause we *are* playing sisters. Besides, if you change your hair color in this town, they call it stretching your range."

Ginger clapped her hands and giggled like the charming child who had once delighted millions. "Ha! You're right about that—they'll say stuff like 'Miss Jellicoe has *finally* matured as an actress.'

The jerks! And you know, I think we'll look real *cute* together. Don't you, Frostie?"

"Adorable," Austin deadpanned. "But before I become transfixed by your joint cuteness, let me go forth and fetch fruit. And whatever you'd like to drink. Ginger, a wine spritzer, I assume. And, Josh, the usual?"

The freshly minted "sisters" nodded their agreement, Ginger with gusto and Jocelyn with a grimace. Her "usual" these days was a diet 7-Up with lime. She hadn't touched a drop of liquor since getting off the plane at LAX. Dreading the extra ten pounds the camera adds to a full-breasted woman with a short torso, she'd gone into training as soon as she hit Mulholland Drive, swimming one hundred laps a day and working out with the previously untouched weights in Austin's basement. Austin, who preferred, on a purely platonic level, fleshy women to cranky ones, wished she would knock it off. But, unlike many of his heterosexual counterparts, he knew better than to say so.

Sliding the glass door shut behind him, he heard Ginger confide to Josh, "Frostie's a gas but he talks kinda funny." He didn't catch her reply, only the sound of Ginger's laughter ricocheting off the glass. Good, he thought, That's a good sign. They're getting on fine and O'Roarke's taking shots at me again. Great. For he had begun to worry mightily.

And he had plenty to worry about, on several fronts. *Free Fall* was his first TV movie script for a major network and his first time out as an executive producer, something he'd sworn he'd never, ever be. Writers can hand in a script, pick up a check, and walk away whistling, which had always been his M.O. and a very good way to maintain one's sanity in Hollywood. But producers never leave the front lines until the bloody finish.

Chopping a honeydew into thin strips, he cursed himself for a fool and not for the first time. The pity of it was he actually cared about this particular script, so deeply that he couldn't bear to see it go through the usual TV meat grinder and come out pulped. So, to protect his baby, he'd become a producer and kissed sweet sanity adieu.

The first battle had been getting the okay to cast Jellicoe. By Nielsen standards, she was washed up, unreliable, and lacked "a nine P.M. time slot sex appeal," as one network mogul put it; all of which was possibly true. But she happened to be dead on,

innately right for the role of Christie. Austin knew it and, thankfully, so did his director, Larry Goldstein. Between the two of
them ranting and raving, Casting Justice had, for once, been done.
Oddly enough, considering that she had absolutely no "TVQ,"
getting Jocelyn approved had been a cinch. In retrospect, Austin
realized that whereas he and Larry both saw it, in trite but true
terms, as "small but pivotal," "The Suits" considered the part of
Anna too inconsequential to bother about. Which led to his
second, more personal concern—his old friend, the Pivot.

The thing that had first drawn him to Jocelyn, back in college,
was her wicked tongue and her great equilibrium. Sophomore
year she had acted in one of his first student plays and they had
both had to endure that most barbaric of all drama school
rituals—the "group critique." Or, as Jocelyn had called it, the
Lord of the Flies Fest. Hiding in the scene shop afterward, shaking
with humiliation and rage, he'd felt a firm thump on the back and
looked down to find Jocelyn offering him the first joint he ever
smoked, saying, "Look, Austin, you can't believe 'em when they
hate you and you can't believe 'em when they love you, either.
Both ends of it are bullshit. The good stuff always falls between
the cracks and you gotta recognize it by yourself or nobody else
ever will. You follow?"

He hadn't immediately but, many tokes later, lying out on the
football field, playing Botticelli, he'd suddenly raised up on one
elbow and stated forcefully, "They were right about the first
act—the structure sucks. But Act Two's fine and those feebs completely missed the ending. And I can see how to make it all
work now!"

"Oh, hey, that's great, Austin! . . . Now was this person ever
involved in politics?"

And that was how it had always been with them—work and
games, games and work. Because, with Jocelyn, they were always
one and the same: she played at her work and worked at her play.
But lately it had changed for her, and Austin missed his play-
fellow. A promising directing job at the Burbage Theatre had
ended for Jocelyn with the death of two company members. This
had been followed closely by the engagement of NYPD Lieutenant Phillip Gerrard, her longtime lover, to another woman.
While Austin had seen Jocelyn get over broken love affairs the
way a steeplechaser gets over a low hurdle, this time she seemed

to be having trouble regaining her stride. And he desperately needed her to be in top form.

He wasn't so concerned about her acting. She could do Anna in her sleep and still be passable. But he hadn't hired her entirely for her acting, though he hadn't admitted it outright. He needed her as an undercover coach for Ginger.

Whether she realized it or not, and she probably didn't, Ginger had been hired to play herself, something she'd never done in the past. Her childhood persona, Jilly of "The Jam House," was just a revved-up seventies version of Shirley Temple, with rock 'n' roll replacing tap dance. "The Jam House" was about an average American family that just happened to be a rock band, featuring Ginger as the youngest singing sibling, who managed to upstage the older cast à la Michael Jackson with the Jackson Five. Unfortunately, once the series was canceled, she hadn't managed to parlay that maxi-voice in a mini-frame into anything more successful. There were a few aborted series, followed by the standard stories of drug abuse, a failed early marriage, and a disastrous bomb of an album called *Ginger Jams*. Then—nothing, until the mid-eighties, when she started popping up in small parts on cop shows, usually as a troubled teenage runaway. Then she got too old to play teenagers and made another bad marriage and fast divorce. After a five-year "hiatus," she turned up in an entirely forgettable low-budget feature titled, appropriately, *Sleaze Street*, playing a young prostitute desperate to move up to call-girl status. Austin had seen it one night at Josh's as a CBS Late Night Special. They were both aficionados of great-bad films. Sadly, *Sleaze Street* did not qualify—but Ginger did. She chewed up the scenery with such ferocity that Jocelyn gasped in awe.

"Oh, it's like the early great-bad work of Kirk Douglas or Burt Lancaster! It's *way* too much. But what commitment. Just think what she'll be like when she can stop acting!"

That had planted the seed for Austin because Josh had a fine eye and a real affection for good-bad acting and where it could lead. And what he needed more than anything else on earth was someone who could get Ginger Jellicoe to *not* act. Larry Goldstein was a good director with a great sense of story and pace and Austin was grateful to have him. But the nature of the TV movie beast allows scant time for things that are taken for granted in stage work, like rehearsal or preparation. He was counting on Jocelyn to be a sort of walking Cliff Notes for Ginger. But would she?

Looking out the kitchen window, he observed his two ladies standing poolside, engrossed in small talk, or at least Ginger was. Even at a distance Austin could see that Josh was absorbed in something else: "imprinting"—that was his name for it. O'Roarke had no name for it since she was scarcely aware of it. But already she had one hip raised with a hand on the other and her head tilted a little up and to one side . . . just like Ginger. Mimicking people was second nature to her; she did it unconsciously whenever she met an interesting type. It was an invaluable trait, but he loved to tease her about it, calling her a "character klepto" or "Ms. Body Snatcher."

Definitely a *good* sign, Austin told himself. Feeling more optimistic than he had in weeks, he dumped all the fruit in a huge salad bowl and started tossing and singing, "They laugh alike, they walk alike, at times they even talk alike. You can lose your mind! When—huh?" He stopped midtoss on the last line of the old "Patty Duke Show" theme. The scene outside his window had suddenly shifted from happy girl talk to something that looked alarmingly like soap opera.

Ginger was sitting on the chaise with her face buried in her hands, shoulders jerking up and down convulsively. The look of surprise and concern on Jocelyn's face as she ineffectually patted the girl's head told him that it was more than a fit of hiccups. Looking up, O'Roarke caught his eye through the plate glass and made waving motions with her free hand, signaling him to stay inside for a bit. He nodded back and, with a sad sigh, carried the fruit salad over to the fridge.

"*Not* a good sign."

2

. . . so one minute everything's fine and the next we're smack in the middle of an Oprah show. Ginger asked me how I learn lines and I said, "In my sleep." I explained how I like to go over a scene a few times right before I get into bed. Then I run over the lines in my head while I'm drifting off to sleep and usually when I wake up I have them down.

Ginger gets this look like I just said I drink blood for breakfast so I made some dumb joke about having to do it that way since I'm a sleep junkie (your description, I believe). She just looked at me with the most woebegone eyes imaginable and said, "Oh, God, you're so lucky . . . I can't . . . I'm afraid to sleep!" And that's when the floodgates opened.

Turns out this girl hasn't had a decent REM cycle in weeks. It's not insomnia—she falls asleep fine—it's nightmares, ones that keep repeating themselves like horrid nocturnal reruns. The kind that are so awful you have to jerk yourself awake to get away from them. But Ginger's always come right back. So now she's afraid to sleep at night. *She's getting by on catnaps during the day . . . which ain't easy when you've got a six-year-old daughter.*

Now Austin thinks it's classic actor-dreams, but I'm not so sure. You and I have had plenty of those and they're usually just one-shot things, pure anxiety overspill. Not the kind that wake you up with the cold sweats and bed-knocker heart.

Theory number two—supplied by our winsome but worldly director, Larry Goldstein—goes, and I quote, "The kid's gone through a divorce and the death of her folks in the last eighteen months. And she's got a lead role that could pull her career out of the crapper—if she doesn't muff it. So what d'you expect—Sugar Plum Fairies?"

This argument, I grant, has some merit. At least it's calmed Austin down, so I'm prepared to buy it. Hell, I'm glad to buy it, Freddie. See, Ginger's one of those sweet, flaky child-women who are always looking for a Tower of Strength, and these days "Lean on Me" is just not in my repertoire. To extend the musical metaphor—"I'm not feelin' too good myself."

But this, too, shall pass. We start work tomorrow so all our mundane little concerns—about life, love, and the ozone layer—will be devoured like so much plankton by that great whale, The Shooting Schedule.

Give the old Fur Bag some catnip for me and write soon.

Miss you madly,
Jocelyn

A grating, mechanical voice spoke in her left ear, making her wince in her sleep.

"It's six A.M. . . . Time to rise and shine . . . Don't roll over or put your head under the covers . . . It's time to get up . . . Right now . . . The early bird catches—"

"Aw, shut up!"

Struggling to an upright position, Jocelyn grabbed the little black box from the nightstand and threw it on the bed.

". . . the worm . . . Get up, sleepyhead . . . You don't want to be lat—"

One sharp kick sent it off the foot of the bed onto the rug, inadvertently hitting the "off" button. Sweet silence reigned as she rubbed the sleep from her eyes and retrieved the mechanical menace from the floor.

"God, it's like waking up in the Twilight Zone . . . I'm gonna get Stegnan for this."

There was a light tap on her door, which then opened a crack, revealing a disgustingly bright-eyed but leery Austin.

"Josh, is there, uh, someone in here?"

"No, some*thing*." She held up the offending object. "A going-away gift from Steve 'Toys-Are-Him' Stegnan. It's called a Nag Alarm. There's a little man inside who sounds like Edward R. Murrow on Quaaludes and he abuses you till you get out of bed. God only knows where Stegnan digs up this stuff."

"Well, you have to admit, it's effective," Austin offered tentatively, trying hard not to laugh. "Saves me coming in here with the garden hose."

"Hey, I'm not that bad. Not everybody bounds out of bed like a spaniel, the way you do."

"That's true, dear," he agreed with feigned sweetness. "Then again, not everybody requires electroshock in order to rouse before noon, either."

"Oh, har-de-har-har," she growled à la Ralph Kramden as she trudged toward the bathroom. "Go catch a worm, Austin . . . then eat it."

"Everybody hates me, nobody loves me. I'm gonna eat some worms. Everybody loves me, nobody hates me. Oh, how my stomach turns!"

The small child in a bubble-gum-pink sundress did a mock pirouette on the toes of her matching pink Reeboks for the big finish. Her fifth big finish. Running her hands through her newly darkened hair, the girl's mother pleaded, "Hilly, please, honey, that's enough now. Okay?"

"No! One more. Just one more time!"

"That's what you said before."

"But this'll be really last."

Taking pity on her fellow thespian, Jocelyn leaned forward in her makeup chair and gently tapped Hilly on her sunburned shoulder.

"Do you know the other worm song, Hilly?"

"Unh-uh . . . Is it gross, too?"

"Oh, very. Extremely disgusting and it's got more words to it. If you worked on it, I think you could really make people blow their cookies."

"Do you know it?"

"I think so. But I need to write it down. Can you go down the hall to Mr. Frost's office and get a pad and a green felt pen for me?"

"Okay. Why green?"

"For the worms, goofus."

Hilly acknowledged this irrefutable piece of logic with a quick nod before whooshing out the door. Ginger Jellicoe beamed her gratitude to Josh in the mirror. "Oh, God, thank you, thank you . . . Frostie's gonna kill you though."

"Nah. Austin *loves* kids," she lied cheerfully. A little petty revenge never failed to raise her spirits.

"Look, I'm sorry I had to bring her along today. Her father was supposed to take her to Knott's Berry Farm but it, uh, all sorta fell through at the last minute . . . That's why she's so hyper. She's usually very well behaved, really."

"Yeah, so am I—until I get stood up. Compared to me, Hilly's a model of decorum," Jocelyn joked, wanting to keep it light and not get sucked into any of Ginger's domestic dramas. Not when they were just about to do their first scene together. But Ginger, already in high neurotic gear, shifted into overdrive.

"See, Tim—her dad—he's usually very good about this stuff. But he's—well, he's been outta work for a while. He's a film editor. Yesterday he got a call to do some free-lance work on an indie and they needed him right away. So, really, it just couldn't be helped. God, I hope Larry's not pissed at me."

"Why should he be? Geez, Ginger, you're not holding things up. But you're doing a good job of making yourself crazy."

"I know, I know I am. It's just that it's the first day and all. And I just don't want anyone saying that I'm being . . . difficult." She whispered the last word as if the room were bugged. "See, I don't have a real great rep in this town and people are going to be watching me on the set. People I worked with before . . . when I was super screwed up, you know?"

Ginger's voice had gone from breathy to husky and there was a hint of moisture in her eyes. With her darkened tresses and a light dusting of freckles showing through her makeup base, the overall effect was reminiscent of Bambi—right after the hunters got Mom—and it made Jocelyn want to scream. Instead she gritted her teeth and spoke rapidly in the general direction of the ceiling.

"In case you're interested, Ginger, it so happens that right now, back in ol' N.Y.C., I don't have 'a real great rep,' either. Matter of fact, I haven't worked in the last eight months. Which is why I'm here—Austin mercy-cast me. Because A—he felt, rightly, that I needed the dough. And B—he knew I was sleeping twelve hours a day and renting old movies the rest of the time. He also knew that the man I'd been involved with for two years is about to marry someone else. And sitting around waiting for the happy nuptials to arrive was doing for me what Jack Nicholson did for Shelley Duvall in *The Shining*.

"So my life's a mess, too, Ginger. But so *what*! So's everybody else's. Everybody standing on that set now, whether it shows or not, is just as screwed up as you or me. So what do you care what they say or think about you? Just do your job and have a good time doing it . . . 'cause, when all's said and done, honey, it still beats working for a living."

Bug-eyed, Ginger sat frozen in her chair, whether with awe or anger Josh couldn't tell. She didn't have time. Someone close by was clapping.

"I love it, I love it! That was so Joan Blondell—early Joan Blondell, I mean. All those films where she played second banana but she'd always have one good scene where she got to wise up the ingenue. The way you said 'honey' was dead on. God, I love Joan Blondell. She's so unsung, you know?"

Both women rotated their chairs in perfect sync toward the doorway. The first thought that crossed Jocelyn's mind was that they must be shooting a Western on the next lot. Why else would she be looking at a cowboy? Not that a lot of people in L.A. didn't affect that look—Rodeo Drive wranglers Austin called them. But this guy looked like the real thing. He wasn't wearing a ten-gallon hat, but everything else fit; the jeans were worn and so dusty they made her throat dry and the brown suede vest, brown now—there was no telling what its original shade had been—was as ancient as the pointy-toed boots with the rundown heels. And the face looked authentic, too; a little weather-beaten, with a strong jaw, a lopsided grin, and crinkles around eyes that were the exact same shade of hazel as her own, she realized with a start. The only thing that was a little off was the hair. It was full and wavy, chestnut with sun-bleached highlights, but too beautifully cut for a cowpoke. The grin tilted a little more as he savored their shock.

"Sorry I'm late, ladies. My jeep had a flat. I'm Jack Breedlove. I'm gonna do your hair."

Something halfway between a shriek and a giggle burst out of Ginger.

"You are? You mean you're the *stylist?!*"

"Uh-huh. Semiretired, though. I'm doing this shoot as a favor to Larry. Nice shade, Miss Jellicoe." He'd loped into the room and begun running expert fingers through her hair, examining the strands. "Did Camille do it?"

Ginger could do no more than nod and gaze and nod again.

"Thought so. She's a great colorist. Now I know you're playing a stuntwoman, so I think what we'll do is cut it shorter in back with lots of layers. That way, no matter how windblown it gets, it'll still fall back in a nice shape. Is that good by you, Miss Jellicoe?"

"Oh, sure . . . I think so. And Ginger's fine."

"Then Ginger it is," he said with a wink. "And you, Miss O'Roarke, is that a perm or your own?"

"My name's Jocelyn and my curls are from my mother."

"Mmm, lucky you. The cut's great, too. Pity we have to put a wig over it."

"A *wig!*" Josh wailed piteously, unable to stop herself. It wasn't just vanity that prompted the outburst, but a craven desire for comfort. Working under strong lights in a wig was like working with a sweatbox on your head; something to be avoided at all costs.

"Sorry. Director's orders. Larry wants me to dowdy you up . . . or down, to be more exact. Your hair's a little too hip for the role."

"Aw, look, can't we finesse it somehow? Like—maybe part it in the middle and pin it back at the sides? That ought to make me look sufficiently June Cleaver, don't you think?"

Jack Breedlove sauntered toward her with a sardonic smile.

"I thought you New York theatre types believed in 'anything for my art' and all that stuff?"

"Honey, this ain't New York . . . and this ain't art," Jocelyn countered, hoping the Joan Blondell touch would work a second time.

It did. Standing behind her chair, Breedlove met her gaze in the mirror and smiled conspiratorially. "Hey, if it's fine with Larry, it's fine with me. I don't get any thrill from sticking a wig on a good head. And you got great hair . . . Let's play with it and see."

Then a funny thing happened.

As Breedlove experimentally scooped up her back curls, his hand lightly grazed the nape of her neck . . . and a cascade of tiny shock waves went shooting down her spinal column.

Gripping the arms of the makeup chair, Josh exhaled swiftly and stared fixedly into her lap, where the cascade had ended in a warm pool of mixed sensations. What the hell is *this*? she wondered. Then she raised her eyes, saw the smile spreading across his face, and stopped wondering.

"Yeah, I think we can work something out."

"Hey, Jack!" Larry Goldstein stuck his already perspiring face in the room. "Do me a huge one and go fondle Brenda's follicles. She's got a major attack of the frizzies and she's driving me nuts."

Breedlove released her curls and gently fluffed them back into shape.

"Okay, be right there. I'll be back in a flash, ladies." With a wave and a nod, he went out the door after the harried director. Ginger craned her neck to watch him saunter down the hall, then swung her chair around to Jocelyn.

"Good golly, Miss Molly, I don't believe it," she whispered like a titillated teenager. "I do not bee-*leeeve* it! I mean, I thought I could tell an AC from a DC at fifty paces. I'd *never* guess that guy was gay!"

"He's not gay, Ginger."

"Josh—he's a hairdresser!"

"Yeah, I know. It deviates from the norm . . . but that guy is not gay."

Ginger's brow furrowed as much as youthful skin could; she seemed to ponder this as a possible violation of some union rule.

"You sure?"

Jocelyn nodded as she reached back to stroke the nape of her neck.

"Trust me."

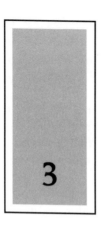

3

"Larry, I'm really uncomfortable with this cross. I have to almost jog to hit my mark on time. It feels so . . . contrived."

For the fourth time, shooting stopped as Brenda Arnold broke character and, for the fourth time, Josh felt Austin's hot breath in her ear as he hissed, "I want her annihilated! I want her to collide horribly with a combine harvester!"

"I dunno. She's tough—the harvester might lose."

This didn't elicit even a ghost of a smile from Frost, though the grip to his right started heaving with choked laughter. But Jocelyn didn't expect Austin to see the humor of it. Larry Goldstein was also mightily unamused and she couldn't blame him, either. A short, wiry man with a receding hairline and a full beard (which, in Josh's experience, so often went hand in hand), Goldstein was a man of boundless energy but not of boundless patience. It wasn't even noon yet and she could see he was already close to the edge.

Scratching his beard as if it were flea-ridden, he approached

Ms. Arnold with a frozen grin that threatened to crack his face in two.

"Brenda, honey, the cross works for me. Okay? It looks just fine an' dandy through the viewfinder. Okay?"

"But it *feels*—"

"Feels? *Feels?* Brenda, this is television. What makes you think I give a rat's turd how it feels?! Just hit the damn mark!"

Brenda Arnold's cheeks puffed out like a blowfish as she drew herself up to her full five feet ten. "Well, really, if that's your attitude, I—"

"That is precisely my attitude . . . Now, let's take it from the top."

"Wait!" A raspy voice croaked seemingly from out of nowhere. Then a short, squat bulldog of a man stepped from behind Camera One. "Larry, Ginger's looking shiny again. Better get her powdered down before we do another take."

The director and the bulldog locked eyes for a moment in silence. Then the bulldog jerked his head around and called over his shoulder, "Makeup!" Goldstein said nothing, just raised both hands palms out and walked back to his chair as Makeup hustled out to blot Ginger. Austin groaned inwardly as Josh nudged his ribs.

"Who is that guy?"

"Buddy Banks—the DP—director of photography. The Suits hired him—not us. But he's very good. Been in the business since kinescope."

"Let me rephrase. Who does he *think* he is? What was that little power play with Larry about?"

Austin sighed the long-suffering sigh of a man who had fought many battles and made many compromises. "Like I said, the network wanted—*insisted*—on Buddy. He's sort of their . . . watchdog around here. Now Buddy doesn't need to work, really. He's got his own real estate company nowadays. Runs it with his wife, Gabrielle Brent."

"Huh?! You mean *Gabby* Brent, agent to the stars?"

"Yup. Gabby—as in 'I'll talk until your ears bleed'—Brent. The only agent who makes you long for the kinder, gentler days of Sue Mengers. She also happens to be Ginger's agent."

"Oooh, I get it. Part of a sweet little package deal?"

"No, part of a big, messy package. She is also Brenda's agent, even though they cordially loathe and detest each other. So, to get Buddy and Ginger, we had to take Brenda."

"Why? If her own agent can't stand her—"

"*Because* Brenda Arnold—before she married Benedict during the War for Independence—was Brenda Banks, Buddy's baby sister . . . Ain't life grand?"

Jocelyn nodded and rubbed Austin's back consolingly. It was a seminal moment for her, though she was hardly aware of it. But looking at her friend's drawn and worried face, Jocelyn, for the first time in many months, actually felt sorrier for another person than she did for herself. Atavistic feelings of fierce protectiveness flickered within as she soothed, "Don't worry. We won't let the fuckers get us down."

Frost nodded in agreement, keeping his gaze on the ground. He didn't want her to see the secret smile tugging at his mouth as he inwardly rejoiced, O'Roarke's back—and I *got* her!

In the next take, Brenda Arnold behaved herself, hit her mark, and was actually quite good as the overbearing mother. Nagging was apparently something she could do easily without feeling the least bit contrived. Ginger, on the other hand, seemed leaden and awkward.

"I just don't understand you, Christie. Why you live like this —risking your life every day! It—it's not normal!"

Ginger gave a feeble shrug and looked in her "mother's" face. "Normal? What's normal—you? The way you live? I don't *want* it, Ma! It's too safe and too . . . too . . . Shit! Larry, I'm sorry. I lost it."

"Cut! That's okay, Ginger," Larry assured her. "You're getting there. Let's take ten, everybody."

As the cast and crew scurried off the set, Goldstein made a beeline for Austin and Josh.

"Frostie—what are we gonna do? She's gone cold. Damn, it's my fault for letting Brenda screw around. Ginger—she's like Stanwyck, you know? But I'm not Capra. I don't know what to *do*, man!"

Jocelyn intercepted a beseeching look from Austin and sidled away from the two men. She knew exactly what Goldstein was up against. Ginger was what was called a One-Take Wonder, like

Barbara Stanwyck in her early years: pure gold the first time out, but downhill from there. Frank Capra, her first great director, used to rehearse scenes without her until he had them down pat, then call her onto the set. Then he'd shoot and print the first take. Getting a One-Take Wonder back up to snuff was tricky business.

She slipped into the makeup room, where Ginger sat slumped in her chair like a rag doll while Breedlove worked on her hair. Seeing Josh, he raised his eyebrows as a warning to tread softly. She gave him an acknowledging nod as she slipped into her chair next to Ginger's and futzed unnecessarily with her own makeup. Without looking up, Ginger spoke.

"I suck."

"Suck is a very subjective term, Ginge," Josh began tactfully. "Compared to—oh, say, Meryl Streep or Gena Rowlands—yes, you sucked the Big Weenie. But then, so do most of us. On the other hand, if we take into account the Suzanne Somerses and Charlene Tiltons of this world, hell—you're golden."

"Josh, you're so . . . mean!" Ginger sounded both shocked and delighted.

"Personally," Jack interjected, "I like that in a woman. Plus Meryl Streep has never had to play opposite Brenda the Hun."

"Oh, you're both *awful!*" Ginger shrieked, then burst into relieved laughter. Josh looked over her head at Breedlove and knew she had an ally. "But Brenda's playing my—our mother. I—my character *loves* her . . . Right?"

"Well, let's leave love out of it for the moment." Jocelyn was talking fast, aware that what had to be fixed had to be fixed in ten minutes. "How were *you* feeling about Brenda out there?"

"Oh, gee, I was kinda upset," Ginger began vaguely, "and I kinda wanted . . ."

"You kinda wanted *what?*"

"Well, just for a second there, I wanted to . . . you know—kick her in her fat gut. A little."

Jack clamped his hand over his mouth and turned away fast. Jocelyn swung Ginger's chair around and cupped her face in both hands.

"That's *it!* That's perfect—everything you say in that scene, you say just to keep yourself from kicking her in her fat gut. Got it?"

Ginger looked like a death row inmate who's just been reprieved, her eyes growing wide with disbelief and wonder. "That's easy. But it's not *acting*, is it?"

"Yeah, it is. And I'm gonna tell you a real big secret that I've been keeping to myself for years, Ginger: Acting *is* easy. It's a damn breeze when you come down to it. What's hard is *Us*. We put ourselves through all kinds of convoluted nonsense and most of it's bullshit. Just feel what you're feeling. And just *do* it."

"Miss Jellicoe—on the set, please!" a voice called from outside the door. Ginger jumped out of her chair and bent down to give Josh a quick, hard hug.

"You're the best. It's like—like you really *are* my big sister." She straightened up and grinned at both of them, "Now I'm gonna kick some ass!" Then she was out the door like Jackie Joyner-Kersee, leaving a breeze in her wake. Jocelyn slumped back in her chair, feeling a little afraid of what she might have wrought. Breedlove plucked a pack of cigarettes out of his grungy suede vest and handed her one. After they'd both taken a long draw, he looked down at her with wry regard.

"Uh, you do know that Mother Teresa has resigned? So there's now an opening—"

"Oh, stuff it."

He chuckled softly and eased his long frame into Ginger's chair. "Sorry. I'm a knee-jerk quipster. Can't help myself."

"That's okay. I know the syndrome."

"Yeah, I bet you do, Blondell."

Arching one eyebrow in her best Bette Davis manner, she asked, "Do I detect a nickname being born here? 'Cause, frankly, I hate monikers. I'm just plain Jocelyn—Josh to my friends."

"Of which, I'm sure, there are multitudes—oops! There I go again. Sorry. But you were very good there—and very . . . generous."

Trying not to squirm under his appraising gaze, she waved a hand dismissively. "Nah, just selfish, really. That's what most altruism is if you look hard enough. I'm vain and I don't like to be associated with failure. So I do what I can to assure a good product."

To her amazement, Breedlove leaned forward, crossed both eyes and blew her a very large raspberry, then chanted, "Liar, liar! Pants on fire!"

Jocelyn bolted back in her seat.

"Geez, what are you? A leftover from 'Twin Peaks'?"

"No, but I make a *damn* fine cup of coffee," he came back without missing a beat. "I can also recognize a good egg when I see one . . . Hey, your hair's escaping. Here, ol' Jack'll fix it." Grabbing a brush, he came around behind her and expertly subdued her recalcitrant curls. "There. How's that?"

"Great." The little tingles were starting again. To distract herself, Josh added, "I look like a genuine Mall Matron."

"Not quite. We need that lacquer finish to make it really authentic," Breedlove said, picking up a can of hairspray that he applied like a coat of spray paint. "Perfect."

The fumes from the hairspray filled the narrow room, which Jocelyn was already finding unaccountably warm despite the air-conditioning. She got up to open a window, only to be met with a smell that made the hairspray fumes seem like a spring bouquet.

"Good grief—what's that?! Skunks in heat?"

Jack walked over and stuck his head out the window to take a test sniff and a look-see.

"Ah—skunk at work's more like it. See that?" He jerked a thumb to the left and Josh leaned out the window, craning her neck in that direction. A languid L.A. breeze brushed her face, bringing an even stronger whiff of the offending odor. Squinting her eyes against the bright sunlight, she saw, next to the studio, a tiny bungalow with an exhaust fan running full tilt in its one small window. Beneath it, oblivious to the stench, a flock of pigeons pecked at the overflow from a green trash can.

"Looks like Buddy's been developing."

"Developing what? We've hardly shot anything."

"Not *film*, silly. Still shots. Buddy's an amateur photographer—better than amateur, really. He's published one book and has another due out soon. That's his darkroom. One of the perks he got from the network for doing this gig."

"What does he photograph—week-old fish?"

"Nah, that's just the chemicals. Banks specializes in candid, behind-the-scenes shots. His first book was called *Hurry Up and Wait*. You know, actors hanging out, trying not to go nuts between takes, doing silly shit. That kinda stuff. Some of it's pretty good, actually."

"Do I detect a damning tone to that faint praise?"

The momentary coldness faded from his face as his eyes lit up. "That's the second time you've used that. How come?"

"Used what? An interrogative sentence?"

"No. That phrase—'Do I detect.' You do a lot of Christie plays in rep or what?"

"It's just a figure of speech," she said with feigned nonchalance, drawing her head back inside the window. This was not a topic she wanted broached. What she did want, the main attraction of this sojourn to Lotus Land, was sweet forgetfulness of her amateur sleuth status. Austin knew, of course. But no one else was going to if she could help it. What she couldn't help, she found to her chagrin, was asking questions, and she hadn't gotten an answer to her last one. "So what's the deal? Is Buddy another Steichen or just stinkin'?"

"Jesus! What a miserable excuse for a pun. And just when I was beginning to like you!"

He leaned one arm on the windowsill, his face just inches from hers, and the tingling was in her feet now. This is just a little harmless flirting, she told herself sternly, but it did nothing to dispel an overwhelming sense of inadequacy. The sad truth was Jocelyn couldn't even recall the last time she'd flirted or been flirted with. The sadder truth was . . . she'd lost the knack.

"Well, that'll l'arn ya," she joked feebly, drawing away from him. "But you still haven't—"

"Okay, okay, Miss Nosy." Breedlove took his cue from her and became serious, staring up at the ceiling a moment. "Banks is good, no question. He's got a real eye, which isn't surprising. The guy *is* a DP. But sometimes it's a real nasty eye—sneaky, too. He snaps people when they're not aware—when, maybe, they'd rather not be snapped. You know, an aging glamour queen without any makeup on. People nuzzling people they don't happen to be married to. Arguments on the set. All that fun stuff."

"Hasn't anybody tried to sue him?"

"Not yet. Better just to ignore it, that's the conventional wisdom, especially considering who he's married to. Hey—this *is* the ultimate company town."

There was a sharp rap at the door, then Austin popped his head in.

"We're ready for your close-up, Miss Desmond."

"Are you kidding? I've only been waiting a scant five hours. You'll spoil me."

"We're just being nice 'cause it's your first day and we know how antsy you New York types are," Austin deadpanned, then broke into a grin. "Ginger just nailed that last scene like an ace . . . What did you *say* to her, you little minx?"

"Nothing much." Jocelyn winked at Jack before sailing out the door past Frost. "She was feeling like a failure but, luckily, I remembered a few quotes from the reviews of your last play—then she felt *much* better."

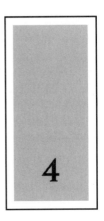

4

"Scene Twenty-five A—take one!"

"Action!"

The clap board clacked inches away from Jocelyn's nose as Camera One dollied in for a two-shot of her and Ginger, sitting on a sofa. In true film and TV tradition, Josh's first scene was one that occurred halfway through the story line. To save on production costs, they were shooting all the "family" scenes at once, in the studio, before going out to do locations. This anti-chronology approach was the biggest hurdle a theatre-trained actor had to overcome and she was concentrating very hard to place herself at the right emotional point. One deep breath and she let fly: "Christie, you got no sense! None at all! You're taking a two-hundred-and-fifty-foot dive off a water tower tomorrow . . . And you wonder why Ma's *upset*?! Geez, why can't you learn to lie a little?"

"I don't *want* to lie," Ginger protested. "Why should I? It's what I *do*, Anna!"

"No, it's not just what you do . . . It's what it does to other people. You gotta take some responsibility for that."

"Meaning I gotta lie all the time? That's a load of—"

"*Cut!* Sorry, ladies, it's not you. We just blew a back light."

"Actus interruptus," O'Roarke intoned solemnly. This was the second big adjustment. Ginger leaned forward and grabbed her acting partner's hand anxiously. "Josh, this is harder—fighting with you. I mean, I *like* you."

"Oh, yeah?" She saw that the grips had replaced the light and they were nearly ready for another take. "Well . . . I think your kid's funny looking."

"You do *not!*"

"Scene Twenty-five A—take two."

"Action!"

They were like two racehorses coming out of the starting gate. Ginger hadn't taken the insult seriously but she had picked up on the implied challenge behind it and went at it hammer and tongs. Larry Goldstein looked over his shoulder to flash a quick smile at Austin, who was rocking back on his heels with smug satisfaction. It looked like all those people who were waiting for Ginger Jellicoe to crash and burn were going to be sadly disappointed. To Frost's practiced eye, it was easily apparent that O'Roarke was the finer technician; her timing, as always, was flawless and her modulations seamless. But Ginger—Ginger had that *thing* with the camera. Whereas Josh dealt with it as a necessary intrusion, Ginger approached it like it was her lover. Her body, always in perfect relation to it, seemed to send out waves of light and heat in its direction. And, in return, the camera simply loved her. Even when her choices were less than inspired, it loved her.

Jocelyn sensed this, Austin could see. Now how would she deal with it? Most actors would tense up, start overplaying in an effort to grab focus. But O'Roarke, bless her crafty soul . . . pulled back. She locked on to Ginger, just like the camera, giving her total focus. Brilliant ploy, he thought, knowing as Josh did that the best acting is reacting. By seeming to subdue herself, she managed to make herself essential. It showed amazing acumen for someone with relatively little TV experience. And Ginger responded to it beautifully . . . until the very end of the scene. Something seemed to pull her eyes away from Jocelyn's and she faltered.

"Anna, you're wrong. I'm not . . . It's not a death wish. It's . . . something else."

Seeing Ginger lose concentration, Jocelyn leaned forward and grabbed her wrist, getting her attention back. She covered Ginger's flub with a quick ad-lib.

"Then what—what is it? Come on, hon, you can tell me."

"It's not about death at all—it's about feeling alive. Really alive. I take chances, sure. But I take them on *my* terms. It's crazy, but—when I'm on a platform about to do a fall—it's the only time I feel in control, like I'm really in charge of my life. Does that sound nuts?"

Back in the moment, Ginger's eyes bored into her "sister's." O'Roarke took a beat, then lifted her shoulders with an air of wry resignation.

"Yeah. But—what the hell—so you're a little nuts? So what? . . . You're Italian."

"Cut! That's a keeper," Larry called out happily. "Thank you, ladies. Thanks, everybody. Let's break for lunch. We'll pick it up at two with, uh, fifteen B—the dinner scene. Okay?"

Cast and crew scurried in all directions before Goldstein had even finished speaking, and the set was nearly deserted by the time he reached Frost, who was scanning the sidelines for the cause of Ginger's distraction.

"Two scenes in the can—not bad for a morning's work, eh, Frostie?"

"You sure we can use that last take?"

"Oh, yeah. We'll just use O'Roarke's reaction shots to cover Ginger's glitch. They were really cookin' there. I wonder why she went up like that."

"Wonder no more." Austin raised one of his storklike limbs and pointed toward Ginger's dressing room, where she stood with Hilly in her arms talking to one of the most godlike creatures he'd ever laid eyes on. "I'd go up like the Goodyear blimp if that crossed my sight lines. Lord, I know they make 'em comely out here, but *that* is almost indecent. Oh, be still, my heart."

"*That*, my friend, is nothing but trouble," Goldstein shot back as soon as he spied the object of Austin's sudden affections. "It's Tim Hayes."

"Are you serious?" Austin asked, arching an eyebrow clear into his hairline. "Ginger's soon-to-be ex? I had no idea she'd married into Greek mythology. And she's divorcing *him?!*"

"Yup. Caught him with his pecker in the woodpile one time too many. Seems Timmy's idea of fidelity means sleeping home four nights out of the week . . . That's a little hard on a girl's ego. Especially when she's trying to get straight."

"It's a lot hard."

Frost's sudden infatuation froze, then melted away. He'd known a few Timmys in his time and knew what havoc they could wreak on a devoted heart. He also knew the high cost of walking away and mentally applauded Ginger for having what it took.

O'Roarke, on the other hand, wasn't so sure. Ginger waved her over as she was about to head out the door. Hilly squirmed out of her mother's arms and came running toward her.

"Lady, you haf'ta teach me the song tomorrow. My daddy's takin' me to Knott's Berry Farm!"

"Hey, lucky you!"

"Josh, this is Tim Hayes, my—Hilly's dad. Tim, this is Jocelyn O'Roarke. She's just the *best . . .*"

The rest of Ginger's accolade was lost on her as Hayes shook her hand and gave her the full effect of his hundred-watt smile. She took in the auburn hair, deep green eyes, and golden skin, but it was more than gorgeous looks that she saw. It was potent charm coupled with the Knowing Look—the look that told each woman that she was Aphrodite incarnate, infinitely alluring and keenly desired. It was an act, of course, but a good one. And Hayes had it down to perfection.

"Boy, this is a pleasure. You two had some serious stuff cranking out there. Couldn't take my eyes off you." To bring his point home, he let those eyes take a leisurely stroll all over her, ending with her face. His smile grew more intimate as he asked, "How's L.A. treating you?" But his line reading implied something more along the lines of: "Is this good for you, too?"

"Not bad. Though mainly I've been holed up at Austin's, learning lines and catching up on my slee—"

She nearly bit her tongue in two, not meaning to mention the "S" word in front of Ginger. But Ginger had knelt down to tie one of Hilly's pink sneakers. It was hard for Jocelyn to tell if she'd heard or if she was at all aware of the little bit of woo Hayes was pitching. She's probably used to it, Josh told herself, that's why she ditched him. Probably doesn't give a damn anymore.

Then Hilly announced importantly, "Mom, Daddy's takin' us to lunch, too!"

Ginger's face turned up to Tim's aglow with surprise and pleasure. "Oh, Timmy, that's sweet."

Oh, yeah, she still gives a damn. Josh knew the signs of love renounced but not relinquished, knew them by heart. And Ginger showed all the symptoms. In that instant her sympathy for the younger woman turned into empathy. So, when Hayes suggested that she join their merry band, she was ready.

"Uh, thanks but I can't. I promised Aus—"

Then a warm hand fell on her shoulder as a man's voice drawled, "Your carriage awaits, Miss O'Roarke. I got us a table at Musso and Frank's."

She spun around to find herself face to face with Jack Breedlove, who smiled down at her with just the faintest trace of deviltry in his eyes. "Let's hustle."

And hustle they did. Before she knew where she was, Ginger had given her a quick hug and an oh-you-rascal-you wink and Breedlove had swept her through the studio doors out into the parking lot. Feeling equal parts relieved and aggrieved, she planted herself directly in front of him just as they reached his beat-up Jeep Cherokee.

"Just for future reference, I don't appreciate being interrupted mid-lie. I've had a lot of practice and I pride myself on my ability to fib with the best of 'em. I don't need anyone to do it for me."

"Ah, see, that's where we differ," he replied, unflappable and unfazed. "Me, I'm basically honest—big disadvantage in this town. So I like to get in a little practice whenever I can. I thought I did okay. But feel free to give me any pointers from your vast stores of mendacity."

"Oh—horse balls!"

"Fine. Hop in. I'm sure you can get some at Musso and Frank's. I think they use 'em in their chili."

"And *damn* fine chili, it is, eh?"

She had to admit, he really did a pretty good Kyle MacLachlan takeoff. And the chili was great. Plus it was damn near impossible, she was finding, to stay peeved with Jack Breedlove. His easy good nature, which had nothing of the standard-issue laid-back L.A. flavor to it, coupled with his quick wit made him an ideal dinner companion. Ripping a crusty roll in two, she dunked a piece into the chili, then popped it in her mouth, eyeing him speculatively.

"Can I ask a dumb question?"

"I dunno," he said before taking a swig of Dos Equis. "Dumb in what way? I mean, are you gonna use bad grammar? 'Cause that really offends me."

"No. Dumb as in I'm sure you've been asked it a thousand times before."

"Oh, that's okay then. I like repeating myself."

"Fine . . . How did *you* come to be a hairdresser?" She was right; he had been asked this many times and he had his answer pre-edited and ready.

"My dad was a barber. Now there's a word you don't hear much anymore: 'barber'—as in 'a guy who cuts hair.' My mother used to be a Las Vegas showgirl. Even after she retired, she was always into wigs in a major way. So it was just something I was always around—hair and wigs. Guess I picked it up by osmosis. It was an easy living, especially in this town."

"Really? Wasn't it hard breaking in? You're not exactly Central Casting's idea of a stylist."

"That's why it was easy. You have to realize how homophobic Hollywood was and is. Now I don't endorse that, but I can't change it either. And I will always be deeply grateful to Warren Beatty for making *Shampoo* because what he did for my business I can't tell you!"

"I see . . . A little tease with a little tease, huh? Is that how you got to semiretire at such a tender age?"

"What an evil mind it is," he said, looking more pleased than offended. "But no. I did my clients' hair, I never did my clients. I just got into another line of business. When it really takes off, I'll never touch a blow dryer again, so help me."

"What's your other line?"

Deliberately misinterpreting her, he grinned lasciviously. "Your skin is like alabaster and your eyes are pure flame— Whoa! There I go again. Sorry, you seem to bring out the wiseass in me."

"Hogwash. Breathing brings out the wiseass in you . . . What's your new business?"

"I raise horses, mainly quarter horses. For private buyers and for studios. If Westerns ever make a comeback, I'll be sittin' pretty. I've got a little ranch near Chesbro."

"You *do*?!"

Jocelyn dropped the rest of her crust in the chili bowl. Sensing he'd just scored big points, Breedlove played it cool. Slouching back against the Naugahyde booth, he off-the-cuffed it. "Yeah, why? Do you ride?"

Sweeping her bread crumbs into a tidy pile, Josh replied quickly, "Yeah, well, no. I *did* when I was a kid. It's an expensive habit in Manhattan, so I haven't much . . . How many horses do you have?"

It was an amazing transformation to behold. Here Breedlove thought he was having lunch with a jaded New Yorker and the next minute he was face to face with National Velvet. He would never have guessed it, but all the telltale signs were there: the flushed cheeks, the bright eyes and heavy breathing. Jocelyn O'Roarke was out-and-out horse crazy. It was, he felt, turning out to be a very good lunch. With deliberate casualness, he replied, "Let's see . . . I've got three good studs—two of 'em with Arabian lines. Six brood mares. We had five foals this spring. I guess about twenty horses in all, not counting the ones I've sold."

Trying to match his matter-of-factness, she nodded several times and slowly reached for her cigarettes. But it was quite clear that she couldn't have been more impressed if he'd announced that he was running for president.

"Twenty, huh? That—that's great."

"Well, it's a nice way to start the day. I've got a little Appaloosa—Brando—that I take for a canter every morning."

Watching her stab out the just-lit cigarette, he realized he'd gone too far. If he'd stuck his tongue in her ear and whispered sweet nothings, he couldn't have gotten her this excited. She lifted her eyes and desperately scanned the room for an out.

"Uh, where are the facilities? This chili's having an immediate impact."

"At the back. To your right . . . You okay?"

"Uh, sure. Be right back." Before you could say "saddle up," she'd slipped out of the booth and was picking her way between tables at top speed. Breedlove leaned out of the booth to watch her progress with an appreciative eye. She stuck out like a Christmas tree at Easter time in the L.A. lunch crowd, not because she was the best-looking woman in the room, not by a long shot. In fact, by Hollywood standards, she was only passable. But, as far as women went, Jack had little regard for Hollywood standards nowadays. His tastes hearkened back to the forties and fifties, when flesh and curves were still in fashion. And those O'Roarke definitely had, along with skin so fair it jumped out against the sea of bronzed bodies all around. A horse of a different color, he couldn't help thinking in equine parlance, and a dark horse, too. For there was no doubt in his mind that this was a lady with an interesting past and a few surprises up her sleeve. He tipped back the rest of his Dos Equis and smiled in anticipation.

"Oh, you have to go see this woman! She's fabulous. She works with crystals *and* acupuncture."

"Wow, what a megacombo. And you lost five pounds?!"

Two Nordic goddesses were applying identical shades of lip liner to their identically siliconed upper lips as Jocelyn quickly dried her hands and slipped out of the ladies' room, feeling like the Sister from Another Planet. In the narrow hallway between the restrooms and the dining booths, she bent down to roll up her sagging sweat socks. A familiar voice resonated on the other side of the oak partition.

"But why do you want me to talk to him? Really, you're his *wife*, for heaven's sake."

"Yes, but I'm also his business partner—which makes me biased in this department. Besides, for some damn reason, he trusts your judgment. Now do we have a deal or not?"

Bending lower, Josh snuck a peek around the corner. All she could see were two pairs of shoes: snakeskin Ferragamos with three-inch heels that had to be hell on the lower back and, along comfier lines, suede open-toed pumps that encased, unless she was much mistaken, the ten little piggies of Brenda Arnold.

"Oh, stop talking like an agent! It's not a *deal*—just a friendly little exchange of favors."

"My ass," the other woman shot back in a voice that dripped battery acid. "Ten grand is no little favor, toots, not when it's *my* money."

"But I—it's just a loan. After all, we're family."

"Right, like foreign aid to Panama's 'just a loan.' Come on, Brenda, for once in your life, just cut the crap. Buddy's not going to lend you another dime unless you get your ass to G.A.—fat chance! Whereas I am offering to pay you outright a—a commission, let's call it, if you can turn him around on the Monte Verde thing. That's my proposition in a goddamn nutshell. It's not friendly, it's not family—it's just business, period. Now I am going to take a pee and powder my nose. And that should give you enough time to either shit or get off the freakin' pot, as your big brother would say."

The snakeskins made clicking sounds, heading in Jocelyn's direction. Jumping up, she lunged for the wall pay phone and managed, in the nick of time, to be engrossed in pseudo-conversation just as the snakeskins came around the corner. Then Gabby Brent sailed past her on a cloud of Chanel No. 9. Tottered past, actually—no one sails on three-inch heels. But the general effect was still impressive, and general was the right adjective since, even with the heels, she stood no higher than five-two but carried herself with a military authority that strongly suggested, if you were in the Shirley MacLaine "past lives" camp, that Ms. Brent had spent one of hers as Emperor of France. Even Josh, no believer in reincarnation, saw the Napoleonic influence. It was there in the small, beaked nose, the pursed rosebud mouth, and that ineffable quality that told others, at a glance, to never, in this life or the next, fuck with this woman.

Taking a different path back to her table, Jocelyn managed to get a look at Brenda, who sat clutching her martini as if it were a life preserver. Maybe it was, and who could blame her, having just lunched with a lioness. It was hard to imagine Buddy standing up to that tiny titan; harder still to imagine what she wanted badly enough to strike a bargain with the despised Brenda. And why was Brenda so desperate for cash? G.A.—did that mean Gamblers Anonymous? Feeling old, familiar wheels ticking again, Jocelyn caught herself. Now cut that out! she told herself à la Jack Benny. Still, when she took her seat opposite Breedlove, the first thing out of her mouth was:

"What's Monte Verde?"

"Huh?" In the space of a few brief minutes, O'Roarke had transmuted again. National Velvet was gone and, judging by the piercing light in her eyes, she'd been replaced by the Grand Inquisitor. "Uh, it—it's just a tract of land. About two hundred square acres up in the hills, above me, I mean above Chesbro. There's nothing on it."

"Are there any plans for something to be on it?"

"Not as far as I know. Shit—there better not be—"

"Uh-huh. Who owns it?"

"Uh, well . . . why do you ask?"

"No reason. Forget it. We should head back." Then it was over, like someone hitting a switch. Poof! End of interrogation. Her eyes were back to their normal wattage as she shoved cigarettes and lighter into her purse. "Let's get the check."

"It's got already."

"Oh—well, how much do I owe you?"

"Nope. My treat."

"No, not your treat," she said firmly, slapping a ten-spot on the table. "We go dutch."

He shoved it right back at her. "No, we don't. My idea—my treat. What is this—some kind of uptight, ultrafeminist trip? What's the big deal about a lousy little lunch?!"

"The big deal is," she began with prim pedantry, "if we go dutch, we're just co-workers eating out. If *you* pay . . . it's a date."

"Oh, gasp, shudder. Perish the friggin' thought! What're you afraid—the columns will get ahold of it? 'New York Actress Dates Lowly Hairdresser!' Well, smell you, lady—'cause your stock's not that high!"

Eyes were turning their way but he didn't notice or care. What he did notice, because it was so uncharacteristic, was that he was breathing hard and experiencing a sharp urge to kick a lady in her keester. He disliked losing his temper and he disliked her for being the cause of it. Then, out of the blue, she started laughing, a deep, throaty laugh that turned up the corners of her eyes and made her look about six years old.

"What's so funny?"

" 'Smell you!' God, I haven't heard that since fifth grade at Saint Augustine's. Mikey Marletta used to say that to me all the time." She paused to wipe tears out of her eyes and put her money away. "Sorry, I'm being rude . . . and a jerk. I, uh—my social skills have gotten a little rusty of late. So, okay, your treat. And the next's one on me. Deal?"

He found himself grinning back at her and nodding agreement as she hoisted her bag onto her shoulder and, still chuckling, headed for the door. Following in her merry wake, he remarked to no one in particular, "You know, I got up this morning feeling really on top of things . . . Well, it just shows to go ya, doesn't it?"

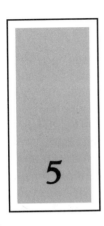

5

"I'm tellin' ya, Gingersnap, I don't know what you been up to lately and maybe I don't want to. But if you don't catch yourself some heavy sack-time soon, I'll have to start shooting you through freakin' *linoleum!* You follow?"

"Uncle Buddy, it's not my fault! I swear I'm in bed every night by ten-thirty. But I just can't *sleep.*"

"So drink warm milk. Take a pill."

"I *can't* take pills. You know I can't. And I've tried milk. I've tried yoga breathing, meditation—I've tried everything! But I have these *dreams.*"

"Aw, dreams! It's just nerves, Ginge, you were always a nervy kid. But you're not a kid anymore. And when you don't get sleep, you look like shit. You can't afford that now."

"I know, I *know* but—"

Ginger's voice trailed off in a series of sniffs and sobs as Jocelyn and Jack stood eavesdropping outside the makeup room door. Josh put her hand firmly on the doorknob but Breedlove stopped her, hissing, "We can't go in there now!"

"You wanna bet?" she hissed back, jerking the door open with barely contained fury. Whatever his motives, Banks obviously knew squat about dealing with an actor's psyche and, given another few minutes, he'd have Ginger's in shreds. Tossing her purse on the counter with a resounding thud, she turned to Buddy, their first one-on-one exchange, and said with a sunny smile, "Ah, Mister Banks, right? Hi, I'm Josh. Listen, Austin's looking for you . . . I think he has some questions about the setup for the next shot."

"Oh, yeah, he's got a better idea?! Christ on a crutch—save me from these pissant writers who think they know something."

Banks was instantly out the door and on the warpath. Jocelyn made a mental note to abase herself to Austin later as Breedlove calmly noted, "Well, you weren't lying about being a liar. You're very accomplished, O'Roarke. Remind me never to believe a word you say."

"That was a *lie?*" Ginger gasped, "But, Josh, why—"

"I, uh—I heard him ragging you and I got a little pissed off. Look, the more you worry about this thing, the worse it's going to get." Jocelyn knew whereof she spoke, having weathered a long spell of sleepless nights in the recent past. "And he wasn't helping any. If he tries it again, just tell him to take a hike, okay?"

"Tell him to . . . ?" Ginger couldn't even get her lips to form the last few words. If Jocelyn had just said Mr. Rogers sold crack to toddlers, she couldn't have appalled Ginger more. "Oh, *no.* I'd never— See, he means well. Uncle Buddy's always looked out for me."

"You mean he's *really* your uncle?" Jack asked, trying hard to imagine a gene pool that could produce both a Buddy Banks and a Ginger Jellicoe.

"No, we're not related. But I've always called him that. Ever since 'Jam House.' He was our cameraman, see."

"But, Ginger, that was a long time ago. It doesn't give him the right—"

Ginger held up a hand to stop Josh before she uttered further blasphemies. "Uncle Buddy is Hilly's godfather. And when my parents got killed . . . " Ginger paused to squeeze her eyes shut for a second. "It was right after I separated from Tim and I—I sort of went off the deep end for a while there . . . Uncle Buddy took care of *everything!* Paid my bills, bought groceries, hired a housekeeper. He's the one who got me into rehab. I mean, I know he can be a little, well, a pain in the buns sometimes. But, Josh, he saved my *life!*"

Staring down at the floor to avoid the "I told you so" look in Jack's eyes and the pain in Ginger's, she muttered, "I'm sorry, love. I thought—well, never mind what I thought. I am an ass and I apologize." She still thought that Banks' approach to the problem was all wrong, but she wasn't about to criticize a man who was a top contender in the Good Samaritan Olympics and who clearly meant so much to Ginger.

"That's okay, honey. And you just wait, I know you'll get to like him. It takes time but Uncle Buddy really grows on you." At that moment Ginger looked so much like Hayley Mills in *Pollyanna* that O'Roarke, to her small credit, didn't even consider using the "Like mold" comeback that was ringing in her head.

Not that she would've had time. The next moment, the doorway was filled with the form of Austin Frost, drawn up to his full six feet four, cheeks aflame and eyes flashing in her direction.

"Miss O'Roarke, might I have just the briefest of words with you . . . *now.*"

Smiling weakly at her cohorts, she got up to follow him into the hall. "Ah, excuse me, you two. Seems I'm late for my two o'clock castigation."

After she'd gone, Ginger looked up at Jack, puzzled. "What's 'castigation' . . . like having an audition?"

"Uh, no. More like having—a root canal."

Meanwhile, out in the hall:

"Are you out of your itsy, meddling mind?! Larry's already got his hands full dealing with Banks. Then you say *I* don't like his shot!"

"Austin, I explained why—"

"Fine, fine! Then you go tell him and have that belligerent little gnome cuss you out for ten minutes. Do you know, he used words that I have actually never *heard* before?"

"Ooo, really?! Like what?"

"I am not here to increase your already extensive knowledge of profanities, thank you. I am trying to get a script made!"

He was obviously not prepared to see the lighter side of the matter. On one hand, she didn't blame him. Producing your own script was an excruciating, thankless task. On the other hand, Austin was getting altogether too huffy for her tastes. When he got huffy, his elocution became very British for some reason. She was fairly sure that, right now, he had no idea that he sounded almost exactly like George Sanders in a snit. But she was not in the mood for George Sanders so she huffed right back.

"Gosh, you're cute when you're self-righteous. Look, Austin, I know you think you've been subtle as shit about all this, but let's get a few things out in the open."

"Meaning what precisely?" If his tones became any more clipped, he was in serious danger of biting the tip of his tongue off.

"Meaning that I know you didn't get me this job just out of the goodness of your heart."

"Of course not. After all, you *can* act—when you're not too busy sticking your—"

"Oh, act, schmact. You wanted someone to play nursemaid-slash-coach to Ginger, right? And who better than good ol' O'Roarke? Have Chutzpah, Will Travel."

"I—I never said that." His accent was drifting toward the mid-Atlantic now.

"But that's what you wanted. Well, fine, you got it. But looking out for someone is a tricky job, especially if you start liking them. You get carried away—*I* got carried away. But I was *right*, damn it! A few more minutes and he would've had her too shook to function. That girl is—she's like an amoeba. Absolutely no protective shield whatsoever. What was I supposed to do?"

They were both leaning against the wall now, winded and not wanting to glare at one another any longer. After a minute, Austin spoke in almost his normal voice.

"Silly twit."

"Dumb twerp."

It wasn't exactly a teary reconciliation, but it was enough to signal the end of hostilities. Jocelyn turned toward him and asked, "So you want I should go make nice-nice with Buddy?"

"Well, if you think you can. Now I'm not being sarcastic, Josh. It's just—sometimes your idea of an apology is someone else's idea of a slap in the face."

"I will ignore that since I know you know better. And producers are renowned for their tactlessness . . . Now where is the little darlin'?" She put a light brogue on the last two words and Frost realized it was safe to tell her Banks' whereabouts. She was probably unaware of it but, over the years, Austin had noticed that, whenever she set herself to be particularly charming, her Irish oozed out. Once, listening to her give notes to a notoriously testy actor, he'd sworn she was speaking Gaelic the whole time, but it had worked. Maybe it would work on Buddy, too.

"I think he's in his darkroom. Know where it is?"

"Yup. Just you leave it to me, boy-o."

Watching her trot out the door, humming "Too-ra-loo-ra-loo-ral," he made a silent prayer. *Sure and begorah, don't muck it up.*

And, in the normal course of things, she wouldn't have. O'Roarke, like any show-business veteran, knew how to get along with or around even the most cantankerous types when required. Unfortunately, she knew absolutely nothing about photography and the delicate art of photo development. If she had, she would never have opened the darkroom door when the little red light was on. She knew, of course, about the red light outside the studio, signaling visitors that a scene was shooting and not to enter. But that was a big light with a big warning sign beneath it. As it was, she never even saw the little red light, and there was no sign anywhere, though she never got to explain that to Buddy. Before her eyes could begin to adjust to the murky light inside, a roar that closely resembled that of a bull moose in battle shook the tiny bungalow to its floorboards. It was amazing that so much noise could come from such a small man. After that, the rest was a blur of sound and fury signifying, in essence, that Josh was a demented she-devil, hell-bent on wreaking havoc and a danger to clean-living Americans everywhere. But she did recall, sometime later, after the nuclear fallout had settled, that Austin had been right: Buddy *did* know words she'd never heard before.

"One more time. Just one more. Please!"

"Okay. But then you're on your own . . . 'Great, green globs of greasy grimy gopher guts, mutilated monkey meat, little birdies' dirty feet. All wrapped up in putrefying porpoise hide.' "

" 'And I forgot my spoon!' " Hilly Hayes chimed in at the top of her little lungs, jumping up and down with excitement. "That's my favorite. I like it better'n your worm song, even—'The worms crawl in, the worms crawl out. The worms play pinochle on your snout . . .'"

"Whoa, pardner! We had a deal, remember?" Jocelyn scooped the child up in her arms to halt her umpteenth rendering of the worm song. "The deal was I teach you the grossest songs I know, then you go to bed. Right?"

In her Little Mermaid nightie, bathed and smelling sweetly of bubble bath and baby powder, Hilly looked as fresh and appealing as an otter pup, albeit an otter with particularly gruesome taste in music. Squirming like one, she tried to avoid O'Roarke's eyes. "I'm not tired yet. You know any more?"

"Hey, Hilla Beans—it's a wrap. Get your fanny up those stairs. Pronto." Buddy Banks came into the living room with a Scotch and soda in one hand and an offensively odoriferous cigar in the other. Hilly, with a child's sure instinct for who can be conned and who can't, slipped demurely out of Josh's arms and headed toward her godfather. But she wasn't above trying stall tactics, even with him. Raising two plump arms and batting her eyes like a little Vivien Leigh, she cooed, "Piggyback, Unca Buddy?"

"Oh—all right. Once around the park, that's it." Putting down his drink and cigar, he hoisted her onto his simian shoulders and trotted up the stairs at a fairly jaunty clip for a man with legs like two beer kegs. As they reached the top of the landing, Hilly's voice drifted down to Josh.

"Unca Buddy, lissen to this . . . 'Great green globs of greasy grimy gopher guts—' "

O'Roarke winced. Terrific, now he can have me arrested for corrupting a minor, she thought, reaching for her glass of Heitz Cellar Pinot Noir. It was her first drink in weeks, but dining with Banks had pushed her beyond her limits of self-denial.

It had been Ginger's masterstroke to make up for the darkroom debacle. At the end of the day's shooting, she'd pleaded, "Please come, Josh. *Please!* We'll have a nice dinner, watch a movie, and relax. You'll see he's not such an old bear. And he'll see you're not . . ."

"Mentally deficient?"

"Well . . . something like that."

She'd agreed, partly because Ginger was one of those sweet,

benighted souls who needed the people she liked to like each other, and partly to keep Austin from booting her out of his house bag and baggage. Although she still felt she'd done nothing really wrong, it had been a less-than-auspicious beginning for her and she'd been prepared to do penance. But she had not been prepared to do the Stations of the Cross, which seemed to be what Banks expected. That or actual groveling and sniveling.

After making humble apologies at the start of the meal, she'd merely received a monosyllabic grunt—it might even have been a belch, she wasn't sure—from Buddy, who had then proceeded to ignore her completely, directing his few terse comments to Ginger or Hilly as he shoveled in his food. Though she'd been starving when she arrived, Jocelyn had found herself too uneasy to do justice to the perfectly prepared seafood paella.

And Ginger, working overtime to inspire goodwill among men, hadn't done much better. But Hilly had saved the day, prattling on about her trip to Knott's Berry Farm, supremely oblivious to the subzero temperature at the table. Banks' only redeeming feature, as far as Jocelyn could see, was that he seemed truly devoted to Ginger and Hilly, though he tended to treat both mother and child as if they were exactly the same age. It had all made for a dining experience that combined the least amount of oral gratification with the greatest amount of dyspeptic aftermath.

Ignoring the tumult in her stomach, Josh lit a cigarette as she prowled around the spacious living room. Ginger's house, best described as Spanish Tudor, a style peculiar to Southern California, lay at the end of Laurel Canyon, tucked cozily behind a row of cypress trees. It wasn't huge, but with a swimming pool in a large backyard, a Jacuzzi, and a private screening room, it was posher than she had expected given Ginger's long periods of unemployment. "Jam House" wasn't in syndication, and even if it had been, it would take more than residuals to keep up a place like this. There was a Tiffany lamp on a teak end table, a thick Persian rug in front of the fireplace, and the bowl on the mantelpiece had to be Lalique.

"We're almost ready." Ginger came out of the screening room and saw Josh examining the bowl. "Oh, do you like that? My father brought it back from Paris."

"Your father had great taste."

"Well, it was his business. He owned an import-export company. Most of this stuff was his. The house, too. It was left to me . . . in their will."

Seeing the sudden moisture in her eyes, Jocelyn said quietly, "Ginger, I'm sorry about your folks—losing them both at once. That's very tough." It was lame, as all such words are in the face of tremendous loss, but Ginger's face lit up with gratitude.

"Yeah, it was—it *is* tough. I mean, it's been a while now, but sometimes I wake up in the morning thinking they're still here —then I remember they're not . . . Can I have a drag?" Ginger was staring at Josh's cigarette with stark longing.

"Have your own. I've got a whole pack."

"Oh, no. Just a puff. I quit but—" She took a quick, guilty look up the stairs, then whispered, "I still get the craving, especially at night. Don't tell Buddy."

"Gosh, that'll be hard, us being so close and all." She allowed herself the one wisecrack as she handed over the cigarette, which Ginger promptly bogarted down to half its length. O'Roarke smiled at her complicitously. "Kind of brings back recess in the girls' john, huh?"

Ginger giggled and exhaled simultaneously. "I used to sneak smokes on the back lot when we were doing 'Jam House.' I always got caught and it was always Buddy who caught me." She handed the cigarette back and made little fanning motions with both hands as they heard the pitter-patter of chunky feet coming down the stairs.

"The kid's out like a klieg light, Ginge. She sang herself right to sleep," Buddy announced, giving Jocelyn a meaningful look as he crossed to the bar to freshen his drink. "She'll probably wake up screaming about worms and shit, though."

"Oh, no, not Hilly. She's just like Tim, nothing fazes her."

Feeling that a change of topic was in order, Josh asked, "So, what's on tonight's viewing schedule?"

"Timmy got one of my favorites—*Arsenic and Old Lace*. Do you like old movies, Josh?"

"Does Imelda Marcos like shoes? It's one of my favorite Cary Grant films. And I think Josephine Hull and Jean Adair win hands down as the cutest killers in film history."

"Okay then—show time," Ginger declared gaily, picking up a fresh bottle of Pinot Noir and leading them into the screening room, which was really a converted den with a long Chesterfield sofa at one end and a projection screen that came down in front of built-in bookcases at the other. It was a cozy setup and much more like real moviegoing than popping a cassette into a VCR. Settling herself at the opposite end of the sofa from Banks, with Ginger in the middle, O'Roarke sank back against the cushions, fully prepared to forget the world and its worries for a few hours while Cary Grant did his elegantly hilarious stuff.

Only it didn't work that way.

Maybe it was because she was so tired, or maybe it was the aftereffect of dining with Dr. Doom. It certainly wasn't the movie itself; she'd loved it all twelve times before. And it was a very good print, even though it had some jumpy frames here and there. But it wasn't working its usual magic for her. By the time Cary Grant was experimentally prodding Raymond Massey's leg with a dinner fork, she was rubbing her eyes, trying to fend off a splitting headache. Even when Grant told Priscilla Lane, "Insanity runs in my family. It practically gallops!" she barely chuckled. This just wasn't like her; she found herself irrationally depressed by her own unresponsiveness and longing for the film to end. What she needed, what she wanted with near desperation at that point was just to crawl into bed and oblivion.

Buddy must have felt the same way. No sooner had Cary proudly proclaimed himself "a son of a sea cook" and gone into the final clinch with Priscilla than Banks got up and hit the lights, making both women blink like surprised owls.

"That guinea Capra really knew how to make 'em," he said, somewhat grudgingly. "'Course, he had help."

"You mean Sol Polito?" Jocelyn asked, then added pointedly, "Yeah, he was a terrific cameraman—another guinea, of course. But he knew how to shoot interiors, didn't he?"

For the first time, Banks looked at her as if she were something approaching a human life-form. But all he said was, "I'll take the reel with me, Ginge."

"Oh, you don't have to, Uncle Buddy. Tim always takes care of it."

One of Hayes' several part-time jobs was with a film rental house; hence Ginger's steady supply of celluloid. It was, Jocelyn supposed, his way of making amends for a misspent marriage. But Buddy seemed set on usurping even this minor role in the family.

"Nah, I'll drop it off tomorrow. It's on my way to the studio. And, speaking of tomorrow, time for botha you to hit the sheets. I don't want to be smearin' my lenses with Vaseline just so's you won't look like death warmed over."

It was the perfect end to a miserable evening.

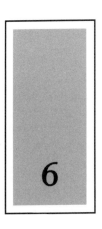

6

Cary Grant was moving in slow motion across the Brewster living room. She watched in happy anticipation, knowing, step by step, what was to come. Move curtain. Look out window. Open window seat. Casually glance down. Close window seat. Sit on it. Beat. Jump up! Open window seat. *Big* take. Slam it shut. Open it again. Double take . . . Perfection.

Only it wasn't perfect; it wasn't right at all because suddenly she was standing in Cary's place, staring down. Then Josephine Hull was at her side, sounding very distressed as she gazed at the body.

"Why, that's not Mister Spinalzo!" That was true and the line was right but the situation was all wrong. And there was nothing remotely comedic about it. Then Josephine departed from the script altogether as she turned to say, "My, she looks so unhappy. Is she a friend of yours?"

"Uh, yes, she—she *was.*"

"Well, I'm very sorry but, you see, we only take gentlemen . . . You'll have to move her, I'm afraid."

Nodding in meek acquiescence, she bent down to lift Ginger's lifeless body. At first she was very heavy and wouldn't budge. Then the real horror started as Ginger's corpse suddenly began decomposing in her hands. She tried but she couldn't extricate herself from the decaying flesh. Josephine Hull started to wail, "Oh, good lord—she's coming *apart!*" Then a black, violent wave of nausea swept up from the pit of her stomach—

Jocelyn made it into the bathroom just in time. After the last of the paella and Pinot Noir had ejected itself forcibly from her insides, she pressed her sweating forehead against the cool enamel tiles and vowed, "No more seafood—ever."

"Did you have a hot date with a steamroller last night? 'Cause you look like shit. But then, I like that in a woman. Makes you look sort of sweet and vulnerable."

"Breedlove, is there anything you *don't* like in a woman? Aside from split ends and dandruff," Josh demanded peevishly.

"Nope, not much. Where ladies are concerned, I'm like Will Rogers—never met one I didn't like."

"Have either of you seen Buddy?" Brenda Arnold, already in costume and makeup, popped her head in the door. "He's not on the set."

"Nope, not me," Jack said mischievously. "Try the darkroom."

"Oh, please. *I'm* not that stupid," was all Brenda offered, with a meaningful glance at Josh, before yanking the door shut. Listening to the angry click of her heels in the corridor, Jack amended, "I take it back. There's one woman I don't like."

"Oh, my gosh, a first! What's wrong with Brenda? She's a bit older than you but she has all the charm of Leona Helmsley."

"I'll tell you what's wrong with La Arnold," he said with surprising vehemence. "She's a big-mouth troublemaker, that's what."

"Fascinating. Tell me something I don't already know."

"Okay, try this on for size. Remember you asked me about Monte Verde yesterday? Well, it turns out it's owned by none other than Big Brother Buddy. I overheard Brenda chewing Buddy's ear off about how he should *sell* the property. Seems some developers want it for a fuckin' housing estate. You know, rows of 'little box houses made of ticky-tacky.' Christ, it would ruin the whole area!"

Jocelyn evinced more surprise than she actually felt but her sympathy was genuine. Horses and tract housing don't mix. "You're kidding. Do you think he'll sell?"

"If Brenda has her way, he will. She was giving him this whole spiel about owing it to Gabby. Ensuring the security of their Golden Years—which is a load of crap. He and Gabby are already golden in the fiscal sense. Brenda just wants a bigger slice of the pie when Buddy's gone—she's all the family he's got left."

"Is she hard up?"

"Shouldn't be. She works enough, thanks to him. She's just a greedy-guts, I'd say."

"More to the point, what did *Buddy* say?"

"Well, I have to hand it to the little fire hydrant—he surprised me. Told her to keep her nose out of his business or else. And no, I have no idea what 'or else' means. See? I *detected* that question in your inquisitive little eyes. Boy, are you always this snoopy?"

"Hey, I'm not the one who eavesdrops on other people's private conversations," she lied blithely. But then, he'd been fairly warned. "So why do you think he won't sell?"

"Well—this is only a guess—but did you see the Greenpeace decal on the side of his viewfinder? I think it's just possible, for all his gruff and grumble, that ol' Bud actually has a conscience. Or maybe Earth Day got to him. I saw him reading a Sierra Club magazine, too. Or . . . he might just love the land, like me. Stranger things have happened . . . and they always happen stranger in L.A.," he ended with an insouciant smile that didn't quite manage to hide the depths of his concern. Then he threw both hands up in a goofy, what-me-worry gesture and began brushing her hair.

There was no denying, though she'd been trying mightily, that Jack Breedlove was an interesting character, a man of parts. And she was starting to find those parts, separately and as a whole, awfully appealing. Now why, she wondered, did that make her feel like a traitorous spouse? Especially since the person she felt traitorous toward, a certain lousy lieutenant, was about to be espoused to another. It made absolutely no sense, she told herself firmly as a ground swell of anger rose up in her; not anger at Phillip, anger at herself for months of languishing like some third-rate Ophelia, longing "to talk to some old lover's ghost." Behind it all was just plain, lily-livered cowardice and she was sick of it.

Tilting her head back, she looked up, pushing aside his brush. "Hey, Breedlove, don't I owe you a meal?"

His eyes flickered once in surprise, quickly followed by that slow grin. "Well, you did say 'next one's on me.' But, since we both know you're a big fibber, I didn't think—"

"I don't *always* fib. Gets monotonous . . . And I know a great little Mexican place near—"

"You're on, lady. Tonight?"

"Yeah. Tonight."

"Morning, Josh . . . Jack. Is there any coffee yet?" Ginger came in wearing the standard star-incognito outfit: tortoise frame sunglasses, head scarf, and a jacket with the collar turned up. Her voice was no more than a whisper as she eased herself into the makeup chair like a geriatric patient. It wasn't hard to guess, even before she took off the dark glasses, that she'd had as bad a night as O'Roarke. With the glasses off, her eyes looking hot and red rimmed, it was clear that her night had been much worse. So bad that Jocelyn was almost afraid when she asked, "Did the fish disagree with you, too?"

"Huh?"

"The paella. I had a major attack of the upchucks around three A.M. Figured it had to be the fish."

"Really? Gee, no, I didn't have any reaction—Hilly either. I just . . . didn't get much sleep again," she murmured contritely, as if she were admitting a heinous crime. "Uncle Buddy's gonna kill me . . . But I'm sorry about the fish, Josh. You feel okay now?"

Touched by Ginger's genuine concern in the midst of her own obvious distress, Jocelyn leaned over and squeezed her hand. "Yeah, I'm fine. I find a good barf can be very cathartic sometimes. And don't worry about Buddy. I'll figure out a way to distract him."

As it turned out, Jocelyn didn't need to figure out anything; the day was so filled with distractions and upheaval on the set that Buddy had no time to fret and fume about his leading lady's skin tone. First, one of the grips accidentally cracked a camera lens, creating a major work stoppage while a replacement was found. Then there was a surprise visit by a Mutt-and-Jeff duo from Standards and Practices, who objected to some of the language in the script and nearly sent Austin into a cataleptic fit. As Jocelyn put it in the letter she was writing to Frederick Revere:

> . . . since Hell hath no fury like a writer/producer scorned. But I don't think Mutt and Jeff had any idea how close they were to meltdown, thanks to Austin's bottomless reservoir of New England reserve. And I must say he's taken it like a champ. He's holed up in his office right now, scribbling away like Mr. Gibbon so we'll all have the new pages by quitting time today. Though, when I went by his door, I did hear a faint voice cry out, "All my chicks slain!"
>
> On top of everything else, our fearless director and our fearsome D/P seem to be on nonspeaking terms with each other at the moment, which makes things go a little slower than their usual snail's pace. It can't be about Brenda—Buddy's not talking to her either. (Like I said, this guy's a real lamb chop.) I get the feeling that Banks is looking to step up in class—i.e., add "director" to his resume—and I wouldn't be the itsiest bit surprised if he had his sights set on Larry's job. Now Larry, having eyes to see and ears to hear and being nobody's fool, probably has the same feeling. Since the network guys, for fear of Gabby, I guess, dote on Buddy, it wouldn't be too tough for him to bad-mouth Goldstein right out of his director's chair . . . Perish the thought! I'm sure Buddy would make Otto Preminger look like a pussycat.
>
> Now, Freddie, there's something I've been meaning to say to you and, since I seem to have all the time in the world just now, I might as well say it: I know you'll be getting an invitation to Phillip's wedding. And I also know that you'll be having misgivings about going out of some stubborn sense of loyalty to me. Well—don't. It won't make things any better or worse for me and it's not fair to any of us. However he feels about me, Phillip thinks the world of you. And I know you truly like him. So go! If it'll make you feel any better, I think I'm nearly done licking my wounds. As a matter of fact, I have—hold on to your seatbelt—a d-a-t-e tonight. Sort of. I'm not sure yet. Really, it's no big deal . . . except all day I've felt like Jack Haley at the top of The Wizard of Oz. I keep wishing someone would run up and oil me or something. I'm afraid all my nuts and bolts have rusted, so to speak. Well, here's hoping it's nothing that a frozen margarita or two can't fix . . ."

"Would you like another margarita?"

"Yes." O'Roarke answered with a fervency that gave the waitress pause. Breedlove merely tapped his bottle of Dos Equis, signaling for another, and gave Josh a knowing, though not obnoxiously so, look.

"It's been a while, huh?"

"What? Since I've had Mexican food? God, yes. It's just not the same east of the Mississippi."

"Don't be thick. You know that's not what I mean. It's been a while since you've, uh . . . gone out."

"Yes," she said again, too chagrined to say more.

"Want to talk about it?"

Playing for time, she savored a mouthful of a truly fabulous chicken *quesadilla* and wondered how in the world one encapsulated two and a half years of personal history into light dinner conversation with a veritable stranger. Finally, deciding to opt for the better-part-of-valor approach, she shrugged and said, "I went out with someone for two years. He wanted to get married. I didn't. So he went ahead and got engaged to someone else. They're tying the knot at the end of the month. I bought them a very nice chafing dish and . . . that's that."

"That's that?!" Breedlove made a face and shook his head. "I don't think so, O'Roarke. You left out all the juicy parts. Like— did you love the guy? And, if so, are you still torching for him? And who the hell *is* this guy?"

"No one *expects* the Spanish Inquisition," Jocelyn intoned in her best Monty Python, but Breedlove wasn't buying the act so she dropped it. "Yeah, I loved him."

"But not enough to marry him?" Breedlove saw her bristle immediately and knew this was a question she'd been asked one too many times.

"I loved him enough *not* to marry him. In the friend, companion, and playmate category, I rate myself very high. In the wife and homemaker department, I'd rank just slightly above Clytemnestra. Okay?!"

Initially inclined to pooh-pooh such gross exaggeration, Jack took heed of her blazing eyes—the hazel had turned to jade green and he knew what that meant—and thought better of it. Instead, he placated, "Ooo-kay, I think we've cleared that up. Which leaves us with: what kind of guy would dump—"

"No, I don't think so, Jack. Let's not do this." She wasn't angry now, just very, very definite. Laying down her knife and fork, she put one hand lightly on his and looked him straight in the eyes. "Listen, I appreciate your interest. And I know it's the done thing—playing Twenty Questions about past loves—when you're trying to get to know someone new. But I've never liked it, never felt comfortable with it. I mean, we could both sit here and tell each other all the things that were wrong with our other relationships and bad-mouth our exes till the cows come home. But it wouldn't really make us any closer, would it? And, for me anyway, it'd feel disloyal and . . . dishonest. I'd just much rather start fresh."

"Well, I think I can live with that," he said softly as he twined his fingers through hers. And he meant it. A veteran of the L.A. Dating Wars, where women, especially actresses, were only too glad to tell you their Life Stories, fully footnoted, in one sitting, he found O'Roarke's attitude blessedly refreshing and intriguing. "So what do we talk about?"

"Hey, there's always horses . . . if you don't mind talking shop."

"Mind—mind?! Does Mario Andretti mind talking engines? Did Hannibal mind talking elephants?"

So horses it was and nothing but horses for a solid hour. Jack caught himself expounding from time to time, but Jocelyn didn't seem to mind. She was a good listener and didn't ask stupid questions. Nor was she soppy about horses like some women, just genuinely fascinated, which he attributed to her Hibernian heritage. Telling her about the spring foaling, when his favorite mare had had a breech birth that had been touch-and-go for sixteen hours, he noticed that she was literally on the edge of her seat, too engrossed to eat or drink.

"But they both made it, right? The mare and the foal?"

"Oh, yeah. He's a fine colt, perfect confirmation. But it was a near thing. So I named him C. C."

"C. C.? For? . . . Oh, I know—Close Call, right?"

"Right! Give the little lady a—"

"Would you like your check?"

Judging by her martyred air, their waitress wasn't just asking; she was giving a heavy hint. Jocelyn blinked twice, as if she'd forgotten where she was, then looked at her watch and gasped,

"Oh, m'gosh, it's late!" She snatched up the check before Jack could even attempt a grab for it and started fishing in her shoulder bag for her wallet. "Shit! I don't believe it!"

"Don't tell me you forgot your wallet. 'Cause I won't believe it either, O'Roarke," he kidded.

"No," she groaned, tossing a piece of magic plastic on the table, which the waitress scooped up like a bird of prey and made off with. "I forgot the new pages! The ones Austin wrote today. We're shooting one of those scenes tomorrow and I haven't learned the new lines yet."

"Hey, relax. It'll probably be hours before they get to it. And Austin says you soak up lines like a sponge."

"No, I have to go back and get them. I like to sleep on a scene before I do it. Plus Austin busted his hump grinding that stuff out. I don't want to show up tomorrow and just wing it."

"All right, all right. I'll follow you back to the studio and—"

"You don't have to do that. It's out of your way."

"Jocelyn, I know you're a hard-boiled New Yorker and all," he said, cocking a skeptical eyebrow at her, "but do you *really* want to go into that big . . . dark . . . deserted studio all by your lonesome?"

"Mr. Breedlove, are you implying that I am, as the guys in my old neighborhood would say, a chicken-livered gullywhumper?"

"Lord, no! Nothing as base as that—whatever that is. I'm just suggesting that you might possibly want some company."

Jocelyn considered a moment before asserting, "Bet your ass."

And Jack was right; the studio was big, dark, and deserted, spooky in the way all such places of frenetic activity are when not in use. According to security protocol, the night watchman should've accompanied them into the building, but he was glued to a Lakers game on his portable TV and only too happy to hand the keys over to Breedlove. Jack unlocked the rear entrance and ushered Josh in ahead of him. Their footsteps echoed tinnily in the corridor as Jack ominously hummed the theme from "Outer Limits."

"Oh, very comforting," she hissed over her shoulder. "Thanks a heap."

"Can't help it. I'm a sucker for atmosphere. Doesn't this remind you of Hitchcock's *Stage Fright*—when Jane Wyman's being stalked by Richard Todd?"

"I'm sure it wasn't nearly as scary as being married to Ronnie," she shot back as they reached the makeup room door. "I must've left it in here. Have you got the key?"

"Right here, madame." He lurched forward à la Boris Karloff and unlocked the door, then turned to her with a mock leer. "Step into my chamber, won't you?"

"Let me guess . . . *Abbott and Costello Meet Frankenstein*, right?" She breezed by him and hit the wall switch. Without the mirror lights on, the room was still fairly dim, but it didn't take Jocelyn long to locate her new pages, lying underneath Ginger's copy of *Glamour*. Tucking the pages into her bag, she turned around to find Breedlove standing very close with a different kind of leer on his face.

"Who's this?" he asked. Placing his hands lightly on her shoulders, he cocked his head to one side and assumed a yearning, wistful air. "'I love you. I've loved you since the first moment I saw you. I guess maybe I even loved you before I saw you.'"

She knew perfectly well that it was Montgomery Clift to Liz Taylor in *A Place in the Sun* and it wasn't a bad line reading. In fact, it was a little too good for mere playacting and she was getting those damn tingles again. For safety's sake, she decided to play dumb and fall back on Joan Blondell. "Uh—Charles Boyer in *Gaslight*? Right before he starts telling Ingrid she's imagining things?"

"Oh, come on," he chided softly. "You know it's Monty . . . and you know you're not imagining things." Very slowly his hands slid down to the small of her back as he started to pull her to him. He was smiling, not leering now, as his mouth came down toward hers. Jocelyn had not kissed or been kissed by a man for longer than she cared to think, but she recognized the Silly Putty feeling in her kneecaps right away. Other atavistic responses were springing back to life with a vengeance as the smell of him, a musky, pinewood smell, reached her nostrils. She wasn't at all sure if kissing Jack Breedlove was a good idea, but it scarcely mattered since all her brain cells, not to mention her willpower, had already gone on sabbatical.

Their lips were just centimeters away from contact when they both heard a heavy, metallic thud.

"What's that?!" Jocelyn sprang away from Jack like a spooked mustang. He put a finger to his lips to shush her. They strained their ears to listen and caught the faint sound of shuffling feet.

"Somebody else is in here," she hissed. Jack shook his head. "I don't think so. Not in the building. Sounds too far away, maybe outside."

"Well, I don't care who or where. Let's get the hell out of here."

Knowing, with tacit accord, that the mood had been broken and the moment was gone, they went out the side door by the dressing rooms. Once outside, they stopped to take a cautious look around.

"That's where it came from—the darkroom."

"But it's after eleven. Why would Buddy be developing prints now? . . . Maybe we should go check."

"Unh-uh, no way," Jocelyn said firmly. "Once burned, twice shy. Either it's Buddy burning the midnight oil—which is perfectly possible since he seems to have the run of this joint—or a vandal. Frankly, I'd prefer the vandal. Let's just tell the night watchman and leave it to him. He's got a gun, he can shoot whomever . . . Frankly, I'd prefer Buddy."

"God! You really are a hard-case New Yorker," he said, only half joking. Her swift transition from pliable female to rock-bottom pragmatist made him a bit uneasy.

"Only in the sense that I know better than to play at cops and robbers. Is not my job, man . . . or yours."

"Now that's a really lousy Freddie Prinze. He always said it like, 'Iz not—' "

"Jack—just go tell the security guard, okay? We can talk the fine art of impersonation later."

"Like at my place . . . tonight?" he asked hopefully, the libidinous glint back in his eyes.

"In your dreams, fella." Jocelyn chuckled as she pulled out her car keys and sauntered toward her rented Acura.

"You know something, O'Roarke? I'm beginning to think you're a scaredy-cat."

"Well, frankly, my dear," she called out as she scooted behind the wheel, "I don't give a damn." Then she revved up the car so Breedlove wouldn't hear the little meow she let out.

7

"Here's a soldier of the South who loves you, Scarlett, wants to feel your arms around him, wants to carry the memory of your kisses into battle with him. Never mind about loving me. You're a woman sending a soldier to his death with a beautiful memory. Scarlett, kiss me. Kiss me once."

Then his mouth came down, hard and demanding, on hers. Only it wasn't Gable's mouth, it was Jack Breedlove's, and she was Vivien Leigh. This time Josh was aware it was just a dream, but that was fine with her; it was a class-A dream. Then Jack started doing things the censors never would've allowed back in '39. And that was just fine, too . . . until a tinny voice butted in with:

"Rise and shine, rise and shine! The early bir—"

Practice had made perfect and Jocelyn nailed the obnoxious alarm clock with one pillow toss. Rubbing her eyes and cursing the gods, she stumbled out of bed and was halfway to the bathroom when Austin knocked on her door and called, "You don't have to get up yet. We've had a slight change in schedule."

Something in the tone of his voice told her that this was not cause for rejoicing. Opening the door only a crack to spare Austin the full shock of her morning face, she squinted one eye at him and asked, "What gives?"

"Ginger's sick. At least that's what her maid told Larry. So we're going to do some pickup shots this morning and your new scene with Brenda in the afternoon . . . So sleep."

It was a tempting offer, but the woebegone expression on Frost's face made it impossible to accept. She flapped one hand in the general direction of the kitchen and said, "Go make coffee. Let me grab a shower . . . Then we'll talk about it, okay?" Austin nodded dumbly and ambled off like Eeyore. Shutting the door, she let her gaze drift back to the beckoning sheets and sighed, "Gone with the wind."

By ten o'clock O'Roarke was wending her way up Laurel Canyon with a stack of paperbacks piled on the passenger seat. Ostensibly, she was on an errand of mercy, delivering light reading to her ailing co-worker; in reality, she was going, at Frost's urging, to do a little covert checking up on their leading lady's condition. She felt like some sort of undercover truant officer and she didn't like the casting at all. But Austin had been eloquent in his pleading.

"All you have to do is just drop by and take a look at her, that's all. If she's really sick—okay, fine. We can work around it. But if it looks like Ginger's, uh . . . slipped back into old habits, Larry and I need to know. And we need to know *now*."

"For chrissake, Austin, what do you expect me to do? March in and ask for a urine sample?!"

"Don't be silly," he'd protested, though there had been just a fleeting pause, as if he were actually considering the feasibility of such a plan. Then his saner self shook off the notion as he soothed, "What's required here is great subtlety and tact—which, of course, you have in abundance. Not to mention a certain expertise in these matters."

"Meaning what exactly?" she'd asked, fixing him with a gimlet gaze. "Since I'm not a physician or a pharmacist—or a narc!"

"Uh, nooo, but you do possess a better empirical acquaintanceship with recreational drugs than most." Seeing the hard set of her mouth, Austin had dropped the fancy phraseology in favor of plain begging. "Come on, Josh, you know what I mean! You could always tell if someone was on 'ludes, or crashing from speed or coked up. I can never tell the difference. And your brother's a doctor and . . . you just have a real eye for this stuff."

"Glowing praise, indeed," she'd said sarcastically. "But what it really boils down to is: you want me to spy on Ginger, be a snitch, and, possibly, get her canned from a job that means everything to her."

"No—not canned. That's the last thing we want. Larry and I fought damned hard to get her cast and we want to keep her. Look, Josh, I know how you feel about all the 'Just Say No' hype and the hypocrisy behind it. But if Ginger's had a—a relapse, don't you think she deserves some help?"

So here she was, pulling up by the row of cypress trees in front of Ginger's place, still feeling like a Judas and praying that Ginger had nothing more than a common cold.

Ginger didn't have a cold. In fact, the first thing that struck Jocelyn, as she approached the sun umbrella that Ginger was lying under, wrapped in a snow white terry-cloth robe with a tall glass of iced tea at her elbow, was that Ginger was looking better than she had in days; she actually looked *rested*. Talking animatedly on the telephone, she waved to Jocelyn with one hand and patted the chair next to her chaise longue.

"Yes, I know the print was due back today but I don't *have* it . . . I told you, a friend of mine said he'd return it. He probably just forgot . . . Yes, yes, I will. I'll make sure he gets it to you by the end of the day, all right?"

Hanging up the phone, she rolled her eyes dramatically. "God, you'd think *Arsenic and Old Lace* was the hottest thing since *Terminator 2* to hear them. Do me a favor, when you see Buddy will you remind him to return it?"

"Sure thing . . . How're you doing, Ginge?"

"God, I feel great, Josh," she said with a guilty smile, "but please don't tell Larry and Austin. They'll think I'm goldbricking."

"Uh—of course not. But how come . . ."

"I slept—really slept—for twelve hours straight! Like a rock—no dreams, nothing. That's why I couldn't come in. Angelina, my housekeeper, tried to wake me at five-thirty and I was just comatose—didn't even hear the alarm and that sucker's loud! I only got up an hour ago. When she told me what she'd done—

bless her little heart, she was just trying to cover my ass—I figured the best thing was to play along. But I'm not slacking off." She picked up a stack of pink pages from her lap and waved them proudly. "I've been going over Austin's new stuff so I'll be letter perfect tomorrow. Just you wait and see!"

Ginger Jellicoe, rested and refreshed, was a sight to see; she looked easily five years younger than she had the previous day. Clean and scrubbed, no makeup on that flawless skin, she looked like a schoolgirl on holiday. Jocelyn eased herself into the patio chair, sneaking a quick look at the size of Ginger's pupils, hating herself for the question she was about to ask.

"You look great, Ginger. I'm glad you got some real rest. Did you . . . take anything? To help you sleep?"

Ginger bolted up as if she'd just been stuck with a cattle prod and shook her head vehemently, holding one hand in the air and the other over her heart.

"Swear to God, no! Nothing. Joshie, on my parents' grave, I haven't taken so much as a Tylenol since I got out of rehab. I have been stone-cold clean—that's why I think I've had so many awful dreams, real gross, suicidal stuff. Seeing myself dead. I figured it was from being clean after so long . . . that and losing my folks. But now, after last night, maybe I've finally gotten over the hump, you know? Maybe the worst stuff is behind me now. What do you think?"

"I think . . . that's great news," she said, mustering a convincing smile to hide the niggling doubt in her mind. Ginger had said "on my parents' grave," and that should've settled the matter. But Austin, blast him, was right; she *did* have an eye for these things. And Ginger's pupils, even in the morning sun, were still dilated enough to make her normally china blue eyes look nearly black; her voice was breathy and her breathing seemed shallow. To Jocelyn, that bespoke more than a sound night's sleep; it spelled barbiturates in big, block letters.

"Hey, Sis, as long as you're here, want to read through our new scene?"

"Hmm? Yeah, sure. Let's give it a shot."

"A house divided cannot stand itself," O'Roarke muttered aptly as she pulled into the studio parking lot. Knowing that Frost and

Goldstein would be anxiously awaiting her field report, she had subjected herself to a long and arduous "examination of conscience" on the drive down from the hills. The single clear conclusion she'd reached was: whatever she said or didn't say, she'd end up feeling like a total shit.

Paradoxically, considering her innate nosiness, Jocelyn truly believed a person's private life was his or her own business and that the ACLU was the second-greatest American invention after the Constitution. She wasn't particularly prodrugs, not since the advent of crack and not in the face of the waste and devastation they engendered, but she was firmly prolegalization for a number of reasons, both moral and economic, not the least of which was a stubborn belief in individual choice, even in the matter of naming one's own poison. If Ginger wanted to take a sleeping pill, which was perfectly legal if she had a prescription, she had the right, even if it was unwise. And was it any of Austin and Larry's business? Not really. Cocaine was Ginger's old nemesis, and she'd seen no evidence of that. On the other hand, she did owe Austin some kind of fealty. But while rehearsing the new scene, Ginger had seemed in top form; shouldn't that be enough? Knowing Austin, she doubted it, but it would have to do for now.

Walking toward the side entrance, something tugged at her peripheral vision. Glancing over at what she now thought of as Buddy's Bungalow, she noticed that the red light was on again, but that wasn't what had caught her attention. It was something small and gray lying on the pavement beneath the exhaust fan in the one narrow window; a dead pigeon. In New York this sight was more common than water-main breaks during rush hour, but in the California sunshine there was something unsettling about it, though she couldn't say why.

Looking around for a way to dispose of the remains, she spotted a copy of the L.A. Times in the trash can next to the window. She pulled out the real estate section and used it to pick up the little feathered carcass. Noting that there wasn't a mark on the bird, she briefly wondered if pigeons were susceptible to sunstroke; or maybe it was death due to smog. Placing the makeshift shroud on top of the trash bin, she wiped her hands none too fastidiously on the back of her jeans and went into the studio.

Her plan, such as it was, was to slip unobtrusively into costume and makeup and hide out in her dressing room until the assistant director called for the "first team" on the set, in order to avoid playing forty questions with Frost. This plan, as so often happened with O'Roarke's schemes, went up the spout almost as soon as she walked through the door.

"Well, at least *you're* here, thank God!" Larry Goldstein stood in the hallway chain-smoking a pack of Camel nonfilters. His hair, what there was left of it, stood out from his head in little spikes. It didn't take an Albert Campion to deduce that, when a balding man tugs repeatedly at his remaining locks, things are not going well. Josh smiled weakly and patted the harried director on one of his hunched shoulders.

"Rough morning, Lar?"

"No, no, it went fine. In fact, it was a little bit of heaven— since I didn't have to contend with Buddy Buttinski."

"How come? Is he sick, too?"

"Only in his mind, sweets, only in his mind. No, he just set up the shots and let Billy—the second unit man—do the shoot, which was just swell by me. Only now we have to set up for the next—your—scene and he's nowhere to be found. And I can't let Billy do it 'cause it'd violate union rules—then Buddy'd have me by the balls but good. Now Brenda's disappeared, too! She's probably closeted somewhere, schmoozing with her bookie. And we *have* to get this scene in the can today without going into overtime or we'll get behind . . . How's Ginger doing?"

"Ah, fine—I mean, better," Jocelyn faffed then, deciding one quick switch deserved another, volunteered, "Hey, I just saw the red light on. Buddy must be in the darkroom."

"Nah, can't be. He always wears a beeper when he's on the set. I've beeped like crazy and he hasn't answered so he must have—" Something in her face made the words fade on his lips; it was like watching a computer, a flesh-and-blood female computer, doing advanced calculus at terrifying speed. Then she sucked in her breath and grabbed his wrist. Goosebumps shot up his arm from where she held him as some of her fear transmitted itself to him.

"Josh, what? What's the matter?"

"Come on," she ordered, half dragging him out the door. Then she was ahead of him, running toward the bungalow as he blinked in the bright sun. She reached for the doorknob.

"Geez, Josh, don't go in there! Buddy'll have a fit." But she wasn't listening; she was pulling desperately at the doorknob.

"Shit! He's locked it. Help me break it in."

"We can't do that!" He hurried over, hoping to avoid disaster. O'Roarke was throwing all her weight against the door now, making it buck and groan. He tried to get between Josh and the door but she was like a dervish now. Spinning around in desperation, she caught sight of an abandoned hand truck propped against the wall. She grabbed the handlebar and aimed it directly at the door; she was going to use it as a battering ram! Larry waved his arms in the air as she started her charge, trying to head her off. An admirable instinct for self-preservation prompted him to jump clear right before the hand truck hit the door with a splintering crash.

"That's it! That cuts it," he wailed, grabbing tufts of hair with both hands. But Jocelyn still wasn't listening; she was knocking away shards of wood and climbing through the shattered door. Then there was a long silence before her voice came to him sounding tired and hollow.

"You'd better come in here, Larry."

The first thing he saw, after his pupils adjusted to the dim light, was the pan. It was on a long, narrow worktable; there was no liquid in the pan, just a single irreparably overdeveloped print. And then he saw what was behind the table. Lying on his back, spread-eagle like a child making a snow angel, his eyes open in mild dismay, was Albert Buddy Banks. It was funny, Goldstein couldn't help thinking, that he looked far more congenial in death than he ever had in life.

Jocelyn had gone to the wall phone and punched in 9-1-1. He heard her voice, oddly calm now, ordering an ambulance, giving the exact location. When she hung up, he turned slowly to her, trying to focus on her face, gauge her reaction. She wasn't hysterical or weepy; she looked defeated and somehow angry.

"The poor son of a bitch," he whispered. "Must've had a heart attack."

Looking down at Buddy's frozen face, her eyes darkened as she shook her head slowly with grim certainty. "I don't think so, Larry. I really don't think so."

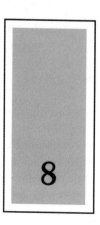

8

"No—no—no! Don't say it. Don't even form the words in your mind. I don't want to hear it. I . . . I just can't deal with this *now*."

Planting a hand firmly over each ear, Austin stared determinedly up at the ceiling and began to hum "What the World Needs Now" loudly. Perched on the corner of the huge oak table that served as his work desk, Jocelyn started making figure eights in the air with one sneakered foot and waited stoically for his hissy fit to pass. Not that she blamed him; a sudden death is always shocking, no matter whose, and the bearers of such news are seldom smiled upon by the recipients. But that wasn't why her old friend looked like he wanted to slay the messenger, i.e., her.

She had left a shaken Goldstein outside Buddy's darkroom to wait for the ambulance and gone looking for Frost, knowing that he'd want to keep news of the disaster contained for as long as possible. And Austin had held up well at the start of her gruesome report. It wasn't until she had described Banks' splayed-out corpse and used the word "hinky" that his nostrils had begun to quiver and he'd snapped.

"Don't say that."

"Huh? Say what?"

"*Hinky*. That's a Zitoism, right?" He referred to the colorful vernacular of Phillip Gerrard's right-hand man, Sergeant Thomas Zito.

"Well, yeah, but lots of cops say hink—"

"Shh! I know *that*. But they do not use—that word—when referring to death by natural causes."

"Uh, no . . . But see, Austin, that's the thing. I don't think Buddy die—"

That was when the fit hit the fan.

Humming like a beehive, he glared at her out of one eye. Frost's capacity for stewing was boundless and since he knew all of Dionne Warwick's hits by heart, she decided to intervene before he got to "Do You Know the Way to San Jose?" Leaning across the table, she yanked one lanky hand away from one ear.

"Look . . . I could be wrong. And it's not as if I *want* it to be a homicide."

"Oh, yes, you do," he shot back peevishly. "You do. That's why you called the LAPD so damn fast. You can't wait—"

"That's not fair, Austin. You *have* to call the police in cases of sudden death. If I hadn't, then it really would look hink—"

"Don't say it!"

"Sorry."

His look of censure was so severe that she was actually experiencing pangs of guilt, which was just crazy since the very last thing in the world she wanted, at this precarious juncture in her life, was to be dragged into an investigation. Austin of all people should know that she'd had her fill of cops and crime scenes and how dearly she cherished her newfound anonymity.

If only it weren't for that damn pigeon.

Reading her expression the way a gypsy reads palms, Frost, a tad calmer now that he'd succeeded in depressing her, broke in on her thoughts.

"What's so suspicious about a dumb dead bird anyway?"

"Not just 'a bird'—a pigeon. You're from New York, you know how tough those suckers are to kill. And there wasn't a mark on this one."

"That's absurd! It could've been a geriatric pigeon. I bet you didn't even think to count the rings on its feet."

Before she had the chance to educate her wayward friend on the marked difference between pigeons and redwood trees, there was a rap on the door, quickly followed by the appearance of a full head of wheat blond hair framing a pair of pale blue eyes.

"Sorry to bother you but I'm looking for Miss O'Roarke." The whole body slouched into the office now and smiled at them with teeth that were headlight white. Jocelyn heard a soft moan behind her: a sure indication that Austin had just experienced instant nirvana. Small wonder—the lanky youth standing in front of them was every inch Frost's notion of heaven with legs: the whole raison d'être for coming to L.A.

Since Josh, who wasn't into blonds, especially ones who looked about the same age as some of her nephews, had retained her powers of speech, the social niceties fell to her.

"You've found her," she said, putting a hand out. "I'm Josh O'—"

Instantly her hand was pressed between two tanned mitts and pumped vigorously. "Right, right! Jocelyn Frances O'Roarke! Wild, just wild, man. I never thought I'd get a chance to meet you. Blow me *a-way*."

Wondering if she were face to face with her very own John Hinckley, she gently extracted her mangled digits from his grasp. But this guy sure didn't have the look of a die-hard theatre buff; he didn't even look like he'd ever been *indoors*.

"Well, gosh—I'm glad you're—blown. But, uh, who *are* you?"

"Oh, shit! Sorry," he said, smacking himself smartly between the eyes. "What a jerk!" Then he grabbed her hand back and resumed pumping. "I'm Dwayne—uh, Detective Dwayne Hamill, LAPD."

If the late, great Danny Thomas had been present, it would've been the perfect moment for the coffee spit-take. As it was, Josh could only make a strangled gurgling sound in her throat. Austin had found his voice, though, and was itching to get into the conversation. Unfolding his stiltlike legs, he sidled forward to shake hands with the Blond Divinity.

"So glad you're here, Detective. I'm Austin Frost. Despite the unhappy circumstances, I must say it's a real plea—*rush* to meet someone so hip to New York theatre. Josh has *long* been one of the undiscovered treasures of the American stage."

"Come again?" Dwayne's blue eyes squinted in confusion, then popped wide. "Oh, yeah, I get it . . . But that's not what I meant. No offense," he added, turning swiftly back to Josh. "I'm sure you're a radical talent an' all. But I don't know diddly about show business. I was talkin' about your work with The Man."

"The *Man?*" She had a sneaking, sinking suspicion of what he was driving at, didn't want to hear it, but was compelled to confirm her worst fear. "What man?"

"Lieutenant Gerrard!" Dwayne spoke the dread words and let them hang in the air for a moment of reverential silence. Austin squelched a wince while O'Roarke shut her eyes and considered the abyss. The detective, however, was oblivious and blathered on, "He *is* The Man, boy! College guy—top of his class. Could'a gone on to make *mucho dinero* but he entered the force as a rookie! Walked a beat and all that shit. Became one of the best homicide detectives in the whole friggin' country! . . . And you *worked* with him on both the Weldon and the Saylin cases, right? I read *all* the coverage. Classic stuff!"

Hamill beamed down at Josh, who was patiently waiting for the floor to open and swallow her up. Austin took pity and intervened.

"Yes, remarkable man, Phillip. No question . . . But shouldn't we be getting down to the, uh, matter at hand?"

"Gotcha." In an instantaneous and amazing *volte-face*, Hamill reached into his back pocket, flipped open a small notepad, and began reeling off data. "Albert 'Buddy' Banks, male Caucasian, sixty-one years old. Director of photography, married to one Gabrielle Brent—I've sent one of my guys to notify the widow —last seen at ten A.M. on the set. Body discovered at one-thirty P.M. in his darkroom by Miss O'Roarke and Mr. Goldstein. No signs of physical violence. That sound right?"

Like Butch and Sundance, Josh and Austin exchanged one brief "Who *is* this guy?!" glance before O'Roarke nodded agreement.

"Yeah, that sounds right, Detective."

A quick grin broke through. "Call me Dwayne."

"Always," she mumbled, then couldn't help asking, "Did you talk to the medics?"

"Sure. They said it might be a heart attack. We won't know

anything more until the ME's had a look. But I need to ask you a few questions, Miss O'Roarke."

"Ask away . . . and it's Josh."

Dwayne nearly melted at this but recovered himself enough to ask the one question that Austin didn't want to hear. "So, Josh, what's this I hear about a dead pigeon?"

9

"Little birdies' dirty feet."

"Huh?"

"Nothing, nothing—I was thinking of a song," O'Roarke murmured as she looked down at the curled-up feet of the defunct pigeon wrapped in the L.A. Times.

"Oh, yeah, I remember that one," Hamill offered.

"Well . . . it is a classic."

"But why did the dead pigeon make you nervous?"

"It didn't at first, not until Larry said that Buddy hadn't answered his beeper—which he would've even if he'd been developing prints in there," she said, jerking a thumb toward the smashed door of the darkroom. "Then I remembered that the bird had been lying right underneath this exhaust fan. It's the only ventilation for the room. And I thought about all the chemicals they use to develop prints and I . . . got a little worried."

"I'd say you got a *lot* worried," Hamill amended, gesturing eloquently from the hand truck toward the smashed-in bungalow door. He ushered her ahead of him into the darkroom. Stepping over the debris in the doorway, she saw that the LAPD had done an efficient clean-up job, though the taped outline on the floor was a pretty effective reminder. Trying not to fixate on it, she watched Dwayne amble about the room, looking more like a kid on a school field trip than an investigating officer as he casually opened a drawer here, a cupboard there.

It reassured her somewhat to spot traces of powder about the room, indicating that the place had been dusted for prints at least. There were, she knew, as many different ways of examining a crime scene as there were detectives, but Hamill's amorphous approach was starting to make her edgy. It was probably just the old L.A.–style–versus–New York thing. And *he* was the professional, she the amateur, but it was all O'Roarke could do not to blurt out: "Do de phrase 'physical evidence' ring a bell?"

So she was taken aback when, after he finished examining a boarded-up door on the inside wall of the room, he turned around, pointed at the taped outline, and said, "Something bothers you about this, huh? You keep trying not to look at it but you can't stop. What is it?"

Giving him points for having good peripheral vision, she answered, "Well, yeah. See he was on his *back* when we found him. Now that I think about it, seems a little odd."

"How come?" His expression was so bland she had no way of knowing if he was testing her or just plain dense.

"If he'd had a heart attack," she began diplomatically, "wouldn't he have first clutched his chest and then crumpled *forward*?"

To her amazement, Dwayne proceeded to do an instant reenactment: an agonized grimace on his face, he clasped his heart and folded like an accordion, ending up half standing with his upper torso across the worktable, next to the developing pan. It seemed that Detective Hamill's methods were closer to Lee Strasberg's than Scotland Yard's. Josh wondered if applause was expected.

His head still on the table, he turned toward her and asked, "Like this?"

"Uh, more or less. Or he could've ended up right in the pan itself, I guess— Please! *Don't* demonstrate . . . It's just that I can't see him doing a dead fall."

"Dead fall?"

"That's what stunt people call it. They can do it, but they train

themselves. It's a tough trick because it goes against our natural
instincts. Even if you were in great pain—like a heart attack—
you'd still struggle very hard *not* to go backward, wouldn't you?"

Resuming an upright position, he gave her a friendly poke and
a wink. "Bitchin', just bitchin'."

"If you say so. Of course, I could be totally off base. Maybe a
massive cardiac arrest *can* knock you off your feet like a thun-
derbolt. Who knows?"

"Yeah, right. Who knows, who cares," he said with a nonchalant
shrug. "What else've you got?"

She couldn't control the surprised laughter that burst out of
her. "What else have I got?! What makes you think I've *got*
anything?"

"Hey, hey, don't get me wrong," he said, waving both hands
as a sign of conciliation. "I, uh . . . appreciate your position here.
Your friend, Mr. Frost, he's gonna be majorly bummed if this
turns out to be a homicide, I know . . . So I also know that you
wouldn'a even brought up the thing about the corpse's position
if you didn't have somethin' harder."

"How, Dwayne, how, on such a brief acquaintance as ours, do
you *know* this?"

Hamill rolled his eyes at the absurdity of such a question before
stating the obvious. "Be-*cuzzz* you've worked with The—"

"The Man," she finished for him, nodding her head sharply
several times. "Okey fucking dokey, I'll tell you what I've 'got,'
but first I'm gonna tell you what you *don't* get . . . which is: I have
never 'worked with The Man.' I just happened to be on hand
when some bad shit went down, that's all. And, since detection
is neither my profession nor my hobby, why don't you just *question*
me as you would any other ordinary goddamned witness instead
of trying to make me play Girl Sleuth in this little two-bit, ro-
manticized scenario you've got going?!"

Dwayne went a little gray beneath his tan, which she found
edifying, but, to his credit, he took it manfully and got right down
to business. Whipping out pen and notebook, he said formally,
"All right, Miss O'Roarke, if you could just tell me your best
recollection of the events leading up to the discovery of Mr.
Banks' body."

It was a good thing, he thought, to have taken that shorthand
course in high school because, after giving him the worst reaming

he'd had since the police academy, O'Roarke settled down and reeled off as clear and concise a statement, including the previous night's disturbance, as he'd ever recorded. But, damn, these New Yorkers sure talked fast.

"So when you and the hair guy—Mr. Breedlove—came out of the studio, was the red light on or off?"

"I'm pretty sure it was off. But you'd better double-check it with Jack."

"If it wasn't Buddy in here . . ." he began tentatively. "What do you think—I mean, do you have any idea what a perp might've been doing or looking for in here?"

"Not really," she said easily, now that her dander had settled. "But I don't know squat about photography or what Banks has been working on. And it really could've been Buddy working late. Like I said, this is all very thin. Hey, maybe the guy just kicked."

Despite her gut instinct, it was a notion that held great appeal for her. But Hamill seemed disinclined to second that emotion. Sweeping his hand around the room, he observed, "There's no sink in here."

"Uh, no, you're right. No sink, nowhere. Should there be?"

"Yeah, it'd be handy. I don't know much about photography either . . . 'cept I once dated a chic—woman who took photos. And all these chemicals they use—developing solution, stop baths, and fixatives—they all gotta be mixed with water first."

Scanning the room, Jocelyn saw what Hamill intended her to see: four plastic gallon jugs of distilled water lined up against one wall and a fifth jug, empty now, on the table next to the developing pan. He was being very calm, very matter-of-fact, but she could tell from the tiny vein pulsating at his left temple that there was one word he was dying to hear from her lips. Considering the lambasting she'd recently given him, she felt it was only humane to supply it.

"So?"

Picking the empty jug up off the table, he held it directly under her nose.

"So if that smells like H_2O . . . I'll eat my board wax."

There wasn't a drop of liquid left in the container but there was a lingering odor—the scent of almonds.

10

"Jesus! You poor kid. What an awful experience! And then Surfer Cop grills you for hours on end, the prick. After you've just had the worst shock of your *life*. Look, honey, maybe I should drive you back to Austin's. You must be really shook."

Pleasant as it was to have a strong man's strong arm around one's shoulder, Jocelyn chafed at the false position in which she found herself firmly planted. But how do you explain to a man, especially one being as sweetly solicitous as Jack Breedlove, that coming upon a corpse, while never a happy happenstance, was not quite the nasty shock that one might reasonably assume it to be? She felt sure that there must be a kind of etiquette for such a situation but, unfortunately, it was ground that Amy Vanderbilt had never thought to cover. Now *there* was a title that would sell, she thought loopily: *Good Breeding, Homicide, and You.*

The notion made her smile until she remembered that it wasn't a homicide, at least not yet. And, even if Buddy's passing had been arranged, it was no affair of hers. So she resolved with a firm shake of her shoulders, causing Jack's arm to slide off.

"Josh, you're shaking. Maybe I should get you a blanket . . . It might be delayed shock."

O'Roarke was thankful that she and Jack were alone in the makeup room. If Austin had been around, he would've laughed out loud at such a suggestion. Still she had to do something, short of telling the truth, to assure Breedlove that she wasn't on the brink of collapse.

Before he could start blanket hunting, she picked up his hand and placed his arm back around her shoulders. Tilting her head back so she could look into those familiar hazel eyes, she said softly, "Don't bother. This is much nicer."

He'd heard how shock could affect people in a variety of odd ways, but Jocelyn's symptoms had to be the oddest. At first, when he'd found her shortly after her interview with the detective, she'd seemed unnaturally calm, a little tired but not overtly distressed. He'd expected the tears to come once they were alone and things started to sink in. But he still couldn't spot a trace of moisture in those clear eyes. What he did see gave him a jolt; he had to be imagining it, but the look Josh was giving him now seemed more come-hither than downcast. It was crazy. Here he'd been dying to bed this woman since the day he'd met her and she'd been nothing but prickly and elusive. So why would she be getting turned on *now?* It just wasn't possible.

"You know, you have an amazing life line," she said dreamily, tracing it down his palm with one languorous finger, ending right at the pulse point on the inside of his wrist. "Not just that it's so long. It also shows great physical vitality."

It was possible.

As big a fan of instant gratification as any man, Breedlove struggled mightily to control his baser instincts. This had to be some bizarre form of delayed reaction, something to do with the old sex-death link. But whatever it was, he told himself sternly, it was not to be taken advantage of or exploited for carnal ends. The fact was Jack Breedlove had A Code about these things and that code stipulated that ladies were to be made love to only when in full possession of their faculties. But the smell of her hair and the way those wavy tendrils were brushing against his neck put the code in immediate danger of crumbling. He had to act fast.

Abruptly removing his arm, he turned Jocelyn to face him.

"Listen, I really—*really* think you should let me take you home now."

"Why?" Disappointment flitted across her face. Then she took a step closer with a wicked glint in her eyes. "You got a hot date later?"

"Of course not! It's just . . . You're not feeling yourself now."

"Nooo, but then I usually only do that in the privacy of the boud—"

"Jocelyn! Cut it out! You're acting . . . weird."

"Weird?!" She stepped back, shaking her head ruefully. "Boy, I must really be losing my touch. Well, I guess it's true—you don't use it, you lose it. But I was kinda hoping that it was like riding a bike, you know?"

She'd done it again, slipped, in the wink of an eye, from a temptress back into Ms. Wisenheimer. Coupled with the hard-on he was getting, it was more than the man could handle.

"For chrissake, Josh, a man just died! How can you be so—"

"So what? Heartless? Unfeeling? You'd like it better if I were sobbing and hysterical? Yeah, you would—well, no can do, fella. But I do apologize for my unseemly behavior. I hope I haven't offended your delicate sensibilities."

"God, you can be such a bitch, O'Roarke."

"Yeah? Well, better a bitch than a basket case—that's always been my motto," she shot back, snatching up her car keys. Part of her was appalled at how badly she was behaving, but that part was somewhere north of Greenland. The rest of her was in the Tropic Zone, burning from the sting of rejection. Her only thought was to get away before she disgraced herself completely.

Breedlove's only thought was he'd be damned if he'd let her.

"A bitch . . . and a coward."

She turned slowly and deliberately before speaking. "I beg your pardon?"

"You heard me—a coward. You know, as in chicken-livered gullywumper."

No one had called her that for a very long time, well over twenty years. But the instincts of an unregenerate tomboy never die, so she threw her keys at his head. They whizzed by Jack's left ear but he just kept talking. "Can't deal with a little real tenderness and intimacy. So you tried to turn it into a sex game, huh? Just to put me off stride."

"Hah!" She pushed past him to retrieve her keys. "You're the one! *You* can't deal with a woman taking the smallest initiative. Why don't you hang a sign—'Only Passive Partners Need Apply.'"

"That's total bull and you know it. But, hey, I forgot—lying's your strong suit, right?"

"Jerk!"

"Liar!"

Jocelyn grabbed for the keys. Then Breedlove grabbed her wrist. Then he grabbed her waist . . . and everything else there was to grab, all at once. It was like a very swift and sensual body search. They were soldered together from chest to thigh with Jocelyn pressed up against the wall. He pinned her wrists above her head, though she wasn't offering the slightest resistance, and began exploring her face and throat with his mouth.

A remote part of him was protesting that this was not according to The Code and not the way he'd wanted it to happen between them, but that part was way far north of Greenland, too. Then it completely disappeared off the map when she deftly bent her head and slipped her tongue inside his ear. They were both breathing heavily enough to seriously deplete the oxygen content in the long narrow room, but way past caring.

As his lips moved farther down her body, Jocelyn pulled her hands out of his hold and buried them in his hair as she arched her body up toward his. He made a sound that was half moan, half growl, then whispered hoarsely, "God, you smell *incredible.* Like cinnamon . . . I just want to eat you whole."

So overloaded by sensation that she actually felt she might faint, she caught one of his greedily wandering hands—the other was busy tugging her blouse out of her waistband—and pressed it to her mouth, inhaling.

"And you smell like . . . almonds."

He was never sure afterward about the next sequence of events. He just had fragmented images of Josh slipping out of his arms, suddenly pale-faced with a stricken look in her eyes; all the signs of keen distress that had been so glaringly absent earlier were there now. Then there were disjointed mumblings about wanting to see how Ginger was holding up and promising Austin that she'd be back for dinner. Then she was out the door and a minute later he heard the sounds of her Acura revving up and peeling out of the parking lot.

Of all the transmutations he'd seen this woman execute in the brief time he'd known her, this one took the frigging cake, he thought. No actress was *that* good; he knew she'd been as close to No Return as he had. What on earth could've brought her back down to it so abruptly?

Still breathing hard, he gazed down sadly at his now swiftly dwindling resources and pondered aloud.

"Either she's a cock teaser . . . or a certifiable schizophrenic."

What was more disturbing to him than either of those possibilities was the realization that he was more set than ever on having her.

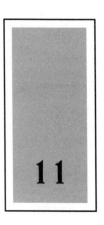

11

"Can you meet me at the Santa Monica Pier?"

Rubbing sleep out of her eyes, Jocelyn frowned down at the phone receiver then demanded, "Who is this?"

"Dwayne—Detective Hamill. I need to talk to you."

"Uh, okay. But what's wrong with your office? Or the studio? Why Santa Monica, for cripes sake?"

"Ah! Good question. Well, for one thing, we need privacy. I don't want the folks at the studio seeing us together right now."

"But your office—it's gotta be closer than Santa Monica."

"Well, yeah, it is. But they just repainted it and it's like toxic in here now—and, uh, I'd kinda like to check out the aggro rookies."

"That's what—green cops?"

"Nah, nah! Young punks on short boards. The kids, they all start out at Santa Monica before going on to the big waves . . . just like I did. You'll dig it."

"Uh-huh. And you're sure that this isn't something we can just discuss over the phone, Dwayne?" she asked with one dwindling ray of hope.

"Oh, no, we should be *mano a mano* for this—sorry, make that *mano a womano*," he amended. "The lieuten—"

"Don't say it, Dwayne."

"Whoops! Sorry, sorry. Can you be there by ten? It's only a twenty-minute drive from where you are."

From past experience of native Angelenos and their unique perspective on time and space when behind the wheel, she mentally added on another twenty minutes' driving time and said, "I'll be there at ten-thirty. And you'd better have a large cup of coffee—medium with one Sweet 'n Low—waiting for me."

"Uh, okay, but you know caffeine's a bad—"

"Shut up, Dwayne."

"Gotcha."

She took Santa Monica Boulevard; it wasn't the fastest route but it spared her driving on the L.A. freeways. She hated them; they were fast and efficient, at least during off-peak travel, but five lanes was too much of a muchness for O'Roarke's taste. There was something about all those shiny cars whizzing along beneath a sky the shade of Gatorade that always made her feel like one of a thousand mechanical lemmings hurtling toward some unseen oblivion. This was Jocelyn's problem with L.A. as a whole; she wasn't given to the typical New Yorker's knee-jerk disparagements but, still, it was too slippery a place to inspire faith, long-term faith, anyway.

On one hand, she loved the romance of Old Hollywood, how it had created itself out of nothing but guts, glitz, and scandal. The glitz was still there, though not with the same panache; there were plenty of good actors out here but damn few who knew how to be real movie stars in the old tradition. As for guts, well, the money men ran things now. The Suits, as Austin called them. Poor Austin—he and Goldstein were holed up with The Suits right now, trying to determine how much time and money would be lost by the inconvenience of Buddy's demise. Then there was the matter of finding a new director of photography. For the sake of expedience, Larry and Austin wanted to give the job to Buddy's assistant, Billy Orbach, a competent, likable kid who could really use the credit and was as obliging as his predecessor had been contentious. But The Suits, of course, would have the final say.

After parking her car on the lot by the kiddie rides, Jocelyn walked out to the pier and spotted Hamill almost immediately. The neon green windbreaker he was wearing made it easy. Clutching a paper cup that she hoped was her coffee, he was hunched over a railing, intently studying a group of boys, seallike in their wet suits, through his Ray-Bans. To Josh's untrained eye they seemed to be paddling about to no purpose.

"A little early for their midmorning break, isn't it?"

"Oh, Miss O'Roarke, hi!" He straightened up, making an odd move with one arm that looked suspiciously like the beginnings of a salute but turned into another bone-crushing handshake. God, this guy should run for office, she thought, snatching her hand away to make a grab for the paper cup.

"It's Jocelyn, remember? This for me?"

"Yeah, I hope it's still hot."

"Doesn't matter. I just want my caffeine fix," she said just to tease him. But Dwayne's attention was back out on the water, his normally sunny expression changed to an almost-frown.

"Aw, geez, look at that turkey! He cut right through that set they're waiting for. Now the waves'll be all gnarly. What a barney!"

"*Pardonnez-moi, mais je ne parle pas surf-ese, mon fou,*" she replied, feeling that one totally unintelligible remark deserved another. Dwayne got the point and pointed toward a narrow speedboat that was cutting through the waves at an amazing clip.

"Those kids were waiting for a set of waves to come in and that idiot just cut through them. Those suckers are powerful and the wake will make the waves too choppy to ride. It's just real . . . bad manners."

"Ah, light dawns. What is that thing? It looks like a gigantic Virginia Slim."

"That's what they call 'em—cigarettes. That one's a Scarab—like the boat Don Johnson used to tool around in on 'Miami Vice'—probably has three hundred and fifty horsepower or more."

"I see—a flying phallus, huh?"

Hamill actually blushed, which surprised and delighted Josh. Looking down at his feet, he stammered, "Well, uh—yeah, kinda . . . I guess. Least I always think those guys are compensating for the lack of—*somethin'*, you know?"

"Spoken like a true detective, Detective," she said kindly, now that she'd had her fun. "Which reminds me—why the hell am I here?"

"Right, right. I wanted to tell you about the lab report . . . And I wanted to thank you."

"For what?"

"Well, if you hadn't found Mr. Banks when you did, we might never've known. The evidence would've just *evaporated* . . . like into thin air. 'Cause there were only a few drops left."

"In the water jug, you mean? A few drops of what?"

Dwayne pulled himself up to his full height and smiled like a proud papa. "HCN—hydrogen cyanide! Just like we figured."

"Oh, goody gumdrops," she muttered glumly, now that he'd confirmed the source of the almond scent, "but I still don't see how it got *in* him. It's a violent poison but it doesn't kill you on the spot. If he'd drunk the stuff, he would've started screaming like a banshee—and nobody heard a thing. Plus he'd have enough time to make it out of the darkroom to get—"

"But he didn't *drink* it, Jocelyn. That's the beauty part—he in-*haled* it!"

"Well, that'd do a number on your mucous membranes, but it wouldn't kill you."

"Not by itself, no . . . Don't you *get* it?"

None of Hamill's laid-back qualities were present now; he was practically hopping from foot to foot trying to contain his glee. O'Roarke was glad that one of them was having a good time but she wasn't used to such puppyish high spirits in an officer of the law. If she'd had a newspaper handy, she would've rolled it up and smacked him on the nose. Instead she fell back on an old standby, verbal abuse.

"No, Dwayne, I don't. Because, as I keep trying to tell you, this is not my line of *work!* And I'm not going to dick around with you, playing Twenty Questions. So why don't you just 'follow your bliss' and cough it up—now."

"Right, I'm gettin' too stoked, sorry," he said, suddenly the epitome of professionalism. "I forgot you don't know anything about photography . . . Thing is, you're right. Hydrogen cyanide by itself isn't immediately fatal. But if it's mixed with *any* acetic acid, it instantly converts to a gas. And one good whiff'll take you out faster than the impact zone at Waimea Bay. I'm talkin' presto nuke-o time. And guess what has acetic acid in it?"

The penny dropped but good.

"The developing solution."

"Bingo! God, you're good . . . See, all the chemicals they use contain acetic acid and they all have to be diluted with water. Banks' darkroom didn't have a sink in it. That's why he had those jugs of water around. Somebody—somebody who knew a little about cyanide and a little about photography—went in there the other night and emptied one of the jugs, then filled it with HCN . . . Then all he or she had to do was wait. It was a very smooth move. 'Cause if you hadn't gone back to get your script that night and if you hadn't found the body when you did, we might've missed this totally. And even if the coroner had found something in the autopsy—we'd have no friggin' time frame for the planting of the cyanide. Thanks to you we do. Now all we have to do is find someone with motive."

"All? That's *all* you have to— Find some*one* with motive?!" Jocelyn plopped down on a nearby bench and regarded him with the sheer amazement that determined youth always inspires in more jaded souls. "Ye gods—Dwayne! There are dozens of people who could've gotten into that room. And Buddy Banks was not a guy with a large fan club. To know him was *not* to love him, see? So you're looking at a list of potential suspects longer than"—she searched for a metaphor that would resonate for him—"longer than the last chord on 'A Day in the Life.' "

"Yeah? Well, see, I was thinkin' that might be the case," he said, tracing one Reeboked foot along the bottom rail. "And I'll be honest with you, Jocelyn, I'm pretty good with physical evidence. But psychology and motivation an' stuff, that's not my strong suit . . . That's why I'm *awful* glad that you're around to help me."

If she had been a younger woman or one less experienced in the ways of cops and the lengths they'll go to to crack a case, she might've succumbed to the look of adoration and expectation on Dwayne Hamill's tawny face. As it was, she almost did. But Dwayne pressed his luck by adding: "Don't you think the lieutenant would want you to?"

Ever so delicately Jocelyn tipped the remains of her coffee over the toe of his Reeboked foot and strode off to the penny arcade.

After a quick mopping-up effort, Hamill followed O'Roarke into the penny arcade and found her engaged in a heated round of Whack-a-Mole, the object of which was to see how many mechanical moles one could whack on the head with a heavy rubber mallet as they briefly popped up out of their holes. Jocelyn had already racked up over one hundred points. It was primitive compared to the other computerized seek-and-destroy games around it, but that was the appeal, he guessed, judging from the small grunts of satisfaction she emitted with each thwack. While no student of psychology, he knew intuitively that it would be ill-advised to interrupt her while she was wielding a heavy weapon. So he slunk over to play his own personal favorite, Rad Mobile.

Several minutes later, as he was negotiating a hairpin turn, he heard a voice heavy with sarcasm. "I find it remarkable that anyone who spends a good five hours a day, most every day, driving a car would opt for *this* as a means of diversion."

"Well, I dunno," he answered unperturbed. "Is it any weirder than someone who doesn't want to dirty their hands helping the police catch a killer but digs slugging little critters over the head?"

"They're not *real* critters." She was beginning to sound more cheerful, especially since he'd just wiped out on the turn. He caught her off guard when he spun around to face her.

"But it's a *real* killer . . . And I need your help. That's real, too."

"Aw, Dwayne, come on! It's like you're the Straw Man—and you think I'm the Wizard of Oz, see? You've got a brain. You don't *need* me. You're doing fin—"

"I do! And it's—it's not what you think. It's not just because . . . of him," he said tentatively, then hastened on. "I need *eyes!* On the set. I have to know how these people behave when I'm not around. See, I think we're dealing with a *stone*-killer—very cold, very controlled. Not someone who's gonna give something away during an interrogation. But after a while, when they think they've gotten away with it, when they start to feel a little cocky, they're gonna slip . . . And that's why I need *you.*"

"Why you little turd," she said, but he could see she was trying not to smile. "You know a lot more about psychology than you let on . . . I bet you've even taken a course or two, haven't you?"

Then she startled him by tickling his rib cage. He chuckled, knocked her hand away, then blushed again. "Hey! Cut it out!"

"Sorry, officer." She gave him a playful slap on the arm. "Come on. Buy me some fried clams."

"For breakfast?!"

"Call me madcap—call it lunch. Come on."

Back on the boardwalk, he watched her scarf down the clams in record time. Licking tartar sauce from her fingertips, she asked, "Is there anybody you've eliminated yet?"

"As far as the time frame goes—yeah, sort of. Your friend Mr. Frost was home all night, we know that for sure."

"He'll be so relieved."

"Banks' wife was at their place in Malibu. The housekeeper swears she got home by ten-thirty . . . But I'll keep an eye out to see if she gets a raise any time soon."

O'Roarke was impressed but restrained herself from patting his back or saying good boy. Plainly it was time to start taking this kid seriously.

"What about Buddy's sister?"

"Oh, man, what a major *chore!*" Dwayne smacked himself in the forehead, a clear indication that he'd met the beloved Brenda. "Nearly did a Zsa Zsa on me just 'cause I asked her whereabouts . . . Don't tell anybody I said it, but some people *should* take 'ludes."

"Mmm, yes. And many. So where about was she?"

"Well, she hated like hell to admit it but she finally coughed up. She was at the tracks. Has the admission stub to prove it, too . . . Now Tim Hayes was working a shoot on Catalina that night. That knocks him out of the water since he was . . . well, out on the water and—"

"Wait, wait! Back up. Which track was Brenda at—Santa Anita or Hollywood Park?"

"Hollywood Park. Said she stayed till the last race and we have a witness who saw her leave then."

"But Hollywood Park's just in Inglewood. You could jump on

42 to 405, go to Culver City, and still get back in time for the last race, couldn't you?"

Again the adoring smile. "*Knew* you'd pick up on that. Yeah, it's a tight squeeze time-wise. And I can't feature bubble-butt Brenda crawling over a wire fence, but it's possible. So we're looking for someone who saw her before the last race."

They were standing by the bumper cars now and an ancient speaker was wafting out a lesser-known Beatles song with John singing lead. It was one of Jocelyn's favorites. She started to hum along as she contemplated the juicy image of Brenda Arnold struggling to mount a fence and missed part of Dwayne's next remark.

"—her housekeeper confirms it, too. But for my money, Jellicoe has the weakest alibi since she says—" Jocelyn jerked to attention as Dwayne's words dovetailed almost perfectly with Lennon's lyrics: "She was only sleeping."

12

"You must tell me every single *word* he uttered! Did he say anything about me?"

"Yes, just a word. But I thought it was very sweet."

"What?! What was it?"

"Innocent."

"Is that *all?*"

"Hey, it's better than 'possible suspect,'" Jocelyn teased, adding, "and he said it with great feeling." Wending her way up the really twisty part of Mulholland Drive, as opposed to the normally twisty part, she didn't dare take her eyes off the road but she could feel Austin's skeptical gaze boring into her.

"He did not. You are toying with me in my hour of need. I find you cruel and . . . unnatural."

That was fine by her. Frost had had a rough morning soothing The Suits. But they'd finally agreed to let Billy Orbach take on Buddy's job so shooting could resume. However, when he'd ar-

rived back home there was a message from Ginger asking him to
come by her place. On her return Josh had found him waiting
in the driveway to enlist her aid. As she wanted to see Ginger
for her own reasons, she'd agreed to take him over, since Austin,
an indifferent driver at best and a peril to public safety at worst,
was feeling too frayed to get behind a wheel. To ease his nerves,
she'd mentioned her meeting with Hamill, and it had worked like
a charm. Neither death nor impending disaster had ever swayed
Austin from an infatuation once he was firmly fixated. It reminded
her of a remark Michael Caine once made about John Huston's
films; they all had one theme, he'd said: "The Improbable chasing
the Impossible—and never getting it." That was a lot like Austin's
love life and certainly the case with arrow-straight Detective
Dwayne. Normally she didn't like to indulge him in these fruitless
obsessions but today it came under the heading of Mercy
Diversion.

"Now I resent that. You've always said that cruelty came very
naturally to me . . . He surfs, you know."

"Does he?!" Frost sighed longingly. "Oh, what I wouldn't
give to wax his board." His eyes glazed as he drifted into a
dreamy reverie that lasted for the rest of the short drive to Laurel
Canyon.

Before they even reached the front door of Ginger's house, it
swung open and a tiny dynamo in Oshkosh overalls came pelting
down the flagstone path toward them. Hilly Hayes catapulted
herself into Jocelyn's arms and without preamble demanded, "How
come Mommie's so sad? She's been crying *all day!*"

"Well, crying's good sometimes, pumpkin," O'Roarke said,
gently pushing one of Hilly's wayward curls behind her ear. "Like
when you scrape your knee and it really smarts? Crying sort of
helps to wash the hurt away, doesn't it?"

The child considered this point gravely before allowing, "Yeah,
sometimes. But she said Unca Buddy's gone. *Where's* he gone?"

Standing in back of Hilly, Austin gave Josh a look that said,
"I wish you well and leave me the hell out of it." She didn't catch
it, didn't even blink or give a "Why me, O Lord, why me?" grimace,
which Frost felt she was fully entitled to; she just stayed focused

on the little girl in her arms and softly answered, "He's gone like your grandma and grandpa are gone, sweetheart. He died . . . so you're not going to see him anymore."

There was no gush of tears; Hilly paled some but was too busy cogitating to cry. "Is died—? Is that like our song, when the worms crawl in and out and play peesknuckle on your snout?"

This time O'Roarke did wince. She'd let herself in for this one and she couldn't duck it. "Hilly, that's just a goofy song. And that's not gonna happen to Buddy. It doesn't happen to anyone, really."

"What *does* happen?" Hilly inspected Jocelyn's earrings closely while still intent on getting answers. "Why can't I see him?"

Holding Hilly with one arm, she used the other to wave Frost on toward the house. This was going to take some time and he was more than happy to follow her directive—he was ecstatic. Josh asked Hilly, "Why don't you show me that rabbit Buddy gave you? And we'll talk some more, okay?" Ginger's daughter wriggled out of O'Roarke's arms, grabbed one of her hands, and promptly started dragging her toward the backyard. As they rounded the corner of the house, Frost heard her ask, "Is my bunny gonna die, too?" Then Jocelyn's reply: "Don't worry. Not until he's good and ready."

He walked up the path slowly, shaking his head. It always amazed him to see this side of O'Roarke and it was a side that few people besides himself, Frederick Revere, and maybe Phillip Gerrard knew existed. For a woman, prickly and caustic by nature, who had always firmly eschewed the notion of childbearing and motherhood, Jocelyn O'Roarke was simply aces with kids. They gravitated to her like ore to a lodestone; not just her myriad nieces and nephews, but any kid who wasn't a total brat and even some who were. Most people would attribute this to a repressed maternal instinct. But Frost had another theory: unlike many actors who loved to psychobabble on about "finding the inner child," Jocelyn had simply never lost hers. She just *knew* how kids felt and thought because she'd never, for an instant, forgotten what it was like. And children sensed it. Come to think of it, it was only with adults, usually of the male variety, that she had problems. That was probably why she was so fond of Ginger and vice versa, he thought. For all her distinctly adult physiology, Jellicoe was just a tall child at heart. Realizing this, he longed for Josh's swift return from the rabbit hutch.

"Frostie! You came!"

Comporting herself with much the same abandon that her daughter had so recently displayed, Ginger came flying down the staircase in a tie-dyed caftan and flung herself into Austin's unexpecting arms. "Isn't it awful? What am I gonna do? He's just . . . gone. And it's all my fault. I just—I can't go on." Less circumspect than her six-year-old, Ginger burst into sobs. Making feeble little "there, there" pats on her back, he tried to absorb this emotional onslaught and order his thoughts. He knew he wasn't functioning at his cerebral best today but what did she mean by "my fault"? Was his leading lady admitting to homicide? Then he remembered that Ginger knew nothing about Hamill's findings.

Holding her at arm's length, he asked, "What's your fault, honey?"

"Buddy! His heart attack. I . . . I think I might've set it off."

"No, no. Ginge, you didn't. I mean, it wasn't—" Screw the bunny hutch, where the hell was O'Roarke when he needed her? He had never before been in the position of having to inform someone that a loved one had been forcibly ushered out of this vale of tears.

He floundered. "Why on earth would you think it's your fault anyway?"

"Stress," she sniffed, taking in a big gulp of air. "That's one of the things that cause heart attacks, right? I think I . . . *stressed* him to death, you know?"

"Oh, honey, no, no, that's out of the question, really," Austin murmured as he led her into the living room and settled her on one end of a cushy wraparound sofa.

"Why?" She sounded exactly like Hilly, and Austin still wasn't prepared to mention the "M" word, so he fudged.

"Uh, for one thing, Buddy was too nast— I mean, he wasn't prone to stress." This wasn't going well. Christ, it's hard to be tactful about the son of a bitch, Frost thought. Then like a true writer, he finessed it by quoting another source. "Like in the Bible where it says it's more blessed to give than to receive? That's what Buddy was like, right?" Ginger nodded forcefully so he forged on. "About everything, even . . . stress. He *gave* it, he didn't receive it. See what I mean?"

She did, but she wasn't willing to let go of her guilt yet. Thumping a cushion with a curled fist, she insisted, "But I sure didn't *help* any! We—Hilly and me—we made a lot of extra work for him. He knocked himself out for us. And what thanks did he get? Maybe *this* much is all." She held her thumb and pointer a hairbreadth apart just an inch or two in front of his face. "And then I go and—"

"Wait, wait a sec," he interrupted, impatiently brushing her hand out of his sight lines. "What do you mean about making extra work for him? Ginge, he was your friend and Hilly's godfather—that's not *work.*"

"No, no, I don't mean that. I mean the other stuff. The legal and business stuff. He took care of all that."

He really wasn't functioning at warp drive today. For a moment there he actually thought that she was referring to her career until he recalled who her agent was. The notion of Gabby Brent sharing the management of one of her clients' affairs with another human being, even a spouse, was beyond ludicrous; it was as unthinkable as Schwarzenegger doing Shakespeare.

"Took care of what exactly?"

"This! All this." Ginger waved an arm in a wide arc, indicating their plush surroundings. He could see she was growing impatient with him but still it made for a nice change from her self-castigation. "Don't you get it? Selling my father's business, managing the estate. Hell, I could never—I flunked tenth grade math, Frostie! Besides, when my parents made their—their will, I was still having, uh, problems. They made Buddy executor."

"They did?!" Austin's brain fog suddenly lifted. He was wholly alert now, so alert he imagined his ears tilting forward like a terrier's. After all, he'd been friends with O'Roarke too long not to recognize a potential bombshell like this one. Plus there was the undeniable fact, though deny it he would if anyone asked, that it would be rather pleasant to "scoop" Josh just once. "So what happens now? I mean, who becomes executor?"

If he'd asked her the square root of four thousand and sixty-three, she couldn't have looked more nonplussed.

"Well, I—I just never imagined that . . . Gee whiz, this is gonna make me sound like such a feeb. But I really don't *know*."

"If I were you, Miss Jellicoe, I'd look into it *real* fast. 'Cause I'm gonna need to know the answer to that one, too."

The voice came from the foyer behind them and Ginger and Austin turned in unison to discover its source. When they did, Ginger froze while Austin melted. Jocelyn was there with a sleeping Hilly in her arms but standing a foot in front of her was, in Frost's opinion, visible proof of the existence of a benign god.

Taking the two steps down from the foyer to the living room, he approached the sofa with an outstretched hand. "We haven't met yet, Miss Jellicoe. I'm Detective Hamill from the LAPD."

"The police?" Undergoing the standard Hamill hand-pump, Ginger blinked once or twice in startled doelike fashion and regarded him with some dismay. "But why—"

Jocelyn broke in, speaking softly but urgently. "Listen, I'm going to put Hilly in bed. She's worn out. But I'll be right back, okay?"

Hamill looked over his shoulder and Austin caught the almost imperceptible nod he gave her; it indicated: *Message received. Will proceed no further until your return.* Eager to help Hamill in any way large or small, Austin wracked his brain for a conversational stall; anything short of "Nice weather we're having" would do. But Ginger beat him to the punch.

"But why the police? Buddy had a heart attack."

Hamill cleared his throat, keeping one eye on the staircase for O'Roarke's return. "Well, ma'am, the police are usually called to the scene in the case of a sudden death, you see."

"Um, okay. But that was yesterday. Why're you here *now?*" she asked, slowly rising and taking a step back from the sofa.

There was really no ducking it. Dwayne scratched the back of his head and stared down at the polished parquet floor for a moment before raising his eyes to meet her gaze. "I'm afraid I have some bad news, Miss Jellicoe. Mr. Banks didn't have a heart attack. He was killed by person or persons unknown, ma'am. So I'm gonna need to ask you some questions."

Tear-assing down the stairs with one hand on a banister, Jocelyn caught the tail end of Dwayne's statement and shouted out, "Austin—*move!* Catch her!"

It was one of those feminine intuition things that make men so uncomfortable. Like a tall pine after the lumberjack yells "Timber," Ginger swayed, then began to topple straight backward. Frost got there just in time.

Cradling her limp form, he was confounded to see Dwayne turn to Josh and ask, "That what you meant by a dead fall?"

Gazing down sadly at Ginger's prone form, she muttered, "Precisely."

13

"So, like on a one-to-ten scale, would you classify it as minor head-butt or a Nagasaki knockdown?"

"In between. Kinda like a five-lane pileup on the Hollywood Freeway," Ginger replied, along with a waffling motion of one hand.

In the annals of criminal investigation, this had to be one of the strangest interrogations ever conducted. *Or maybe it's just 'cause we're in L.A.,* Josh thought. *Or maybe it was just because it wasn't Phillip Gerrard conducting the interview,* but she swiftly suppressed that notion. Whatever the reason, the questioning of Ginger Jellicoe by Detective Dwayne beggared description.

After regaining consciousness and getting over her initial hysteria, Ginger had asked that Jocelyn and Austin be allowed to remain and Dwayne had blithely acquiesced. (Phillip would've put his big flat foot down but she, like Scarlett, just wasn't going to think about that now.) At any rate, it made little difference. Ginger and Dwayne, about the same age and children of Southern

California both, seemed to speak a common language and, as far as she and Austin were concerned, it might as well have been Esperanto.

Following the standard questions about her relationship to the deceased, Dwayne had quizzed her about their last meeting. Jocelyn was surprised to hear, since Ginger hadn't mentioned it when she'd made her sick call on the day of Banks' death, that Buddy had stopped by the previous evening to have a word that ended in a row. That's what she and Hamill were discussing now.

"So what got it started?"

"Well, give me a second to process this, okay?" Ginger said in standard twelve-step vernacular, pressing a finger against each temple. "First I need to share with you—just in case you've never read a tabloid or ever watched 'Entertainment Tonight' once in your life—that I've had a substance abuse problem in the past, okay?"

Dwayne just shrugged a shrug that was the West Coast equivalent of "So, new?"

"Yeah, right," Ginger agreed. "Anyway, Buddy came over after work to see Hilly—my daughter. And I always keep a box of Cuban cigars here for him. He went to get a cigar and he found . . . a couple'a joints in the box— Now I had *no* idea how they got there! And I told him that grass was *never* my drug of choice. I mean, I was always your basic cokehead. Maybe a few pills on the side. But marijuana's just too retro for me, you know?"

"Dig it . . . So wha'd he do?"

"Oh, got epically gnarly with me! Now Buddy used to chew me out a lot, but this made me nuts 'cause—well, it wasn't the trust issue. Once you've been an addict, you can't really expect people to trust you a whole bunch. It was more a *stupid* issue. Like did he think, if I was gonna start taking drugs again, I'd be zomboid enough to stash them in *his* cigar box? No way! And I told him so."

"So wha'd he do then?" It wasn't what O'Roarke would call a deeply probing question but it seemed to suffice.

"Nothing. I mean, he didn't say anything—but then Buddy never apologized for shit, no matter what. He just paced around for a while, very stoked up. Then he opened the cigar box, took the joints out, and slammed it shut again—still not saying boo. Then he shoved a bag in my hand and said something like, 'I'll

take care of this.' And he just walked out without even seeing
Hilly."

"What was in the bag?"

"Oh, just chamomile tea. He knew I'd been having trouble
z-ing. And Gabby, his wife—my agent, she swore by this stuff."

"So what do you think he meant when he said he'd take care
of it?"

"I dunno. If he didn't believe me, he meant he'd find out who
my supplier was, I guess. If he *did* believe me, then . . . shit. I'm
not sure."

"Then he meant to find out who planted the numbers on you."
Jocelyn knew she'd just spoken out of turn but Dwayne didn't
seem to mind. He just followed her lead.

"Do you have any idea who'd want to do that—screw you up
with Banks?"

"Aw, that's silly, guys." Ginger made little flapping gestures
with both hands as if to *shoo shoo* the notion away like a dirty
pigeon. "Nobody would do a—" Seeing dubious looks all around,
she stopped and rose from the sofa to confront the three of them.
Hands on hips, there was actually something akin to a steely glint
in her eyes. "Hey, look, I'm not, like, totally *dim*, you know? I
mean, Buddy always treated me like a kid and that was okay 'cause
he knew me since I *was* a kid. But I grew up in this goddamned
town—in this goddamned business. And I've been jerked around
and screwed with plenty. So, Christ! Give me some credit. I know
the friggin' score. Hell, there's not a day I don't go to the set
ready to duck and roll. But this is not the business—this is my
home! The only people who come here are my friends and my
family—folks who are on my side. You get it?!"

If little Linda Blair had just walked in and rotated her little
head, Hamill and Frost would've looked just about the way they
did now. But O'Roarke wasn't shocked; in fact she was rather
pleased for Ginger's sake. Jellicoe fell into that category of young
women that Josh thought of as career Good Girls, girls whose
sense of self-worth depended on the perceptions of others, on
being "nice," being liked. Girls who, owing to the demands of
their persona, are constantly forced to swallow their anger. She
was long past due for a major uncorking. Jocelyn was only sad-
dened to see how quickly she scrambled to put the cork back in
place.

"Oh, gosh! Sorry, sorry, sorry. I—I'm just not myself. I know you're only trying to help. But it's . . . Can we do this later, maybe? I'll, uh, I'd be happy to come to your office, Detective. But right now I'm just wiped."

Blushing again, Dwayne said that was fine but asked if he could take the cigar box with him for closer examination. For a second there Ginger looked like she was going to blow another gasket but the Good Girl was back in control and she conceded demurely. Josh was gratified to note that Hamill took pains to slip the box into a plastic evidence bag while Ginger wasn't looking. It had a smooth lacquered surface, the kind that takes prints well. But it would only disturb her to know that he intended to have it dusted. Like his idol, Dwayne seemed to know that discretion was the better part of good police work.

Once they were outside the house, Austin, who'd been mum longer than was his wont, became suddenly convivial. "I'm right over on Mulholland. Would you like to stop by? I thought you might have some questions for me, Dwayne . . . You don't mind if I call you Dwayne?"

"Nah, that's cool," he said with a shrug before turning to Jocelyn. "You gonna be there?"

"Sure. Austin's too cheap to hire a cook. That's why he has me around. I'll make some guacamole. How's that?"

Frost was glaring at her, his eyebrows arched into matching chevrons, but his face relaxed into bliss when Dwayne said, "Bitchin'."

"Would you like to take a dip? I'm sure I have, uh, something your size."

They were poolside on the patio now. O'Roarke had returned with the promised guacamole and a couple of cold Dos Equis just in time to hear Austin's invitation and watch him dreamily calculate Hamill's trunk size. Dwayne squinted down at the sunlight dancing on the chlorinated water and shook his head.

"No, thanks. I only like to swim in the ocean."

"Oh, right, of course. Josh told me you're into surfing. That's a sport I've always wanted to take up."

O'Roarke swiftly shoved a nacho chip piled high with guacamole into her face to keep from screaming with laughter at the
mental image of Austin hanging ten. It was amazing what love
had wrought since, up to now, Frost's idea of strenuous exercise
had only extended as far as running to catch a cab, and then only
if it was pouring rain. The big fibber was ignoring her pointed
glance in a big way, but Hamill was oblivious to their little
vaudeville act.

Plopping down on a lounge chair, he opened his trusty notebook, flipped through several pages with one hand as he scooped
up dip with the other, then asked, "As far as you know, Mr.
Frost—uh, Austin—was Larry Goldstein on the set all morning
the day of Mr. Banks' death?"

It was an abrupt segue and not at all what Austin had been
anticipating, but he took a sip of beer, then answered carefully,
"Yes, as far as I know. I was up in my office doing some rewrites
part of the morning. But Larry got a scene in the can that morning
so he had to be there most of the time. Uh—why do you ask?"

"Checking, just checking. We still haven't verified his alibi for
his whereabouts the night before, see."

"Well, where did he say he was?" Frost was keeping his voice
perfectly level but Jocelyn saw that telltale green tinge in his
pallor and she felt for him. Larry was his director and his partner
on this project and Austin was a very loyal fellow. Cut a friend
and he'd bleed.

"Said he was at a test screening for the new—what's the name?
Yeah, the new Bertrand Blier film. But he says he went by himself
and nobody saw him there."

"Oh, Larry sees everything. And he's not dating right now. So
that's perfectly possible."

It wasn't *perfectly* possible since Jocelyn had heard Goldstein
holding forth on more than one occasion on "overrated Frog
filmmakers," but she wasn't going to bring it up now. Austin took
another sip and tried to sound casual as he asked, "Why are you
so interested in Larry anyway?"

"Like I said, we're just checking . . . But he drives a red 'eighty-
eight Audi, doesn't he?"

Asking Austin the make and model of a car was like asking a
deaf man to hum a few bars from *Aida*. So O'Roarke reluctantly
filled in the gap.

"Yeah, he does. Why?"

"Well, it's no big thing. Except we've heard that Banks was making a lot of noise about Goldstein not being up to his job on *Free Fall*."

"Big deal," Austin snorted derisively. "Buddy was a DP looking to step up in class. There's a guy like that on every shoot."

"Yeah, I'm sure," Hamill agreed pleasantly.

But O'Roarke was catching on to his style now and, sensing there was unpleasantness to come, asked, "So, Dwayne, why're you so interested in Larry's car?"

"No reason . . . Only the screening was in Studio City and didn't let out till midnight. And there was a red 'eighty-eight Audi spotted parked on the Pacific Coast Highway at eleven-thirty."

"So wha—" Austin's question was cut short by Jocelyn's waving hand.

"When'd you find this out, Dwayne, ol' buddy, ol' confidant? This morning?"

Frost hadn't the faintest idea what was transpiring between them. But he saw Hamill swallow hard and place one hand over his heart.

"Swear to God, not till after you left the pier, okay?"

"Ooo-kay." She stretched the two syllables out for a ten-count before asking, "So where on the Pacific Coast Highway was this car seen?"

Feeling like he was standing in front of an X-ray machine, Dwayne tried not to squirm as he answered. "About a quarter mile from Gabby and Buddy's place in Malibu."

Placing his beer mug down on the arm of his deck chair, Frost nodded his head very slowly as if fearful of it falling off his shoulders. "I see . . . I see. Well, that's very, uh— Will you excuse me? I've, uh—gotta swim."

Jocelyn waited until he was at the very edge of the pool before calling out, "Austin, your watch isn't waterproof and . . . you're still in your street clothes, honey."

Nodding numbly Frost made a sharp right-angle turn and headed for the nearby cabana without so much as a backward glance at Josh or the object of his affections.

The object whispered, "Is he all right?"

"Not at the moment, no."

"What's the matter? Did I upset him? I mean, is it like a sensitive artist thing?"

"Not exactly. It's more like a my-career-is-over thing."

"Aw, no, it's not that bad . . . is it?"

O'Roarke just shook her head and sighed as she handed him a chip.

"Dwayne—have some more guac."

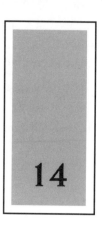

14

" 'He discovereth deep things out of darkness and bringeth out to light the shadow of death.' And so must we, in the shadow of Albert's death, strive to bring the light of God's love into our own personal darkness to dispel our sorrow . . ."

"Tricky segue. This guy should try out for 'Star Search.' He could bill himself as the Ultimate Spokesperson," O'Roarke whispered, trying to get a rise out of her friend. But Austin just pursed his lips and shook his head like an offended church deacon. Yesterday's immersion, after Hamill had dropped his little bombshell, had failed to render Frost born again in any sense of the word. He had simply holed up in his den with his old Peggy Lee tapes and left Jocelyn to answer all calls. Not that there were many since Dwayne had managed, quite miraculously, Josh felt, considering how swiftly the old gossip mill turned in Hollywood, to keep the homicide investigation under wraps thus far. Still it hadn't been easy taking calls and writing down messages with Peggy in the background, repeatedly asking: "Is that all there is?" But Austin was entitled to a good wallow—as long as it was over by twelve-thirty when they were all due back on the set. Death or no, the shoot must go on.

The modern, streamlined chapel on La Brea was as nondenominational as the smooth-faced clergyman delivering Buddy's eulogy and just as bland as the eulogy itself. Nothing he'd said so far gave the slightest indication that he'd ever met Buddy or knew anything about him. But maybe that was for the best, Josh considered, since someone better acquainted might have had trouble keeping a straight face. She was having a little problem in that area herself but then she always did, always had. Inappropriate behavior in houses of worship had been the first manifestation of her own fall from grace. Growing up Catholic, she'd done all right while the mass was still being said in Latin, which made it mysterious enough to keep her in check. But as soon as they'd switched to English, she, like Peggy, was forced to wonder: "Is *that* all there is?"

Fortunately the rest of the congregation seemed to have themselves well in hand. At least they were behaving in a manner befitting the occasion. Ginger, with Tim beside her, was sniffling into a hanky. They shared the front pew with the family; that is, Brenda and Gabby. O'Roarke noted with interest that the widow had maneuvered to have Ginger beside her so that Brenda was placed at the opposite end of the pew. La Arnold's face was out of her sight lines, but Josh thought she could detect signs of offended dignity in her ramrod posture and the red flush on the back of her neck. Gabby's face she could see. Though she looked drawn and tired, she was dry eyed and composed; her expression gave away nothing.

Austin's gaze had been Ping-Ponging from Larry to Gabby for much of the service. But if he was hoping to glean signs of suppressed passion he was out of luck. Goldstein had come late and taken a pew toward the back all by himself. Josh's hunch was that he was surreptitiously working out the day's shooting schedule. The only person who had arrived later than Larry was Hamill, who had slipped into the last pew unobserved by all except Josh and was doing a splendid job of blending in with the paneling. She was sure he was making notes, too.

The only person who seemed to share her lack of reverence was young Billy Orbach, the new DP. Positioned directly across the aisle from Austin and Jocelyn, he looked, not happy as a lark by any means, but sort of serene. And O'Roarke did catch him biting his lip when the minister mentioned Buddy's "constant commitment to helping others up the ladder of success."

There was just one individual present whose deportment she hadn't observed—because she was too mortified. Jack Breedlove was sitting directly behind her and, after making such an ass of herself at their last encounter, she still hadn't found the guts to face him or a plausible way to explain why the odor of almond shampoo had made her shy like a spooked mare in a barn fire. But Breedlove, not a man easily put off, was making his presence felt. When the preacher switched from the Old Testament to hipper references such as "Death ends a life, but it does not end a relationship," Jack goosed her by whispering, "Gene Hackman in *I Never Sang for My Father*." She wanted to hiss back, "I *knew* that," but didn't have the nerve. Besides, the minister was going for his big finish now.

"So, once again, art mirrors life, just as Albert tried to do with his photography. Though he is gone from our midst, be comforted by the knowledge that your relationship with Albert, the joys you shared, the mutual love you felt, that relationship goes on in this life . . . and the next. Amen."

Then they were all filing out. Gabby was first, her expression a little less inscrutable now as she muttered under her breath, "I *told* him to use 'Buddy.' 'Albert'—Christ!" Ginger followed behind, leaning heavily on Tim, then Brenda with eyes that looked both moist and angry boring into the back of the younger woman's skull. Now it was Austin and Josh's turn to leave. Chicken-shit to the last, she clamped on to his arm and kept her gaze down. But Jack came right alongside her. Pitching his voice low so only she could hear, he rolled his eyes toward the preacher then up to the chapel ceiling as he said, "Do you think it would be tacky to ask if *He* validates?"

Luckily she had a hanky of her own handy and managed to stuff it in her face just in time. Tears streamed down her face as she shook with suppressed laughter and had to lean on Frost in order to stay erect. And it only got worse when she heard one of the grips whisper, "Geez, O'Roarke's takin' this harder than anybody! Go figure."

But it was worth it. Breedlove's impish impiety restored her perspective. Any man who could make the ultimate Hollywood joke at a funeral deserved acknowledgment. He also deserved a swift kick in the pants. But when she got outside and turned around, expecting to find him behind her, he was gone.

Austin was tugging her toward the car.

"Come on. We've got to get back to the lot."

The others were going on to the cemetery. But the funeral lunch or wake, as it were, was to be held at the studio and Austin was in charge. This was Gabby's idea; always the pragmatist, she knew it would make up for lost production time and, as she'd brusquely told The Suits, "Buddy'd be pissed as hell if anybody else's funeral cut into *his* shooting schedule. So this'll do him fine."

"Wait, wait." Jocelyn hung back. "I want to talk to Jack."

"Well, you can't," Austin said testily, jerking his head in the direction of the chapel foyer. "He's busy." And so he was. At that moment he was deep in conversation with Dwayne Hamill and, judging from his expression, he'd ceased finding things funny.

"Turn right here. No, no, go left—*left!*"

"I *can't!* I'm in the wrong lane. Why the hell did you say turn right if you wanted me to go left?" Jocelyn snarled, turning off Venice Boulevard onto Overland.

"I meant here is the exact place where we turn—but I was *pointing* left, plain as day," Frost hissed back.

"Plain as—? Austin, I'm watching the road, not your friggin' hands, for chrissake!" She ground her teeth as she took another right on Regent Street to get back to Venice, trying to smother several other pointed remarks she wanted to make about Frost's deficits as a giver of directions. One of them slipped out anyway. "And 'right here' does *not* mean the exact place from whence we turn. That's so feeble—even for a writer."

"Well, fine. That's fine," he said, crossing his arms over his chest. "We'll just be late then. Lovely."

"Oh, we will not. Keep your diaper on."

Without further assistance, verbal or otherwise, O'Roarke managed to find their destination, a smoke shop on Washington Boulevard. Like most writers, Frost was a creature of habit who cherished his small daily rituals. For instance, he could not go to work without stopping here first for a pack of Marlboros and *The New York Times*. Normally Jocelyn was understanding about such things but she'd been chauffeuring Austin around for two days and now felt she deserved either a raise or a reprieve.

For his part, Austin was still smarting over the writer crack; he unsnapped his seatbelt and wrangled his way out of the car without so much as asking if she wanted a pack of cigarettes. Not that Josh needed a smoke at the moment since she was already fuming. Among the many topics on her growing list of grievances was Austin's ingrained impracticality. In all of Los Angeles with its thousands of relatively straight roads, why did a man who only liked to drive on deserted open roads choose to rent a house in a part of town that looked like a Chutes and Ladders board? Well, she'd had enough. Tonight she'd park Frost's beat-up Volvo somewhere on Franklin Avenue and drop him off there in the morning. Knowing that it was often the tiniest of straws that finally breaks the camel's hump and that more marriages and friendships have come unglued in cars than anywhere else, she thought this the safest solution. And if Austin didn't like it, he could damn well hire a driver.

Mentally rehearsing the little speech she intended to give, Jocelyn didn't see Frost leave the shop. She hadn't even gotten to the "we're both under a lot of strain" part when he plopped down beside her. The rest of it went out of her head when she saw the expression on his face.

"What? What is it? What happened?!"

Looking as if his favorite pup had just had a run-in with a Mack truck, Austin just shook his head woefully and dropped a newspaper in her lap. It wasn't *The New York Times;* actually it wasn't even a newspaper in the proper sense of the word—it was a rag. This one, printed on particularly lurid ocher paper, had the typical banner headlines about male Siamese twins sharing one penis and the latest Elvis-spotting. But in a small box at the bottom of the page was a blurry picture of Ginger, clearly taken in her pre-rehab days, next to boldface print that read: "Jellicoe Jinxed! First Drugs—Now Murder!"

"*Jesus!*" Jocelyn swatted it off her lap as if it were a cockroach. "Those schmucks—fucking, filthy little leeches! Goddamn, I tell you, there's the scum of the earth, then there's the slime beneath the scum . . . And underneath that are *those* guys," she yelled, stabbing a finger down at the fallen tabloid. "Two-legged jackals. Walking, talking excretia!"

Like everyone else in the entertainment industry, O'Roarke had no fondness for the tabloid press. But this was the first time someone she knew had been the object of one of their slurs and she was beside herself with fury. She reached for the paper but Austin snatched it away before she could tear it to bits; she had to content herself with banging both fists on the steering wheel.

"Josh, take it easy. It's a rental, remember."

"I don't care! Why didn't you let me rip it up?"

"Because I haven't read the whole thing yet," Austin answered with admirable restraint. "And I need to. Something like this was bound to happen sooner or later. I just wish it could've been later and . . . not this way. Now that it has, I have to control the damage—for Ginger's sake."

Jocelyn looked at him with wonder; after all, she'd seen this guy go ape-shit over a mildly unfavorable review. Now the man of eccentric habits was suddenly exhibiting signs of rock-bottom pragmatism.

"God, Austin, you're being amazingly . . . adult."

"No, I'm just being a producer. It's my job. But thanks, Josh."

"Huh? For what?"

"You curse extremely well, kiddo. It's like a two-for-one deal. You swear so good that I . . . don't need to, see?"

"Oh."

"Come on, tiger," he said, giving her knee a genial pat. "Let's go face the music."

15

"Who picked this candy-assed music? What is it . . . friggin' Debussy or somethin'?"

With a plate of designer sushi in one hand, O'Roarke found herself eye-to-almost-eye with the Widow Banks. It was their first meeting and though Gabby was slightly the worse for drink—to the tune of three gin and tonics tossed back in swift succession—it did nothing to diminish the force of her personality.

"I, uh, don't know. On both counts," Josh hastened to add. "I don't know who picked it. And I don't know if it's Debussy. I'm pretty ignorant about classical music and—"

"Wellll, good for you! Wha's your name anyway?"

"Jocelyn O'Roarke. I'm—"

"I know! You're the one who busted in an' screwed up Buddy's prints. Shit, was he mad 'bout that." Gabby let out an unnerving cackle, then patted Jocelyn's arm. "Is's okay. You can make it up to him. Help me eighty-six this garbage."

Having attended her first wake at the age of six, Jocelyn was well versed in funeral etiquette, and what it boiled down to in such situations was: Do whatever the family wishes. So, ignoring the scores of stares directed their way, she took one of Gabby's jewel-encrusted hands and led her into the sound booth. Pointing to a stack of cassette tapes and CDs, she said, "See, they've got a ton of stuff here. What would you—what do you think Buddy would like to hear?"

Polishing off G&T number four, Gabby sucked on an ice cube, considering. "Me, I'm into the New Wave stuff. But Buddy was in a musical time warp. He liked the big bands—swingtime, that kind'a shit, you know?"

Josh rifled through the stacks like a desperate squirrel needing a nut fix. "Ah, here's Tommy Dorsey doing 'In the Mood' and . . ."

"Good. Play it."

Brent's delivery was as clipped and hard as Bogart's and O'Roarke actually got a shiver, imagining the specter of Dooley Wilson smiling down as she dutifully slipped the CD into place.

As the opening strains came up, Gabby beat time on the console with one hand as she looked through the four-by-four glass window, delighting at all the surprised faces on the set turned their way. "Wha's their problem? They think this is a goddamn *wake?!*"

"Uh, yeah, I think they do, actually. Hard to blame them really. But, you know, they'll take their cue off you," Jocelyn offered tentatively. "Just tell 'em how you want to play the scene."

"Okay." Without further ado, Gabrielle Brent kicked the sound booth door open with one spike-heeled foot, stuck her head out, and yelled, "*Dance,* you shitheads! Dance!"

DeMille couldn't have gotten a faster response. They moved, sluggishly at first, but then some of the grips, stalwart party animals all, grabbed the wardrobe and prop girls and started cutting rugs in earnest. Josh watched Tim Hayes lead a whey-faced but game Ginger onto the floor. By now she'd heard of the tabloid story and, though it had obviously pained her, Jocelyn had been surprised by her contained response. She'd simply shrugged her shoulders and murmured, "Well, I've been to this zoo before." The oddest pairing on the floor was Larry Goldstein dancing with Brenda, who towered a good five inches above his balding dome. They moved desultorily around the floor, both firmly staring at the sound booth window. And Gabby, in turn, seemed to be studying them as she asked Josh, "How well did you know my husband?"

"Not well at all, Ms. Brent."

"Screw that—it's Gabby. But you knew him enough to, uh, form an opinion, huh?"

"Just a first impression, really," she began, prepared to lie her ass off if necessary. "And you know how misle—"

Gabby stopped her by clamping a hand on her shoulder. "Oh, honey, just can the crap, okay? I'm askin' 'cause you're a rank outsider. I *want* your first impression. Give."

Gabrielle Brent was a mightily compelling woman. All the platitudes Josh had ready to roll off her tongue melted away and she heard herself say, "He was very professional, extremely good at his job . . . as well as cantankerous, rude, and domineering. But I think he really cared for Ginger and Hilly."

She half expected to get the remainder of Gabby's drink tossed in her face, but the older woman just kept her eyes on the dancers.

"You forgot to mention stubborn as a friggin' mule, toots."

"That, too."

"An' somebody killed him for it."

For the first time there was the faintest tinge of emotion in that steely voice, but Jocelyn couldn't identify its source. "I doubt it. Innocent children are murdered every day, aren't they? And through no fault of their own. So you really can't think of homicide as a reflection on a person's character. That's too easy. Usually it's a matter of a person being in the wrong place at the wrong time . . . Or just being in someone's way."

For a moment Gabby's gin-induced fog seemed to lift. Her eyes widened and snapped to attention as she regarded Josh with something between astonishment and fear. "What the *fuck* are you talking about? In someone's way? *Whose* way?"

Gabby's voice cracked like a bullwhip and Jocelyn flinched like a stunned calf. As she tottered threateningly toward her, O'Roarke reminded herself that good funeral protocol forbade one's punching out the grieving widow's lights.

Then the door swung open.

"As Deborah said to Yul—shall we dance? Who wants to trip the light fantastic?"

And there he was; her deus ex machina, better than Dudley

Do-Right and Clark Kent rolled into one. Jack Breedlove's toothy grin dispelled the mounting tension in the small room and she blessed him for his great timing. Gabby snorted, "Well, it ain't me, babe," as she unceremoniously shoved Josh in his direction, then slammed the door shut behind them.

Whisking her out to the center of the floor, he asked, "What was that all about? I mean, for a moment it looked like you were Anastasia. Then it looked like you were a dirty Bolshevik. What giveth?"

"I haf not the fainteth," she lisped back. "She's a tough lady—and tough to read. But I think she's afraid of something—or someone."

Over Jack's left shoulder, O'Roarke watched Larry Goldstein make his way to the sound booth. He knocked softly on the door before entering. Josh swung around to get a view of the window. She could see Larry speaking rapidly with both hands held out, palms open, in a gesture that was meant to be either comforting or supplicating. But Gabby had her back to the glass, her head bowed low.

"Uh, Josh, you're leading."

"Oh—sorry. I wasn't thinking."

"Just the opposite, I'd say. Looks to me like you're in mental overdrive. What's up with you, O'Roarke?" From the tone of his voice and the tension in the sinewy arm around her waist, she sensed what was coming. "More to the point—what's up with *us*?"

"Look, Jack, I, uh—I know I've been acting like a jerk. And you deserve some kind of explanation. But, God, I really can't think about it now."

"Uh-huh, I see. Well, when do you think you *can* think about it—tomorrow at Tara?" His bantering air did little to conceal his frustration. She felt like a louse and worse, a tease, so she swiftly changed the topic.

"I saw you talking to Hamill. What did he want?"

Breedlove shook his head and gave a dry chuckle that was more rueful than amused. "Shit, Gabby's not the only tough nut around here. Okay, we'll play it your way—for *now* . . . The Boy Detective wanted my recollection of the night when we heard noises in Buddy's darkroom. To see if it jibed with yours, I guess."

"That all?"

"No. Actually he kind of threw me for a loop. Asked if Buddy had ever said anything to me about selling his Monte Verde property—since it's so close to my place. He never did, of course. But it surprised me."

"Why?"

"Exactly—*why*? I mean, why's he even interested in Monte Verde?"

This was getting sticky. Jocelyn wished she'd just kept her mouth shut and waited to ask Dwayne himself. But Jack expected some reply so she looked down at her feet, then up at the ceiling, anywhere but at him as she said, with all the casualness she could muster, "It's, uh, hard to say. He's just fishing, I guess. Poking around for, you know . . . possible motive."

"Motive? *Whose* motive? You mean he thinks Gabby might've bumped off her own husband just so she could sell that land?! That's nuts."

"Not really, not to a cop," she said, more easily now, relieved that Jack hadn't taken the implication personally. "Cops go by statistics. See, strangers really don't kill strangers very often. Ninety percent of all homicides are family affairs. So they always look to the spouse first."

Breedlove stopped moving to the music and stared down at Jocelyn. There was something in her voice, not coldness, but a certain matter-of-factness that he found deeply disconcerting. But before he could ask how she came by such grisly knowledge, Gabrielle Brent emerged from the sound booth with a sweaty-faced Goldstein following in her wake and went straight for the makeshift bar with all eyes upon her. She grabbed another gin and tonic, then turned to face the expectant crowd.

"Okay, it's a wrap on the wake, folks. This guy's got a schedule to keep," she announced, jerking a thumb in Larry's direction. "You've all been swell and I appreciate it—so would Buddy. But do me a favor. No more friggin' flowers, huh? They make me sneeze. If you wanna make a gesture, send a contribution to the American Film Institute. He'd like that." With that she turned on her heel and marched, with no trace of inebriation in her gait, toward the exit, pausing only long enough to tap Ginger on the shoulder and mutter, "We'll do lunch, kid."

Then she was gone. From somewhere behind her, Josh heard Tim Hayes say admiringly, "What a broad." He'd been dancing with Brenda Arnold, who now followed her sister-in-law's exit with an icy stare. "What a coldhearted bitch is more like it. She never gave a damn about my brother," she hissed back, intending her words for Hayes' ears only. O'Roarke heard and took care to give no sign. But Jack couldn't help turning around. Brenda caught his critical gaze and demanded, "What the hell are you looking at?!"

Looking her up and down as if she were a particularly unpleasant lab specimen, he answered calmly, "I don't know. You tell me—what *am* I looking at?"

Hayes turned a chuckle into a cough as Brenda flushed redder than the Red Queen. Jocelyn half expected her to yell, "Off with his head!" But she seemed to have lost her voice and her nerve for the moment. She turned to Tim, apparently expecting him to defend her dignity. When she saw that there was no help coming from that quarter, she sailed off to her dressing room, like a galleon in heavy seas. Tim grinned at Jack then gave a low whistle.

"Wouldn't want to be in your shoes, fella. Ol' Bren holds a grudge the way a camel holds water. She'll make your life hell from here on in."

"I doubt it. I do her hair. So I have a sort of immunity. She gives me shit—I give her a rat's nest."

Hayes hooted, giving Jack a buddy-buddy slap on the back. "Way to go, man! Gotta keep the upper hand any way we can, right?" Then, seeing Jocelyn's back go up, he hastened to add, "But you know, Bren's not all that bad, really. She's just a little nervy right now."

"Gee, I wonder why." O'Roarke dripped sarcasm from every pore. "Do you think it's because her brother was murdered—or just PMS?"

Whether he was inured to irony or merely unaccustomed to censure from any female, Tim just shrugged and said, "I think she's worried about the will. Buddy was getting tired of paying her debts. Told her if she didn't shape up, he was going to change it."

Even though he'd just told the lady off, Breedlove didn't consider gossiping about La Arnold in very good taste, given the time and place, and was just about to say so when Jocelyn asked, point-blank, "Who told you that?"

Her blunt query caught Tim off guard. "Well, hey, I don't like to tell tales out of school, you know. Let's just say a little birdie."

"You've *been* telling tales already, Tim. If you can't back them up—that's slander. Or plain bullshit. So who's your birdie?"

Stunned by her chutzpah, Breedlove saw no reason on earth why Hayes should answer her, save for the fact that her eyes were boring into him like a mining drill. Apparently that was reason enough for Tim, who swallowed hard then stammered, "Christ, I didn't mean anyth— . . . Look, fact is, *she* told me, herself. Okay?"

"Ol' Bren, you mean? My, my, you do get around, don't you?"

Tim started to make protesting noises, then abandoned the idea in favor of a hasty retreat. "I, uh, think Ginger needs me . . . Gotta go."

Once he was out of earshot, it was Jack's turn to wax sardonic.

"Golly, gee, even in a town famous for tacky behavior that was a pretty impressive display."

"Yeah. Aside from the fact that he's blindingly handsome, I don't know what Ginger sees in that guy."

"I meant the *both* of you, actually. Him for shooting his mouth off and you for grilling him like—like a fifth-rate Sam Spade! Why don't you give it a rest, O'Roarke. Let Hamill earn his paycheck."

The fifth-rate crack really stung but Jocelyn, realizing that she'd overplayed her hand, swallowed her indignation.

"I . . . guess you're right. I was out of bounds there. Still, don't you find it interesting that Brenda would confide in *him?*"

"Not really. She's had a few Scotches, they were dancing together, and he is, as you pointed out, 'blindingly handsome.' That would do it for most women." He spoke evenly but Josh caught the faint tinge of jealousy in his voice that both flattered and amused her.

It had long been O'Roarke's contention that the armchair psychologists had it all wrong when they ascribed envy of physical beauty as a particular frailty of the female sex; it certainly didn't hold true in show business. She knew women in her profession who might kill to have Michelle Pfeiffer's lips or Kathleen Turner's legs, but it didn't keep them from acknowledging or appreciating the considerable talents of those ladies. You'd have to look long and hard, however, to find two SAG actors who would freely admit that Mel Gibson or Robert Redford could act worth a damn.

According to O'Roarke's theory, men are the real peacocks and they deeply resent birds with brighter plumage. That's why Newman had to wait so long for his Oscar.

Unaware that he was confirming her pet theory, Jack squinted in Tim's direction and mumbled, "'Course the guy's a piss-poor editor, you know."

"Really? But he's working on something now, isn't he?"

"What—that gig out on Catalina? I bet he's like the editor-slash-cook-and-dishwasher on that shoot. It's just a two-bit indie, non-union, I think. Probably never get out of the can—especially if he cuts it."

"Oh. Well then, it's nice he has other talents . . . to fall back on, huh?"

She kept her voice carefully bland, but Breedlove caught the mischief in her eyes. He clamped a hand on the nape of her neck and gave it a playful shake.

"Whoa, boy—to the *moon*, Alice!"

16

" 'Moon River, wider than a mile. I'm crossin' you in style some-day. . . .' Shit, I shouldn't be doing this! You are such a bad influence." Ginger dropped the tennis racket she'd been pseu-dostrumming and dissolved into hiccupy giggles.

"Aw, no, don't stop! That was terrific. *Very* few people can do Audrey Hepburn as Holly Golightly. You owe it to posterity, Ginge."

O'Roarke wasn't being facetious; it really was a good Hepburn impression. Everybody and their aunt could do Kate, especially in gay bars, but a decent Audrey was a rarity and she'd been amazed and delighted by Jellicoe's version.

"No! You're *awful*," Ginger shrieked, smacking Josh's arm as tears of laughter coursed down her cheeks. "We're both awful. I mean, we're supposed to be *sad*."

They were in the makeup room, on one of those interminable breaks, this one caused by a chirping cricket that had gotten into the studio and was wreaking havoc with the sound track, a not uncommon occurrence in Hollywood. All the grips were on a search-and-destroy mission, but they hadn't found the bugger yet.

The work had been going well, especially Ginger's. Despite the funeral and the nasty jolt from the tabloid press, she'd thrown herself into the first scene and nailed it in one, to the great relief of all the eggshell-treaders around her, particularly Austin. When the treacherous cricket made its unwelcome presence known, he'd turned to Jocelyn, begging, "Please, please, don't let her go cold. Do *anything!* I don't care what. Do that history of oral sex thing you made up."

"No! That was just for Sadie Sitwell—it was the only way to get her up for Wednesday mats . . . But I'll think of something."

What she'd hit on was seventies television, a topic near and dear to Ginger's heart. After analyzing the best and worst that decade had offered viewers—and Jocelyn had found Ginger's observations remarkably savvy—she'd fallen back on the only impression she'd ever mastered. It chronicled the transition of Mary Tyler Moore from Laura Petrie ("Oh, *Rob!*") to Mary Rich-ards ("Oh, *Mr. Grant!*"). It was brief but effective and had inspired Ginger to share her far superior Hepburn Golightly. And O'Roarke was not about to let her high spirits go down the tubes.

"Look, Jelly—we're not *supposed* to be anything. It just doesn't work that way." She could see that Ginger was a hairbreadth away from swapping giggles for guilt and knew it was time to deliver the real goods. "When my dad died, I had all these friends from New York calling me in Saratoga to offer their con-dolences—which was very sweet. But they were kind of shocked when I told them I couldn't stay on the phone 'cause I was in the middle of a pinochle game."

"You were playing *cards?*"

"Yeah. We all were . . . my sister and brothers and me. Dad had taught all of us young, from the cradle, I think—I don't really remember a time when I didn't play cards. And I guess my friends thought it was strange but it felt okay, like it was the right thing to *do* then. So maybe—I can't say 'cause there's just no set rules for this—but maybe this is the right thing for now."

There was a long moment where Ginger, still waffling, looked at her as if she'd sprung an extra head. Then the penny dropped and she grinned broadly.

"You know, Buddy liked impressions. He could do a real mean

Bogart. And he also did," she leaned forward and lowered her voice conspiratorially though they were completely alone, "he did an awesome Gabby. You know how she kind of sounds like a man anyway? Well, he'd call me sometimes and I'd think it was *her!* It was a riot. And the sneaky pictures he'd take—they were a scream."

"Sneaky pictures?"

"Yeah. He liked to catch people when they weren't looking. He had a whole set on Gabby—I bet she still doesn't know about it—when she was, like, bleaching her mustache or screaming at a producer on the phone. Real silly stuff . . . He did that all the time—with everybody."

"He did, huh? What a joker," O'Roarke murmured, her mind several light years away. Recalling what Jack Breedlove had had to say on this same topic, she wondered who else Banks had snapped at an inopportune moment. There was that ruined print in the fatal developing pan. What had become of the negative? Hamill probably had it, she told herself. But if he didn't, it could still be sitting in the darkroom. The police had the room sealed but some yellow tape wasn't going to stop anyone who wanted to get their hands on it badly enough.

The sound of a faint *splat* followed by a chorus of cheers signaled that the cricket had been croaked. In unison, both actors swung their chairs toward the mirrors and did some hasty primping as Jack, who'd been drafted into the insect search, came through the door, brush in hand. More adept at impressions than Ginger and Josh combined, he squinted his left eye, arching his right brow dramatically.

"By jiminy, we found the Great Wee Cricket and he'll haunt my dreams no more!" It was a very creditable rendition of Gregory Peck as Ahab but O'Roarke wasn't about to say so.

"Uh, don't tell me . . . Victor McLaglen, right?!"

"Tch, there's no envy so petty as that of the jaded old pro toward the gifted amateur, is there?" He directed his comment to Ginger while briskly back combing the crown of Jocelyn's head.

"Ow! That hurt."

"Well, you know what the song says," he teased, verbally and literally, catching her eye in the mirror. "We only hurt the ones we lo— Ow!"

She'd caught him right on the kneecap with the heel of her Cobbie Cuddler and not a moment too soon. Judging from the goofy grin on her face, Ginger was starting to notice the heavy chemistry in the air. This would not do; whatever it was she'd gotten herself into with Jack Breedlove, it had to be kept private. And it wasn't just a matter of personal preference. To snoop effectively, it was crucial that she keep a low profile around the set, which would be impossible if she and Jack became a known "item." Despite herself, O'Roarke couldn't help but recall Phillip's comments on the pitfalls of working undercover: "It's just incredibly exhausting—I hated it in the end. Because, even in the most harmless situations, you have to maintain the lie, be what you're not. Even with people you like a lot—or you'll get nowhere. But it still makes you feel like pond scum."

It also lent new dimension to the concept of staying in character, something she'd never had trouble doing in her work. But, in real life, it was a damned uncomfortable feeling.

Taking his cue, Jack mock-limped over to Ginger with a wry smile. "Geez, these New York artistes! Just can't take a joke. How do you stand it?"

"Aw, give her a break," she said soothingly, still rooting for romance. "Joshie's just a pussycat, really. You should see her with my little girl! Hilly thinks she's cuter than Miss Piggy."

Breedlove threw back his head and howled as Jocelyn applied a fresh coat of lipstick, blotted her lips, then, in her best Bankhead baritone, growled, "Words I shall treasure always, dahling." Then she switched to a screechy falsetto as she yanked Ginger to her feet. "Now, Kermie, my co-star and *moi* must go and make celluloid magic for all my adoring fans."

So Ginger returned to the set ready and rarin' to go, to the delight of all concerned, specifically Larry and Austin. The two women had, by now, learned each other's acting rhythms and developed their own working shorthand. Goldstein, like any good director, saw this and wisely kept out of their way. Resuming their marks for the kitchen scene—two sisters drying dinner dishes and dishing family history—Josh asked Jellicoe, "You want to lead or follow?"

"Follow. You push the buttons. Make me work to get my lines in, okay?"

"Gotcha . . . That good by you, Larry?"

Goldstein graciously extended his arms wide and said, "Ladies, your pleasure. Let's see how it plays."

It played just fine. Watching them work effortlessly off each other, Austin started to relax for the first time that day. He even started to have fun; knowing, as no one else present did, that Jocelyn was a youngest child, he keenly appreciated how well she assumed the stance of a kindly but wiser-than-thou elder sibling, subtly hinting that she knew what was best for baby sister. And Ginger, an only child in real life, bristled and went careening off the deep end, just as if she'd been under this woman's thumb all her life. It was exactly what Frost had envisioned when he wrote the scene and it was immensely gratifying to see it delivered back to him in perfect form.

At the end of the take, Goldstein turned to him and said, "I say that's a keeper. If you don't, you're blind." Austin smiled and nodded his approval, though with some constraint. He and Larry hadn't had a private moment all day. There were questions he sorely wanted to ask his director. But, dreading what the answers might be, he hoped to persuade O'Roarke to do a little fishing on his behalf.

Then she walked off the set, directly up to him, bent on pursuing her own agenda.

"Can I use your office? I need to call Hamill."

"About what?"

"A bunch of stuff. I can't explain now."

"Well, uh, okay . . . But I was hoping you could find a minute to corner Larry and ask about Gab—"

"Now?! That's nuts, Austin. Besides, if he's making patty cakes with Gabby, he's not going to tell me. You're his partner."

"All right—all right! Point taken . . . But I'm just not *used* to this sort of thing."

"Well, I can't help you with that, Austin. It's nasty business, always is. If you can't deal with it, leave it to the cops. They will, eventually. But you can't look to me to be your personal Pinkerton service."

She knew she was being brusque, maybe even brutal. But, now that her work for the day was finished, she was firmly fixated on the possible contents of Banks' darkroom and the necessity of contacting Hamill posthaste. Aside from that, she was getting just a tad tired of being Austin's nursemaid. After all, it was his career that was on the line here; so it was time for him to pull his own weight, detection-wise.

Frost obviously had other notions. Drawing his shoulders back like a heron with seriously ruffled feathers, he huffed, "Well, forgive me for my presumption! I had the silly notion that you might want to spare me further unpleasantness. But you must, as always, please yourself."

He sounded so veddy British and she was getting so very tired of it that she spoke without thinking. "You know, the job you hired me for—as opposed to the other jobs you've expected me to undertake—specifies only that I act. So I will now go up to your office, all the while *acting* like I don't think you're a total ingrate. How's that?"

"Fine. As you're clearly no use to me here," he shot back.

"Fine. I'll tell Dwayne you send your love." With all the disdain she could muster, Jocelyn spun around and headed for the stairs, torn between rage and laughter. Her fights with Austin never failed to contain a degree of archness and artificiality that rendered them both infuriating and ludicrous at the same time. But they always managed to stop short of the downright petty, thankfully. No matter how miffed, Austin wouldn't think of refusing her the use of his office.

Not that it did her any good.

"Yes, yes, I heard you. Detective Hamill isn't there, got it. But can't you just beep him and . . ." She was on the phone with one of L.A.'s Lamest, who'd been carrying on as if Dwayne's where-abouts were a matter of national security. The Boy Wonder had obviously not thought to share with his fellow officers the fact that Jocelyn was assisting the investigation since the geek on the other end of the line was treating her like a pesky ex-girlfriend who wouldn't take the hint. "I realize you can't give it top priority. How about you just give it a *try*, okay?" She hung up in disgust. Knowing she'd be lucky if Hamill got her message before nightfall, she grumbled, "Should've lied and said I was from Paramount. *Then* it'd be top priority."

Of course, the grown-up thing to do was to go back to Austin's, make a loaf of cornbread as a peace offering, and wait for Dwayne's call. She told herself this quite firmly, trying to ignore the inchoate plan that was struggling to coalesce in her brain. Fishing her car keys out of her bag, she headed for the door, yanked it open— and there it was, gleaming in her mind's eye.

The boarded-up door to the darkroom.

The day of the murder, she had watched Hamill examine it. The killer hadn't entered that way; it was simpler merely to jimmy the lock on the outside door. But that didn't mean it couldn't be used as a point of entry. According to her calculations, the inside wall of the darkroom abutted the wardrobe room. Banks had probably boarded it up himself. But had he done it on *both* sides? There was only one way to find out.

Luckily the cast and crew were feeling the pressure to make up for lost time so all hands were on deck for the last scene of the day, a long heart-to-heart between Mother Brenda and Daughter Ginger. And, since Brenda tended to sweat like the racehorses she was so fond of playing and had to be constantly supplied with fresh dress shields, both the wardrobe mistress and her assistant were on the set. So no one saw Josh slither by with the hammer and crowbar she'd filched from the tool room tucked under her outsized denim shirt.

Three walls of the wardrobe room were covered by clothes racks, including the one next to Buddy's bungalow. The clothes racks were on wheels but groaning under the weight of dozens of costumes, so it was no mean feat to wheel one of them away from the wall, single-handedly and without the rack's making a racket. But O'Roarke's labors were rewarded. The door was there and unboarded. Better still, there was no lock on it!

Not that it did her any good.

The wood of the door and frame was old and dried out, but the same was obviously not true of the boards on the other side. The old wood had warped enough to allow Josh to open the door an inch or two and slip the tip of the crowbar into place, then press against it with all her might.

"Give, goddamn it, give!"

Thirty minutes later she was still pressing as well as sweating and cursing while her shoulders and forearms screamed for mercy. Buddy had been an indifferent carpenter, nailing the three boards across with large gaps between them. The top and bottom planks had given way fairly easily but he'd obviously put his heart into hammering the middle one. The sucker just wouldn't budge; it was as obstinate as the man who'd put it into place.

Jocelyn, at the urging of her aching tendons, was on the brink of conceding defeat when she heard footsteps heading her way. From the spate of angry Spanish accompanying the footsteps, she knew it was Marie, the wardrobe assistant. Hoping her tirade would mask the noise, Josh yanked the clothes rack back into place, wedging herself between it and the door frame with the crowbar digging painfully into her back.

Still frothing in her native tongue, Marie came into the room and started rummaging through drawers. Though she knew little Spanish, she caught the words *loco* and *porquo* and guessed that Marie was in search of more dress shields for La Arnold's pits. The way her luck was running, Jocelyn wasn't too surprised to find a maribou boa, part of one of Ginger's outfits, directly under her nose. This was all she needed. One good sneeze—and O'Roarke was an Olympian sneezer—and she'd be exposed like a low comic in a lesser Feydeau farce.

But the gods were merciful; the little Mexican spitfire found the shields and stormed out of the room a moment before O'Roarke let loose with a sneeze that probably sent some nearby seismologist into a panic. Where it sent Josh, however, was smack against the crowbar with propulsive force. She heard a cracking sound and prayed it wasn't her lower vertebrae.

It wasn't. She registered this fact when she opened her eyes and found herself, on her posterior, in Buddy's darkroom.

"Hence the phrase 'putting one's back into it,' " she groaned, dusting the seat of her jeans as she got slowly to her feet.

The room was murky, lit only by a single shaft of light coming through the one window, so it took her a minute to find what she was looking for—the enlarger. It was on a table placed at a right angle to the counter where the developing pan had been. That's where the negative would be, she knew. But where exactly? O'Roarke didn't even own a camera and her education in film developing began and ended with one visit to the Eastman House in Rochester at the age of nine. So it took her a while to decipher the machine, and find the sliding plate at the top that held the negative—if there was one.

But there wasn't.

"Idiot, dummy . . . total twit!"

Of course there wasn't. Of course Hamill had had the smarts to remove it. She never would've bothered to look if it had been—if it had been Phillip's case, she finally admitted to herself. What had she been thinking? Dwayne copied Phillip's techniques more closely than De Palma tried to copy Hitchcock's and to better effect. Had she been subconsciously trying to prove that she was a better investigator than the both of them? A bitter Freudian pill to swallow.

Still, the little *putz* hadn't seen fit to mention the negative to her and for this she would make Hamill suffer. To relieve her angst, she gave the table a swift kick, causing the enlarger to jitter precariously toward the edge. Grabbing it with both hands before it could fall off, she saw something flutter to the floor.

She picked it up delicately by one edge.

Whether it had been beneath the enlarger or inside it some-where, she couldn't tell. It was a torn piece of celluloid, though not a negative. Even Josh could see it was too stiff and thick, and there was another torn fragment attached to one end with some-thing resembling chicken scratches on it. It might be a piece of a slide but she couldn't be sure.

With her free hand, she dug into her pocket and pulled out her wallet. Flipping it open, she carefully slipped the celluloid frame into the plastic sheath that held her driver's license.

A clue, a palpable clue, she thought, relieved that her efforts had not been for naught. Of course, she would hand it over to Hamill—as soon as the little twerp returned her call. But it had been a long, hard day and she was due for that long swim.

Then she heard someone scream.

17

"It was! It was *him*—in the window. He looked right at me! Oh, God, it was awful . . ." Ginger's voice faded as her shoulders started to shake convulsively. Burying her face in her hands, she sobbed softly as Larry Goldstein patted her back ineffectually.

"That's okay, sweetie, you just let it out. This is all my fault, Ginger, really. I'm a schmuck and I could kick myself. Never should've worked you so hard—today of all days. The strain just got to yo—"

"No!" Ginger's sobs stopped abruptly as she glared up at her director. "Okay, so I'm tired—we all are. But I'm not nuts and I'm not imagining things. Geez, after all the acid I've dropped, don't you think I *know* when I'm hallucinating? This wasn't . . . this was *real!* I saw Buddy's face."

Jocelyn caught the long-suffering look Goldstein shot Austin's way. Frost caught it, too, and returned it in kind as he mangled a cigarette that he was digging out of a nearly empty pack. Racking his brain for the right words to soothe his star, he pulled a Dunhill lighter out of his shirt pocket.

"Austin, you're about to light the filter."

"Oh! So I am. Thanks."

The three of them were alone with Jellicoe in her dressing room; O'Roarke had been included at Ginger's insistence, much to the chagrin of Brenda Arnold, who was probably standing outside with an ear plastered to the door, along with sundry other members of the cast and crew. Not that you could blame them, really. Ten minutes after they'd wrapped for the day, Ginger had bolted out of her room in full-blown hysterics, shrieking at the top of her lungs that she'd seen Buddy's ghost. For people whose paychecks were riding on Jellicoe's ability to function and make it through the shoot, this was not an auspicious sign.

"Darling, I'm sure you saw *something,*" Frost began tentatively, handing Ginger a cigarette much the way a mother gives a baby a pacifier. "But let's not rush to any morbid conclusions, eh? Look, even with all the security on the lot, I'd bet my laptop that some paparazzo or tabloid scum snuck in somehow. Now think, love, what drew your eye to the window? Did you hear a shutter click or see a flash, maybe?"

Larry smacked a palm against his forehead as if he'd just remembered he could've had a V-8. "Frostie, brilliant! Why didn't I think of—"

"No, guys. It won't play." Jellicoe took a deep drag, then continued more calmly. "I'm not psychic or anything but I got a real sixth sense about those assholes. My flesh starts to crawl and I *know* they're around. You need a telephoto lens to catch me, boy, 'cause I've had practice. Besides, I didn't see anything at first . . . I heard something."

Her eyes were starting to well up again so Josh picked up the ball.

"What did you hear?"

"Buddy's voice—what else? I'd know it anywhere. He said my name—well, his pet name, Gingersnaps. Nobody else called me that but him, ever. That's when I turned around and saw him—just his face, sort of floating there." She waved her hand weakly in the direction of the window, suppressing a shudder. "And he started to sing to me."

"*Sing?*" Goldstein ran a hand over his five o'clock shadow in an attempt to mask his incredulity. "Sing what?"

"An old song. It was one of his favorites. He taught it to me when I was a kid and we used to do it as a duet every Christmas. You know the one." She hummed a few bars, then sang in a shaky voice, " 'It's gettin' late . . . But, baby, it's cold outside.' . . . And then I just—lost it."

Her voice broke as she shut her eyes, wrapping both arms tightly around her body against the sudden chill that seemed to hang in the room. Josh felt it and was fairly certain that Larry and Austin did, too, given the way they both snuck glances at the window.

Then Ginger reached out for Josh's hand and asked, "Do you, like, believe in ghosts? Or do you think I'm nuts, too?"

She wanted to avoid this topic more than Bush wanted to avoid domestic policy, but there was no escape. Goldstein and Austin were imploring her with spaniel eyes to tread carefully but, since her days at the Burbage Theatre had given her a nodding acquaintance with spectres, she couldn't, in good conscience, dismiss Ginger's question lightly.

"No, I don't think you're nuts. And, yes, I do happen to believe in ghosts. I've even read up on the subject, uh, recently. *But*, like Austin said, I wouldn't necessarily jump to that conclusion. According to experts, and that's a pretty amorphous term in these matters, remember, someone who dies . . . unexpectedly—well, it takes them some time to realize they've actually, uh, passed on, see?"

"What does that mean?"

"Well, honey, I don't mean to be crude, but Buddy's barely cold, right? I just don't see how he'd be up to a full-fledged manifestation right off the bat. It doesn't usually work that way."

"Then what do you think I saw?"

O'Roarke did, in fact, have an incipient theory about that, but it wasn't one that she wanted to share with the world at large. She was spared further explanation when the door burst open to reveal Brenda Arnold, puffing like an asthmatic dragon on the warpath.

"For chrissake! Will you people wake up and smell the goddamn coffee? I can't believe this claptrap. Ghosts, my ass! Hasn't anyone here ever read *Freud*? It's guilt, pure and simple. Sure, she saw Buddy's ghost—the way Macbeth saw Banquo's. Guilt—I'm not saying she *did* it. But I'd stake my life she was the *cause*. The only times my brother ever got into hot water was because of her and she knows it!"

Before any of them could react, a tanned hand clamped down on Brenda's shoulder and spun her around. Tim Hayes had materialized out of nowhere with hellfire in his eyes.

"You stupid, lying cow! I don't know what the fuck's goin' on here but I know about hot water, babe. And you got your brother into plenty of that, paying off your bookies, huh? And those guys don't play nice, do they, Bren? Maybe the tab got too high and they offed him so you could inherit and pay your bill? Ever think of that—that *you* might be the cause, baby sister?"

If she'd been a betting woman like Brenda, O'Roarke would've made it five-to-one odds that Hayes was about to get his ears boxed. And she would've lost. To the amazement of all onlookers, and there were plenty at this point, Ms. Arnold struggled vainly for a retort then folded like a house of cards. Hayes' attack had caught her off guard and right in the solar plexus. It was all she could do to give him one baleful look before bursting into tears and running down the hall.

Unfazed by her dramatic exit, Tim turned to Ginger, holding out one hand. "Come on, sugar. You can fill me in on the way home. Let's go have dinner with Hilly."

Jumping up, her face flooded with relief and gratitude, Ginger grabbed her tote bag and Tim's hand, then turned to give Jocelyn a quick kiss. "Tell the guys not to worry," she whispered, nodding toward her director and producer. "I'll be fine now."

Then they were gone, leaving Austin and Larry to play scissors-paper-stone to see which one would go to coddle La Arnold. Austin's paper lost to Larry's scissors. Still peeved with her but desperately wanting her assistance, he turned to Josh and asked stiffly, "Care to join me?"

"Not on your life." It wasn't sheer vindictiveness on her part, just plain dread of Brenda coupled with her keen desire to get in touch with Hamill. But she couldn't expect Austin to see it that way. And he didn't.

"Fine. You just go on home," he replied tartly. "Larry can give me a lift."

"Fine. See you later then," she returned in kind.

Watching Austin turn heel and march huffily out the door, she was led to conclude one of two things: either she was a total bitch, a possibility that had been suggested to her once or twice before, or that men, whatever their sexual inclination, tended to believe that women were created primarily to cater to their needs. But it was a fairly easy conundrum to resolve, really: to refuse to cater was to be a bitch. Well, she could live with that all right. She'd been living with it ever since she'd turned Phillip Gerrard down and lost him. The pain of that loss had knocked her for a loop but it hadn't made her recant. Men, as lovers or as friends, were a very expensive proposition. And, while she didn't entirely hold with Gloria Steinem's assertion that "A woman without a man is like a fish without a bicycle," she had to admit it was easier to swim upstream without the encumbrance.

Walking out of Ginger's dressing room, she ran smack into an encumbrance.

"You do have a genius for being in the eye of the tornado, don't you, O'Roarke?" Breedlove grinned down at her provocatively.

"Yeah, call it the luck of the Irish—and most of it's bad."

"Well, we can do something about that, you know. I don't want to speak out of turn here but it looks to me like you and Frostie could do with a brief sabbatical from each other."

He'd obviously caught Austin's irate exit so there was no point in prevaricating. "Yes, Jack, you're right. We are not currently our favorite people. But this, too, shall pass. Meanwhile I just want to get in a few laps before—"

"Wouldn't you rather go for a ride? I've got a sweet little bay mare that's a great mount. If we left now, you could ride for a good hour before dinner—and I'm a great cook, by the way."

"Oh, you swine, you," she hissed.

"What're you talking about?!" Breedlove was all mock innocence now. "I make a friendly offer and you start callin' me names, geez!"

"A bay mare! You're not playing fair and you know it," she insisted.

"Yes, I am. I have been from the start," he said, suddenly serious, leaning in close to her. "Before any of this shit started. I let you know right away who I was, what I had . . . and what I want to have. You're the one who keeps tap dancing around it."

"I'm not tap dancing! I mean, you have to admit the atmosphere around here isn't exactly conducive to romance."

"Right. That's why I say we blow this popsicle stand, sister," he Bogarted back; he really was a good mimic as well as charming and oh, so easy on the eyes. Still she wavered until he added, "Of course, if you'd really rather go home and wait up for Austin—"

"Right—we're outta here!" She grabbed her purse, then stopped. "But I have to make a call first. I'll meet you in the parking lot in five minutes, okay?"

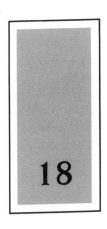

18

Ride a cockhorse to Banbury Cross,
To see a fine lady upon a bay horse;
Rings on her fingers and bells on her toes,
She shall have music wherever she goes.

"That's wrong. It's 'To see a fair lady upon a *white* horse.'"

"Hey, it's my horse so I'm entitled to a little poetic license, okay? God, what a hard-ass little hairsplitter you are."

Jocelyn urged the mare up the hill and drew alongside Jack who was riding Brando, his Appaloosa. He stopped when they reached a small plateau and turned west to face the setting sun. She needed the breather. Jack was an excellent horseman and it had been so long since she'd last ridden that it was all she could do to keep up with him, though Peg was as obliging as he had promised.

Taking a deep gulp of air, she grew dizzy, not so much from exertion as sensory overload. This was about as close to heaven on earth as she'd ever gotten. Growing up in the East, O'Roarke had ridden horses on farms as a kid and on sedate bridle paths as an adult, but this was her first experience on horseback in the wide open spaces. A whole new ballgame; forget about going to church or meditating, in her book, *this* was a religious experience.

No wonder he's such a carefree guy, she thought, watching Jack lean forward to rub Brando's neck. He does this every *day!* This was freedom incarnate and the best way possible to keep a sound perspective on the world and all its woes. At this moment, watching the sun sink with the smell of horses' sweat and saddle soap in her nostrils, she felt something that she hadn't felt in ages: that life was filled with limitless possibilities. Sudden tears pricked her eyes as she realized, with a deep, sharp pang, how long and how desperately she'd missed that feeling.

Rubbing a sleeve across her face, she saw Jack regarding her quizzically.

"What's over that hill?" she asked, pointing to the north.

"Funny you should ask," he said, looking less carefree than he had a minute ago. "That's where Buddy and Gabby's property starts—Monte Verde, all five hundred acres of it. I wonder what's going to happen to it now."

"Now that Gabby has sole control, you mean? That's assuming that she does, of course."

"Well, hell, she must! I can't picture Buddy leaving it in Brenda's hands."

"No, probably not. Actually, I was thinking more about Ginger. He really did adore her. If he wanted to protect the land, he might've just left his interest to her."

"That's cold comfort. If Gabby's hot to sell, I can't picture Ginger standing up to her."

"Oh, I don't know. She's very loyal—and she's got more guts than people give her credit for."

"Yeah . . . maybe," he said doubtfully, turning Brando around. "Come on. We should head back before it gets too dark. I don't want you hitting any gopher holes. Just stay right behind me."

She was happy to oblige since it was such a pretty vantage point, given the fluid conjunction of rider and mount. Mentally tipping her hat to the Freudians, she pulled on Peg's reins, sighing, "O happy horse, to bear the weight of Antony!"

Breedlove's ranch house was uncannily close to what she'd

imagined: sparse, tasteful, and functional, with Navajo rugs on the pine floors, woven Mexican wall hangings, and some very good Indian pottery. But there were a few eccentric touches here and there, like the Pee-wee Herman doll wearing a button that read WANKERS UNITE—FREE THE PEE, and a wall clock, obviously handmade by Jack, that had faces of old, grade-B movie stars instead of numbers on it. Joan Blondell was at one o'clock, she noted, followed by Claire Trevor and Ida Lupino.

Then there was one small guest bedroom that had been converted into a mini–Wig Museum, filled with white Styrofoam heads sporting everything from thirties bobs to sixties beehives up to eighties punk cuts.

The large kitchen with a huge butcher block island told her he hadn't been fibbing about his culinary skills. And the filled floor-to-ceiling bookcases everywhere attested to a man with far-flung, eclectic interests.

Since Jack had told her nicely but in no uncertain terms that he would single-handedly prepare their repast, Burritos à la Breedlove, Jocelyn felt free to indulge in one of her favorite pastimes—book snooping. Slicing jalapeño peppers on his island, Breedlove watched her run her hands and eyes over his reading material. Tom Clancy and the other espionage boys only rated a cursory glance but his extensive collection of books on film and television received close attention, especially *Hidden Messages*, an exposé of subliminal advertising in the fifties that she pored over for several minutes. Then he lost sight of her when she got on her knees to inspect the lower shelves. There wasn't a peep out of her for the next thirty minutes and he started to get a bit nervous. Had she found his set of erotic Japanese lithographs? And, if so, was she repelled or intrigued?

After popping the burritos in the oven, he took a pitcher of margaritas out of the fridge and two frosted glasses from the freezer. He filled them, then sauntered over to investigate, joking aloud.

"Now I bet you're going to beg to borrow that pictorial history of the hairdos of Mamie Eisenhower—of course, it's just *one* photo. But those bangs of hers *are* classic. So I'm afraid it's out of the question. Lend a book, lose a friend, I always say . . . Josh?"

Sitting cross-legged on the floor, O'Roarke was giving her full attention to the large book open on her lap, one that Jack had forgotten was there. It was *Hurry Up and Wait*, Buddy's first book. Josh raised a hand to accept the drink but kept her eyes on the page before her.

"He really was quite good, wasn't he?" she said with faint surprise. "And I like that he only used black and white. But, lordy, you were right—the man was vicious!"

She was looking at a photo of Bette Davis on the set of "Hotel." It must have been taken during the pilot episode because Davis had suffered a stroke shortly after and been replaced by Anne Baxter. Leaning far back in a chair while being made up, she had her remarkable myopic eyes shut and her hands clasped loosely across her midriff. Buddy had taken the shot from a high angle, which had the eerie effect of making Davis look like a corpse being prepared by morticians.

"And he wasn't any nicer to his own kith and kin. Look at this." She flipped a few pages and stopped at a photo of a young Ginger tête-à-tête with a younger Gabby, probably taken during the last season of "Jam House." Shot from an unflattering low angle, it made Brent, with a cigarette dangling pugnaciously from the corner of her mouth, look like Edward G. Robinson circa *Little Caesar* while Jellicoe, pubescent but sweaty and pallid with her eye makeup smeared, resembled a poster child for Phoenix House.

"I think Buddy was an Arbus wannabe, 'cept he didn't identify with his subjects. Just skewered them."

This wasn't, to Jack's thinking, an auspicious start to a romantic evening. Kneeling beside her, he reached down to remove the book, but Josh grabbed it back.

"Wait, wait! Look at that guy there, the one staring at them. It's hard to tell 'cause he's got hair—but isn't that Larry?"

"Goldstein? Nah, it can't—" Jack leaned forward and squinted at the grainy face in the background. "Well, I'll be damned, it could be . . . but so what? You gotta remember, this is a *very* small town, Josh. We all go way back together. That's why it's dangerous to make enemies."

"Well, Buddy obviously didn't feel that way. He must've made a barrelful," she remarked as she reluctantly let him put the book back on the shelf.

"Yeah. But he was good at his job. *And* he was married to Gabby—that gave him a lot of immunity." To change the topic, he nuzzled her ear and asked, "You getting hungry?"

Alone with Jack at last, she was suddenly feeling shy, which is why she blurted out, "God, yes! I could eat a hor— Oh, sorry. Bad choice. But, yes, I'm famished."

"Good. Let's eat."

Burritos à la Breedlove might not have impressed Julia Child, but Josh felt Calvin Trillin would love them almost as much as she did. They brought tears to her eyes, thanks to the liberal layering of jalapeños, and a glow to her insides, though this might've been abetted by the chef's wit and charm and his generous refills of margaritas. Preceded by a quirky but tasty endive-and-cucumber salad with salsa dressing and followed by fresh *bonuelos* powdered with sugar and cinnamon, the meal was "an elegant sufficiency."

Sated and dreamy, Jocelyn lolled on the polished-burlap sofa and watched Jack make Mexican coffee and bring it over to the oblong, glass-topped coffee table.

"That was a *great* dinner."

"Glad you liked it." With catlike economy, Jack handed her a cup, slid onto the sofa, and slipped an arm around her shoulders. "Who was it that said, 'A great meal is often the prelude to great love'?"

Jocelyn laughed so hard she nearly spilled her coffee. When she finally regained her powers of speech, she punched his arm and said, "Sue Ann Nivens on the old 'Mary Tyler Moore Show,' you nit! God, does that mean I'm Lou Grant?"

"Shit, you're right! And here I thought I got it from some M. F. K. Fisher book . . . Well, O'Roarke, it just proves that we're a match for each other."

"No, it just proves that your other women were pop culture illiterates, is all," she snickered.

"Good god almighty! What're you made of—asbestos? I have wined you and dined you but . . . Do you have a *single* romantic bone in your body, woman?"

Jack spun her around to face him with a hand on each shoulder. His eyes were blazing now, the hazel almost turned to gold and she knew what that meant. But she was feeling heady and brazen and couldn't resist teasing, "Gee, I dunno. I never thought of those particular sentiments as being in one's *bones*, you know? I always figured they resided in, uh—other places."

But Jack Breedlove was up to her baiting. With a dangerous smile, he replied, "Fine . . . Let's go looking for them."

And he did with swift dispatch. It was more than she'd bargained for but not more than she wanted. And she was ready, more ready than she'd known, to meet him, caress for caress, as they groped, fondled, and engulfed one another. The glass-topped coffee table shuddered, bringing coffee cups precariously near the edge, as they tumbled together off the sofa onto the floor. Articles of clothing went flying in every direction as, in some far corner of her brain, Jocelyn noted that here was one guy who really knew how to unhook a bra—and a lot more. But there was another part of her brain, farther distant, faintly protesting, *But it's not Phillip!* Not that it mattered anymore; animal instinct was sweeping past history and all other mundane considerations aside. And it felt wonderful.

Then, just as his mouth was executing an extremely interesting exploration of her lower belly, the phone began to ring.

"Jack, uh, your phone—"

"Forget it," he murmured. "The machine's on."

"Yeah. But . . . I think it might be for me."

"Josh! *Now?*" He looked at her with passionate incredulity.

" 'Fraid so . . . It might be important."

With less good grace than McEnroe after a bad call, he snatched up the receiver and barked, "Yeah?" His eyebrows jerked up when he heard who the caller was, then tossed the cellular phone to her with a curt, "You were right."

"Josh, I got your message. What's up?"

"Uh, hi, Dwayne." Getting to her feet, she hastily slipped her shirt back on. "Can you hold on just a sec?" She turned to Jack, tapping the phone lightly against her heart three times. "Mea culpa, mea culpa, mea maxima culpa. I've got to take this in private, Jack."

"Hey, that's cool," he said with as much sarcasm as a man can muster while pulling his pants on. "I wouldn't want to eavesdrop on you and *Dwayne.*"

Reaching for a cigarette, she watched him stalk off in the direction of the bedroom before turning her attention back to Hamill.

"You still there?"

"Sure. Hope I'm not interrupting anything."

"Uh, not anymore. Look, I did some hunting around today . . ."

Dwayne listened in silence as she recounted the day's adventures, starting with her sortie into the darkroom and ending with Ginger's suspect apparition. If it had been Gerrard at the other end, she would've been interrupted by a twenty-minute lecture on the illegality of disturbing a crime scene and the dangers of solo snooping, whereas Hamill was merely impressed by her initiative and anxious to get his hands on the new evidence.

"Hot damn! We missed it completely. Didn't really look for anything else after we found the negative in the enlarger."

"Yeah, well, you might've mentioned it to me, Hamill."

"Sorry, slipped my mind. They just developed it this afternoon. That's why I wasn't around when you called."

"Well, what the hell was it?!"

"A picture of his sister with a guy. The boys in the photo lab think it was taken from a distance with a zoom lens. I took a print out to Santa Anita and showed it around. Thought I might find someone who saw Brenda *during* the races."

"Did you?"

"Nope—but I did find out who the guy was. This bookie I know, Easy Eddy, placed him. His name's Randall Boggs, aka Boogie the Beast. No record, but he's a known cruncher."

"Cruncher as in bones?"

"Right. A free-lance enforcer for anyone who's having trouble with welchers."

"You think somebody sicced him on Brenda?"

"Could be. Or maybe Brenda was looking to sic him on somebody. Rumor has it he accepts the occasional contract. And they looked kinda cozy in the picture. So I'm meeting with Banks' lawyer first thing tomorrow to find out how big a chunk ol' Bren stands to inherit."

"Well, not to burst your bubble, but, if I were you, I wouldn't bet my badge on it."

"Why not?"

"Look, essentially Buddy was poisoned, right? Now I don't hold with the theory that poison is a woman's weapon. But it is a subtle form of homicide. If this guy's a muscle man—well, it's just not his style, is it?"

"Guess not." Hamill's voice was heavy with disappointment. "But I'm still gonna check him out."

"By all means, he's got to know something. While you're at it—if you can spare the manpower—you might want to put a tail on Jellicoe."

"Why? You think she faked that scene in her dressing room?" Dwayne asked eagerly, all his youthful exuberance restored.

"No, I don't. She saw something all right," Josh answered evenly, careful to mask her protective feelings toward Ginger. "But I don't think it was Buddy making a cameo appearance from the Great Beyond. This may or may not have anything to do with the case but . . . I think someone might be trying to *Gaslight* the girl."

"Huh?"

If it had been Gerrard at the other end, she wouldn't have had to give a quick plot synopsis of the 1944 film that had secured Ingrid Bergman's first Best Actress Oscar, but such are the vicissitudes of dealing with kindergarten cops.

"Oh, I get it! Ex–drugstore cowgirl trying for a comeback and somebody wants to push her toward the funny farm."

"Right. You could have a terrific career writing headlines for *Variety*, Dwayne—that's the gist of it. So, when you speak to Buddy's attorney, find out if she's in the will, too. It might tell us something."

"Far out. But, listen, I need to get that—whatever it is you found in the enlarger—like, pronto. I could drive out now and—"

"*No*, Dwayne," she said firmly, grinding out her cigarette. "Unlike you and your illustrious role model—who shall go nameless, right?—I have other priorities in life. And I'd like to get back to them . . . if that's possible. Just call me after you see the lawyer. I'll come by your office, okay?"

"Okay, cool. And thanks, Josh, for everything. I just gotta say—you do The Man proud."

He hung up quickly, before she could bite his head off. It was just as well, she thought; there was other work at hand. A fire, once doused, was hard to reignite, especially where the male libido was concerned. But O'Roarke, once a seeded player on the Manhattan dating circuit, was beginning to feel like Jimmy Connors at the 1991 U.S. Open; she still had a few good shots left.

Tiptoeing over to the liquor cabinet, she found a bottle of Fundador and filled two snifters. Then she rifled through Jack's CDs and spotted Don Henley's *Building the Perfect Beast*. And perfect it was; first cut on the A side was "The Boys of Summer." She slipped it into the player, then unbuttoned the top of her shirt.

Jack was lying on the bed watching the Sports Channel—very tough competition. But, knowing the song by heart, she timed her entrance superbly. Gliding through the door, she shimmied in front of the TV screen, melding her voice with Don's as he pleaded, "But, babe, I'm gonna get you back. Gonna show you what I'm made of."

But Breedlove was no easy mark. He took the snifter from her proffering hand grudgingly. There was an even chance that he'd just go back to watching the Padres and her feminine self-esteem would go right back to the gutter it had been wallowing in for months. But then, just as she was about to retreat, he grabbed her wrist.

"Want to tell me what that little conference call was all about?"

"Uh, no. Not right now. But I will . . . later."

"You don't make it easy for a guy, O'Roarke, you know that?"

"Yeah, I guess you're right. But I don't mean to," she demurred, half apologetic, half provocative. "Though there's some would say harder is better."

"Really? How interesting." That dangerous glint was in his eyes again as he carefully placed his snifter on the bookcase headboard with one hand while the other snaked up her arm. "Well, if you're one of them, lady, you're about to get your wish."

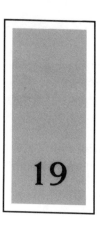

19

"Phillip! What in the world are you doing here?"

Gerrard came toward her with a sad smile on his face. "I was worried about you," he said, gently brushing her cheek with his knuckles, his old familiar greeting making her ache with remembrance. "Thought you might need some help, kiddo."

Kiddo? Phillip never called her kiddo. For that matter, he never, ever wore a hat, but he was wearing one now, a fedora. Though she had to admit it looked right with the trench coat. Trench coat?

"But how did you get here?"

Instead of answering her question, he crossed to the crystal decanter and poured himself a glass of wine. Holding it up, he winked at her and lisped, "Here's looking at you."

Rooted to the floor, she waved her hands in sudden panic. "No! Don't drink that—it's poisoned!"

"Oh, now why would you say a thing like that, dear?" Jean

Adair was at her side now, all lace and smiles. "That's my best elderberry. Isn't it, Mortimer?"

Cary Grant bounded down the stairs and draped his arms around Jean and Josh's shoulders. "Well, I'll be a son of a sea cook! Phillip Gerrard, as I live and breathe. Wait till you hear what this little filly of yours has been up to." Grant gave her a playful nudge, then called over his shoulder, "Hey, Jack! Someone here I think you should meet."

"No! I don't . . . *want* that." She struggled to break away from the Brewsters and get to Phillip but couldn't manage it. There were heavy footsteps on the stairs now, made by cowboy boots. Gerrard gave her another wink as he raised the poisoned wine to his lips. Just as he was about to drink it, he said, "Watch out for these guys, love. They're real ladykillers."

Alarms went off all over the place as he downed the drink while she looked on helplessly.

"Josh—Josh, wake up. Call for you."

"Huh?" She bolted up in bed, then, realizing she was topless —bottomless, too, for that matter—made a wild grab for the sheets.

"It's a little late for maidenly modesty, don't you think?" Freshly showered, Jack Breedlove handed her the cordless phone with an ear-to-ear grin on his face. "I know first mornings are weird but, if it'll help, I still respect and esteem you as much as ever—more, actually. *Lots* more." Then he kissed the tip of her nose and headed off to the kitchen, whistling "What a Difference a Day Makes."

Totally discombobulated, she fumbled for the phone, which had gotten lost in the tumbled sheets, finally managing to track it by the little giggling sounds that were coming through the receiver.

"Hello?"

"So he *is* straight! You were right, Joshie . . . Was it fun?"

"Ginger?"

"Yep. Sorry to butt in but I wanted to call before I got to the set."

"How'd you know I was here?"

"Austin told me."

"God, why didn't he just take out an ad in the trades?"

"Aw, don't be mad. I begged him . . . I wanted to thank you for yesterday—for sticking by me when everyone else thought I was, you know—losing it."

"Well, you're not losing it, Ginge. You're no crazier than I am," she said groggily, then winced as the full force of the dream came back to her. At that moment, O'Roarke was pretty sure that she could beat out Ginger in the "a few sandwiches short of a picnic" sweepstakes.

"You know, I'm beginning to think you're right, Josh. 'Cause even with all the shit that's been going on, I've been sleeping *great* lately! And I think it's thanks to you—your support . . . Of course, last night I had a little help," Ginger said coyly before breaking into girlish giggles.

"What kind of help?" It couldn't be drink or drugs; she didn't need to see Jellicoe's pupils to know that only the sober and chemical-free could sound this disgustingly perky at five-thirty in the morning.

"Well, Sis, let's just say that"—more giggles—"we *both* got our oil changed last night."

"Ahh, I get it." It wasn't a euphemism that Jocelyn was wont to use for the sex act but, in California, everything referred back to cars. "Tim spent the night?"

"I'll say! My therapist will kill me when I tell her—*if* I tell her. But he was just being so sweet and sharing. It was like the old days . . . So how about you?"

"How about me what?" She knew perfectly well what Jellicoe was driving at but it was just too early in the day to be playing Betty to her Veronica.

"You and Jack! Like, did the earth move under your feet? Did the sky come tumbling down?" And when automobiles were not used as a sexual metaphor, earthquake imagery was the next best thing. Made sense, which was more than O'Roarke felt capable of at present.

"Uh, can't really say right now."

"Oh, he's there, right? Okay, I'll catch you later. Kiss kiss."

And he was there, leaning in the doorway, bare-chested in his faded 501s, blithely announcing, "Coffee's on and we're having fajitas for breakfast, okay?"

By all that she held sacred, she should be feeling the way Ginger sounded and, on a purely physical level, she did. Thanks to Jack's imaginative and generous ministrations of the previous night, she felt like her body had been given back to her, more pulsing and alive than it had been for months. Why then that lousy, guilt-infested dream and the subsequent *tristesse?*

"Great. I'm ravenous. Just let me jump in the shower first," she said, trying her best to sound game.

"Wait a sec." Her best wasn't good enough judging from Jack's furrowed brow as he came to sit on the bed beside her. Massaging her thigh under the rumpled sheet, he said, "You look down. Now I don't mean to sound like a conceited bastard—but I don't think it's 'cause of last night. You're a very straight-on lady and you'd've let me know if you weren't having a good time."

"Yes, you're right. And I was—and it was more than a good time, Jack."

"Glad to hear it, 'cause it was everything I'd hoped for and then some. So—'what is the cause of your sorrow?' Is it that guy?"

"Jack, I told you—"

"Come on, Josh! I know you hate the Spanish Inquisition—but I need to know where I stand here. Are you done with it or not?"

Good question. She grabbed a pillow and held it against her stomach while staring up at the spackled ceiling for a long moment.

"Yeah, I'm done with it. It's just—you're the first person I've been with since . . . then, see? And that's kind of scary 'cause it brings up a lot of old *stuff*, you know? So this is going to sound nuts but—if last night hadn't been so wonderful—I wouldn't be missing him so much right now. Does that make any kind of sense?"

Still unable to meet his gaze, she shifted hers to a framed animation cel of Rocky and Bullwinkle on the far wall while Jack let her words sink in. Finally his hand moved over hers as he gently drew the pillow away.

"I don't know if it makes sense but I know it's honest—which is more important. And I know it means you don't take these things lightly—which is good. 'Cause I don't want you to," he said as he slipped in under the sheets beside her. "And I know, for sure, that you're not on call today so I'm going to be late for work, for once."

"All right, Peg, bear with me. I think I've got it down now. 'One—Fuck guilt. Two—Don't make such a case out of everything. Three—Who said it was fair? Four—Who said it was easy? Five—Why you? Why not?' Oh, come on, lazybones, just to the top of the next hill and then we'll head back, promise."

The little bay shook her head and made a soft snuffling sound, the equine version of a Bronx cheer, before responding to O'Roarke's request. But Jocelyn, her spirits considerably lifted after Jack's unique notion of a wake-up call and a hot shower, paid not the slightest heed.

After a massive breakfast, Jack had suggested, "Since you *insisted* on driving up here in your own car and you're not working today, why don't you stick around and take a morning ride before going back to Smog Central?"

She'd jumped at the suggestion, though not purely out of love of horseflesh. While Jack had been putting the finishing touches on their fajitas, she'd put in a call to Hamill, who, true to his sun-drenched nature, asked her to meet him at Topanga Beach, of all places. Since Breedlove was still in the dark about her dealings with Dwayne and the time was not yet ripe to let there be light, she'd been rifling through her mental Filofax of fabrications, trying to come up with a plausible excuse for her detour. It had been a great boon to her digestive system not to have to fib to a man who'd made love to her and then made breakfast.

Still, there'd been a lingering twinge of guilt, which is why, after Jack's departure, she'd done the dishes before going to saddle up Peg. That's when she'd spotted Lester Colodny's Commandments stuck on the refrigerator door. Number one had caught her eye immediately with its apropos sentiments. Whoever this Lester guy was or had been, he was on to something and O'Roarke, always one to follow the most subversive path to enlightenment, had instantly seized on him as a soulmate, deciding to commit his teachings to memory there and then.

Nearing the top of the hill now, Josh recited, " 'Six—Don't press, let it happen. Seven—They can kill you but they can't eat you. Eight—If you don't want to be crucified, don't hang around crosses.' Ha! Take *that*, Sister Mary Timothy. 'Nine—Wherever you are, at any time, in any place, you can always reach out and touch . . . a schmuck.' Oh, *shit*."

Colodny was, indeed, a prophet of some ilk, because there before her eyes was a Land Rover coming toward her over the bumpy terrain, shaking its passengers like martinis. And those martinis were none other than Gabby Brent and Larry Goldstein accompanied by a rotund man with a seasick expression.

Peg came to a halt just as the Land Rover did. Gabby, at the wheel, leaned forward, shoving her Ray-Bans back to squint at Josh accusingly while snapping her fingers as a memory aid.

"Christ almighty, it's what's-her-face—O'Riley! What the hell are you doing up here? I hate to tell you, kid, but they aren't planning a sequel to *City Slickers*. Or is this one of those desperate-actor ploys to get an agent? In which case, I have to give you two points for initiative, doll . . . I mean, this *is* new but—"

"Psst—Gabby! It's O'Roarke, not O'Riley."

"Huh?" Brent swung around to glare at Larry, who was sunk low in the passenger seat, looking nearly as bilious as the fat guy in the rear.

"Jocelyn O'Roarke," he said more firmly, giving Josh a weak stab at a smile. "And I really don't think she's trying to, uh . . ."

"What he's trying to say, Gabby, is I don't ascribe to the Sean Young school of auditioning," Josh said tartly as she dismounted and led Peg toward the Land Rover. Yesterday she'd made allowances for the effects of drink and distress but today the Widow Banks was sober and back in rare shark form. It was time to eat or be eaten. Locking eyes with the older woman, she added, "I'm just here as Jack Breedlove's guest. Which reminds me—his land goes on for another five acres, doesn't it? So . . . aren't you folks *trespassing?*"

It was immensely gratifying to watch Brent drop her gaze, though, to her credit, she didn't start squirming in her seat like her male companions. Not wanting to lose the upper hand, O'Roarke chose to extend it to Tubby in the backseat with a sunny smile.

"Hi! I'm Josh."

"Oh, uh, pleased to meet you. I'm Thatcher Pruitt. And I hope you don't think we meant to—"

His hand felt like a dead eel but she shook it heartily and

pressed on. "Now that name sounds awfully familiar. Help me here. Thatcher Pruitt of . . . ?"

"Ah, yes, maybe . . . of Prescott and Pruitt Developers, actually. Have you heard of us?"

"No. But I can guess," she said brusquely before swerving back to Goldstein. "So, Lar, what brings you up here at this hour? Aren't you afraid the Culver City troops will falter without their Fearless Leader?"

"Well, no. I mean, we're doing some wild-tracking first . . . They don't need me for that. And I should be back in time for the first setup."

"Still makes a hell of a long day for you though," she breezed on, knowing that she was fishing but not sure for what. Clearly with Pruitt along, this was not some secret lovers' tryst. But then how *did* Goldstein fit into the picture? "Well, I guess you're smart to get out of the city—just blow off all responsibility and clear your head."

"Uhh, it's not exactly that, Josh," Larry began uneasily. But Pruitt finished for him.

"Oh, no, not at all! Larry's been working very hard—burning his candle at both ends, you know? He put us in touch with Mrs. Banks and his advice on this project has been inval—"

Confronted by the dual spectres of Doom (Gabby) and Gloom (Larry), Thatcher sputtered to a hasty halt. But Jocelyn had heard enough. Goldstein was in bed with Gabby, all right, at least in the financially figurative sense. Brent was hot to sell Monte Verde and Goldstein had helped her set up the deal. If Buddy had known about it, it would account for much of their on-set friction and maybe something more.

It was time for a false exit so Jocelyn swung herself back up on Peg with an easy, "Well, it's been real, all. Though, if you think you'll get Breedlove to sell, I'd say you've got an ice cube's chance in hell. But I've got to get back. Austin'll be wondering where I am."

As she expected, Goldstein scurried out of the Land Rover and made a grab for the reins. A startled Peg nipped him and Josh rubbed her velvet nose in approval.

"Geez! That *hurt*," Larry yelped, jumping back.

"Yeah? Well, as a wise man once said, 'Why you? Why not?' "

"Huh? What's that supposed to mean?"

"Nothing. What do you want, Larry?"

"Hey, Josh, I know this all looks kinda funny but, really, it's just business . . . Do you haf'ta say anything to Frostie about it?"

"No, I don't. And I won't. It's not my place. But you *haf'ta*, Lar. He's your partner. You owe it to him. And if you don't come clean with him then, yeah, I might get a little loose-lipped in the wrong quarters."

"What does that mean?"

"Guess."

Having picked up a trick or two in her time with Gerrard, she'd learned that a veiled threat was always better than an explicit one. And this one seemed to make an impact; Larry jumped away from Peg as Gabby regarded Josh with a baleful though somewhat respectful glance and Pruitt stared fixedly down at his feet while twiddling his thumbs like a Dickens caricature. When Josh tugged on the reins, Peg, suddenly obliging, did a very nice heigh-ho-Silver-and-away turn, providing her rider with the best exit she'd managed in years.

Looking over her shoulder, she narrowed her eyes at Goldstein and asked, "Who is that masked realtor?"

20

"Whoa! Who is that barney? Anybody dropped in on me like that—I'd wax his board with Crisco, man."

"Dwayne—?"

"Oh, sorry, Josh. What I mean is—that guy on the long board was already riding the wave and that twerp came in front of him and stole his ride. It's just not *done*, you know?"

"He is beneath contempt, I'm sure," O'Roarke agreed, recapping a tube of Almay sunblock SPF 30 after having covered every millimeter of skin exposed to the UVs beating down on Topanga Beach. "But could we possibly get back to the *will*, Dwayne?!"

"Uh, sure, sure. But let's walk, okay," he said, slipping off his Docksiders and motioning for her to follow suit. Despite the strong sun, the sand felt cool under her feet as she tried to match her stride to Hamill's loping gait. "I 'preciate you coming out here, Josh. It's just that I think best near the ocean—gets your alpha waves going and you need your alphas to help you see the Big Picture, crime-wise, right?"

"If memory serves, the lieutenant—or shall we just call him Allah?—usually gets his alphas going with a shot of Jack Daniel's. But to each his own, eh?"

At the mention of Gerrard, Dwayne shot her a surprised glance but nobly restrained himself from pursuing the topic. Actually she'd surprised herself as well but chalked it up to the subconscious aftermath of that bizarre dream of hers.

"So what'd the lawyer have to say?"

"Not lawyer—lawyersss. To the tune of three. Man, those dudes are twisted. Acted like Banks' will was some big state secret I was trying to steal. But I managed to make 'em cough up," Hamill said, a heretofore hidden toughness in his tone. "Those guys get so cranked up over a couple'a lousy millions—well, twenty, I guess."

Jocelyn stopped so fast, she kicked sand in her own face. "Twenty?! Buddy's estate is worth twenty mil?"

"Yeah, give or take a few—definitely take after death duties and those guys get their cut, I'd say. Still, a nice sum considering that it's not even factoring in his wife's income."

"I'll say! He and Gabby must've done better than I thought with their real estate business."

"They did okay," Dwayne said with a blaséness she found amazing in a guy who couldn't be earning more than fifty grand a year. "But that's not the bulk of it—not by a long shot."

"Then what is?"

"Now here's where it gets interesting. Remember Ginger said Buddy was the executor of her parents' estate?"

"Sure. And an executor gets a fee but not to the tune of twenty mil—"

"Wait, wait! She also said that he oversaw the selling of her father's business, right? But he never sold it, Josh. Jellicoe Import-Export is still a going concern! And Buddy—as executor and Ginger's financial manager—was still getting a cut of the profits."

"Well, shiver me timbers and blow me away! You think he was skimming her?"

"Hard to tell yet. They ran a lot of numbers by me and I'm no accounting whiz. She was definitely receiving quarterly payments from the business. Maybe she was getting her fair chunk, maybe not. But if I was her, I'd hire an accountant, pronto."

"Christ, it's hard to fathom. I could see Buddy pulling a fast one on anybody—except Ginger. She was always the Beauty to his Beast."

"Well, we're still speculating here. But if he *was* scamming, he must've had a real bad conscience . . . 'cause he certainly made it up to her."

"How?"

"That Monte Verde property? Turns out it doesn't belong to the company—his and Gabby's. Buddy held sole title to it—and now Ginger does. He left it to her, free and clear."

"Oh, ye stars and little fishes!" Her hunch confirmed, O'Roarke fell back once more on maritime imagery as she narrowly missed treading on the bare midriff of an unsuspecting sunbather. "Uh, sorry . . . God, Gabby's going to blow a gasket over that. She must've just assumed that she'd get the deed."

"Well, she gets plenty, but not that."

"What about Brenda? How did she make out?"

"Okay. Enough to pay off her gambling debts and then some —if she doesn't blow it. Plus the rights and royalties to his books."

"Well, that's not what Brenda will consider a real nest egg given her luck with the ponies. But, you know, it means she has ownership of all the materials to his new book. So watch your step, she might own that negative I found."

"Nah, don't worry." Dwayne patted the jacket pocket where Josh's piece of darkroom booty now resided. "I don't know what the hell this *is* but I'm pretty sure it's not a negative—too large and too thick. Whatever it is, I'll get it blown up fast as I can."

"Speaking of physical evidence, did you turn up anything on that cigar box?"

"Yeah! That's another weird one. Almost no discernible prints on it, which is no big surprise. I talked with Jellicoe's housekeeper—she cleans that place, top to bottom, almost every day. And we haven't taken prints from all the parties involved yet, either. But what we did find was pretty conclusive."

"Conclusive—when you haven't even taken prints?" Jocelyn tried her utmost not to sound dubious—but really.

"In this case, yeah," Hamill answered, oblivious to her skepticism. "See, the only clear prints were very small ones. So they'd have to be—"

"Hilly's."

"Right. Now it could mean absolutely nothing. Kids touch everything in sight, I know—I always did. But somebody's got to ask her about it just the same and . . . I, uh, I'm not good at questioning kids, Josh." A pleading note came into his voice as he added, "They're like hard-core felons—they can smell a cop a mile away, even in plainclothes. Only they don't get hostile, they get scared—and I hate it. It's the worst part of the job for me, you know? I love kids but I'm just no good at playing kiddy cop. And she seems to really like you, so do you think you could—"

"Yeah, gotcha." She did and she didn't like it but she saw his point and she'd live with it for Hilly's sake. "I'll ask her, Dwayne. Just don't push for this. I'll have to wait till the time's right."

"Oh, sure, sure, no *problemo* at all," he assured her. Then that disarming blush suffused his cheeks. "I bet Gerrard knows how to handle this kind of thing all right. Guess I'm just a weak sist— uh, a coward."

That cut it.

Hero worship had gone far enough. O'Roarke grabbed a shoulder and spun him around to face her.

"Drop it, Dwayne! Don't do this . . . to you or me or *him*. Phillip's a damn fine cop but he's just a man, okay? And, for your information—and no one else's—he's a man I've seen weep because he had to drag a child up on the witness stand in a wife-murder case. If there were any way in heaven or hell he could've avoided it or passed the buck, he would've, gladly. That's not being a weak sister, Dwayne, that's being human."

The blush subsided as another light filled his face. Ever so delicately he placed a hand on her arm and said quietly, "Thanks for telling me that. And if I ever tell another soul, may I never live to ride the Banzai Pipeline." Having no notion where or what the Banzai Pipeline was, O'Roarke could see from the sudden pallor beneath his tan that Dwayne had given her his most sacred oath. He swallowed so hard his Adam's apple bounced, then added, "I guess I don't have to tell you that the LAPD has some pretty macho guys on the force. And some of 'em give me awesome amounts of flak 'cause I surf and I don't hang out at the same bars and I'm, uh—"

"Different." She was going to say human but decided in favor of diplomacy.

"Yeah, right. And I don't mind, really. But sometimes it makes me feel like I'm maybe not right for the job, you know?"

"Oh, you're right for the job, Dwayne. You're tenacious as a rat terrier and that's the chief qualification as far as I can tell. But compared to the average, garden-variety cop—yeah, you're somewhat, um, atypical. And I have kind of wondered how you got into this line of work."

"Through the back door, I guess," he said with a chuckle. "I sure wasn't planning on it! All I ever cared about was surfing, and that's the crowd I hung with."

"Not a strongly law-and-order-oriented group, I'd assume."

"Yeah, right! But I had this buddy, Mac the Quack we called him 'cause he was always prescribing pills or weed for whatever ailed you. He was a dealer but very nickel-and-dime stuff. Till he got into a coke deal with some very heavy people. When they tried to shortchange him, he made a stink . . . and got blown away. And I didn't think the cops would try very hard to get the guy."

"Sure. One pusher whacking another never rates as a high priority."

"Well, it bugged me. 'Cause, deep down, Mac was a very aloha guy, see? And I *knew* who deep-sixed him. Hell, everybody knew! It was just a matter of taking the time to build a case. I just didn't want to see this slime bucket walk so I got in touch with this one detective, Harvey Soames—an epic dude—and we built one . . . and it stuck. Next thing I knew ol' Harvey had me taking the entrance exam. Then, for a few years, we were partners."

"Where's Harvey now?"

They walked along the edge of the water, letting the wave foam tickle their toes. "He retired two years ago. Lives in Hawaii now. Drops me a line now and then to let me know how the surf's cranking at Waimea. I miss the old fart." Squinting, Hamill looked out to the horizon as if he were trying to spot his ex-mentor. "You know, I never thought of it before but I guess that's when I started following the lieutenant's moves. Just needed to know there was somebody else out there who cared about doing it right. Sounds crazy, huh?"

"No, it sounds eminently sane and reasonable . . . and decent. And that kind of thing really pisses some people off, you know, 'cause it makes them look bad. But they're the crazies, Dwayne, not you."

"Yeah, I guess," he mumbled with less than total conviction.

They were standing still now, shoulder to shoulder, looking out over the waves, but Josh didn't need to see his face; she could sense the strong emotions working in him and was overcome with a rare rush of maternal feeling. Slipping her arm through his, she gave it a good, hard squeeze. "No, don't guess—*know*. 'Cause I'll tell you, if you ever transferred to Manhattan, Phillip would snap you up in a second!"

"Aw, you're just being nice," he protested, but the blush was back and he sounded markedly cheerier.

"Nice?! Oh, gag me. Dwayne, you should know by now, I am never nice. Nice gives me hives," she chided him playfully, eager to avert what could become a tender moment.

"Yeah, you are." She kicked sea foam in his face. "Okay, okay—*decent* then. And you're real good at picking up on . . . stuff. I can see why the lieuten—"

"Oh, look!" O'Roarke spotted a welcome distraction and pointed to a boat that was cutting through the waves at top speed. "Isn't that a—you know—a scabbard?"

"A *Scarab*. Yeah, look at that sucker go." Dwayne's eyes followed its high-velocity progress. "Man, those things hardly touch the water. The Porsches of the waterways."

To ensure that their tender moment was safely past, she egged him on by asking, "But they can't travel that fast at night, can they? It'd be too dangerous."

"Sure they can! They're radar-equipped. Even in fog conditions, they can do thirty knots if the traffic's not real heavy. That's why the drug runners use 'em. They're filthy machines, all right."

"That one looks pretty immaculate to me."

"No, no, Josh. Filthy means awesome—epic. Get it?"

"Ah, how foolish of me . . . Well, we should be heading back, huh?"

"Right on." Following her lead, Hamill tore his gaze away from the boat and began trudging up the beach. "I gotta get the physical evidence back to the lab . . . But, Josh? Just so you don't go off thinking I'm a clueless California airhead—that was a cute diversionary tactic—but I *still* think you're a real sweetheart of a lady for what you said back there," he said, dropping a bronzed arm around her shoulder as he gave her a knowing wink and his most winning smile.

"Oh, damn. Well, shit—I like you, too, okay? For someone with so many disgusting natural highlights in his hair, you're pretty sharp . . . a filthily aloha guy. How's that?"

"Not bad! I tell ya, when this mess is over, O'Roarke, I'm gonna get you a board and get you up on a wave."

"You think so? In that case, Dwayne, I take it all back—you *are* crazy."

21

" 'Let's go surfin' now. Everybody's learning how. Come on and safari with me.' "

"You're crazy! Totally friggin' nuts!"

Breaking off her raucous rendition of the Beach Boys classic, O'Roarke, fresh from her fifty laps in the pool, stopped toweling her hair and cocked an ear in the direction of the living room. She'd gone straight from her car to the cabana and hadn't noticed that Austin was home. But he was and obviously upset with someone. "There's no way in hell we can afford to take that risk."

"Get real, Austin. We can't afford not to. We're behind schedule as it is!" That someone was the ubiquitous Larry Goldstein, sounding as perturbed as his partner. "Look, everything went smooth today. No scenes, no upsets, right? And she's agreed to do the stunt—hell, she *wants* to! Tomorrow's our first day on location. It'll save us time and money."

"Not if she breaks her neck, it won't. Screw the money, Lar. An ounce of prevention is worth a—"

"A pound of manure! Frostie, I swear this stunt's so safe my grandmother could do it. She's playing a stuntwoman, for chris-sake! If you want the character to have a shred of credibility, we gotta have one lousy sequence where we see *her* doing a stunt. And this is the safest one in the script. Jesus, you know that. And you're the one who was always going on about verisimilitude."

"Yes, but that was before Buddy died and our leading lady started having hallucinations. Now is not the time to ask Ginger to jump off a bridge!"

"It's a very low bridge with a very big airbag underneath it. And, like I said, she's game. In fact, I think she needs to do this—call it a rite of passage—and we shouldn't deprive her."

A long hallway ran between the kitchen, where Jocelyn now stood dripping on the tile floor, and the living room, where all hell was currently breaking loose, which led to the bedrooms, Austin's and hers. Caught between the devil of an argument that she wanted no part of and the deep blue her skin was about to turn, she decided to try to pussyfoot her way past them.

And she'd almost made it past the living room archway when Austin said doubtfully, "I don't know . . . I'd like to ask Jocelyn what she thinks."

"Oh, come on, Austin! I know she's your friend but what does she know? She's so busy screwin' her brains out with Breedlove, she could care less—"

"Hey!" Frost's sharp tone cut Larry off. "Watch your mouth. Whatever's going on with Josh and Jack is their business, all right? And it's never been my experience that sexual activity necessarily lowers one's IQ. In Jocelyn's case, I'd say it's quite the opposite, actually."

Warmed, emotionally if not physically, by her friend's chivalry, Josh felt she must reward it—hell, she *wanted* to reward it; Gold-stein was starting to seriously piss her off. Wrapping her towel around her goose-pimpled shoulders, she stepped backward into the archway and tried to keep her teeth from chattering as she beamed at both men.

"He's right, Lar. I do some of my best thinking on my back, which, I'm sure, is true of many women, contrary to popular opinion. Also, for future reference, postcoital euphoria in no way clouds one's short-term memory. Which reminds me—don't you have something you'd like to tell Austin about you and Gabby and Monte Verde? Why don't you just catch him up while I slip into something dry?"

Slinking as far down as was humanly possible in an Eames chair, Goldstein nodded weakly, rubbing the hand that Peg had nipped. "Yeah, sure . . . I'll do that."

Leaving her door open while she climbed into a fresh pair of jeans, she couldn't quite hear what Larry was saying, but Austin's response rang out loud and clear.

"Slow down. Let me get this straight—you're working on a real estate deal with Gabby? When did this whole thing start?"

Again, Goldstein's reply was indistinct but it didn't matter.

"A year ago! Jesus, Larry, why didn't you tell me?"

Wanting to be there for the good part, Josh grabbed her U.S. Open sweatshirt and pulled it over her damp head as she hustled back down the hall. Goldstein was up on his feet, pacing the polyurethaned oak floors and mangling his hair with one hand.

"Take it easy, Frostie. It's just a little thing I had going on the side. Had nothing to do with the production at al—"

"Until somebody killed Buddy," Austin interjected sharply. "Now it has *everything* to do with it. You should've told me."

"I didn't want to give you *tzuris*. You worry too much as it is. And I'm telling you now—it's no big deal! I'm just a small cog in the wheel—a middleman."

"To the tune of what?" Josh asked as she sauntered over to a window seat.

"Huh? What you mean?"

"Well, maybe you're just a really altruistic guy . . . And maybe I'm Marie of Romania. What I mean is—what's your cut?"

"It's called a commission, Jocelyn. Geez, you make it sound like—"

"How much, Lar?"

"Uh, the usual . . . ten percent."

"From both parties?" Goldstein just nodded so she pressed on. "That makes it twenty percent. Of how much—how much is Gabby asking for Monte Verde? Just a ballpark figure will do."

"Well, nothing's been set yet. But I'd say . . . around seven mil maybe."

"So your cut—excuse me, commission—would be about a hundred and forty grand, right?"

"Yeah, about." He qualified his answer with a casual, waffling motion of one hand while Josh and Austin exchanged a sour glance. By normal standards, certainly by O'Roarke's, one hundred and forty thousand dollars was a tidy sum. But, even if Larry was lowballing them, by Hollywood standards it amounted to what Mike Ovitz probably spent on valet parking tips in the course of a year. There had to be more to it.

From the speculative and slightly repulsed look Austin was now giving his partner, Jocelyn guessed that he was contemplating the illicit-love angle again and getting no joy from images of Gabby and Goldstein locked in the throes of passion. Larry caught his expression and demanded defensively, "Why're you looking at me like that? Like I'm some kind of . . . insect!"

Confrontation was never Austin's forte and whatever gruesome carnal visions had flitted through his mind's eye seemed to have rendered him momentarily speechless as he merely threw his hands up in front of his face, shaking his head sadly.

"What! What's bugging you?"

"Not to put too fine a point on it," Josh waded in where Frost feared to tread, "but I think he's wondering if you've been sleeping with Gabby."

"Me? *Schtupping* Brent?!" In a movie, say a horror flick of the *Friday the Thirteenth* ilk, the camera would now dolly in on Goldstein for an extreme close-up; the kind they use when the victim (Larry) spies the ghoul just as it's about to hack him into a thousand bloody pieces. It seemed that the images this notion conjured up for him were a hundredfold worse than Austin's. "Are you out of your friggin' *mind*?! Where'd you get that idea?"

"From a little bird named Hamill, actually. The night before the murder—when you were supposed to be at that screening—your car was spotted near her Malibu house."

Head hung low, he now looked ready to be hacked to pieces as he groaned, "Ah, shit. I'm fucked."

"Oh, Larry, how *could* you?" Austin had found his voice at last. "Don't you see the position this puts you in?"

"But it was business—nothing more! And not just the real estate thing. That's why I didn't want anyone to know. For a while now I've been wanting to switch agents—give my career a boost— that's why I got involved in the Monte Verde deal in the first place. Pruitt's an old tennis buddy of mine and I knew he was interested in the property. I thought if I got him and Gabby together, she'd take me on as a client . . . But I didn't want Felix to find out beforehand, see?"

"Oh, for pity's sake! Of course, I see. Why didn't you say so at the start," Austin replied, both exasperated and relieved. "Hell hath no fury like an agent scorned. And, yes, Felix would've had your guts for garters if he'd gotten wind of it—and I wouldn't blame him, by the way. He's been very good to you."

"Yeah, but he blew that 'L.A. Law' gig I was up for, remember?"

"You don't know that for a fac—"

Carefully placing two fingers between her lips, O'Roarke blew a short, piercing referee's whistle to call a halt to this insane digression.

"Hey, I don't want to poop on your party, boys, but I'd say you're still wading in shit's creek. Cops don't know from agents' egos, Larry. All they're gonna see is a blown alibi and possible motive."

"Motive? You mean for killing Buddy?" Aghast, Goldstein faced her with his hair tortured into spikes, making him look like a middle-aged version of Yahoo Serious. "Why would they suspect me?"

"Oh, gosh, let me count the ways," she said, lifting up a hand and starting with the pinkie, "A—*schtupping* or not *schtupping*, you were in cahoots with his wife. Buddy didn't know squat about this Prescott and Pruitt bid, did he?"

"Um, no, Gabby said he had some sappy idea about building his dream house up there for their retirement or something."

"Uh-huh. Which leads us to B—you two were far from sympatico on the set. Because C—he was The Suits' darling and maybe gunning for your job. So D—if he *had* found out what you and Gabby were up to, he would've spared no pains to screw you over royally. Which means E—you would've been out of a job and a hundred and forty grand to boot . . . Some folks might call that probable cause."

"Oh, geez. I am well and truly fucked, huh?"

"Wait, wait!" Austin leapt to his feet with the fire of salvation in his eyes. "No, you're not. Okay, so you lied about where you were that night, but they know you were in Malibu. You couldn't be two places at once—so you couldn't have been in the darkroom planting the hydrogen cyanide. Right?"

"Right! Oh, you brilliant, beautiful *boychik*, you!" Goldstein grabbed Austin in a bear hug, then beamed at Josh. "I love this crazy guy. See, O'Roarke, I'll explain everything to the cops and it'll be cool. Oh, man, I thank you guys, really. It's such a relief to get all this crap out in the open. A mammoth friggin' weight has been lifted, I tell ya."

"Well, yes, it has been a cleansing experience," Austin said with more reserve. "But let's make sure it doesn't happen again, Lawrence, all right? I don't think my stomach lining could handle it."

"No way! It's one for all, all for one from here on in, guys." In the full bloom of good fellowship restored, Goldstein magnanimously clapped a hand on Jocelyn's shoulder and asked, "So, getting back to business, what *is* your take about this stunt thing? Think Ginger's up to it?"

She heard Austin suck in his breath in anticipation of her response. But she merely shrugged, neatly managing to dislodge Larry's hand, and said mildly, "If she says so. You haven't pressured her at all?"

Goldstein placed one hand over his heart and raised the other. "May I lose my Guild card—swear to God."

"Well, she's a grown woman. If she wants to do it—let her."

Then he was gone in a flash, practically dancing his way out the door. Austin saw him to his car and came back, via the kitchen, with a glass of buttermilk, a recent capitulation to his uneasy digestive tract, in one hand and a Rolling Rock in the other. He handed her the beer, along with a cigarette and a loopy grin. It was his way of making peace, she knew, just as she knew she was going to have to disturb it.

"Well, thank God that's cleared up, huh? So how was your, uh, date?"

"Date was fine . . . But he's not out of the woods, Austin."

"Why not?!"

"Even if his car was at Gabby's, it might be an intentional false lead—which would be very clever: create a false alibi and then give yourself a better one. He could've parked his car in Malibu and taken another car to Culver City. And Larry knows the layout like the back of his hand; he'd have no trouble skirting security."

"Nah, I see a flaw here." Instead of plunging back down into the depths of despair, he spread himself out full length on the sofa, balancing the buttermilk on his stomach. "It lurks within that phrase 'very clever.' Larry, bless him, is a good director. Not highly analytical but a wonderful sense of pace. And he's a bright enough guy . . . but not *very* clever. Not in the way you mean. He's just not up to devising that devious a scenario."

"He might've had help."

"Gabby? Are you really serious, Josh? I know she's a gorgon in Ferragamo heels, but I can't see her killing her own husband for a lousy land sale."

"Uh, Austin, remember Harold Tewes?"

"Well, of *course*," he began irately, but his face fell as the memory sank in. "Oh . . . right."

"Right. Compared to Gabby, Harold was a pussycat, and he did away with his spouse just to be rid of her." O'Roarke was referring to the first time she and Frost had encountered homicide; it had also been the first time she'd met Phillip, but she wasn't about to dwell on that. "Who can even begin to imagine what it was like to be married to Buddy the Shutterbug all those years?"

"I take your point. Might've been like a long-running Strindberg play—a distaff version. Or maybe he snapped her once too often in early morning light."

"Maybe. In any case, Gabby *is* clever enough to pull it off."

"Oh, no question. Rumor has it she changed her name to Brent from Borgia—she's a genius at getting other people to do her bidding." Austin sipped his buttermilk gloomily, then pulled himself upright in protest. "But I still don't see Larry as her henchman. People only *say* they'd kill for a good agent; they don't actually do it! God—Sunset would be littered with corpses. And, yes, Larry has a temper and he detested Buddy with a vengeance. I can even imagine him bludgeoning the little bastard in a moment of passion. But he's not capable of something like this . . . something so premeditated—so cold. No, Josh, he'd have to be hypnotized or subliminally brainwashed . . . like Lawrence Harvey in *The Manchurian Candidate.*"

Despite her doubts, she had to smile at her friend's boundless loyalty. Not that there wasn't merit in his argument. His casual assessment of the killer was cannily close to Hamill's and there was something else he'd said that was tickling the back of her brain even as she heard herself reply: "Well, no, hypnotism doesn't work that way. You can get a guy to crow like a rooster but you can't get him to kill . . . unless the subject's already so inclined."

"Lord, you are so literal sometimes," he groaned, flopping back to a reclining position. "I was merely dramatizing a point."

"Yeah, don't you always," she answered warmly, then clapped her hands. "Come on, let's table this morbid discussion and get something to eat."

"Oh, I don't know." Austin sighed, placing one hand, Camille-like, to his brow. "I feel too drained to go out."

To save him from being sucked down to the lower depths, she kidded, "Nice line reading. But it doesn't hold a candle to Ludlam's Marguerite."

At the mention of the late and deeply lamented leader of Manhattan's Ridiculous Theatre Company and one of Austin's personal idols, he perked up instantly. "Okay, then how's this?" Stretching a feebly imploring arm toward her, he mimicked the silky Ludlamesque growl, "Throw another faggot on the fire, Nanine!"

"Close, close—but no cigar."

"Well, what do you want? Charles was a genius," he said with fervor. "I mean a *real* genius! As opposed to the way the word is bandied about in this town . . . God, Josh, remember him in those pearls and that spaghetti-strap dress with all his chest hair spilling out of the top? Too brilliant."

"I always remember him in *Irma Veep*. Constantly twirling that curl around one finger—only there was *no* curl on the wig—he just made you see it. Thought I'd wet myself laughing."

Austin nodded. "I think Madeline Kahn's right—he *was* the funniest man in America."

Frost's emphasis on the past tense reawakened their mutual sense of loss; another great artist claimed by the AIDS plague. Jocelyn swallowed hard before saying, "And he was just about to do that production of *Titus Andronicus* at the Public. The best bad Shakespeare play in the canon—would've been a stitch."

They both nodded in silent accord. Adding to their sadness, O'Roarke's mention of the Public Theatre stirred up a swell of homesickness for that "dirty town" they both loved as much as Lancaster's Hunsacker. Finally Jocelyn asked, "What if we stay home and I cook something?"

Food, the ultimate panacea, succeeded in rousing Austin's interest.

"Will you make your country-fried pork chops?" he asked hopefully.

"Honey, that recipe's from the pre-cholesterol-consciousness days. I make that and the American Heart Association will raid the house."

"I don't care! They're delicious and well worth risking thrombosis for. Besides, I need comforting food tonight. For tomorrow we go On Location!"

"Okay, fine. You got it," she said, getting up and heading for the kitchen. "But we're both going to swim laps tomorrow as penance. Deal, Camille?"

"Sure. And can you fix me a martini while you're at it?" he asked, setting the buttermilk aside. "Oh, and see if the paper's here, okay?"

"You're pushing it, Austin," she threatened even as she swerved toward the foyer. Opening the front door, she found the *L.A. Times* on the doorstep along with a less reputable journal. Reentering the living room, she dropped both papers on his lap, then pointed to the tabloid.

"Jesus, what're you doing subscribing to that rag?"

"*I* don't. The guy I'm renting from does. Just toss it in the back closet," Austin said, fastidiously holding out the scurrilous pages between thumb and forefinger. "I've had enough of this muck."

"Oh, yez, Miz Scarlett. I'll sure 'nuff do that," she mammy-ed back, snatching the paper out of his hand. "You jis rest yo' little bones."

"Yes, I'll do that, Hattie." He came back with Vivien Leigh. "An' you rustle up a heap'a po'k chops so big that, as Gawd is my witness, I'll never go hungry *again!* . . . Not bad, huh?"

"Oh, damn it all to hell."

O'Roarke had her back to him but it was clear, from the sudden slump in her shoulders, that she was no longer at Tara.

"Josh, what is it? What's wrong?"

Grim-faced, she spun around, tapping a finger on the bottom of the front page. "Take a gander."

It was a small banner in the left-hand corner but you couldn't miss it. Austin flipped to the inside story and scanned it rapidly. Raising his eyes to meet hers, he whispered ruefully, "Well, looks like the jig is finally up, huh?"

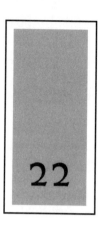

22

"Geez, have you read this?" Billy Orbach asked excitedly.
" 'Actress-Detective on the Trail of Banks Killer . . . East Coast
actress and director Jocelyn O'Roarke, a member of the tragedy-
plagued *Free Fall* cast and one-time companion of Detective Phillip
Gerrard, whom she aided in solving several celebrity murder cases
in Manhattan, has been secretly assisting the LAPD in their on-
going investigation of the Albert Banks slaying at Culver City.
Though neither Ms. O'Roarke nor investigating officer Detective
Dwayne Hamill could be reached for comment, confirmed sources
say that it was O'Roarke who discovered the body and that her
input has been crucial to the case from the start of this—"

"Can it, Billy. I've heard it. Everybody on the damn set has
heard it, all right?"

"Okay—but, man, what a mindblower! Talk about karmic
cohesion."

"No, let's not. Let's talk about squat."

Since the woods were filled with folks willing and eager to dish
this latest piece of dirt, Billy shrugged amiably and sauntered off,

leaving Jack Breedlove to stew in his own juices, as he had been doing since the tabloid article was thrust in his face promptly upon his arrival. Normally Breedlove would have been in high spirits because he liked being on location and this one, in Malibu Creek State Park, was just a short hop from his ranch. Just a brief hour ago, he'd been happily driving down Las Virgenes Road, whistling with anticipation at the prospect of seeing Jocelyn again. Now he found himself angry for reasons he hadn't even begun to sort out and dreading her arrival.

"Hey, Jack, how's it feel to be dating the nineties version of Miss Marple?" Tim Hayes kidded as he approached him with the offending rag opened to the inside story, complete with pictures. "Gotta say, she's a big improvement over what's-her-face. That old English broad with eight chins."

"Margaret Rutherford," Breedlove supplied between clenched teeth, then, trying to soothe his soul with trivia, added, "Played Marple in four MGM films in the early sixties. First was *Murder, She Said* directed by George Pol—"

"Yeah, yeah, that's the one. Boy, did you take a look at this?" With gleeful obtuseness, Tim shoved a grainy photo under Jack's nose. It was a shot of Jocelyn, more decked out than he'd ever seen her, in an off-the-shoulder wrap and evening gown, being helped out of a cab by a dark-haired man in an impeccably cut suit. "That's the ex. Tough act to follow, I'd say."

Wishing that Hayes would go play in a missile silo as much as he wished he could bring himself to tear his eyes away from the page, Jack fell back on the last resort of threatened male vanity and muttered, "Looks short."

"So what? So's Newman."

"Come on—he's no Newman." Trying to hide the note of protest in his voice, he shoved the paper back at Tim, who proceeded to assess it with the kind of clinical expertise that is the special province of those born beautiful.

"Well, no, he's not what I'd call classically handsome but he's not half bad. And he's got that thing some women like better than looks. You can see it even in a crappy print like this."

Hating himself for uttering the words, Jack asked, "What thing?"

"I dunno . . . depth, I'd guess you'd call it. You know, like Bogie had—only this guy's definitely better looking than Humph. And that suit's a killer, man." Hayes gave an admiring whistle before delivering the coup de grace. "Style and depth—a winning combo with the ladies, boy. Opened more portholes than a ship's steward, if you know what I mean."

At that moment Jack would've dearly loved to open a large porthole in Hayes' head, if only to let some of the gas escape, but he was too dispirited to do more than growl, "What are you doing here, Tim? Thought you were working a shoot out on Catalina."

"Aw, I canned it. It was a lousy gig anyway," he said, still absorbed in the article. "I was supposed to be assistant editor but they had me doing all sorts of shit—ferrying equipment and crew back and forth from Avalon to Isthmus Cove all the time. Those indies are a drag. Besides, Ginger's real stressed right now so I figured I should stick close—make sure she doesn't backslide before the Big Test."

"What test? You mean her stunt today?"

"Huh? . . . Oh, no, she's cool with that. Hell, she's looking forward to it. After being straight so long, it'll be a high for her—a legit high. No, I was talking about the other thing." With an uncharacteristic display of circumspection, Tim looked around to make sure there were no eavesdroppers in the vicinity before continuing. "See, Buddy was the executor of her folks' estate. Now that he's dead, there's a codicil in the will that says Ginge can become executor *if* she passes a drug test. Her old man—whoa—he was one thorough bastard, I'll say that for him."

Glad of the change of topic, Breedlove asked, "And if she doesn't?"

"Then the court appoints an executor—which would be a major drag for her . . . Hey, look at this!" Something on the page caught his attention. He pointed to a bottom paragraph as he gave Breedlove a chummy poke in the ribs. "You're out of the woods, Jack. El Gerrardo's engaged to another girl. Whew—Rebound City, man! The best time to catch 'em, you lucky dog, you."

Having the presence of mind and just enough self-restraint to keep from bouncing the leading lady's ex-spouse off the side of a nearby trailer, Jack contented himself by stretching out one large hand to slowly and deliberately extract the newspaper from Hayes' grasp and mangle it to a pulp.

"Speaking of dogs, you son of a—"

Tim jumped back, protectively holding both hands in front of his precious features. "Hey, hey, sorry! Really, Jack—no offense meant to you or O'Roarke. She's a hell of a bro— uh, lady. I mean, I don't know her very well but Ginge, she thinks she's Queen Shi—ah, thinks the world of her. And I do, too. Honest. I know I crack wise too much but she's helped Ginger over some very rough spots and I appreciate that."

"Uh-huh? Well, you've got a real strange way of showing it, sport," Breedlove replied, gratified by the younger man's palpable fear and secretly pleased to have a scapegoat to vent his unfocused anger on.

"Look, I'm an asshole sometimes, okay? And women like O'Roarke—the real smart ones—they spook me some. They look at you different . . . like you're a walking X ray, and I can't handle it. I'm not *used* to it, you know?"

"To use your own description—it's called depth, Timmy."

"You're right. Yeah, I guess that's what she's got. And, well, I'm very *low* on it, see," he said with a shrug and a sudden, disarming smile that succeeded in appeasing Jack and even restoring his sense of humor. But Hayes seemed to feel the need to prolong his self-abasement. "But you're not like me. It doesn't threaten you and I kinda envy that—no, I *do!* I mean, hell, it must be pretty damn interesting to be around. And you get to be in on all the inside stuff, too."

"No, I don't. That's between her and Hamill," Jack said curtly, unwilling to admit exactly how far away from the inside stuff he really was.

"Aw, come on! You must have some idea which way the wind is blowing—you can tell me," Tim whispered with a just-between-us-boys wink. "Like, have they stumbled onto Brenda's boyfriend yet?"

"Brenda *has* a boyfriend?!" Breedlove was too surprised to feign prior knowledge.

"Sure, I saw her at the track with him. Guy named Boggs—a very shady dude, I hear. I don't know if Buddy knew about him but, if he *had*, he would've pitched a major fit for sure. Buddy liked to keep all his womenfolk on a very short leash, that I do know."

"Including Ginger?" He hadn't really meant to press the matter, but Jack, normally the most laissez-faire kind of fellow, was experiencing an atypical surge of inquisitiveness that was feeding on Tim's casual indiscretion. At the back of his mind, he chalked it up to some sort of subliminal side effect from hanging out with the perpetually nosy O'Roarke; somehow he'd contracted the driving Need To Know.

"Oh, the shortest! Are you kidding? Ever since 'Jam House,' " Hayes said with a short laugh. "Shit, why do you think Ginge got so into drugs? It wasn't like a rebellion against her folks. It was a Buddy rebellion. He only put up with me 'cause he knew I was trying to get her straight. I mean, she loved him, sure. But he drove her abso-fucking-lutely crazy sometimes. It was always, 'Gingersnaps, *when* are you gonna grow *up?*' " He barked out an impeccably Buddyesque line reading, then added, "Plus, she was always worried about losing Hilly."

"To Buddy? How could that happen?"

"Not to Buddy—to me. For chrissake, I'm her *father*, man," Hayes said with the first signs of temper. "Not that I'd sue for custody or anything. Ginge and me, we've always tried to keep our personal shit away from her. But, as executor, he could've had her declared an unfit mother, if he thought she wasn't flying straight, then I'd have sole custody. I always told her it wouldn't make any difference—she could see Hilly whenever she wanted—and she shouldn't let Buddy hold it over her head. But she's a mother, you know, and it scared her to death."

"*Timmy!*"

Both men spun around to find themselves confronted by a trembling, tight-lipped virago in a makeup smock and hot rollers.

"I've been looking everywhere for you. Your, uh—agent's been calling. And, Jack, I need you, too. My hair's going to burn off at the roots if you don't uncomb me," Ginger said with uncommon asperity. "If that's not too much to ask . . . And you can both spare me that 'oh, women' look while you're at it, okay?"

Caught in the act, Hayes couldn't refrain from ruefully whispering, "Like I said, Jack, O'Roarke's done her a world of good."

"I heard that, Tim," Jellicoe exploded. "And I heard a little more than that, for your information. And I think you both *stink!* How's that? Jesus Christ, it's bad enough to have your life picked over like a Thanksgiving turkey in those goddamn rags, but to hear your own so-called friends get in on the carving, that's too much. I mean, I'm used to it but Joshie isn't. And if either one of you throws any of this crap in her face—well, I'll make you wish you'd been born without nuts. Is that clear?"

"As crystal," Jack rejoined. Even though he felt Jellicoe's indignation was probably as much for her own sake as Jocelyn's, he still applauded her fervor while savoring the stark dread it struck in Tim's breast.

Watching Hayes scurry off in the direction of Ginger's trailer, Jack held the door of the makeup trailer open and ushered her in with a gallant bow.

"Cut the crap, Jack," she said, giving him a withering look as she stepped inside. "I'm still pissed at you and I don't charm all that easy. I lived with Timmy the Charm King for five years, remember?"

Putting a towel around her shoulders, he gave her a tentative pat on the back which she ignored. "Look, Ginger, I don't want you to get the wrong impression. We were just talking . . ."

"Oh, sure! When men do it, it's 'just talking,'" she shot back in a fresh burst of temper. "But if women do it, it's 'Oh, God, they're gossiping *again*.' That's what you were doing, Jack . . . Why can't guys ever own up to their own shit, huh?"

Chastened, Breedlove mumbled, "I'm not sure—I think it has something to do with the Y chromosome." Adroitly whipping hot rollers out of her hair, he marveled at this whole new side of Jellicoe's nature. It wasn't just star temperament. Maybe Hayes had been right in suggesting that some of O'Roarke's ingrained feistiness had rubbed off on her impressionable young friend. But Jack thought there was something more to it; something to do with that short leash Buddy had kept her on for so long and the sudden, liberating effects of finally slipping the lead. Or maybe she'd just had another bad night.

Running his fingers through her hair to loosen the curls, he asked as casually as possible, "Get a good night's rest, did you?"

"*Yes*, just fine, thank you," she said sarcastically, letting him know that she'd caught the implication. And he had to admit she certainly didn't look like someone who'd been missing her REM cycle. "I've been sleeping fine ever since—well, for days now. So this is not me being a morning grouch—this is me being *mad* at you . . . I thought you liked Joshie."

"I did—I mean, I *do*," he protested, muddled by this sudden shift. "It's just . . . a little weird, you know? To find out that the girl of your dreams is Joe Friday."

"Yeah, well, it does kinda blow the mind some." Ginger relented and gave him a small smile. "You mean you really didn't know a thing about it?"

"Nope, clueless as the day is long," he admitted wryly. "Hell, who'd ever think a lady with a mouth like hers could keep a secret—and what a secret!"

"There you go again! Male ego, I tell ya." Mrs. Pankhurst's latest convert clicked her tongue and regarded him severely. "Sure, women are more open than men about lots of stuff, but that doesn't mean we don't have hidden, uh . . ."

"Depths," Jack suggested, as it seemed to be the word for the day.

"Yeah, right—depths. And you can bet your blow dryer—*all* women have secrets, Jack. That's a fact."

"Yup, a fact that keeps *all* men scared shitless almost constantly. But don't tell anyone I told you," he whispered conspiratorially, eliciting a delighted chuckle from his leading lady.

"You're a very bad boy, aren't you, Breedlove? Don't try to deny it 'cause I've got a sixth sense for bad boys . . . just ask my divorce attorney."

The unmistakable irony in her last remark made him blink with surprise. But he was starting to get a kick out of the new Jellicoe. Then, suddenly, she turned back into the old, beseeching Ginger, asking in that little-girl whisper of hers, "So what're you gonna do when Josh gets here? You won't give her a hard time, will you?"

"Tell you the truth, I don't know what I'm going to do. I haven't had a chance to sort any of this out yet."

"Well, just try not to make her feel badder than she does already. It's such a lousy thing, seeing your personal life in print—only they never get it right, of course. They don't want to. And it always makes you feel like you wanna die—even now, I still get that way, and I grew up with it. But Jocelyn, I think she's a very private person really. It's gotta be tearing her up bad."

Despite his hunch that anyone in such close proximity to New York's hottest homicide detective must have had prior exposure to the glaring rays of public scrutiny, Breedlove couldn't, in the face of Ginger's keen concern, bring himself to raise the issue. Besides, she had a point. Up to now, he'd been fretting over his own wounded feelings and, though he was loath to admit it, subconsciously storing up choice phrases for O'Roarke's ears only, phrases like "false pretenses," "betrayal of trust," and "calculated manipulation," to name but a few. But he hadn't really stopped to consider how she must be feeling, how she must be dreading the day ahead. While part of him, the Y-chromosome part, still felt that she deserved whatever licks she had to take, another more chivalrous part wanted to play Lancelot to her Guinevere and save her from the burning pyre of public censure, if only— and this was the part he wasn't quite owning up to yet—to prove he was a better man than the sartorially splendid but obviously shallow Gerrard.

"You're a wise woman, Miss J." He smiled down at her as he worked dabs of sculpting mousse into her forelocks. "You can't penalize people because they have a past. Who doesn't, right? And Jocelyn doesn't know what this town is like when it's feeding time at the zoo and you're today's piece of meat. Guess it's up to us to try to keep the wolves at bay, huh?"

"Oh, wow, what a sweetie pie. Really, I mean, move over Alan Alda!" Ginger leaned back in her chair and gazed up at him with melting eyes. "I knew you'd come through. You're just like Timmy. He can be a real prick sometimes—well, through most of our marriage, actually—but when things get rough, he's an absolute brick."

And just as thick, Jack thought; he didn't care for the comparison—clearly Jellicoe's newfound enlightenment hadn't yet extended to her former mate—but he was still warmed by her praise and grateful for her insight into Jocelyn's plight. Now he was ready to face her, more than ready; he was champing at the bit to lend a shoulder for her to lean on.

Mirroring his anticipation, Ginger glanced at her watch and exclaimed, "Gosh, it's almost six. I hope Joshie gets here soon. I want to see her before we do the first scene."

With superb, if unintended timing, O'Roarke came through the door in classic New York fashion, like an express train at rush hour. "Sorry, sorry, sorry. Would've been here sooner but I, uh, got sidetracked." Yanking off her flight jacket and tossing her purse in a corner, she turned to face them and asked with un-nerving directness, "So what's the verdict? Are you talking to me or should I consider myself a social leper and just upchuck and die?"

Breedlove's Guinevere fantasy deflated faster than the *Hindenburg*, but Ginger jumped out of her chair and threw her arms around Jocelyn.

"Of *course* we're talking to you, you silly! And I can't tell you how sorry I am about that rotten story getting leaked."

"Yeah, and I'd love to know the SOB who leaked it, just so I could shove every yellow page down his gullet. But, hey, them's the breaks."

"Right on, sister," Ginger agreed. Jack half expected her to raise a fist in a power salute. "But don't worry too much about it, hon. Trust me, you're in the Land of Short-term Memory. It'll blow over in a day or two."

"Uh-huh, right, thanks, love." Josh patted Ginger's arm distractedly as her gaze kept drifting toward the trailer window. Then, out of nowhere, she asked, "Is Brenda on the set today?"

"No, hon, she's not on call," Ginger said gently while signaling Breedlove with her eyes that this was a sure sign of O'Roarke's distress. "Remember? We're doing the scene where you tell me she's had a heart attack right before I do my stunt."

"Yeah, that's what I thought."

Billy Orbach stuck his head inside the trailer and said, "Ginger, you ready? We need you on the set."

"Oh, sure, be right there," she said, pulling off her smock to reveal the jumpsuit underneath before giving Josh and Jack a coy wink. "Besides, three's company, right?"

Still fixated on the window, Jocelyn hardly seemed to notice Ginger's departure or Jack's presence, which irked him mightily as her whole manner was so at odds with his imagined scenario. He gave a sharp whistle to draw her attention.

"Huh? What is it?"

"That's what I'd like to know," Jack answered, sounding more peevish than he'd intended. "With all the shit that's gone down since last we spoke, you come in here wondering where's *Brenda*?"

"Oh, Jack, I'm sorry." O'Roarke seemed to come to her senses, though she still kept an eye on the window. "Look, I had this whole spiel ready to try to explain things to you but, like I said, I got sidetracked."

"By what, for chrissake?!"

"By a guy I saw hanging out near Ginger's trailer—I just saw a photo of him—a guy named Randall Boggs, known by some as Boogie the Beast."

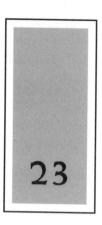

23

"NO! Goddamn it to hell, no! I cannot believe this. A *storm* front? This is friggin' California, for cryin' out loud. This is not supposed to happen!"

Larry Goldstein was dancing around like a dervish, pulling at his thinning locks with demented disregard as his AD tried to calm him.

"Look, I'm sorry, it wasn't in the forecast, Lar. But it's supposed to be heading down from Frisco. Should hit here in about two hours. What do you want to do?"

"What the fuck do you think I want to do?" Goldstein demanded frantically. "I want to get the damn stunt shot done before we lose the friggin' light, you numbskull! Get it set up—*now*."

The long suffering AD raised his megaphone to announce, "People, we're skipping Thirty-five A and going straight to Thirty-six A. Apologies to the waiting cast but, please, let's move it as quickly as possible, folks."

And they did. Thirty-odd men who had spent most of the morning playing gin and sipping bad coffee suddenly galvanized themselves into a single working unit that would make an ant colony look sluggish. But this was the nature of location shoots, where you were, literally, at nature's mercy.

If Larry didn't get Ginger's big jump in the can today, they'd go dangerously over budget and over schedule; something to be avoided at all costs and the crew knew it. Lights were set up on the bridge and the air bag was inflated in less time than it took to fry an egg.

Striding past her, Goldstein muttered brusquely, "Sorry, O'Roarke, we may not get to your scene . . . Oh, shit, why me, O Lord, why *me?*"

"Why not," she answered rhetorically, as Larry was already out of earshot. But Jack wasn't and he raised his eyebrows in surprise.

"You've been reading Lester's Commandments, haven't you?"

She nodded. "Sure, I'm not your average New York infidel. I recognize real wisdom when I see it. I even memorized them— got up to Number Ten: 'We do the best we can and if that isn't enough, it'll have to do until the Real Thing comes along.' That right?"

"Yeah, that's right," he admitted grudgingly. They'd made their peace back in the trailer and he had stayed by her side since to discourage tactless inquiries from the peanut gallery, but Breedlove was still feeling far from sanguine as fragments of their tête-à-tête replayed in his brain like postgame highlights. Chief amongst them was O'Roarke's maddening refusal to apologize in any way for her subterfuge.

"Sorry for what? For not telling you about confidential conversations with Hamill?" she'd asked calmly. "That's silly, Jack . . . Besides, it could've compromised the investigation."

"Why? Were you afraid I'd tell tales out of school? Look, I may have a silver tongue but I know how to keep a secret, too."

"That's not the point," she'd maintained patiently. "*You* could've been compromised as well, don't you see? It would look very bad for you to be privy to undisclosed information in case you were to come under, uh . . . suspicion yourself."

His jaw had dropped as her words hit him like a shot in the rib cage. "Let me get this straight. You're saying you thought *I* might've had something to do with . . . killing Buddy?!"

"No, not me—the police. They have to look at anyone with a possible motive. It's their job, love."

"Possible mo—? Me? Jesus Christ. I didn't like the guy but I had no reason to want him dead." He'd been truly aghast, and Jocelyn's matter-of-factness had done nothing to allay his outrage.

"Well, hypothetically, you did have a reason—if, say, you thought Buddy was getting ready to sell Monte Verde. Least, that's how the cops would see it."

"But I was with you when—whoever it was—broke into the darkroom!"

"Which gives you a perfect alibi." Jocelyn had nodded before reluctantly adding, "Only . . . cops hate perfect alibis, Jack. Makes them nervous. Then they start thinking about accomplices and stuff. And how really clever you were to have someone handy to witness you *not* being in the darkroom at the crucial time, see?"

"*No,* I don't see! This is crazy—it's Kafkaesque." His voice had risen half an octave, sounding, even to his own ears, like someone guilty as sin. "Wait! Hold on a damn second—I couldn't have set it up that way. I didn't know we'd be going back to Culver City that night. We only went because you forgot your pages."

"Right!" Smiling like a teacher proud of her pupil, she'd given him an approving pat on the back. "Now you're getting it. And that's exactly what I would've pointed out to Hamill had the topic come up . . . which it never did. So relax, dear."

"My God, does your mind always . . . work like this?" Her smile had faded when confronted by the look of repugnance in his eyes. "Christ, Jocelyn—it's just so *cold.* I mean, I like a woman with a dirty mind but not *this* dirty."

"Can't be helped," she'd said with a casual shrug that her eyes belied as they'd locked on to his. "Murder's sort of like nuclear fallout, Jack. *Everybody* gets contaminated whether they know it or not. And the first casualty is our innocence. You can't stay innocent about people—even the ones you care for—because it's a luxury you can no longer afford, a dangerous luxury."

"Uh-huh, I see—I think. It becomes a kind of—of willful ignorance, like a kid shutting his eyes so he won't see the bogeyman." He'd spoken haltingly, feeling like an alien in a harsh rather than brave new world. "Only, in this case, the bogeyman's real and he *wants* you to keep your eyes closed."

Standing on tiptoe, she'd given him a soft kiss on the lips and whispered, "You constantly amaze me . . . Go to the head of the class."

Drawing her in close, he'd asked, "So where do we go from here, Teach?"

"To the set—I want to find this Boggs character."

But Boggs was currently nowhere to be seen; a keen disappointment to Josh, but Breedlove, as her unofficial bodyguard, was secretly relieved after hearing her describe him as "about six-four, built like a linebacker—looks like Jack Palance's ugly baby brother." In his youth, Breedlove had had his share of fights, usually in barrooms and almost always with some lovely's jealous boyfriend, but in recent years he'd come to ascribe to what he called the Rockford Philosophy, inspired by one of his favorite actors, James Garner in "The Rockford Files." What this credo boiled down to was: Don't go looking for trouble. Let it find you. And Jack thought it was a sound one, but here was Jocelyn, clearly not in a Rockford frame of mind, tugging at his sleeve.

"Come on. Let's go down to the bridge. We haven't looked there yet. And I want to see them blow up the air bag."

By the time they reached the bridge, the bag was fully inflated. Jocelyn walked around it, frowning faintly.

"Not very big, is it? I thought it would look more like the one in *Lethal Weapon*. You know, in the scene with Mel and the jumper."

"No chance. Since that was a tall building. This is a low bridge. Also, that was a big-budget feature and this is TV."

"But it's safe, huh?"

"Sure. It's more than adequate for this stunt. Honey, look, the bridge is hardly higher than the roof of my house. Don't look so worried. You don't want to spook Ginger."

"Hell, she looks anything but spooked." Josh chuckled, pointing to their approaching star. "She looks like Amelia Earhart ready for flight."

Watching Jellicoe walk up to the bridge, Breedlove had to acknowledge that Hayes knew his girl. That reckless buoyancy from her Jilly days was back in her step and, as a joke, she'd thrown a white silk aviator's scarf around the neck of her jumpsuit. Cheers and applause from cast and crew greeted her as she took her place on the bridge, waving to the crowd below with a campy beauty queen smile pasted on her face.

Whipping off the scarf, she yelled down to Goldstein, positioned at the foot of the bridge near Billy Orbach and his boom camera, "Lar, I know I told you I'd *die* to play this part. But, shit, I never thought you'd take me seriously!"

More cheers and guffaws as Larry, trying hard to contain his anxiety to get the shoot over with, joked back, "But, Ginge, it's in your contract. Guess you didn't read the fine print, huh? . . . Come on, babe, let's nail this sucker in one. Okay?"

"Okey-goddamn-dokey, Lar."

The AD called for silence as Ginger hit her mark. Eyes bright with the wind tossing her hair, she looked like an impossibly beautiful bird eager to spread her wings in first flight.

"Told you that haircut would play great in the wind," Jack observed proudly. Josh shushed him as Larry shouted, "And—action!"

And she took off fearlessly. Nothing fancy, just a straight drop down, but her body alignment was poetry in motion. If a strong gust of wind, precursor of the approaching storm, hadn't suddenly come up, she would've hit the bag dead center. As it was, she landed over to the right but still well within the safety margin.

But then her body rose up from the air bag in alarming trajectory, accompanied by a loud bang that sounded like some Gargantua with an enormous pitchfork popping the Goodyear blimp. Like Jack Nicholson in *The Two Jakes*, Ginger flew, slo-mo, head over heels through the air. Watching her, Jocelyn couldn't scream, move, or breathe, so great was her terror. Luckily Jack could and already had. They'd been standing near the right side of the air bag and, just as it popped, he'd taken off in a jackrabbit sprint, reaching the sidelines just as Ginger came down for a landing—directly on top of him.

For a long moment, they lay in a motionless heap, the shocked spectators still immobilized. Then the crew sprang into action with Jocelyn hot on their heels. She got there in time to see Ginger, shaken but seemingly intact, stagger to her feet, holding her hand to a cut on her forehead and staring numbly down at Jack's prone figure.

"Aw, holy geez, did I squish him dead?" she asked tearfully.

On her knees, cradling his head, Jocelyn shouted, "Jack! Come on—open your eyes, love."

Behind her, she heard Billy Orbach whisper, "Cripes, he looks like Ray Bolger dismantled, huh?"

The ultimate movie buff, Jack revived at this reference to *The Wizard of Oz*. Opening one eye, he grinned weakly and came back with the appropriate line, "Yeah—that's me all over."

In tandem, Jocelyn and Ginger burst out laughing, then promptly burst into tears as they helped him to his feet.

"Ginge, let me lift him," Josh sniffled. "You might be hurt."

"Nah, I'm just a little banged up is all," she sniffled back, hoisting one of Jack's arms around her shoulder. "Hell, he saved my life. Boy, I owe you big time, Breedlove."

But then the first aid crew descended on them, stretchers and all, shunting O'Roarke aside as they loaded Jack on one stretcher and made signs for Ginger to take the other.

"No, really guys, I'm okay. All I'll need is a little Mercurochrome . . . and some Ben-Gay."

"Miz Hellicoe, *por favor—pleeze!*" Rolling huge chocolate eyes, a Mexican orderly implored her, making it clear that his future in health care depended on her acquiescence. So Ginger hopped on a stretcher and gave Jack an encouraging wink as she snapped her fingers and shouted, "Okay, men, mush . . . or hike or whatever it is. We've got a wounded hero here."

The first aid team trotted up the hill in double time just as Larry reached Jocelyn's side, pale and panting.

"Oh, shit, is she going to be all right?"

"Looks that way. I think Jack got the worst of it . . . What went wrong, Lar?"

"Swear to God, I have no idea. That air bag is brand fuckin' new, Josh. And we tested it right before the jump and it was fine! Christ, I'm gonna go out and buy Jack an Arabian or something . . . she could've been killed."

"Damn straight she could've been killed! Thanks to you, Goldstein, you little prick." The vocal equivalent of carbolic acid seared the air just as the sky started to turn dark and threatening, almost as threatening as the diminutive Medusa in heels who stood, Ferragamos planted far apart, glaring at them.

Goldstein's surprised gasp was drowned out by the first roll of thunder. Then he swallowed hard and spoke up. "Gabby! I didn't know you were here."

"Of course not. I don't think you have the balls to try to kill a client of mine under my nose. Nice try, Lawrence, but you blew it—as always."

"Wha—what're you saying?" His color had gone from pale to puce as the tendons in his neck bulged. "You can't possibly think I had—"

Only the pandemonium triggered by the storm's swift approach kept this exchange from taking center stage. The crew was too busy, racing to tarp or take in various pieces of expensive equipment, to pay heed to Brent's reply.

"What I think, bucko, is you were trying to jinx the works and put Ginger out of commission so you can walk way from this fucking five-star fiasco and still get your hands on the insurance. Or should I say—collect your pound of flesh?"

The first drops of rain hit the dried earth with a hiss as Larry visibly winced at the anti-Semitic barb. Well, that cuts it, Jocelyn thought, taking a careful step backward, watching Goldstein's chest heave with powerful emotions. A strong wind blew up just as the director did.

"Why you—you evil-minded old bitch! After all I've done for you."

"You mean, all you *tried* to do," she countered, lifting her chin pugnaciously.

"Shut up! Just shut your big mouth or, I swear, I'll pop you one right on your lipo-sucked jaw, lady. One more word—one more *syllable*—and I'll have you in court so fast your fat head'll swim."

"Children, children, take it easy," O'Roarke interceded, seeing that Gabby was unwisely about to make a comeback and Larry was fully prepared to make good on his threat. "I hate to spoil your fun but we're standing in a potential lightning field here. Don't you think you'd better take it inside?"

As if to demonstrate her point, there was another roll of thunder as the rain started to fall in earnest. As she'd hoped, self-preservation won out over blood lust and Jocelyn was able to herd them back toward the trailers; Larry walking stiff-backed with both hands shoved deep in his chinos while Gabby held hers ineffectually over her head to protect an already ruined coiffure.

About to start up the hill behind them, Josh took a parting look at the treacherous air bag, which now looked like a giant, squashed squid. Out of the corner of her eye, she saw something move in the distance; a figure that must have been standing in the underpass beneath the bridge began to move up an incline, heading north, away from the set.

There was only one person around who'd have reason not to seek shelter in the trailers.

Jocelyn took off at a fast clip. Luckily the ground wasn't yet wet enough to interfere with traction and O'Roarke had the ability, common to many New Yorkers used to crossing against the light and dashing through closing subway doors, to put on a mighty burst of speed when needed.

When she reached the underpass, her quarry was halfway up the steep hill with his back to her, moving slowly. Spotting a footpath on her left with a gentler incline, she veered toward it, trying to keep her panting low as she gained ground. She still couldn't see his face but the height and breadth of the man left no doubt in her mind. Just as her lungs were about to burst, she stopped short and used the last of her wind to shout out.

"Hey, Boogie! What's the rush?"

"Whodafuck'reyou?" It came out as one word, but O'Roarke managed to decipher the question.

"A friend of Brenda's, man," she answered as she sauntered up to the hulking monolith with an insouciance that was one hundred percent pure bluff. "We met at the track once—Santa Anita, I think it was. Don't you remember?

"Wha'syourname?" He looked down at her, way down, with dead eyes, and she stopped a judicious three yards from him as the words of her old friend Tommy Zito came floating back to her from a conversation years past.

"The thing you gotta know, Josh, is felons fall into three categories: Pros, who're probably the safest to come up against 'cause to them it's just a job, see? Desperadoes—usually strung-out junkies or what youse bleedin' hearts call extremely underprivileged—and they're more dangerous but give 'em what they want and they'll blow. But then there's the Dead-Eyes, that's what I call 'em . . . the psychos—the *real* monsters. They're just in it for the thrill. You can give 'em your watch, your wallet, and your wife and they'll still waste you just for kicks. See, they're all dead inside already and they want you to join 'em."

She didn't need Zito's confirmation to tell her which category Randall Boggs fell into, though she would have keenly appreciated his presence at the moment. Curling up her hands, the way one does around a vicious dog so it can't smell the fear sweating out of your palms, she managed to stand her ground and answer.

"Josh O'Roarke. When I saw you on the set, I thought maybe Brenda had sent you up here with a hot tip. She knows I love a sure thing—hell, who doesn't, right?"

Fortunately, cognitive thinking was not Randall's big thing so he merely knit his single brow and said, "Nah, Brenda dinnit say nothin' about you. And I don't 'member you, iver, lady."

"Aw, now I'm hurt. I thought you never forgot a pretty face, Boogs," she said flirtatiously; a distant part of Jocelyn's mind wished her old acting coach, Harry Toth, could be there because this was *acting*. "So, if not me, who'd you come up here to see then?"

"None a' your damn business—nobody," he barked back, then added with what he obviously thought was a brilliant riposte, "I jist wanted some air."

"Really? Just any old air or did you have something more specific in mind? Like, did you come here to suck up some *air bag* air, Boogie?"

"Huh? I don't know what you're talkin' about." He took one step toward her and she took two steps back.

"I'm talking about one short poke of a knife followed by one big bang. You *do* have a knife, don't you?" The rain was pelting down now, getting in his eyes. Jocelyn moved off to his left side before adding, "So maybe someone asked you to come up here to take the wind out of Jellicoe's sails, huh? For a price, of course—which means it's not really *your* fault. But it didn't come off and you don't want to be left holding the bag, do you, Randall?"

"Crazyfuckinbitch!"

The use of his Christian name was a miscalculation on her part as it seemed to inflame him. Her second miscalculation was in moving to the left, as Boggs turned out to be a southpaw. He sprang toward her, delivering a solid blow to her midsection. Jocelyn deflated faster than the air bag and, with the ground now sufficiently slick and muddy, went tumbling backward down the steep incline. When she finally stopped rolling, she found herself just a few feet away from the underpass. Wiping mud from her eyes, she looked up to see if Boggs was coming after her to deliver the coup de grace. But, mercifully, he was right where she'd left him, standing in the wind and rain with arms outstretched in a bizarrely crucifixlike pose. He shouted out something that sounded like: "Dumb broad—I was jist doin' the usual!" Then he was gone, hightailing it over the crest of the hill with remarkable speed.

Too tired to move or call out, she let her head drop back in the mud. All she could do, as faintness and aftershock overtook her, was dimly contemplate Lester Colodny's Eleventh Commandment: "If you drop dead in the next five minutes, somehow they'll all muddle through."

24

"You poor dear. Did Jonathan scare you? I'm sorry to say, he's always had appalling manners."

"Let's not mince words—he's appalling period, especially now, with his new face . . . He looks just like that Boris Karloff person."

"Oh, it's you two, again . . . So I'm dreaming, right?"

It was the Brewster sisters, back by popular demand. Jean Adair smiled down at her benignly while Josephine Hull brought a glass to her lips, murmuring, "In a way. You've had a nasty shock. You'll feel much better after you've had a sip of our wine."

"Aw, geez, give it a rest, girls. You're always pushing this stuff." Dream or not, Jocelyn rose up in protest, attempting to push the glass away.

"Come on—*drink* it!" Josephine's voice shifted gears gratingly as she forced some of the liquid down Josh's throat. "It won't kill you."

She'd never tasted elderberry wine but she knew instantly that this wasn't it; it was brandy, quite a good brandy actually, but unfortunately most of it went down her windpipe. She bolted up, snorting and hacking.

"Damn, that *burns!*"

"See? I told you it would bring her around."

"Joshie, honey, you all right? God, I was getting worried. You looked at us so funny just now."

Blinking away scalding tears, O'Roarke regained full consciousness only to find that Jean and Josephine had mutated into Ginger and Gabby. She looked around, trying to get her bearings, but it wasn't easy with Brent thumping her on the back as if she were a large infant with gas.

"Where—? Ow! Knock it off, will ya . . . Where am I?"

Obviously they were no longer on location but in a bedroom, a rather stunning bedroom with a high, oak-beamed ceiling and watered-silk wallpaper. To her right was a large casement window through which she could see the rain coming down in sheets now, so heavily that she couldn't make out any terrain. Then she realized there was no terrain; the window looked out on the ocean.

"Welcome to Brent's Infirmary on the Beach," Gabby said by way of wiseass answer as she rose and plucked a Sherman Oval from a mother-of-pearl cigarette box, giving Ginger room to relieve her maternal feelings.

Putting one arm around O'Roarke's shoulders, she drew her close, brushing damp tendrils off her cheek. "You're looking better now, sweetie. Boy, when they brought you in, you were pale as a ghost."

"How could you tell under all that muck? She looked like one of those otters after the *Valdez* spill," Gabby said, sounding more concerned for the otters than O'Roarke. "Which reminds me, you'd better get cleaned up, kiddo. You're starting to smell up the place."

"Why don't you go see about dinner, *Gabrielle?* I'll take care of Josh, okey-dokey?"

Taken aback by Jellicoe's tone and use of her full name, Brent blew a few smoke rings as she regarded her client closely for a tense moment. Then she chuckled dryly and winked as she headed for the door. "Good idea, kid. I just don't *do* the Clara Barton bit real well . . . Oh, there's a fresh robe in the bathroom, O'Roarke.

And I'll have Miriam find you something to wear. We'll probably have to burn your stuff. See ya downstairs."

Unlike her agent, Ginger did do the "Clara Barton bit" extremely well and Jocelyn, too woozy to give Gabby the parting shot she so richly deserved, was content to let her. In no time, Ginger had drawn a bath and led Jocelyn into a sunken marble tub brimming with bubbles in a bathroom that looked like a set from *Juliet of the Spirits* and was about the size of her living room. After shampooing Josh's matted hair, she ran to fetch the brandy snifter and cigarettes. Handing both to her patient, Ginger then lit a Sherman for herself as she plopped down on the truly throne-like "throne."

Lying back on an inflated rubber pillow shaped like a seashell, O'Roarke took a sip of brandy, making sure it went down the right way this time, while marveling at her companion's amazing resiliency. After all, of the two of them, Jellicoe was the one who'd had the real brush with death that day. But, other than a small, egg-shaped bump emerging under the Band-Aid on her forehead, she seemed relatively fit and in fine spirits, her only anxiety seemingly on Jocelyn's behalf.

"I feel so bad, Joshie. After the accident, everybody was fussing so much over me and Jack, well . . . it was a while before we noticed you weren't there. Larry was running around like a madman, making sure the crew got packed up before the storm got worse. Then, when we were getting ready to leave, Jack started yellin' 'Where's Josh?!' So Billy Orbach and Tim went out to look for you. When they carried you back, you looked half drowned. I was scared to death and Jack was mad as hell, boy."

"Then he must be feeling better." Josh grinned, feeling light-headed with relief.

"Oh, yeah, much. I really knocked the wind out of him and he might have a cracked rib or two but they got him patched up and back on his feet . . . But, Josh, what were you *doing* out there?"

"My guess is she was confronting a known felon! Right, O'Roarke?" The bathroom door was only open a crack but the nose and partial chin that was wedged in it were distinctly Breedlovian. "Goddamn, I turn my back on you for one second and you run off to make small talk with a maniac! Woman, if we weren't both feeling so shitty, I'd tan your hide."

"Oh, golly, I love it when you talk tough, Big Fella." Jocelyn giggled despite herself. The brandy combined with the Fellini-esque setting and the rising steam from the tub was fogging her mind, disordering her sense of priorities. She jerked herself up and turned on the cold water, placing her head under the gilt spigot. Turning the water off, she shook her head clear as Ginger wailed, "What maniac?! Who're you talking about?"

"Tell you in a sec." O'Roarke grabbed a loofah and started scrubbing herself vigorously. "First, you tell me how we ended up *here.*"

"Oh, well, we have *you* to thank for that," Jack hissed through the crack. "By the time Billy and Tim found you, it had gotten really torrential. We had to travel at a snail's pace and then, when we got to Big Rock, there was a huge mud slide across the road. Impassable—there's no way they'll get it cleared before morning and we all have to be back up at Malibu Creek at dawn. So the ever warm and gracious Gabby agreed to bivouac us here for the night. Swell, huh?"

"Oh, don't be such a grouch. This way we'll all get to sleep later," Ginger shouted back. "It'll be fun—like one big pajama party."

"Yeah, sure. The three of us, Gabby, Tim, Larry, and Brenda," Jack growled. "We can roast marshmallows and play Truth or Dare."

"Brenda! What's she doing here?"

"Came up early in the day," Ginger said with a grimace. "Wanted to collect some of the material for Buddy's new book, she said. Timmy's real bummed. He just can't stand her."

Her wits finally gathered, Jocelyn absorbed all this information with a growing sense of unease. It had already been, to put it mildly, an overly eventful day and, given the volatile mix of personalities gathered under one roof, it didn't look like the evening was going to be a cakewalk, either. She felt that storms were raging within and without and, if she didn't get in touch with Dwayne Hamill pretty damn quick, the whole roof could blow.

"Ginge, hand me a towel, would you?"

About to toss her a towel the size of an area rug, Ginger suddenly clasped it to her breast. "Wait a minute. What about this maniac person?"

"Jack'll fill you in. I've gotta make a call."

"Oh, sure," the nose in the door sniffed. "Why me? Why not?"

"Boggs was there? No wonder I couldn't find the son of a bitch! And he *bit* you? Oh, man, I'm sorry, Josh. But at least I can pull him in for A & B now. Then I'll grill him like a cheese sandwich."

"Fine, fine. But until you get hold of the air bag, this is all just speculation," Jocelyn whispered. She was on the phone in Buddy's den, which had walls as thick as a bunker's, though this did little to lessen her anxiety about the proximity of prying ears and eyes. "Did you get a blowup of that slide I found?"

"Yeah, finally. Only it wasn't a slide—it's film, *movie* film. Half of a frame with another half-frame spliced onto it with what looks like the top part of some letters written in. It's hard to describe, Josh— Hey, does Ms. Brent have a fax machine up there?"

"Do sharks have teeth? What do you think?" Mercifully the fax machine was in the den with the number clearly labeled on its side; the only serendipity of the day.

"Good, give me the number and I'll send it out to you tonight. It's the best I can do. If they get the roads clear, I'll try to get up there by morning."

"And if the roads aren't cleared?"

"I'll try to get a helicopter, if I can. But whatever happens, you just lay low. Whoever's in cahoots with Boogie . . . well, you're an identifiable threat by now. So be cool, Josh."

"Don't worry. I'm fresh out of bravado. And it could all be nothing, Dwayne. Ginger's accident, genuine or planned, might have nothing to do with Banks' death—or with Boogie."

After a long pause, Hamill asked carefully, "That what your gut tells you?"

"Uh—no, just the opposite, actually. But I can't see how it all ties together, either."

"Me, either—yet. But I know it does," he said with quiet conviction.

"Yeah, me too. Fax me fast, pal."

Jocelyn hung up just as the housekeeper, Miriam, Gabby's very own Mrs. Danvers, flung open the door and announced, "They're waiting for you, miss."

Despite her many shortcomings, Gabrielle Brent was no slouch at putting on a spread. Entering the long dining room, O'Roarke was amazed by the variety and profusion of victuals laid out on the glass-topped dining table with wrought-iron legs. In the center, a large candelabrum, also of wrought iron, shed soft light on platters of chicken *piccata*, bowls of risotto and braised Belgian endive, and a large tureen of seafood bisque. The lady had to have a larder the size of a van to serve up such a feast at such short notice, not to mention a hell of a deep-freezer. But Gabby sat at the head of the table, clad in a fuchsia silk caftan, casually dipping a crescent roll in her bisque and chewing on it as if this were just a potluck meal, which, for her, it probably was.

Everyone else sat there like the condemned having their last supper.

Slipping into her place between Larry, strategically placed at the opposite end of the table from their hostess, and Tim, Josh hoped against hope that this impromptu dinner party was not going to rival Ginger's for first place in her memory book of grotesque gourmandizing.

Then Hayes, one of those empty barrels who like to make the most noise, played havoc with her faint hopes. Reaching for a bottle of Heitz Cellar chardonnay, he totted up his wine glass, took a long sip, and grinned across the table at Brenda Arnold, saying, "Hey, Bren, did you hear? Josh ran into an old buddy of yours today—well, *he* ran into her's more like it. Randy Boggs. Can you beat that?"

"Wha'?" La Arnold's eyes popped wide as she nearly choked on a piece of *piccata*. A complicated round of intense glances was exchanged which, had they been charted in ink, would've formed a mandala in midair. It went like this: Jocelyn directed an accusing glare at Jack, who answered with a disclaiming blink or two before visually passing the buck to Ginger who, pink-cheeked and clearly pissed off, shot daggers at her ex then swung her beams toward Josh to beg forgiveness. All this ocular pantomime gave Brenda time to swallow her chicken and find her voice.

"Old buddy! Tim, really, the way you put things," she said with a tinny laugh. "He's just an acquaintance and *barely* that . . . I can't imagine what he'd be doing up on location."

"I didn't say *where* she met him," Tim drawled back, ignoring

Ginger's *shush* signals, having a heck of a good time at the older woman's expense. "But it happens you're right. He was at Malibu Creek. 'Course, I thought he had to be looking for *you*."

"Listen, you son . . . you silly man, you know perfectly well that at every racetrack there's a—a certain element present," Brenda replied, trying hard to sound blasé. "People you'd never know socially but who happen to know a thing or two about horseflesh. So there's no way you can avoid, uh, consorting with them occasionally, is there?"

"Consorting occasionally! Hah!" Gabby's bark of mirth surprised them all. Having passed on the wine in favor of Scotch stingers, she had seemed oblivious to the conversation at hand. "Real ritzy talk, toots. You been screwing Alistair Cooke lately or what?"

"Or what, I'd say." Tim's veiled insinuation was nearly drowned out by Gabby who, delighted by her little joke, was doubled over with laughter. But Arnold caught his very mean meaning as did Josh. Brenda bit her lip but made no attempt to answer, though her ample frame fairly vibrated with repressed emotion. If she were modeling for a portrait, Jocelyn decided, it would end up being titled *Fear and Loathing in Lotus Land*.

But all actors, even sorry ones like Ronald Reagan and Brenda Arnold, know how to brazen things out; helping herself to more risotto, she turned to O'Roarke and inquired calmly, "Did Mr. Boggs actually *say* that he'd come to see me, Jocelyn?"

"Uh, no, no, he didn't," she said swiftly and truthfully, as anxious as Brenda to change the topic. "He said very little. Which seems to be his style."

"Well, there you have it," she announced triumphantly. "End of discussion."

But it seemed that discussions at chez Brent didn't end until the hostess said so. Snatching up her sister-in-law's verbal gauntlet, Gabby came back with, "Well, Bren, all I can say is, if this guy's some racetrack tout, you better cut out the consorting real quick. Unless Buddy's new book sells more copies than the friggin' Bible, your betting days are numbered, kiddo. 'Cause he sure didn't leave you enough to support your little habit for long, huh?"

The mini-Medusa had struck again and turned her opponent to stone. Then the stone started to crumble and Josh found herself actually feeling sorry for Brenda, who shrank back in her chair, desperately searching the faces around her with stricken eyes, looking for a savior. But the pickings were scant. Goldstein was too worn out to brave Gabby's wrath twice in one day while Tim was clearly enjoying the scene he'd created; Ginger, also near tears, was closely examining the floorboards for a possible opening to swallow her up, and poor Jack was just too appalled for coherent speech. Clearly this was a situation where only a rank outsider could intervene.

So she did.

"Well, hey, here's to the Hostess with the Mostest," Jocelyn said, lofting her wineglass high. "Considering that you weren't expecting company, it's truly amazing that you could whip up this little in-house version of *Long Day's Journey* on such short notice, Gabby. Though you did have some help from ol' Timmy here." She paused briefly to give Hayes a short, sharp jab in the ribs. "And that fifth of Scotch you've put away. See, I know you're bereaved but you're also *drunk* and behaving like an asshole. And since all of us are tired and none of us *wants* to be here, it might occur to you to put a sock in it and spare us the family drama. So give it a rest, lady . . . you've collected your ten percent, okay?"

There ensued a silence that seemed to last as long as the *Götterdämmerung*. All eyes were riveted on Gabrielle as she rose unsteadily on her platform espadrilles and tottered down the long length of the table toward Josh with a stinger still clenched in one tiny hand—a stinger that everyone, including O'Roarke, fully expected to see flung in her face.

Willing herself to meet Medusa's gaze, Jocelyn had to admit the broad was a magnificent monster who knew how to play a scene to the hilt. Raising the glass high, she brought it swiftly to her lips and tossed it back in one shot.

Slapping the empty glass down on the table within an inch of Josh's elbow, she gave her a curt nod and said, "I like you, kid. You've got balls."

25

" 'I've been to a marvelous party. With Noonoo and Nada and Nell. And we came as we were. And we stayed as we were. Which was *hell*.' "

Ofttimes through the years, in moments of stress, Jocelyn O'Roarke had sought solace in the wit and unfailing flippancy of Noël Coward. And she did so now, ensconced once again in Buddy's den, waiting anxiously for the fax from Dwayne and silently cursing him out for his pokyness.

After Dinner at the O.K. Corral had ended, Gabby had blithely invited the shaky survivors into the rec room to watch an old movie. Personally, Josh had thought her choice of Cary Grant and Joan Fontaine in *Suspicion* thematically unfortunate. But at least it put an end to further conversation and allowed her to slip away unnoticed once the lights were dimmed.

When the fax machine finally began to hum, she jumped to her feet and snatched the thin, shiny papers out with eager fingers. Dwayne had scrawled a message on the cover sheet that read:

"Had it blown up but don't know how clear it will be. Call me PDQ if it means anything to you."

On first glance, it meant *bubkes*. Gabby's machine wasn't state of the art so the resolution was none too good. It took Josh a minute to separate and distinguish the two half-frames. Finally the top half coalesced; it looked like a man's legs from the knee-caps down with something attached to them from the right side. After closer inspection, she saw that the attachment was a hand holding something against the right leg; she wasn't sure what, but the visual composition itself was eerily familiar to her—a pose she'd seen before and more than once.

The bottom half-frame was even more obscure; it appeared to be a printed message, but only the tops of the letters were there. She squinted hard, trying to play connect-the-dots with the sawed-off letters, but they remained as inscrutable as characters in the Chinese alphabet.

It was more maddening than a crossword puzzle only half filled-in and Cary's voice seemed to taunt her through the thick walls as she heard him murmur, "Hello, monkey face."

"Can it, Cary," she muttered to herself. Finally, here it was, her one and only found clue making a monkey out of her. But it had to mean *something*.

Her only recourse, she decided, was to resort to the tactics she used when tackling a particularly knotty *New York Times* crossword, i.e., light a cigarette, sip some wine, and stare at the ceiling.

She did this for a while, listening with half an ear as Cary and Joan thrashed out their marital problems in the car on the cliff. Shortly after, she heard footfalls on the stairs and knew it was time for Plan B—go to sleep and come back in the morning with a fresher eye and brain. It had worked before, though she had the feeling this nut was going to be a lot harder to crack than a five-letter synonym for aggravation.

But before she could reach the door, the synonym walked in; Gabby, mellower now, but still in her cups and impossible to bypass. Jocelyn surreptitiously stuffed the fax into her bra as her hostess plopped down on a leather recliner.

"Wondered where you were. Don't you like Hitchcock?"

"Adore him. But the studio made him change the ending and I've seen the light bulb inside the milk glass a hundred times."

"Yeah, bet you have. You're one of the clever ones," Gabby

replied vaguely, hauling herself out of the recliner to wander about the den. Pausing at a low table beneath a casement window that held a glass-encased topographical map of the California coastline, she stared down at the map for a moment then looked up suddenly and asked, "You think I'm an A-one bitch on wheels, don'tcha?"

"Uh, Gabby, don't do this now, okay?"

"*Don'tcha?*"

"Uh, let's just say I think there are members of CRIPS who fight cleaner than you do sometimes."

"Sure, but they're just in the street wars, not in show biz."

"Good point."

"Did ya look at this?" she asked, jerking her head toward the glass case. "Buddy made it himself."

Approaching the table, O'Roarke saw that the three-dimensional map was a highly detailed picture of the coast from Carrillo State Beach down to Corona Del Mar including Catalina.

"It's, uh, very nice. He did an excellent job. I didn't know he was a cartographer." Seeing the blank look on Brent's face, she quickly amended, "A mapmaker, I mean."

"Well, he wasn't. This is the only one he ever did," Gabby said quietly, waving the smoke from her Sherman away as she stared fixedly at the map. "It was, well, partly a joke and partly a . . . a sentimental gesture, I'd guess you'd call it."

Surprised by this sudden change of mood and topic, Jocelyn snuck a sideways glance at her hostess, trying to gauge if this was just the Scotch talking. But Brent appeared to have something on her mind. Normally more direct than a guided missile, Gabby was working up to whatever it was with uncharacteristic circuity. And she clearly wanted to be coaxed, but O'Roarke wasn't sure how or in what direction.

"What was the joke part?"

"Ah, he had this crazy idea that when he retired—which I told him would prob'ly be never—he'd buy a big ol' cabin cruiser and we'd spend our days either in that Xanadu he said he was gonna build in Monte Verde or cruising up and down the coast. He built this to prove he wasn't just bullshittin'."

"And the sentimental part?"

"There," Brent said. With one manicured talon she tapped

the glass directly above Catalina. "That's where we spent our honeymoon."

"Really? I thought the local joke was if you went to Catalina, you'd meet people from every part of the country *except* L.A."

"Yeah, that's mostly true. But, hell, we were just kids with hardly two nickels to rub together back then. So we drove down to Redondo Beach and hopped the ferry. Took forever in those days—now they can pop out there in no time in those copters and things. We couldn't even afford a hotel room, so we slept on the beach at Avalon. You ever been there?"

"No, but I'd like to go. Is it nice?"

"Well, tell you the truth," Gabby said with a dry laugh, "I haven't been back since then, so I don't know what it's like now days. But it was gorgeous then all right. We had just enough money to go to the Casino. Has the largest circular dance floor in the U.S., you know that?" Brent didn't wait for a reply; she was too caught up in reverie. "It was just . . . real lovely. With this huge wraparound terrace looking over the bay. We went out there just before sunset. Buddy spotted a whale blowing his spout—said it reminded him of me when I got pissed at him."

The memory made the older woman chuckle but the laughter went on too long and started to teeter dangerously toward the brink of sobs. But Brent made a supreme effort, drawing in a long breath as she dug her nails into her palms. When she swung around to face Jocelyn, there was just a single tear making its way slowly down one powdered cheek.

"See, I've *always* been a tough bitch, O'Roarke, in case you were wondering. I wasn't some sweet young thing who got hardened by Tinsel Town over the years. I came out of my momma's belly clawing and scratching. And it was a good thing, too, or I'd've ended up on the funny farm the way she did. See, it's not that nice guys finish last. They *don't finish* at all. That's my belief and Buddy understood it. He *knew* me and he never tried to change me. Sure, he could be a royal pain in the butt lots of times. But he took me as I was, warts and all, and he stood by me every bloody step of the way . . . So now it's my turn."

"Your turn to do what?"

"That's it—I don't know what to do! I'm a shrewdie but I'm not a chess player like you. I don't know from psychology and motivation and all that crap. But you—you're the type that stares through people's skin till you can see what makes 'em tick. Frankly, you give me the creeps . . . No offense, I mean that as sort of a compliment."

"Flattered, I'm sure." And in an odd way she was. For one thing, Josh felt fairly certain that she was one of the few mortals who had ever gotten a glimpse of Brent's vulnerable side. Of course, Gabby's vulnerable side was pretty armadillolike compared to most folks', and there was still the outside chance that the sly old fox was just trying to lead her down the garden path by a different route. But at least it was comforting to know that she had managed to intimidate this she-devil to some small degree. "But, before I swoon from such praise, suppose you come to the point. What do you want from me, Gabby?"

"I want you to tell me what to do. I can't keep going around lobbing grenades every which way like I did tonight. Doesn't seem to do much good."

"Lobbing grenades? Whoa, Nelly! Are you telling me you're pulling these stunts on purpose? That little massacre at mealtime was *planned*?"

"Well, yeah, in a way. Same as my tussle with Goldstein on location. Though I wouldn't say *planned*. I just keep pressing people's buttons to see if I can flush the bastard out."

"Uh-huh, I see. But do you have any idea who the bastard *is*?"

"Nah, not a clue. But it's one of this bunch, all right. Has to be. That's why I got so mad at Buddy's wake when you said something about him being in somebody's way. Well, everybody he was blocking is right under my roof tonight."

O'Roarke thought Gabby's observation was fairly accurate, more accurate than she intended since she, herself, was also among the blockees. But a strong sense of self-preservation forbade her saying so.

Instead she asked, "What about Hayes? How was Buddy blocking him?"

"He wasn't. I was only thinking of him as a—what's it—an accomplice. Like if Ginger put him up to it. Which I doubt."

"You mean you doubt Ginger had anything to do with it?"

"No! What're you, nuts? She had the most to gain. I just don't think Timmy would go along with it. He's too much like me," she said with an almost affectionate smile. "That boy goes out

on a limb for nobody but himself. Besides, he's just a butterfly—
a Good Time Charley. Doesn't have the stomach for it . . . Nice
buns, though."

"So who's your top contender then? Brenda?" Josh asked, watching closely for Brent's reaction.

Gabby took a long, thoughtful draw on her cigarette before
responding in a dispassionate voice, "If the woman weren't dumber
than a post, I'd say yeah, definitely. Buddy always looked out for
her 'cause she was all the family he had left, but he didn't really
care for her much and she knew it. There was no love lost there."

"If that's so, Gabby," Jocelyn said, deciding it was time to take
the petite bull by the horns, "why were you ready to pay her off
to pressure Buddy to sell Monte Verde?"

"Oh, say, you *do* get around, don't you, cupcake?" Brent was
definitely surprised but not overtly outraged. She even raised her
glass to salute a fellow she-devil. "You're even slicker than I
thought. Well, sweets, it may boggle your evil little imagination,
but I didn't like to *bock* my husband about business. Brenda, on
the other hand, loved to. And she usually got results. Buddy was
being a damn fool about Monte Verde—he was never gonna
build that house up there! And we stood to make a packet on the
sale. I thought Brenda's whining might tip the scales, that's all . . .
Does that make me *your* top contender?"

Before Jocelyn could come up with a decent reply, the door
cracked open to reveal Brenda Arnold's cold-creamed face.

"Sorry to interrupt. Gabby, Miriam says Sam Cohn's on your
private line. He's sorry it's so late but he's interested in that
Hispanic writer of yours for the Meryl Streep film."

A tiny bolt of lightning shot through the door and all that
remained of Gabby was a mixed odor of Scotch and Ysatis. Josh
made to follow in her wake but, before she could reach the door,
Brenda had it shut with her considerable bulk wedged against it.

"We *have* to talk," she gasped in high melodramatic dudgeon.

"We do? Why?"

"Because I don't want you to get the wrong impression. About
me . . . or about Randall."

"The only impression I have about Boggs is the one he left in
my gut. And it's gonna be very hard to eradicate, Bren, 'cause I
really *hate* being punched out, you know?"

"Oh, but that had *nothing* to do with me, Josh!"

"Yeah? Tell my abdomen that—it's not going to feel better till it has somebody to blame. All I know is, I just mentioned your name to this hulk and the next second I was rolling down a hill. I figure that was Boogie's version of a chivalrous response."

She expected protestation, some vehement denial, but Brenda, distracted from her initial purpose, merely blushed like a schoolgirl and gasped dreamily, "Really? How sweet . . . maybe he was just being overprotective."

"Well, golly gee, maybe he was—but at *my* expense. So you damned well better tell me what the hell he was protecting—*now!*"

O'Roarke's caustic line reading yanked the other woman back to unromantic reality. Brenda tenderly massaged her greased forehead, trying to marshal her scattered thoughts. But Jocelyn poured on the eye contact until the other woman blurted out, "I have no idea, honestly! You have to believe me, Jocelyn. I don't know what he was up to but I'm sure Randall would never hurt Ginger . . . or anyone intentionally." She added the last words hastily in an attempt to cover her blunder, but O'Roarke was on to her in a flash.

"So you think Ginger's accident was intentional—and you weren't even there. But Boogie was—yet you're sure he had nothing to do with it. How interesting . . . what gives, Brenda?"

"No, no, you're putting words in my mouth," she protested, fidgeting her way across the room to a worktable strewn with photos and the galley proofs of Banks' last book, "I just meant—well, I don't know what you've heard about Boggs, but he has a bad reputation in some quarters—"

"Some *head*quarters, you mean," Josh inserted, positioning herself by the glass case that was kitty-corner to the worktable. "Like the LAPD's."

"Well, it's undeserved! He's never even been indicted," Arnold asserted as if this were proof of a noble character. As she busied herself organizing the pages and photos, she became less timorous and more defiant. "But I'm sure that Ken doll masquerading as a cop has told you all sorts of slander. So when I heard about Ginger's accident, I guessed you'd assume the worst."

"Yeah, right. Lucky thing Boggs *knocked* some sense into me, huh," O'Roarke said, laying on the sarcasm with a trowel. "Now I see the guy's just a pussycat. In fact, I'm so taken with the little dickens, I've got Hamill out looking for him now. I want to shake his hand . . . right before I press charges."

"You wouldn't do *that?!*" Brenda went pale beneath her cold cream, which made her face look like a waxwork dummy's.

"Oh, but I would. See, I've got a vindictive streak a mile wide. So it looks like Boggs is going to get indicted after all . . . unless you tell me what he was really doing up on location."

"I'm not sure." All her bravado vanished as she thumbed listlessly through a pile of photos to avoid Josh's gaze. "But whatever it was, someone else put him up to it. It's true Randall's something of a one-man collection agency—for bookies mostly. I suppose somebody forgot to pay their tab and he was sent to, uh . . . jog their memory."

"Uh-huh, well, who do you think he was sent to 'jog'? Come on, Bren, you're a player. You must know who the heavy bettors are in the company."

"Well, Billy Orbach bets, but he's lucky as sin. Little twerp played a thirteen-to-one long shot on an Exacta last month and it came *in!* Can you believe it? Unlucky *thirteen*—on two nags that hadn't won a purse all season and they come in," Arnold sniffed disgustedly. "Had to be a fix."

As soon as she'd started talking horses, Brenda's whole aspect had altered; the color had come back to her cheeks and there was a keen glint in her eyes that O'Roarke had never seen before. This was the world where Brenda Arnold truly lived and breathed and where she bore little resemblance to her posturing prima donna persona.

Fascinated by the transfiguration, Jocelyn had to quell her actor's instinct to soak up interesting character quirks and ask, "Who else then?"

"Oh, hell, half the damn crew, I'd say. Most everybody likes a little flutter now and then," Brenda rattled on with the assured air of a true expert. "Even Miriam likes to place the odd bet, but she's just a gut guesser—bets on a horse named Bright Jewel, even if it's a real dog, 'cause her grandmother's name was Jewel or because it sounds pretty. A total dilettante. Where somebody like— Oh, *shit!*"

Arnold, who had continued to leaf through photos as she delivered her discourse, came to a full stop as an eight-by-ten glossy caught her eye. Stepping in to see what could have possibly distracted the other woman from a topic so dear to her heart, Josh saw three photos fanned out in Brenda's trembling hand. On the left was a head shot of little Hilly Hayes staring into the camera with huge, wounded eyes; her usual esprit nowhere in evidence, she came off like a poster child for Tiny Tots with Clinical Depression. On the right was a picture of her dad, shirtless and unshaven with a joint dangling from his lower lip, bent over an old-fashioned splicer, looking dashing, dangerous, and extremely decadent. But Brenda was staring at the center photo, an artfully grainy study of herself in a makeup smock, wearing a nylon wig cap that made her look like a pinhead, glued to the pay phone at the Culver City studio with a glazed and desperate expression on her face.

"He must've taken that just a week ago—the day Everybody's Baby went down the tubes in the fifth and I dropped a bundle," she hissed hotly. "Goddamn little spy! The hell with him—it's *my* book now and this is history." Breathing hard, Brenda ripped the photo to shreds and shoved the remains into the pocket of her robe. Feeling O'Roarke's eyes upon her, she quickly swept up the rest of the pictures and the galleys and deposited them in a nearby file cabinet before Josh could get a better look. With one sharp twist, she locked the cabinet drawer and pocketed the keys.

Before Josh could get a word in edgewise, Arnold swung around to face her and table all further discussion.

"I'm really very tired now, Jocelyn," she said, becoming her old pompous self. "I'm tired of this whole stinking mess and I'm tired of *you*, frankly. If you have any more questions for me, you'll have to get the Ken doll to ask them—officially . . . And I'd *love* to see him try."

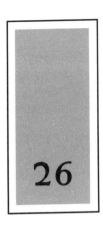

26

" 'I'd *love* to kiss ya, but I just washed my hair.' "

Having just plopped her weary and aching bones down on the bed, Jocelyn looked up to find Jack Breedlove standing in the doorway, fresh from the shower with a towel wrapped around his waist and another one rubbing his damp hair. Too tired for sexy repartee, she mumbled, "You do a good Bette, fella. You'd be the envy of every female impersonator in New York."

"Ah, but I'm more versatile. I can do *men*, too. Like—'Clear the gate, asshole!' "

Despite intense fatigue, Jocelyn jerked up against the head-board. "Clear the gate" was the expression every DP used at the beginning and end of each take to make sure the camera lens had been checked for minor obstructions, a stray hair, or a smudge that would mar the final print. The "asshole" part had been Buddy's special addition and Jack had eerily rendered the phrase in his exact intonations.

"God, cut it out! That's too spooky."

"Sorry, I thought you'd heard that one already," Jack said, casually easing himself down on the edge of the bed. "It's nothing new. Almost every guy on the crew can do it. Like almost anyone can do 'The calla lilies are in bloom again.'" Dropping the well-known Hepburn quaver, he added, "It was Buddy's signature phrase."

Thinking about it, it made sense; Buddy had had the kind of basso profundo growl that was easy to mimic, Jocelyn realized belatedly. If she placed her voice low enough, she could probably pull it off, too, which only added to her conviction that Ginger had not imagined a voice at her window. But how many people knew that "Baby, It's Cold Outside" was their special song? And who had the skill to whip up a Buddy mask?

Jack gently interrupted her train of thought with, "Don't tell me, let me guess—you're not even remotely pondering how cute I look in a towel, are you?"

"Uh, sad to say, no . . . though you really *are*, Breedlove. Damn fetching. But, truthfully, my libido is at low ebb just now."

"Thought so. You look done in, angel, 'cept I can still see those mental wheels spinning." He gave her thigh a friendly pat and offered, "Anything you want to mull out loud?"

After a moment's consideration, she drew Hamill's fax out of her bra, ignoring his Groucholike leer, and handed it to him. "What do you make of this?"

"What the hell is it?"

"A blowup of a film frame I found in Buddy's darkroom."

"Oooh, wow, as in 'a crucial piece of evidence,' huh? I'm honored," Breedlove bandied but focused on the paper with immediate and total concentration. His tone altered completely when he handed it back to her after a careful inspection. "Well, I don't know what to make of the hen scratchings at the bottom. But the top half looks awful familiar—I just can't place it!"

"Yeah, that's what I feel, too," Josh said, fired by his corresponding impression. "Like it's an image I've seen before, more than once, and seen recently."

"It's too bad the fax is so damned grainy." Jack had caught her fever now. "I can't make out what the hand on the right is holding against the leg and I think that's the key."

"Right, right! But this is good, Jack. If we both feel this way, it means whatever this is is in our mutual frame of reference—

which can't be too large. I mean, we've only known each other a short while and we don't have all that much in common."

"We don't?" Breedlove asked dejectedly, his inchoate detective impulses momentarily squelched by romantic egoism. "I kind of thought we were soulmates."

"Now be sensible. Whatever our natural affinity, we come from two very different parts of the country," Jocelyn maintained with what he felt was heartless logic. "And two different cultures—"

"Now don't pull that high-falutin' New York artiste garbage on me. We're both in show biz, kid. And so was Banks—so my guess is this is from some old movie."

"Okay, that's a reasonable assumption. But what old movie, and why was Buddy cutting it up? And why was it tucked inside his enlarger?"

"Hey, slow down! I'm new at this." Breedlove chewed his lower lip and leaned back against the headboard. "Okay, it was inside the enlarger 'cause he didn't want anyone—or someone in particular—to find it. How's that sound?"

"Brilliant," Josh agreed, giving him a sleepy but encouraging smile. "Now let's get back to Name That Flick . . . What is the hand holding?"

"Beats me. The resolution's so bad! It could be a stethoscope, maybe."

"Against a *leg?*" she mumbled faintly, too tired now to focus properly on the hand or anything else. "That's silly."

"True. Very silly, which means it could be from a Marx Brothers movie. Didn't Groucho impersonate a doctor in one of them? Let's see—wasn't *A Night at the Opera* or *A Day at the Races*. Maybe one of the early ones, like *The Coconuts* or *Animal Crackers*, huh? . . . What do you think?"

For reply, Jack got a soft snort that segued into a delicate but definite snore. Glancing down, he found his lady sleuth had been bludgeoned by the sandman; her cheek rested against his shoulder as she breathed deeply with lips parted in a soft O. It was, to him, a rare and lovely sight: Jocelyn O'Roarke with her dukes down. Feeling tender and protective—and more than a little horny—he did the gallant thing and pulled the comforter up to her chin gently, so as not to disturb her.

"Shit. Now *I'm* wide awake," he whispered, his eyes straying back to the nagging fax in his hand. But after a few more minutes of fruitless scrutiny, his head fell sideways and he joined her in dreamland.

Slowly she moved toward him in something long, flowing, and gauzy that revealed, teasingly, as much as it concealed. Holding out her arms, she said in a hush, "Come here, love. I've been waiting so long for you . . . all my life."

"Hold on. Just a sec," Jack said, shaking the fax that was still clenched in his hand. "I've almost got it!"

"Mmm, I knew you would." She slid both arms around his neck, enveloping him. "'Cause you're twice the man he is. Now we can be together."

"Oh yeah, baby, yeah." His arms went around her waist greedily but he didn't want to lose sight of his discovery. "Just give me a minute. I think I see what's in his hand."

"Later, later." Bending over him, Jocelyn breathed hotly in his ear, then ran the tip of her tongue around it. "I need you *now*."

He groaned in pleasure and surrender, giving himself up to her caress.

"Jack! Wake up. Come on, Jack, I need you awake *now!*"

Still half in dreams, he saw Josh hovering above him and raised his hands to cradle her breasts. But she caught his wrists and yanked him upright.

"Listen, there's been an accident. We've got to get downstairs fast!"

His skull bumped against the headboard, bringing him to full consciousness. Lights were on in the house and he could hear several pairs of feet scurrying down the corridor. Seeing that he was fully awake, O'Roarke, still fully dressed, was already heading for the doorway. He reached out to grab her hand.

"No, wait. Don't go down without me."

"You're still in your *towel*, love," she reminded him while squirming to get free.

But Breedlove held fast and scanned the room until he spotted a fluffy, terry-cloth guest robe draped over a chair. Setting her loose, he grabbed it and managed to pull it on and knot it before she'd reached the bottom of the stairs.

There was a small crowd consisting of Gabby, Larry, and Brenda standing in the open doorway of Buddy's den. Inside, stretched out on the Aubusson carpet, was Tim Hayes, eyes closed, with his head cradled in Ginger's lap. Hayes looked bad, but the room looked worse, like someone had gone through it with a thresher. Books and papers were scattered everywhere, the glass case was on the floor, its contents shattered, and the file cabinet was gaping open.

"Timmy, honey, please wake up. Just open your eyes, honey, *please.*" Tears spilled down her cheeks as she ran her hands through his hair, trying to coax him to consciousness. Then she brought one hand up and gave a small shriek when she saw the large, wet, crimson patch on her palm. "Oh, my God! Oh, *no*, they've killed him, too!"

"Good thing Miriam knows how to get out bloodstains," Gabby Brent growled. She stood in a jade green Dior dressing gown with matching sleep mask pushed high up on her forehead in front of the fireplace in her immense cathedral-ceilinged living room, expertly taping a large gauze patch to the back of Hayes' head. "That rug costs twenty grand, kid." Taking a swig from a brandy snifter, she handed the remainder to Hayes, then chuckled humorlessly. "Talk about a stuck pig, huh? But head wounds are always like that, bleed like crazy. And it'll hurt like hell, too, but you'll live to break more hearts, don't worry."

It wasn't exactly the Florence Nightingale approach but Brent's brand of nursing seemed to have a more salutary effect on Tim than it had had on O'Roarke. He downed the contents of the snifter and handed it back to Gabby with a feeble smile.

"Fill 'er up, barkeep."

"Oh, Timmy, no. You might have a concussion," Ginger pleaded, gripping the arms of the wing-back chair she'd been ensconced in ever since Gabby had brusquely taken the first aid kit out of her shaking hands.

She still had the shakes but the color was coming back to her cheeks finally, which was a relief to Josh. Like Gabby, she knew that head wounds always bleed profusely and that Hayes was in no danger of imminent demise. The gash at the base of his skull was fairly shallow, but the fright his injury had given Jellicoe might well be more than her sorely tried nerves could bear. And, compassion aside, Jocelyn didn't want her unraveling now when it was so crucial to nail down the order of events.

Whisking the refilled snifter out of Brent's hand, she handed it to Jack for safekeeping and turned to Hayes.

"Tim, what were you doing down here anyway? Can you remember anything?"

"Yeah, I think so. I was up in bed—couldn't fall asleep. Guess it was from all the excitement today. So I came down here to get something to read," he said, jerking a thumb in the direction of the built-in bookcases that covered one entire wall. "But I heard something. Sounded like it was coming from Buddy's den."

"What kind of noise was it?"

"I dunno. Kinda sounded like metal scraping, I guess . . . Anyway, I went out into the hallway and saw that the door to the den was partway open."

"Do you remember if the lights were on or off?" O'Roarke asked, ignoring the various disgruntled faces around her.

With the exception of avid Jack, her newfound Watson, the rest of the group seemed ill-disposed to interrogation at two-thirty in the morning. Goldstein, red eyed with hair standing at attention, was trying to look suitably somber and concerned while sneaking furtive glances at the Waterford clock on the mantel, no doubt wondering what havoc would be wreaked upon his shooting schedule by all this. Finished with her patch-up job, Gabby looked surprisingly blasé about the whole thing, as if ransacking and assault were nothing out of the ordinary, and ready to pull down her sleep mask. While the hatchet-faced Miriam silently circulated with a tray of assorted beverages like a somnambulant cocktail waitress, Brenda skulked near the fireplace, slugging back brandies and blinking her puffy eyes like a hoot owl on the verge of hysteria. Hardest to ignore was Ginger who, for the first time, looked on Jocelyn with keen disfavor for hounding her wounded hero. But O'Roarke kept her eyes locked on Hayes', hoping to extract every drop of information she could before aftershock hit him.

"Off, I'm positive," Tim, seemingly the least perturbed member of the party, stated flatly. "'Cause I remember flipping the wall switch and . . . man, the place looked like a cyclone had hit it!"

"Now think—what did you do next?"

"Lemme see . . . oh, yeah, I saw the file cabinet wide open. That spooked me 'cause I knew the stuff for Buddy's new book was in there."

"How'd you know that?"

"Oh, *Jesus*, Josh! Get off it. He's only been in this house maybe a jillion times," Ginger burst in with the ferocity of a mother tiger shielding her cub. "Of *course* he knows where that stuff is!"

"Really?" Keeping her tone carefully bland, she turned to Ginger. "So you knew, too?"

"Sure I did," she answered, discomfited by Jocelyn's sudden shift but still defiant, making a sweeping motion with one hand to include the others. "*Everybody* did. Just like everybody knew Buddy kept it locked up all the time. It's no big thing! So drop the Perry Mason bullshit, okay?"

"Okay, sorry I asked," O'Roarke said mildly, concealing her concern. It wasn't Jellicoe's anger, which was fueled by protectiveness, fear, and a confused sense of betrayal, that troubled her; it was the younger woman's strong resistance to her line of questioning. Too experienced to be blinded by her own affections, she also couldn't help recalling Phillip's oft-repeated belief that: "The ones you have to watch the most are the ones who're most put off by questions. For whatever reason, they really *don't* want you to get to the bottom of things. And they may or may not be the perp—but they've got something invested in *not* finding the answers." What did Ginger have invested that was powerful enough to keep her from wanting to find out who had attacked Tim?

"Hey, Ginge, cool it," Hayes intervened, giving her a soothing smile. "She's just trying to help clear things up, babe."

Instantly chastened, Jellicoe folded herself up in the huge armchair and gave Jocelyn a hangdog look and a mumbled, though not altogether convincing, apology.

"Okay, Tim," O'Roarke resumed. "What happened next?"

"Okay, so I started to head for the cabinet, right? . . . Then I must've heard something, I guess, 'cause I stopped dead in my tracks and started to turn around. Out of the corner of my eye, I caught someone coming up on my left. Then—*wham!* Just like they say, I saw stars, man."

"Uh-huh." Drawing the syllables out with a long, worried sigh, Jocelyn waited a moment before asking, "Did you get even the *faintest* glimpse of a face before you went out?"

Now there was no distraction or inattention in the six faces that turned toward Tim as one. It was hard to tell if he was having trouble remembering or just relishing the drama of the moment, but Hayes took his own sweet time answering. Putting an exploring hand to the back of his head, he winced slightly and the pain seemed to jog his memory.

"Yeah, yeah, I think I did . . . But it seems crazy."

"Forget about crazy. Who did you see?"

Tim looked blankly around the room as if he were searching for a certain familiar face but not finding it. A sweat broke out on his forehead as the reality of his close call seemed to finally sink in; for the first time since regaining consciousness, Hayes looked frightened. Mopping his face with his T-shirt, he swallowed hard then stared, wide-eyed, up at Josh.

"Swear to Christ, for the life of me . . . it looked like Buddy."

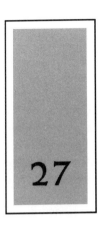

27

"Okay, buddy, let's try it again . . . Why'd you take a poke at the lady?"

"Shit, I keep tellin' ya, I never did. Okay, mebbe I sorta shoved her and she, like . . . slipped."

"Yeah—right down a forty-foot embankment. And you split. Didn't even go down to give her a hand up. I don't call that polite, Boogie. Do you?"

Seated in a straight-back chair in Dwayne Hamill's freshly painted office, Randall Boggs, unshaven and exhausted, hands clasped and hanging between his splayed knees, regarded his inquisitor with a dawning and wary respect. No stranger to the hardline tactics of L.A. cops, he'd figured this punk with his Pepsodent smile and Coppertone tan would be a comparative piece of cake. But the kid had had him in his office for three hours now; he hadn't laid a hand on him but had, instead, badgered him ceaselessly with knotty questions that Boggs' sluggish brain was having a hard time fielding. He wanted a drink and a smoke real bad and didn't know how much longer he could keep dodging bullets.

"Look, I dinnit know whodafuck she was and she was actin' real crazy. I jist wanted to git away from the broad."

"Well, according to her sworn statement," Dwayne fibbed smoothly, "she was just asking what I've been asking you for the last three hours—what the hell were you doing there in the first place? And I'm starting to get a little crazy, myself, Boogie, so why don't you just cough up, huh?"

Hamill had made short work of tracking a half-smashed Boggs down in one of his favorite dives on the strip in the early hours of the morning but, after calling Brent's Malibu home to find that Josh had already left and was en route to location, he was working in the dark with very little real evidence. If Randall didn't crack soon, Dwayne, a scrupulous by-the-book player, might have to let him walk. Luckily for him, Boggs had no scruples and, therefore, never suspected that Hamill might.

"Lissen, I don't know nothin' about no accident. I mean, I's jist as surprised as the next asshole when that bag blew out under that broad. An' I don't like being around that kind a' scene, you know? So's my business was finished—so I jist wannid to clear out quick, see?"

"Fine, fine. I'm totally copacetic with that, Randy. Just be a pal and tell me what your business *was*."

More than anything else, it was this weird cop-kid's unfailing good cheer that was wearing Boogie down. Used to abuse, he simply couldn't cope with such relentless affability.

"Geez—gimme a break! Somebody owed somebody some dough an' they ax'd me to go ax about it. Nothin' heavy . . . I tried to tell her it was jist the usual. C'mon, you know the score."

"Sure I do," Dwayne agreed sympathetically, "and I know a guy's gotta make a living somehow. And maybe, just maybe, I can persuade Ms. O'Roarke not to press charges. But first, you have to tell me *who's* the player you were trying to squeeze?"

Though devoid of scruples, Boggs did have a hazy sense of outlaw professionalism. Giving Hamill a stricken, offended look, he cried, "Hey, lay off, will ya? I got a reputation to protect here! Whad d'ya want from my life?"

"Way I see it, Randall," Dwayne drawled, leaning back in his chair, "it's gotta be one or the other—your, uh, 'reputation' or your life . . . as in one to five with good behavior."

"What do you *mean* you don't know where she is?! It's your business to know." Austin Frost, just recently apprised of the past night's events, spit fire into the crackling phone line and Larry Goldstein, the reluctant messenger, fired it right back.

"No, Austin, it is *not!* I know you're upset about the accident and what happened at Gabby's last night and you're frustrated because the roads are still blocked and you can't get up here. But I'm the one stuck up here with only half a crew and a leading lady who has eye-baggage down to her kneecaps, trying my friggin' best to juggle the shooting schedule so she can rest and we don't fall irreparably behind and go down the goddamn *tubes!!* So don't *hock* me 'cause your nosy friend has made herself scarce . . . When I see her, I'll tell her to call you, all right?"

"Larry, Larry, it is not all right," Austin protested. "Don't you get it? Forget the shooting schedule—forget everything! And get a *clue.* You've got a killer up there, don't you see? Jocelyn knows it—she must. And the killer *knows* she knows. I have to talk to her."

"Well, what can I do?" Goldstein asked distractedly. "After last night's ruckus, she locked herself up in Buddy's den till dawn. Came out this morning looking grim as hell."

"Did she say anything, anything at all?" Frost was swiftly losing what little trust he had left in Larry but was desperate for any scrap of information. "Did she say what was missing?"

"We're still not sure—the place was such a wreck. But Jocelyn did mention that some photos Brenda had shown her were gone. Said there was a pile of ash in a wastebasket—like they'd been burned. But I don't know what the photos were of."

"And you didn't ask?!"

"No! There was no time. Breedlove just scooped her up like a Saint Bernard and drove her up here in his Jeep. I haven't seen her since."

"What did Dwayne say?"

"Who?"

"Detective Hamill, you nit! She must've called to tell him about the assault."

"Nope, couldn't. When we got up this morning the phone lines were out at Brent's."

Austin groaned inwardly. It was the last thing he wanted to hear; it meant that whatever Jocelyn was up to, she was working on her own without the benefit of Dwayne's counsel. Though he had a high regard for O'Roarke's amateur standing as a snoop, in the past she'd usually let herself be guided by Gerrard's more cautious approach to crime solving. Left to her own devices up in Malibu Creek Park, and given her flair for the dramatic, she might resort to extreme, not to mention unsafe, measures.

"Look, if you can't find Jocelyn, get ahold of Breedlove and have him call me right away." Frost spoke slowly and deliberately, trying to convince himself that he was forming some helpful plan of action. "I'm going to call Hamill and see if he can get up there somehow."

"It'll be tough. The grips say the roads are still—" But Austin was off before Larry could finish. Billy Orbach walked by, whistling happily now that the skies had cleared, with a viewfinder in one hand.

"Hey, Billy, have you seen O'Roarke or Breedlove?"

"Nope. I've been setting up the reflectors for the first shot," he said, squinting approvingly with a slight air of self-congratulation up at the brilliant, cooperative sun. "You know, it's so clear now, we might get too much light bouncing off that back panel."

"Oh, no, we can't have that, Bill," Goldstein said with alarm, instantly forgetting Austin's instructions. "We won't be able to see the flames. Let's check it now so we don't have to reposition it later."

"By Jove, I think I've *got* it!"

There was no one around to appreciate Jack's flawless rendition of Wilfred Hyde-White's Colonel Pickering, but at that moment he didn't care; he was too caught up with the thrill of victory.

Alone in the makeup trailer, waiting for Ginger to wake from her much needed beauty sleep, he'd taken the fax out of his pocket for reexamination. Concentrating on the bottom half-frame, he'd determined to decipher the truncated message printed on it. Grabbing the clipboard check-in sheet, he'd ripped out several blank pages, copying the half-letters on each page several times. It had been slow going at first and frustrating as hell, like trying to reconstruct a tyrannosaurus rex from a few odd pieces of tailbone—or attempting to hook up a VCR without an instruction book. But he'd stuck with it, endlessly experimenting with every possible letter formation that suggested itself.

Such patient diligence was not typical of Breedlove—unless he was dealing with an unbroken colt or a foaling mare—but he had strong incentives; the basest was a keen competitive need to prove he was as good a man as the seemingly omnipresent Gerrard, but stronger and more urgent was his desire to solve the case before his lady love got herself hurt . . . or worse, since she was, in his estimation, skating on very thin ice.

After helping her sort through the wreckage in Buddy's den in the early hours of the morning, he'd fallen asleep for half an hour in the recliner, waking to find her gone. Panicking he'd run through the house looking for her and finally spotted her from the dining room window. With her back to the house, she'd stood, hugging herself to ward off the dawn's chill, on the flagstone path that led down to the beachfront, staring out at the ocean.

"What're you looking at?" he'd asked softly, draping a blanket around her shoulders. She'd turned to him with a slight start and he could see from the dark circles under her eyes that she'd gotten no sleep at all.

With a wan smile, she pointed to a lone speedboat, far from shore, skimming the waves. "Look at that guy. Out there at the crack of dawn. I just don't get it. Guess I'm too much of an earth sign, huh?"

"Nah, you're just not nuts," he'd answered, rubbing her arms with both hands. "That guy there is 'the need for speed' incarnate. They get addicted to it. Me? I'd rather ride a bronco with a burr under its saddle. Those things are dangerous."

"God, don't we sound like two middle-aged cranks," she'd chuckled.

"Speak for yourself, old lady," he'd sniffed in mock offense. "I prefer to think of it as a healthy sense of self-preservation . . . Besides, even young Turks like Tim don't like those machines."

"How do you know?"

"He told me," Jack had answered, glad to speak of inconsequentials for the moment. "That's why he quit the Catalina job. They'd had him schlepping stuff all around the island in one of those things and he got fed up with it."

"I didn't know that." Squinting her eyes to catch a final glimpse of the boat as it sped out of view, she'd observed, "You'd think he'd be just the type . . . like Ginger."

"Like Ginger?! How's that?"

"You know, the high-risk types, thrill junkies. I think that's a big part of the bond between them. You saw Ginger yesterday. She was all hyped to do that stunt. Wasn't much fazed by the blowout, either."

"Yeah, come to think of it, you're right. Though I don't see Ginger as the totally fearless kind."

"She is and she isn't. Ginger's afraid of people—angering or disappointing them. She's got the child star's need to please. That pressure, along with the cheap thrills, is probably what got her in over her head with drugs. Her bogeymen are all in her *mind*. But when it comes to the purely *physical*, she's got guts for days. More than Tim—I bet she'd *love* to own a Scarab."

Surprised by the note of clinical detachment in her voice, Jack had snuck a look at Jocelyn's face and glimpsed something that startled and disturbed him; her whole demeanor bespoke a complete and profound objectivity that was beyond all claims of personal liking. Feeling like Kevin McCarthy in *Invasion of the Body Snatchers*, he'd realized with a jolt that all emotion had been drained out of her, leaving behind only an implacable will ensconced in a walking, talking human shit-detector.

Without meaning to, he'd whispered, *"La belle dame sans merci."* And she'd caught it.

"What? Did I say something that shocked you?"

"Uh, no, not what you said . . . Just *how* you said it, I guess."

"Oh, I see . . . sorry, Jack. I know the feeling." Rubbing the small of his back consolingly, she'd added gently, "Used to happen to me a lot with Phillip at first. It's like—where did the *person* go, huh? All I can tell you is you get to a point where your mind and your emotions *have* to part company. It's like coming to a fork in the road and you've got to cho—"

"That's *it!*"

O'Roarke had nearly jumped out of her skin at this sudden explosive exultation from Jack, who was scrambling to pull the fax out of his shirt pocket. Her casual remark had finally triggered something in his archival film memory. Trying to hold the paper open against the ocean breeze, he'd stabbed a finger toward the center of the top half-frame.

"It's not a stethoscope and it's not the Marx Brothers! It's a *fork*, Josh. See? That hand is poking a fork into that leg . . . Well, I wasn't too far off. I *knew* it had to be a comedy and I was right!"

"Oh, you clever, clever boy, you," she'd exclaimed, hugging his waist. "I've been such a dunce. Of course it is. It's Raymond Massey's leg and Cary Grant's hand. It's—"

"*Arsenic and Old Lace*," he'd crowed, too pleased with himself to let her finish, then reeled off, "Frank Capra. Warner Brothers, 1944. The Epstein brothers rewrote Joe Kesserling's stage play. Big fight over having to change Mortimer's 'Thank God, I'm a bastard' to 'I'm the son of a sea cook.' Geez—*how* could I have missed it?!"

"And Sol Polito was the cameraman," Josh had added, though with nowhere near his enthusiasm. In fact, she'd looked as if she'd just seen a ghost. Then her attention had shifted back to the house, which was beginning to show signs of life. Tugging his sleeve, she'd started back up the flagstone path, pulling him after her. "Come on! We've got to get up to location right now."

"Sure, sure. Just hold on a sec," he'd said, hanging back to stare at the fax. "We're on a roll. Maybe we can crack the bottom frame, too."

"No, no time. You can work on it once we're up there."

"*Me?* What about you? Don't you think it's important?"

"Oh, absolutely. My hunch is it's the whole key to why Buddy was killed."

"Well, then shouldn't we take the time *now* to—"

"Can't. Too risky," she'd shot back with an adamant shake of her head. "Besides, I think I already know who."

"You *do?!*"

But she'd already gone inside to change back into her own clothes. Once inside the Jeep with him, she'd refused to discuss her hunch, pleading fatigue; a plea that she had justified by leaning back against the headrest and, to Jack's frustration and amazement, promptly falling asleep. As soon as they'd reached the location, her eyes had instantly popped open and she'd hit the ground running, pausing only long enough to call over her shoulder,

"Keep working on the bottom frame. I'll meet you in the makeup trailer later."

"When?"

"After I talk to somebody about a cigar box." And then she was gone.

"Well, serves her right," Breedlove said to himself with no small satisfaction as he eagerly sketched in a series of letters that, unlike his earlier efforts, finally looked like they were shaping up to something more than gibberish. "She's going to miss out on the Big Revelation."

To be honest, he had to admit it pleased him mightily to have broken the code, so to speak, all on his own. He was beginning to understand how intoxicating this detective business could be; in the thrill of the moment his writing hand actually started to shake as he traced in the final letters. When he read the message he'd reconstructed, the pen fell from his hand and bounced across the floor. He didn't pick it up; he couldn't, because now his hand was shaking in earnest.

"Jack? You in there?" There was a light tap on the trailer door but the voice wasn't Jocelyn's; it was Ginger's. Wearing a terry-cloth robe, she stepped inside, looking rested but still befuddled by sleep. Jack spun around to face her, shoving the printed message deep into the back pocket of his jeans.

"Sorry. Didn't mean to startle you," she said, seeing the surprised look on his face. "You ready for me?"

"Yeah, sure. Just take a pew. I'll be right with you."

"Well, you've got your work cut out for you," Jellicoe said with a yawn as she settled into the chair. "My hair got all mushed up while I was napping."

"Uh, that's okay. We'll fix it," he answered uneasily, placing a towel around her shoulders. "It's more important that you got some rest."

"Oh, I did, I did," she said with another kittenish yawn. "Went out like a light. It's funny, isn't it? . . . Considering that just a while ago I was like a freakin' insum—what's the word?"

"Insomniac."

"Yeah, that's it. And even with all that's happened, I haven't had a single nightmare in *days* . . . Go figure." Catching his drawn face in the mirror, she added, "But you sure look like you've had some lately. What's the matter, hon?"

"Uh, nothing . . . just the, um, usual. You know," he fudged then segued into a Sam Jaffe impression. "Man, Woman, Birth, Death, Infinity—all that garbage."

"Hmm, well, if you ask me, it's probably from hanging out with Joshie," she said between pursed lips, the kitten becoming a bit of a cat. "Don't get me wrong. I know she's just trying to help. But sometimes she just makes it worse, the way she stirs things up all the time."

Normally he would've been offended on O'Roarke's behalf by such base ingratitude, but at that moment he could do no more than mumble, "It's just her way, Ginge."

"Yeah, I guess . . . Boy, that feels good," she purred with half-closed lids as Jack lightly massaged her scalp. "I could go right back to sleep. But don't let me, okay?"

"Okay."

He worked swiftly with sure hands despite the sensation that the hidden piece of paper was burning a hole in his pocket. One glimpse of it, he felt sure, would wake Ginger up faster than a dip in a polar lake—unless she'd seen it already since, whoever penned it, its message was clearly meant for her.

And its meaning brooked no misinterpretation; short, to the point, and brutal, it read: YOU KILLED YOUR PARENTS.

28

"You leave message, hokay?"

"No, no, Angelina, it's not okay. I know it's early but I *have* to talk to her. *Por favor?* It's important."

Sequestered in the back of a van with a portable phone she'd wangled from the key grip, Jocelyn heard the receiver being laid down at the other end followed by a fading mutter of Spanish imprecations. After a few endless minutes, she heard the soft patter of little feet approaching, then a scrambling sound as small hands wrestled with the phone.

"Who is it?" Hillary Hayes' voice came through the line faintly but sounding fully awake.

"Hilly, it's me, Josh, remember?"

"Uh-huh. Is my mommie there, too?" she asked hopefully.

"No, sweetie, not right now. But she's around," O'Roarke answered in her most reassuring tones. "I'll have her call you later, okay?"

"Okay, but I might be at school. I'm bringing my bunny for show an' tell."

"Hey, that's terrific. You two will be a big hit. Now—"

"Can you teach me a bunny song? You always know good songs."

It was a safe bet that never in the annals of crime had someone on the brink of identifying a murderer had to pause to sing "Here Comes Peter Cottontail" to a key witness. But O'Roarke knew better than to try to duck the request. Thankfully Hilly was a human sponge and a remarkably fast study. Three minutes later she was parroting back, "Hip, hip, hopping, hopping on down the lane . . . Is that right?"

"Just perfect. You're gonna wow 'em."

"Yeah! Will you tell my dad?"

"Sure thing . . . Now, Hilly, I want to ask a *very* important question that only you can answer, okay?"

"Uh-huh, what is it?" As Jocelyn had hoped, she sounded very grown up now, her voice filled with a pleased sense of self-importance.

"Do you remember when I came to your house for dinner?"

"Sure," she scoffed. "We sang the worm song . . . and Unca Buddy wasn't deaded yet."

"That's right, honey," she said gently. "Now the next day, when your mommie was at work, did anybody come by the house?"

"Lotsa people come to my house all a' time," Hilly said with a note of confusion.

"Right, right. But I'm thinking of someone who came with, uh . . . a present. Like something to put in your Unca Buddy's cigar box?"

"Oh, *yeah!* I 'member that," Hilly answered, her self-confidence restored. "And with a present for Mommie, too—a secret present."

"*Really?* And what was that?" Jocelyn held her breath waiting for the answer.

"I *tol'* you—it's a secret."

"Of course, of course it is." Her mind raced around looking for an incentive strong enough to overcome the scruples of a child who was bright and well on her way to being nobody's fool. "Well, look, the only fair thing is I tell *you* a secret and then you can tell me yours. How does that sound?"

"Uhhh . . . that's okay, I guess. But it's gotta be a *big* one."

"Definitely, that's only right. Now let me see . . ." O'Roarke racked her brain for something sufficiently juicy as sweat trickled down the back of her neck. If Hilly didn't opt to someday follow in her mother's thespian footsteps, it was eminently possible, given her inchoate negotiating skills, that she would grow up to put both Gabby Brent and Mike Ovitz out of business. Finally inspiration struck. "Okay, I don't like to say this 'cause you'll think I'm a sissy but—you know what a bat is?"

"Sure, I seen 'em at night—like black mouses only with wings."

"That's right. Well, I pretend I'm not—but I am really, really afraid of them."

"Really? So much they make your tummy hurt?"

"Yup, I've even thrown up once or twice." Jocelyn confessed the simple, unvarnished truth, knowing anything less just wouldn't suit the works.

"Well, you don't hafta be," Hilly counseled sagely. " 'Cause they never, never go in your hair Ang'lina says."

"I know, and she's right. But I can't help it—they just scare me."

"Well, tha's okay, Josh. I won't tell."

Compassion coming from a small child is a very powerful thing and Jocelyn felt hot tears suddenly pricking her eyes. Part of it was due to fatigue but the other, stronger part had to do with self-disgust at the manipulative bargain she was striking with the one totally innocent victim in this whole sordid mess.

Still, she had no choice but to see the business through; swallowing hard she whispered, "Thanks, that's very nice of you . . . Now can you tell me about the secret present?"

"It was tea—a special kind. Better'n what Unca Buddy brought Mommie. So I threw his in the garbage and put the good kind in the Tea Can on the counter."

"I see . . . But what made this tea special? Did it have a special name?"

"I think so—it was a sleepy-time tea, see? 'Cause Mommie was awake too much at night."

"Well, that makes a lot of sense." And it did, more than Hilly could ever imagine. Cloaking her voice in blandly neutral tones, she said, "What a good idea . . . So, honey, who gave you those nice presents?"

"I don't give a good goddamn about Dan Quayle being in town! No political assassin in his right mind would waste a bullet on that twerp—hell, it's in their best interests to keep him *alive*. And one friggin' copter isn't going to make any difference anyway."

Bellowing in the face of his superior officer, Dwayne Hamill was amazed at what was coming out of his own mouth and how little he cared, for the first time in his career, about the repercussions.

"Hamill, get a grip. All you've got is a signed statement from a highly questionable witness," Lieutenant Mellson barked back. "And you want to go flying up to Malibu Creek Park on a *hunch*? For chrissake, man, the roads'll be cleared in an hour or so."

"And it'll take another two hours to drive there," Hamill insisted. "And by then it could be too *late*."

"Why can't you just call and have the suspect put under arrest?"

"By *who*, Mell? A five-foot-five *actress* shouting 'citizen's arrest'? I don't have enough solid evidence to call in the state troopers but, I'm tellin' you, if we don't get up there fast, we stand to have another homicide on our hands . . . And if we do, Mell, we're going to look bad in the press—*real* bad."

The threat of bad PR won out over prudence. Mellson yanked a receiver out of its cradle and grudgingly ordered a helicopter to be put at Hamill's disposal. Hanging up, he glowered at this maverick who also happened to be the most promising detective in the unit and thundered, "Okay, you've got it. But it's *your* ass, Surfer Boy. If this turns out to be a wild-goose chase, I wouldn't show up to work tomorrow if I were you."

"Fine," Dwayne agreed. "If I'm wrong, I'm gone."

"That's right. And if, by any chance, something happens to the veep, you'll—"

"Know that I've done my country a favor."

"Okay, let's get this road on the show!" Larry Goldstein stood with hands on hips trying to organize the pandemonium around him while Billy Orbach, anxious not to lose the best light of the day, jogged in place beside him like a boxer loosening up for a match. "Jesus, cut it out, Billy. You're making me nervous."

"Sure, Lar, sure. Sorry." The young man apologized, making a serious effort to quell the ants in his pants. "But listen—are we gonna do the car crash first? 'Cause the light's really good right now—look." To strengthen his case, Billy ended his appeal by pointing at the sun.

"William, I'm standing here sweating like a mule—I do not *need* to look. I *know* the sun's out, okay?" Goldstein growled. "We're going to do the sisters scene first—tight with one camera. That way—"

Billy went back to his sun dance. "But . . . but we might lose—"

"*Look!* It's a short scene. With any luck—and I'm damn well *due* for some—we'll nail it in one. *Okay?*" Larry's voice boomed and his eyes bulged. Orbach, who had up to now considered his boss a relatively stable sort, shrank back from this near apoplectic vision. The terror in his puppy dog eyes brought the director back to what was left of his senses. "Besides, our P of P needs more time to rig the charge."

"Oh, right, gotcha." Comprehending all, Billy bobbed his head up and down so rapidly his neck looked like a loose mattress spring. *P of P* was shorthand for the Prince of Pyro, aka Washington Marshall, one of their special effects crew. Marshall was a hulking black man whose specialty was igniting things. He was meticulous at his job, always had been. But ever since a minor sulphur explosion during the filming of *Backdraft* had singed off his eyebrows and, as an aftereffect, completely destroyed his sense of smell, Marshall, basically a sensualist who had had a keen and appreciative nose, had become a trifle testy and painstaking in the extreme. So neither Goldstein, Orbach, nor anyone else interested in living to retirement age was about to tell Washington to hustle his butt. "I'll, uh, see if the ladies are ready," Billy offered feebly.

But he didn't have to; Jellicoe and O'Roarke, both in full costume and makeup, were already approaching. Giving them the once-over as the lights were adjusted, Larry noted that Ginger looked rested and ready after her nap but Jocelyn looked like hell. It wasn't just fatigue, but a certain grimness had settled around her eyes and mouth; this might have troubled Goldstein the man but it suited Goldstein the director just fine as the scene they were about to shoot was a showdown between the warring siblings.

Maybe it was just a matter of actors preparing but the two women, with Jack Breedlove hovering between them like a referee, already seemed to have heard the call of battle. None of their usual playful bantering was in evidence as they studiously avoided each other's eyes while Breedlove's gaze ricocheted from one to the other like a nervous chef watching two pots that were simultaneously on the boil. Of the two, Jellicoe appeared to be percolating more rapidly, hopping on one foot then the other and doing elaborate stretches like a dancer warming up, while O'Roarke stood perfectly still and stared at the ground as if she were some latter-day druid contemplating invisible runes.

"All right, ladies, we're ready to roll," Larry called out to them. "You know what we need here—I want to see the dam *burst!* So give me a little blue-collar Krystle and Alexis, okay?"

In their first show of unity, both actors disgustedly rolled their eyes to heaven with identical expressions that read: *Oh, spare me.*

Fine, so I'm not friggin' Mike Nichols, Goldstein groused inwardly as the women hit their marks and the clacker clacked, then shouted, "Action!"

"Christie! Oh, Christie, thank *God* I found you!"

On the sidelines, Jack watched Jocelyn grab Ginger's arm, looking suddenly as flushed and winded as if she'd just sprinted a mile. Despite all that was weighing on his mind, he couldn't help but be fascinated, as he always was, by such technical virtuosity; the way fine actors could bend their bodies, their very physiology to their will. It was all the more amazing considering that he'd had a brief few minutes alone with Josh to whip her hair into shape and share his recent discovery with her. With the AD calling her to the set, she had only a moment to study his handiwork before giving the paper back to him with a hurried, "You done good, Jack. This clinches it. Now keep it hidden and stay close. Something's about to go down but I don't know what—or when."

"Anna, what're you doing here? What's wrong?!"

"It's Momma. She took a bad turn in the night . . . her heart. They're doing the bypass right now. Come on, we gotta go."

Ginger whipped her arm away from Josh's grasp. "I—I can't. Not right now . . . I'll come soon as I can. After I finish the stunt."

"Finish the stunt?! I—I can't believe you. Have you lost your *mind?*"

"Look, Anna, she's in surgery. I can't do anything to help her *now*. But I should be there by the time she comes to, okay?"

"No, it is *not* okay. After all she's done—? Who *are* you? You're not my sister."

"Anna, stop it! I *have* to do this—it's important. All my life, whenever Momma's whistled, I've come running, haven't I?" Ginger pleaded desperately for understanding with tears sliding down her cheeks. "Just *once* I have to be me first and a daughter second."

"Don't kid yourself. You're no daughter," O'Roarke shot back with pure venom. "You're just a self-centered little *bitch!*"

There was a short, sharp *crack*, like a twig snapping, as Ginger raised her hand and brought it down against Jocelyn's cheek— at least, it *should* have been her cheek. From experience, Jack knew that all staged slaps were executed by lightly smacking the palm of one's hand against the hollow of the cheek while the slapee took care to hold their lower jaw loose for minimum impact. But from the sound Jellicoe's blow made coupled with the way Josh's head jerked up, he knew that Ginger had caught her squarely on the jawbone. O'Roarke blinked and shook her head briefly but, war-horse that she was, stayed in the moment.

"And that just proves it, doesn't it, Christie," she said between painfully gritted teeth. "So you just go *be you*—whatever the hell that is. 'Cause you're no damn use as a daughter. And you're no sister of mine."

With that she stepped out of frame as the camera came in for a close-up of Ginger's quite convincingly tormented face.

"Cut! . . . and *print*. Thank you, ladies, that's a keeper," Larry announced as the crew gave the performers a rare, spontaneous round of applause, not that either one was paying much notice. A hefty welt was rising on Josh's jaw. Jack yelled out for somebody to bring some ice and hurried over to her but Ginger got there first.

"Joshie, I'm sorry. I don't know what happened," she said, re-verting back to her little girl gush. "I guess my hand just . . . slipped. Did I hurt you bad?"

"Nah, it smarts a little but it's not bad at all," she reassured her.

The fact was it hurt like hell. But even as she felt around for loosened molars, O'Roarke realized that in some strange way she didn't really mind the pain; she was even glad for it. It evened the karmic score in a way since she was fairly positive that, before the day was over, she would cause far greater pain than this.

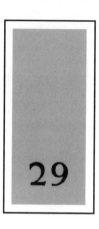

29

"Can I get you anything, Ms. Brent?" A sweet young extra in high-cut shorts and a halter top asked, beaming hope through every healthy pore in her astounding body. "Some coffee or an éclair maybe?"

"Not a goddamn thing, toots. I'm fasting," Gabby replied dismissively as she lit one of her Shermans.

"Really?! I fast, too, you know," the ingenue gushed. "Every Wednesday. I find it very cleansing—physically and mentally, don't you?"

"Nope. It's a bore and I only do it when my ulcer kicks up—when I'm aggravated. Like *now*."

Under Gabby's threatening glare, the young actress curled up like a pretty potato bug and rolled away. Waving a hand to disperse the cloud of smoke hovering above Brent's head and below his nostrils, Jack Breedlove observed, "Another starlet nipped in the bud, eh, Gabby?"

"Aw, fuck her and the little pink cloud she floated in on," Brent growled, though with no real anger. Watching the fresh young thing flirt with a hunky prop man, her mind seemed to be elsewhere as she casually observed, "Those breasts can't be real. They don't even move when she walks . . . Not a bad implant job, though. At least they don't stand out like torpedo tits."

As it was a well-known fact that Gabby herself had been, once or twice, under the cosmetic surgeon's scalpel, Jack could have come back with a snappy "it takes one to know one" retort but his mind was also preoccupied; O'Roarke had done another one of her vanishing acts. With an ice pack planted against her jaw, she'd slipped away soon after her scene was finished. His guess was that she was trying to contact Hamill. But Washington, the Pyro Prince, had just successfully blown up a car and Goldstein, on a hot streak now, was already setting up for Ginger's next shot; the one where she'd take her stunt double's place and emerge from the burning vehicle. Breedlove, still in the dark as to who Jocelyn's number-one suspect was, felt aggrieved that she wasn't on hand to enlighten him.

Pacing restlessly, Brent seemed to pick up on his concern as she abruptly demanded, "Where the hell's O'Roarke anyway? I hear Ginger really laid one on her. Sorry I missed that." She chuckled dryly but without malice.

"Well, if you ask nicely, I'm sure Larry will let you see the rushes," he shot back. "She's, uh, probably lying down in a trailer with her ice pack."

"Oh, come off it! It'd take more than one slug from Ginge to put her down—it'd take a *tank*. So don't bullshit me, Breedlove. What's she up to?"

At the end of his tether, Jack sighed wearily and looked her straight in the eye. "Gabby, even if I knew—why the hell would I tell *you?*"

Two small jets of smoke shot out of her nostrils as she regarded him with surprise. After a tense moment, she took another long drag before answering.

"You're an asshole, Jack. But I'll say one thing for you—you're a fast study."

"Yes, yes, I get it! He's not there. But where *is* he? I need to get in touch with him right away."

"As I told you, miss, Detective Hamill isn't available. He's, uh, in transit." Unfortunately the cop on the switchboard was not a fast study and Jocelyn, after hearing him reel off the same statement three times, was ready to tear her hair out in frustration.

"Okay, he's in transit. Fine. But this is an emergency, you id— . . . I mean, you could patch this call through to him, couldn't you?"

"No, sorry, that's against regulations, miss." Jocelyn let out a hiss that, coupled with the static on the line, sounded like a nest of angry vipers getting ready to strike. It was enough to take some of the starch out of his collar, prompting him to add, "Anyway we're having trouble with some of our equipment. We wouldn't be able to reach him at that distance and altitude."

"Altitude? You mean he's in the *air*? Great, that's great." She sighed with relief. "Then he must be coming by copter. How long will it take him to get here?"

"I'm sorry," the rookie said, reverting to his by-the-rules stance, "I can't divulge official—"

"Okay, okay! Just tell me this—*hypothetically*, how long does it take a helicopter—any ol' helicopter—to travel from Los Angeles to Malibu Park? Be a sport, just make a wild guess."

"Well, um, I'd say about half an hour—that's if the weather's good and there's not too much air traffic. But that's just a guess."

"Fine, fine. Now could you make another guess as to approximately what time Hamill left the—"

"No, ma'am, I couldn't. That's officia—"

"You could if you'd take out that stick you've got up your ass," Josh yelled into the receiver, but to no avail. A fresh burst of static drowned out the voice on the other end and the connection was broken. She slammed down the phone, knowing that there was no point in calling back.

At least she knew that the cavalry was on its way. But she didn't know if they'd arrive before the Indians attacked. How could she, since she didn't know when or where the Indians would strike. Of course, there was the possibility that she was wrong; that there wouldn't be another murder attempt made. But it was a faint hope at best; Dwayne wouldn't have commandeered a copter if he, too, didn't think that disaster was imminent.

The burning question was: How do you cut the Indians off at the pass if you don't know where the pass *is*?

"Now listen up, lamb chop. I'm gonna s'plain it all again so you don't git spooked, okay?"

"Wash, you don't have to. I know the drill. And I'm not spooked."

The Prince of Pyro shook a long index finger in Ginger Jellicoe's face and warned, "You say that now, girl. But it'll be diff'rent when the camera's rollin' and your sleeve's all in flames. So I will reiterate and *you* will pay close attention."

"Yes, sir, Mr. Prince, sir," Jellicoe quipped, hanging her head in mock humility. "I am all ears."

"Okay, we got you in this asbestos suit. But sewed on here, on the right sleeve, is the burn patch—a couple layers of linen. So we're gonna set off a smoke bomb right by the car, okay? Just before you run into the smoke, Benny'll light the patch. And it's gonna go up like Watts, sugar."

"Like what?"

"Forget it, you're too young. But it will burn, baby, believe me. And it's gonna feel *real* hot. Just remember, it takes a good three minutes to burn through the linen—plenty a' time. And there'll be me and a whole line of bucket boys to douse you soon's you get out of frame. All you gotta do is stand still and let us soak you good. You got that?"

"Sure. You're gonna water-bomb me and enjoy every minute of it, huh?"

A slow smile spread across Marshall's serious face as he allowed, "Well, yes, angel, tha's true—since it's as close as we'll git to a wet T-shirt contest on this gig."

"Oooh, Marshall, you naughty man," Ginger laughed, vamping him with fluttering eyelashes. Spotting Jack and Tim helping out with the water buckets, she called out, "Hey, fellas, we're gonna have a wet T-shirt contest after this shot!"

"Great idea," Hayes yelled back. "I'll go tell Gabby and Brenda to get ready." The crew broke into a cacophony of hoots and whistles as Tim kept up the joke by marching purposefully, bucket in hand, toward the trailers. Pausing by the backup gas tanks, he turned around to ask with elaborate politeness, "Ah, is this to be a formal affair—or should they come braless?"

In one voice, the crew answered, "Braless!"

"Right." Tim made a deep bow then added, "As I always say—*braless* is more."

The bucket boys broke into approving applause as Hayes turned the corner. Giggling, Ginger looked up at Washington as she jerked a thumb in their direction. "Men. They're pond scum . . . but you gotta love 'em."

"What do you mean, you can't *land?*" Dwayne Hamill asked in alarm. His stomach was churning with anxiety and he was on the verge of airsickness. An hour in a helicopter had proven to him, beyond all doubt, that he was wholly a creature of earth and water, meant to ride waves, not air currents.

"Well, look, we can only land on flat ground," the hard-pressed pilot pointed out. "And the only flat ground nearby is the location site."

"So land *there,* for chrissake."

"I can't right now."

"Why *not?*"

"Because they're filming."

Steeling himself to look down, Hamill saw that the pilot was right. In L.A., even civilians know when cameras are rolling. Dwayne saw what looked like a Tonka toy car in flames with a tiny mushroom of smoke alongside it. Two figures were poised between the car and the smoke; one figure raised an arm while the other touched something to it. He could barely make out the orange patch of flame that appeared. Then the figure with the orange patch went headlong through the smoke, running straight toward the camera. As the copter circled, he watched with growing alarm as the figure veered from the camera and headed toward a line of waiting men. They were all holding something, cans or buckets he assumed, which they raised as the figure approached them.

Suddenly, out of the corner of his eye, he spied someone running pell mell, right in front of the camera, toward the figure with the orange patch. From an aerial view it was hard to judge, but the running figure seemed to hit its target in a perfect midsection tackle. They fell to the ground together, rolling in a flurry of dust and flailing limbs.

"Land! Land *now*. I don't care where, I don't care how—just land," Hamill shouted urgently. "It's going down."

Following orders, the pilot banked the chopper at a stomach-tilting angle and headed for the top of the closest hill. Dwayne nearly wrenched his neck trying to look over his shoulder and follow the action below. But even with his 20/20 vision, he couldn't make out much and started to curse violently.

"Hey, don't go ballistic on me now, man," the pilot pleaded as he negotiated the tricky landing. "Look, there's a pair of binoculars in the glove compartment."

Fortunately they were Konicas with self-adjusting focus so Hamill was able to zero in instantly on the unfolding pandemonium. The two figures had risen from the ground; the one in the jumpsuit with the still smoking sleeve was Jellicoe, who seemed to be chewing out her assailant, a sweaty, begrimed Jocelyn, as people converged on them from all directions. Dwayne lost sight of the two women for a moment, then O'Roarke elbowed her way through the crowd and headed toward what Hamill now saw was a bucket brigade with an irate Ginger hot on her tail. Waving one arm to silence Ginger, she called out something to the men with the buckets.

No one paid the slightest attention to the chopper as the four men, obviously following her instructions, placed their buckets on the ground. Dwayne watched Josh walk over to the first bucket, pulling something out of her shirt pocket. A second later he saw a pinpoint of flame rise from her hand before she dropped the match in the bucket. The Konicas were truly first-rate and Hamill was even able to make out the faint wisp of smoke that rose from the bucket when the match was extinguished.

The blades of the landing copter were churning the air, sending a stiff wind down the embankment, but O'Roarke raised a shielding hand, lit another match, and dropped it into the second bucket. Dwayne imagined that he could hear the hiss as it hit water. They were just about to set down and the chopper was bucking from side to side but he managed to keep the binoculars fixed on O'Roarke. He saw a red-faced Gabby Brent in high dudgeon approach her from the sidelines, but Josh barked something over one shoulder and the tiny titan stopped in her tracks.

Just as the copter's runners touched ground, O'Roarke stepped up to a large, black man and dropped the third match into his bucket. Then a blinding column of flame shot up in the air, obliterating everyone and everything from Hamill's view.

"What the hell was *that*?" the startled pilot asked as his hand nearly slipped off the landing gear.

Before the pilot could even shut off the rotating blades, Dwayne hit the ground running. Without the binoculars, all he could see was smoke rising from below. Reaching the edge of the small plateau, he looked down and spotted the bucket brigade back in action, trying to douse the flames with sand and water. They were having a fair amount of success but the smoke still billowed around them, making all the figures shadowy and indistinct. Hamill headed down the slope full speed. Years of practice on the long boards had given him the sure footing of a mountain goat and he never broke stride until he was halfway down the hill. Then he spotted a figure moving frantically through the clouds of smoke, heading in his direction.

There was another gust of wind and the running figure broke through the smoke and came into clear view just yards below him.

"Hold it right there! Police," Hamill said, whipping his .38 Special out of its shoulder holster. It was the first time in his career that he'd drawn on anyone. The fact was Dwayne hated guns and the thought of having to actually fire into human flesh sickened him. To avoid such necessity, he put steel into his voice as he said, "Just stand perfectly still. If you run, I'm gonna have to shoot. According to the book, I'm supposed to aim for your knees. But this sucker has a nasty kick so I might hit you a little higher up, you know?"

The running figure came to a screeching halt. As Jocelyn had earlier observed, Hamill was no slouch when it came to human psychology. The only thing the man before him feared more than facing a murder rap was the possible loss of his family jewels.

"Hey, stay cool, man. I'm not going anywhere."

Sweat trickled down his face, making rivulets in the dust and grime. Holding his hands up and away from his body, Tim Hayes looked up at Hamill with one of his winning smiles.

"I just wanted to get away from all that damn smoke, that's all."

"No, Tim, I don't think so. See, I've been talking to your pal,

Boogie," Dwayne said easily, keeping his .38 hovering between Hayes' knee and groin area. "You were the one he came to see yesterday. He says you're in hock up to your eyeballs to a certain bookie."

"Aw, come on, Sarge—so what? If bein' in debt's a crime, you're gonna have to lock up half the country, right?"

"No—just you, Tim. And not for gambling. Turns out ol' Randall's a big fan of Ginger's. Did you know that? He's had a crush on her ever since her 'Jam House' days. So he hung around to watch her do her stunt . . . And he saw you spike the air bag."

What was left of Hayes' sangfroid crumbled as he stared aghast at Hamill. Finally his hands fell to his sides as he shook his head ruefully.

"Shit, I knew it—I knew you and that gonzo bitch would find a way to stick it to me."

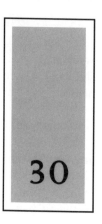

30

"Martin! Good to see you."

The maître d' at Cafe des Artistes grinned delightedly at the tall, distinguished man who had just wafted through the door of the elegant restaurant on West Sixty-seventh Street.

"Always a pleasure to see you, Mr. Revere. It's been a while."

"Too long, far too long," Frederick concurred graciously. "I don't get these old bones up above the theatre district much these days. But I've been staying in the neighborhood—apartment-sitting for a friend—and I couldn't miss the chance to enrage my doctor by indulging in some of George's excellent wines. Is there any Beaujolais Nouveau still to be had?"

"For you, of course," Martin said, nearly purring as he led the renowned actor across the room, causing the noontime diners to sit up and take note. "Your table's ready and your, uh, guest is here."

"So he is," Frederick said merrily as he raised a hand in greeting. "Punctual as ever, old boy. And a sight for sore eyes, I must say."

All eyes, sore and otherwise, turned toward the short, stocky man sitting in the corner booth, avidly inspecting the nude murals that graced the walls. Turning beet red, he bolted up in surprise but managed to mutter, "Iz good to see you, too, Freddie. Thanks for takin' the time—"

"No, no, *you're* the one with the busy schedule," Revere said as he slid into the booth. "Ah, Martin, you can bring the Beaujolais any time." The maître d' melted away and he turned back to his companion. "Time is something I have plenty of these days, especially with Jocelyn away."

Few could segue as gracefully as Frederick Revere. In a few brief sentences, he'd come right to the topic he knew was uppermost in his friend's mind; in fact the point of this impromptu reunion, he strongly suspected. His suspicions were confirmed as Sergeant Tommy Zito jumped in with both feet.

"Yeah, right! Have you heard from her lately? All I know is what I read in the papers—and that ain't much. See, I don't have any pals on the LAPD so . . . I was wondering, uh . . ."

"What the scoop is on the Banks case?"

"Well—yeah. That is, if you don't mind me askin'. And if it'll make you feel easier—it's just *me* askin', if you know what I mean."

"Point taken," Frederick said, suppressing a smile as he nodded his head gravely, "And, yes, I spoke to her last night. But it's a long story, Thomas, one that should not be embarked on with an empty stomach. So let's order. I suggest the bouillabaisse. It's quite splendid."

"Now let me get this straight," Zito said, digging into the last mussel on his plate with gusto. "This guy was tryin' to drive his wife nutso using sub-*what?*"

"Subliminal suggestion. I myself have never been to a drive-in movie but Jocelyn tells me they did it there all the time until it was outlawed. A single frame of film flashes by before the conscious mind can record it, but the subconscious takes it in. They'd cut in a frame of a tall, frosty Coca-Cola or a big bag of popcorn and the audiences would run like lemmings to the concession stands . . . Is that true?"

"Oh, yeah, I remember now. Worked like a charm, too. This Hayes guy is a sicko but he's no dummy," Tommy said, nodding as he wiped his mouth with the napkin he had tucked inside his shirt front. "You got a woman who's recently lost both her folks and gone cold turkey to boot—still grieving and probably feelin' some guilt. She'd be a perfect target . . . But how did Josh tumble to it with just two lousy half-frames to work from?"

"She didn't until she recognized the frame from *Arsenic and Old Lace*. That was the movie she'd seen at Ginger's house with Banks. That night *she* had a violent nightmare but chalked it up to an upset stomach. Now Buddy, who had been an editor as well as a cinematographer, would've spotted something awry even as he watched. That's why he insisted on taking the film with him."

"And when he found it was peppered with poison pen notes aimed at Jellicoe he confronted the perp instead of takin' it straight to the police, right?" Zito nodded knowingly. "Always a *big* mistake. So the guy sneaks into his darkroom and fills a water jug with hydrogen cyanide while everybody thinks he's out on an island. Gotta admit, that was very slick."

"Oh, yes, very. Then, once he knew it wasn't safe to keep gaslighting his wife, he proceeded to set her up as the fall guy. That was also *slick*," Revere said, wrinkling his nose with distaste, "especially the way he used his own daughter to do it."

"The schmuck!" Tommy brought a fist down on the table, rattling the silverware and making heads turn. "Killin's one thing but making a little kid put grass in the cigar box so Banks would find it, then having her slip her mother tea spiked with downers to weaken her alibi—we're talkin' *major* scumbag here."

"Alas, yes, but fortunately he got rattled and got sloppy as, uh, scumbags usually do."

"You mean that little scene he faked at the agent's house, right?" Zito said with a knowing wink, then, "What the hell was he looking for anyways?"

"Jocelyn's theory is that it was a seek-and-destroy mission with several objectives," Revere answered, preparing to tick off points on his long, tapered fingers, "Firstly, he was trying to find the print of *Arsenic and Old Lace*. Remember, Banks never returned it to the rental place. It wasn't likely to be there but he was desperate to get his hands on it. Secondly, there was Buddy's cache of possibly incriminating photos—like the one of Hayes bent over a splicer—that might point a finger in his direction if the film *was* found. And lastly but, Jocelyn thinks, most importantly, there was—"

"The map in the glass case!" Tommy snapped his fingers triumphantly, then smacked his palm against his forehead. "A' course!
I mean, if he was just out to ransack the den, *why* knock it over
and make all that noise? He didn't want anyone lookin' at that
island."

"Catalina. Exactly, Thomas." Revere picked up his cue smoothly
and, not to be done out of his grand revelation, hastened on. "It
was an excellent piece of work, Josh says, showing the coastline
precisely. Now the ferryboats go from Redondo and Long Beach
to Avalon, which is at the southern end of the island. But Hayes
had been at Isthmus Cove to the north. It's just nineteen miles
from there to the San Pedro marina."

"But O'Roarke saw the map *before* he wrecked it, right?"

"Yes, but at that point, she hadn't yet heard about Hayes having
access to a—what's the word?—oh, yes, a Scarab, much less that
he even knew how to pilot one . . . But, in any case," Frederick
said, rubbing his hands with anticipation, "she already *knew* he'd
faked the whole thing because—"

"Because me and Phil took her to the Schmitz lecture!"

"I beg your pardon?"

Zito was filled with the pride of a proud papa and too excited
to notice that he'd just upstaged the star.

"Dr. Leon Schmitz, a top gun at some limey university. He's a
head specialist—not a shrink. The other kind."

"A neurologist," Frederick supplied, magnanimously ignoring
the "limey" remark.

"Yeah, that's it. Came over and gave a lecture at NYU. Talked
about this famous case—in South Africa, I think it was—
where a guy said some crooks broke into his place, tied him up
and knocked him out, then shot his wife dead. Under cross-
examination, he described everything that happened right up to
the blow on the head. That's how they nailed the sucker . . . See,
Schmitz says the brain's just like a computer." Zito gulped down
some Beaujolais as he warmed up to a favorite topic. "It stores
everything, even if we don't know it's in there. And it's true! Like,
we'll get a witness to a crime and they can't remember shit about
how it went down 'cause they're too shook—they can't *access* that
file, get it? But you bring in a good hypnotist and put 'em under
and bingo! They come up with amazing stuff—like the full license
number on the getaway car—'cause it's all *in there*, see?" Tommy

tapped a stubby finger against his forehead, then raised it and paused dramatically. "And the *only time* the brain will, like, permanently *lose* a file is—"

"After a blow to the head that renders the person unconscious." Frederick knew it was rather mean to steal Thomas's thunder but, really, he had been looking forward to telling this bit himself and it did make up for the limey crack. "So Jocelyn knew that anything that happened five to ten minutes *before* Hayes was struck would be irretrievably erased from his memory. Hence, since he, like the South African bloke, remembered *all* . . . it had to be a lie. And that little bit about the attacker looking like Banks really tipped the scales. She realized then that Tim must've staged that Banquo's ghost scene at Ginger's dressing room window."

"Right." Zito grinned ungrudgingly as he topped up both their glasses with the last of the wine. "Boy, we went to that lecture —what?—almost two years ago. O'Roarke don't need no hypnotist, she's got a memory better than an elephant's. Man, the way she pieced this thing together! It'd blow Phil away."

"Now, Thomas, be fair. It's not as if she didn't have help. Her young detective friend dug up the hard evidence when he went over Hayes' condo with a fine tooth comb and found the latex mask he'd made of Buddy's face. Odd that he'd keep that."

"Oh, you'd be surprised, Freddie, what they hold on to. See, they can't tell anybody how smart they've been, so it gives 'em a thrill to keep little souvenirs . . . Lucky break for Hamill. Not to take anything away from the kid. He sounds all right. Did a good job pumping Boggs and following the ol' money trail. It'll always lead you to it . . . I'm talkin' about the trust fund now. That's what Hayes was after, huh?"

"Hilly's trust fund, yes, that was his chief objective from the start," Revere concurred, admiring his friend's astuteness. "That's why he doctored all those movies. If Ginger had a breakdown or fell off the rehab wagon—or worse—he would've had no trouble gaining sole custody and getting his hands on the loot, as they say."

Tommy let out a low whistle. "Geez, that Jellicoe's one lucky dame. If O'Roarke hadn't been on the scene, she'd be history."

"Well, yes, that's one way of looking at it," Frederick agreed, shifting uncomfortably in his seat, reluctant to give Zito bad news.

"Unfortunately, it seems it's not Ms. Jellicoe's way. I gather she now views Jocelyn as some sort of . . . catalyst of doom."

"What d'ya mean?" Zito demanded, instantly on the defensive. "She oughta be down on her *knees* to Josh. She saved her friggin' life!"

"Of course. But, Thomas, you have to appreciate the bitter irony involved here . . . and the fact that human beings are less than rational at times. In Ginger's mind, Jocelyn also *destroyed* her life. She took away the husband that she believed still loved her—and her oldest friend as well."

"You mean Banks? I don't follow . . . Look, dinn't you say O'Roarke even got Gabby Brent to hire accountants to check the books and prove Buddy hadn't been skimming from Jellicoe's business?"

"Yes, she did. Ginger was very relieved about that. Seems she's even decided to take up the reins of the family business herself. But—"

"So what's she got to gripe about then!?"

"*But* she doesn't know Josh had anything to do with that. She was led to think it was all Gabby's idea . . . which was Jocelyn's idea."

"Aw, man, two damn peas in a pod," Zito groaned, shaking his head in frustration. "Her and Phil—sorry, I gotta say it—the both of 'em would stick pins in their eyes before lettin' anybody know they did 'em a good turn, right?"

"Right," Frederick agreed ruefully, then added, "But it's part of their charm."

"Oh, yeah, it's *real* cute." Tommy oozed sarcasm as he slathered butter on a roll. After a moment's ruminative mastication, he said, "But I still don't see how the hell she could blame Josh for what happened to Banks."

"It's convoluted, but bear with me. You see, normally Ginger watched those old movies all by herself—as Hayes well knew. The only reason Jocelyn and Buddy were present that one night was because Josh had burst into his darkroom earlier in the day and he'd thrown a fit. So Jellicoe arranged the impromptu little dinner party to reconcile them—which fatefully led to Banks' murder and all the rest."

"But—but . . . the guy was out to *ice* her!"

Frederick didn't like the way the veins in Tommy's neck were bulging. Fearing that a bit of roll was about to lodge in his friend's windpipe, he signaled Maurice to bring another bottle of Beaujolais. "True, true. But you're underestimating the capacity—the deep desire—some folks have to just let sleeping dogs lie . . . People just don't *want* to know the worst about those they're fond of, even if it's in their best interest. That's a large part of what masochism is all about. And they don't *thank* those who, well . . . rouse the cur, so to speak."

"Yeah, okay, I get what you're saying." After swallowing the last of the roll, Zito finally agreed. "It's one thing if I tell somebody their ex was out to whack 'em. I'm a cop and it's my job to deliver the bad news. They might not like it but it's not personal. When it's a friend, it's a lot stickier, I guess . . . How's Josh takin' it?"

"Not too badly. She *hates* it but she understands. Her chief consolation is, whether Ginger appreciates it or not, she's spared little Hillary from potential ruin—both financially and emotionally, I'd say. And at least she has the gratitude and support of her friends . . . *this* time," Revere added, obliquely referring to the Burbage Theatre debacle, a sore spot in Zito's memory as it marked the end of Jocelyn's relationship with Phillip Gerrard and, in Tommy's secret opinion, a low point from which his friend and superior officer had never completely rallied. Part of him longed to say as much to the old actor but loyalty, both professional and personal, forbade it.

Instead he asked, "You mean ol' Frostie, Hamill, and Goldstein, the director? They all came through?"

"Yes. And this Breedlove fellow. Jocelyn says he was instrumental in—"

"Oh, yeah, yeah," Tommy said dismissively. "The guy who broke the code—the fairy hairdresser."

"Thomas, don't try to play the Sicilian bigot with me," Freddie warned as he whisked the uncorked wine bottle from the hovering Maurice with one hand and waved him away with the other. "You can read between the lines as well as I can. This boy's clearly straight as an arrow and clearly smitten with our Josh. We should both be happy for her, eh? . . . As happy as we are for Phillip and Trish—"

"Now, see, that's the thing, Freddie," Zito broke in, throwing caution to the wind. If he didn't speak now he had a gut-sure instinct he'd curse himself to the end of his days. "And I'm tellin' you this totally off the record—just between us two—*you* can be happy for Josh, okay? But, from where I'm sittin', these days there's no joy in Mudville, *capisce?*"

"Really? I'm sorry to hear that," Frederick murmured politely, stroking his mustache to mask his rampant curiosity. "Do tell."

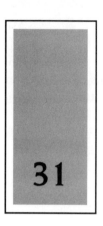

31

"Stop jerking me around, Frostie, or I'll nail your lily white hide to the wall . . . Now be a sport and tell me where she is."

"For the last time, Gabby, I don't *know* where Josh is," Austin said wearily as he pruned the azalea bush on his patio with clippers in hand and the cordless phone tucked under his chin. "Just leave a message and I'll give it to her—if and when she calls in." The fact was he hadn't heard from O'Roarke in nearly three days, during which time his phone had been ringing off the hook, almost always for Josh, and he was getting a tad tired of playing secretary.

"It'll be too late," she protested with an almost plaintive note in her voice. "I've set up an audition for her for the new David Lee sitcom. She's gotta be over at Paramount first thing tomorrow."

"You what?!" Austin came perilously close to lopping off the top of the shrub as his pruning shears jerked upward in his hands. "Gabby, what're you up to? She has an agent."

"Yeah, yeah, I know, some East Coast *putz* who hasn't gotten her a job in months, right? Well, he can have the commission if she gets it. It's a good part, could become a running character on the show."

"Well, Gabrielle, that's really very . . . sweet of you."

"Please, I just ate. Sweet, my ass," Brent said with a brusque snort; Austin could almost see smoky wisps from her Sherman coming through the receiver. "She's right for the part and I just thought . . . I owed her one."

"Gosh, it's kind of like the end of *Pollyanna* with you in the Jane Wyman role." Frost couldn't resist ribbing her and, now that *Free Fall* had wrapped, he could afford to do so. "Joshie'll be so glad."

"Hey, where do you get off being such a wiseass," she sputtered. "If O'Roarke hadn't been tailing Tim when he filled that bucket from the gas tanks, your leading lady and your whole damn production would be history. As it is, you'll probably end up with a twenty share in the ratings, what with all the free publicity. Seems to me you owe her one, too, turd ball. So just cough up and tell me where she is."

"Texas."

"Huh?! Why the hell . . . *Where* in Texas?"

"Who knows? It's a big place. Somewhere around that thing they call the Panhandle, I believe."

"What the fuck's she doing there?"

Putting down the pruning shears, Austin plopped down on the chaise longue and reached for his cigarettes and a mug of tepid coffee; one needed stimulants to deal with Brent early in the day. "Shopping, I guess. At least that's what Jack's doing. Somebody's auctioning off quarter horses at bargain prices. He wants to pick up a few for the ranch and he invited her along."

"Well, I'll be damned," Gabby said, ignoring the muttered "Probably" at the other end. "So they're still hot and heavy, huh?"

"I dunno," Austin answered, casually noncommittal. "He bribed her, really. Said if the stock was good and the price was right, he'd buy one just for her . . . that's as near as I've ever seen her come to actually swooning."

He made light of it but the truth was Austin was deeply grateful to Jack for spiriting Jocelyn out of town. Fortunately that fateful day at Malibu Creek Park had been her last day of shooting, especially fortunate since Ginger had made it clear that she would, under no circumstances, be on the same set with O'Roarke; an attitude that he'd found inexcusable but Josh had seemed to take in stride. Until the morning she'd gone to Hamill's office to give her full deposition. To Dwayne's dismay, some incompetent departmental paper-shuffler had unwittingly scheduled Jellicoe's appointment immediately after O'Roarke's.

Miraculously managing to avoid the pack of photographers who had been dogging her, Ginger had swept into the precinct headquarters with little Hilly in tow just as Jocelyn was leaving. Jocelyn had been braced for the cold shoulder from the mother, but it was the daughter who had nearly undone her when, breaking free of Ginger's hold, she had run up to Josh and blurted, "Mommie says you made them take my daddy away. Is that so?"

"No, honey, the police did that. They had to," O'Roarke had managed to whisper, stroking Hilly's head as her eyes burned into Ginger's back. "Someday I'll tell you all about it . . . or your mother will."

Once safely back in the car, Josh had immediately sunk into one her rare black-Irish funks. Austin had been hoping for a bout of tears; O'Roarke could be a four-star weeper when she got going, but she usually emerged from a crying jag cleansed and with her normal aplomb restored. These funks of hers had always been a different and more dangerous matter, symptomatic of the kind of merciless self-castigation that former good Catholics did so well.

She had been so despondent that she'd allowed Frost to drive, a clear sign that she had lost her zest for living. In a feeble attempt to distract her, he'd even taken the long way home, going past Bad Boy Hill, that stretch of Mulholland Drive where Beatty, Nicholson, and Don Henley reside, the last being of chief interest to O'Roarke. But that day she hadn't even glanced out the window when they'd passed his house.

Breedlove, bless his canny soul, had been waiting for them when they got back and Frost had backed his plan for the Texas trip to the hilt.

"Well, good, that's good. A trip's just what she needs," Gabby said after a long pause; either Austin was having aural hallucinations or there really was a tinge of maternal concern in her crusty voice. "But if she should get back tonight, you tell her to get her butt over to Paramount tomorrow. Could mean major bucks."

"Okay, will do," he said. There was just no saying no to this woman.

"Who knows, maybe if she gets this job she'll stick around here, huh?"

"Maybe . . . and then you can adopt her, Gabby."

"Aw, screw you."

There was a sharp click at the other end and the line went dead. No sooner had he put the phone down than it started ringing again. But the azaleas were also calling and Austin decided to let the answering machine on the kitchen counter pick up since he was nine-tenths certain the call wouldn't be for him.

It wasn't. But even through the sliding glass door, he recognized the voice; it was a distinctive, deep male baritone that even the tinny quality of the machine couldn't disguise.

"Hello, Austin. It's me . . ."

" 'It's me,' " Frost sniffed huffily and addressed the innocent azalea, "Don't you just love men who call after you haven't heard from them in several light years and say 'It's *me*.' The nerve."

But there was no denying who "me" was and he had a sudden, angry urge to give "me" a piece of his mind. Snatching up the phone, he pressed the talk button and, in his most mid-Atlantic tones, said, "Why hallo, Phillip. Long time, no speakee, eh?"

"Hello! Earth to O'Roarke. Come in please."

"Huh?"

"I said, do you want to go to Mulholland Drive or should we just drive straight up to the ranch? We could get there in time for a sunset ride."

"Uh, that sounds great, but I'd better get back to Austin's. He probably thinks I've run off to join the rodeo by now."

"Okey-doke," Breedlove said without rancor. At least he'd gotten her to speak and that was something.

The three days in Texas had been a great success, he'd thought. As soon as they'd stepped off the plane Jocelyn, chameleonlike as most actors, had instantly transformed into the Girl of the Golden West. Like a curious three-year-old, she had peppered him endlessly with questions about all things equine, from fetlocks to foaling. And every night she'd made love with the wild abandon of a horny teenager. Between answering her questions by day and her carnal appetites by night, Jack had wound up in a state of slaphappy exhaustion. But it had been well worth it both for the three quarter-horses he had picked up for a song at auction and for the salubrious, not to say libidinous, effect it had had on Josh, whose energy and avidity never flagged—until they'd boarded the plane for LAX.

Right after takeoff she had fallen asleep and remained near comatose until the steward came along to make her fasten her seatbelt and upright her seat. And ever since she'd been about as zombified as Brando's performance in *Apocalypse Now*.

Jack knew he was looking for trouble but couldn't keep from asking, "Uh, are you just real jet-lagged or have I suddenly developed major B.O. or something?"

"Oh, no, no, Jack! It's nothing to do with you. I, uh, I just had some weird dreams on the plane."

"Not the Jellicoe variety, I hope."

"No. Mainly they were about . . . home."

"The kind where you're a kid again in your parents' house, you mean?"

"No, the kind where you're just dying for some lox from Zabar's but Zabar's isn't on the block where it's supposed to be."

"Hmm, I see," Breedlove said uneasily. "Well, my interpretation is it's one of two things. Either you were hungry 'cause you slept through lunch—and missed a delectable mystery meat casserole, by the way—or, and I think it's the less likely of the two, you're maybe just a touch . . . homesick."

Jocelyn said nothing for a minute, just put her hand on his shoulder and gave it a squeeze.

"You're an awfully dear man, you know that?"

"Oh God, no," he groaned. "So where's the 'but'? After an opener like that there's *always* a 'but.' "

"Well, you're wrong, smartypants. There's no 'but.' I'm just not used to being with someone who's, well . . . so easy to be with."

"Uh-huh, which means you're either bored—or scared."

"Neither. Tell me, did you take a *lot* of psych courses when you were in college?" she asked with her old teasing smile. Jack's dread abated and he started feeling hopeful again.

"No, but I bet *you* did," he joked back, then tsked, "See, once again female chauvinism rears its nasty little head. A man shows the slightest degree of sensitivity—a soupçon of insight—and the woman ridicules him. Secretly fearing, of course, that he's trying to storm the bastion of that most hallowed preserve—feminine intuition!"

"Yeah, right!" Jocelyn gave a deep, throaty chuckle that sent shivers to his loins as she ruffled his hair playfully. "You are so full of shit, Breedlove. The nineties version of Teddy Roosevelt. Speak softly and carry a big *shovel*, eh?"

But her little joke backfired as the reference to Teddy catapulted her memory back to *Arsenic and Old Lace* and the murder which, by tacit consent, neither of them had mentioned in the past three days.

Jack shot her a sidelong glance and said softly, "Ginger's going to come around after a while, love. She's too decent not to. And when she does, she's going to want—no, she's going to *need* to apologize to you. To your face. So for her sake, not to mention yours truly's, it'd be kind of grand and generous of you to stick around for a bit."

"God, I don't know, Jack," she sighed as she massaged her temples. "I hope you're right about Ginger. But the cold, hard financial fact is I'm out of work again and I don't have the cash to rent a place out here and—"

"Hey, that's no problem! You can—"

"No! I can't," she broke in fast so she wouldn't have to reject his offer. "And I can't keep sponging off Austin either . . . I really need my own place. It's the way I've always lived and I like it."

"Sure, sure you do. But don't forget, you're the new kid in town right now," Jack said eagerly as he turned the Jeep into Frost's driveway. "We're talkin' Flavor of the Month, see you at Spago, and all that *Premiere* magazine crap. And there's *no* damn reason why you shouldn't take advantage of it while it lasts. Hell, you're good, Josh! Why not let these clowns pitch their high woo your way?"

"If they pitch it half as well as you do, I just might enjoy myself," she said, getting out of the car quickly as her thoughts raced ahead. There was no denying that Jack had a point. After the undeserved shellacking her career had taken in the wake of the Burbage Theatre incident, maybe she was due for a break or two; God knew she could use one.

Grabbing her suitcase, Jack followed Josh up the path to the back patio, whistling an upbeat version of "Come Rain or Come Shine" and enjoying the rear view of her bouncing gait. He came through the sliding glass door just a moment later and immediately sensed the tension in the room.

Frost was hunched over the kitchen counter with the phone embedded in his ear and an overflowing ashtray at his elbow, sure signs of a lengthy conversation. He hadn't said a word to Jocelyn, but there was an eloquent gravity in the look he gave her.

"Uh, hold on. She just walked in . . . Josh, it's for you."

She didn't ask who it was, didn't seem to need to, just nodded her head once or twice as she took slow steps toward the counter.

As soon as she took the receiver, Austin leapt to his feet, grabbed two cold Molsons out of the fridge, and with amazing economy of movement whisked Jack back out to the patio, sliding the door shut behind them.

Breedlove took a long swig from the bottle before saying, "It's him, isn't it?"

"Uh, yes, 'fraid so." Austin lit a fresh cigarette off the stub of the old one before grinding it out under his heel. "Look, I could've lied —just hung up and not told her. Believe me, I thought about it for maybe a second. But it's her life, Jack, and Jocelyn does not take kindly to *anyone*, even her nearest and dearest, playing God in it."

"I know. You did the right thing," Breedlove said magnanimously, then spat out, "But what the fuck does he want anyway?"

"Mainly just wants to see how she's doing. Listen, you can't ignore past history. A lot of water's gone under that particular bridge," Austin said, jerking a thumb toward the kitchen. "And Phillip knows that after a case is resolved there's always a certain kind of angst that follows. He just wants to see how she's handling it."

"Bullshit! He didn't give a damn about her angst last time. You told me so yourself. Why can't he just leave her the hell alone?!"

"Maybe he will. Or maybe she'll make him," Austin offered hopefully. "She's not real big on granting second chances, you know. After all, enough is enough."

"Not according to Colodny's last commandment." Jack gave a gloomy glance toward the kitchen where Josh stood with her back to him.

"Which is?"

Before answering, Jack killed the rest of his beer and wiped his mouth on his sleeve.

"It's never enough."